Caesar's General

Alex Gough is an author of Roman historical adventures. His first two series, The Carbo Chronicles and The Imperial Assassin, were written as a result of a lifelong obsession with ancient Rome, and his upcoming series will follow the story of Mark Antony in his rise to power.

CAESAR'S GENERAL

ALEX GOUGH

CANELO

First published in the United Kingdom in 2024 by

Canelo
Unit 9, 5th Floor
Cargo Works, 1-2 Hatfields
London SE1 9PG
United Kingdom

A CIP catalogue record for this book is available from the British Library.

Print ISBN 978 1 80436 209 9
Ebook ISBN 978 1 80436 208 2

Eagle used by permission of Original German Militaria
https://originalgermanmilitaria.com/product/german-railway-train-eagle-by-j-z-large-size-reichsbahn-adler/

Cover design by Blacksheep

Cover images © Arcangel, iStock, Shutterstock

Look for more great books at www.canelo.co

Printed and bound in Great Britain by Clays Ltd, Elcograf S.p.A.

To my family

Prologue

Antony felt the breeze of the arrow as it passed his cheek, and he laughed out loud. He never felt so alive as when he was in the heat of battle. The archer who had nearly skewered his eye was out of his reach for now, but a line of warriors were grimly braced to receive the cavalry charge, their shaggy blond hair, soaked by the drizzle, plastered across their faces.

As usual, Antony was first to crash into the defenders, his muscular mount bashing aside the burly warrior before him, Antony using his *spatha* to bat the Gaul's spear aside. He slashed downwards and roared in triumph as the blade bit into the angle between the warrior's shoulder and neck, a spurt of bright red blood rewarding the stroke.

To Antony's left and right, his mounted comrades impacted the enemy line a heartbeat behind him, and the cavalry wedge split the Gauls like an axe cleaving through a log. Then he was into the pack, slashing around him, his sword smashing into hastily raised shields and iron helmets, parrying spear thrusts, biting deep into flesh and bone. Blood and gore sprayed out, as if he was a butcher in a hurry to finish his day's work and get to the Circus in time for the race.

The battle didn't last long, if you could call it a battle. Antony knew that this little punitive expedition was too small, too one-sided, to make it into the commentaries that Caesar regularly sent back to Rome to publicise his victories. But that made it no less real, or less dangerous, to Antony and his men.

Antony reined in his horse and looked around him. The enemy had numbered no more than two hundred, and had proven little challenge for the veteran cavalrymen. At least half of them were dead or incapacitated. Any who had attempted to flee had been run down and massacred. Only those who had thrown down their weapons and surrendered were spared, and soon they were being bound and corralled, to be added to the massive stockpile of slaves that the Gallic war had created.

Antony glanced down. His breastplate had an ugly gouge across it that would take his armourer some time to work out. He did not remember the stroke that had inflicted it, nor the one that had slashed his outer thigh. He wiped the blood away with his palm to inspect the wound, nodded when he saw it was only superficial, and then summoned his *Praefectus Equitum*, Gaius Volusenus Quadratus.

'Casualties?'

'One dead, half a dozen seriously injured, Legate.'

Antony nodded. Pleasingly light. He gave the order for the men to form up to begin their journey back to their base. As they left the field of battle, Antony took a look behind him, and let out a sigh.

'Something wrong, Legate?' asked Volusenus.

'The war in Gaul is nearly over, Prefect. The campaigning season's finished for the winter. Caesar's command will soon be at an end.'

'Time for a well-deserved rest for everyone, then, sir?'

'I suppose so. It will be time for me to begin my political career. It's going to be years before I get a chance to lead an army into battle again, if ever.'

He shook his head.

'Life,' he said, 'is about to become much less exciting.'

November DCCIII AUC (November 51 BC), Northern Gaul

Caesar had left Antony in charge of fifteen cohorts – two and a half legions – and ordered him to hold down the territory of the Bellovaci, a tribe of the Belgae who had always acquitted themselves admirably in combat. Despite the crushing defeat that Caesar had inflicted on the Gauls at Alesia the previous year, the country was still not entirely pacified. The Bellovaci had, sensibly in hindsight, not fully committed themselves to Vercingetorix, and so had retained enough manpower to muster a large army. Their leaders were Correus and an Atrebatian called Commius, who had been a thorn in Caesar's side for many years.

Formerly an ally of Caesar during his expedition to Britannia, Commius had helped with the negotiations for the British chieftain Cassivellaunus' surrender, but then had changed his loyalties and switched sides to support the Gallic leader Vercingetorix at Alesia. He had developed an even deeper hatred of the Romans after Caesar's second-in-command, Labienus, had lured him into a trap, assuring him of safe conduct to negotiate a peace, and then attempting to have him killed. But Gaius Volusenus Quadratus, the cavalry officer Labienus had tasked with the assassination, who was now Antony's Praefectus Equitum, only succeeded in wounding him.

A few months previously, Correus and Commius had planned an ambush that might have annihilated a large proportion of the Roman forces in Gaul. But Caesar's spies warned him, and he turned the ambush against the Bellovaci, inflicting a heavy defeat in which Correus was killed and Commius fled to the Germans. The Bellovaci had sued for peace and given hostages, freeing Caesar's forces for an orgy of near genocidal slaughter in the territory of the Eburones – revenge for a defeat the tribe had inflicted on Caesar years earlier. Antony had no regrets at being left behind at that time – there was no honour and no thrill in hacking down unarmed farmers and their families. But he was more frustrated when Caesar had marched south to deal with a revolt of the Carduci and Senones tribes, and left him behind to keep watch over the thoroughly cowed Bellovaci.

Antony had decided to overwinter in the territory of the Atrebates, near the coast across from which, on a clear day, could be seen the cliffs of Britannia. He settled himself in for a prolonged period of boredom, interspersed with bouts of heavy gambling, heavy drinking and heavy petting with some of the most alluring of the local courtesans.

That evening had, in fact, included all three of his favourite activities that didn't involve holding a sword. He had lost a small fortune gambling on a sure thing in the boxing ring, then won half of it back by challenging the winner of the bet to a drinking match. Given the amount he had drunk, that he was able to not only walk back to his quarters unaided, but also satisfy the voluptuous wife of a local merchant who had been flirting with him outrageously all evening, was a matter of personal pride.

That said, the booze had well and truly kicked in when, in the early hours of the morning, there was an urgent knocking at his door. It was the startled yelp from his companion that actually woke him, and the unfamiliar surroundings and the unexpected commotion disorientated him for a few moments. His dream about wrestling Neptune on the rocking deck of a trireme – the sea god having caught him with his wife Salacia – merged with reality to the extent that he gripped the bed to prevent himself being washed overboard.

The knocking came again, and he groggily called for whoever it was to enter. The merchant's wife screamed again and disappeared under the blankets just as the door swung open. Gaius Volusenus Quadratus stood stiffly in the doorway, eyes straight ahead, carefully avoiding paying any attention to the trembling mound beneath the bedcovers.

Antony attempted to speak and found his mouth had gummed up, as if it was full of a sour liquid with the consistency – but not the taste – of honey. He reached for a cup of wine that sat on his bedside table and swilled down the mouthful that had somehow gone undrunk. He worked his tongue over his lips and tried again.

'Volusenus. What can I do for you?'

'Legate, it's Commius. He has attacked again.'

Antony sat up abruptly, in the process pulling the covers aside and revealing the naked woman beneath. She desperately wriggled herself deeper to preserve her modesty, if not her identity. Volusenus affected not to notice. Antony's head spun, but he worked to keep his voice even and clear.

'Give me a full report.'

'Do you need a moment, sir? Shall I fetch your personal slave?'

'Get on with it, Volusenus.'

'Yes, sir. A messenger just arrived, sent by the centurion who was leading a foraging party. When the man was dispatched, the century was under heavy attack from Commius' cavalry, and greatly outnumbered. The messenger thought it likely they would be wiped out.'

'When was this? Where?'

'The attack began only around three hours ago. Some twenty miles north.'

'Twenty miles? Commius is growing bolder.'

Commius had recently re-emerged from the forests of Germania with a small but tough collection of Germanic and Gallic cavalry riders. Since Labienus' treachery and Quadratus' failed assassination attempt, he had made it his mission to make life miserable for any Roman soldiers he came across. Given that Caesar was way down south in Gallia Narbonensis, settling local legal and civil disputes and dispensing rewards to the province, which had remained loyal throughout Vercin-getorix's revolt, it was the men under Antony's command who were taking the brunt of Commius' harassment. As yet, Antony had not been able to pin down these highly mobile marauders, who were no doubt secretly assisted by the local Atrebates tribe.

But now Commius had grown too bold, and had struck too near Antony's camp. Maybe it was a deliberate provocation; maybe Commius was boosting his own men's morale by showing he could attack the Roman lines wherever and whenever he chose. Whatever the reason, it was a chance for Antony to strike back, if he was swift.

'Summon a cavalry wing. Every man who isn't mounted before I am is to be given half a dozen strokes of the vine stick.' Antony threw his legs over the side of the bed, got to his feet, put his hand out to steady himself, and staggered across the room, his flailing arms ripping the bedcovers clean off his nocturnal companion, before he pitched head first into the bedside table, which split apart under his weight. He found himself face down on the cold tiled floor, surrounded by wood splinters and shards of pottery, with the world revolving madly.

Volusenus hurried over and helped him back to the bed, where he sat down heavily, leaned forward, and retched. The vomit splashed Volusenus' *caligae*, but he made no sign that he had noticed, calling instead for a slave to fetch water. Antony groaned and put his head in his hands.

'Sir,' said Volusenus urgently, 'we must move quickly.'

'Yes, yes,' said Antony. 'I just need a few—'

He vomited again.

'Sir, let me lead the cavalry. Your evening's meal has clearly not agreed with you. I was always told never to trust the oysters in these parts.'

'It should be me,' protested Antony.

'No one will think worse of you, if you are too ill to ride out. Besides, I have a score to settle with Commius. I don't like leaving a job unfinished. Please, sir, let me take this command.'

Antony considered arguing further, but he knew it would be futile. He had prodigious powers of recovery from the effects of wine, and within a couple of hours he would be fit enough to compete in a chariot race. But every moment of delay was a chance for Commius to escape and, in all probability, to take more Roman lives another day. Antony grudgingly acquiesced.

'Mars be with you,' he said. 'Go.'

Volusenus saluted and hurried out. Antony groaned and lay on his back, his forearm across his eyes. His stomach roiled and his head spun. He heard the merchant's wife – What was her name again? – tiptoeing around the bedroom.

'I don't suppose you're up for another round?' he said, more in hope than expectation.

Without a word, she gathered her clothes and slipped away.

–

Antony waited anxiously for Volusenus' return, alternately beseeching his ancestor Hercules for his blessing, and cursing Liber Pater for the evil effects of wine. Nor did he spare himself from censure – not for having been drunk, but for having been too weak to lead the cavalry despite his inebriation. He paced the camp, berated the legionaries for any examples of bad discipline or poor equipment maintenance he came across, and shouted at the slaves. Everyone hurried to do Antony's bidding, fully aware that he was both concerned for his men's safety and badly hungover.

It was early afternoon when a messenger from Volusenus arrived back in camp. He was directed straight to Antony's headquarters, where he was received immediately.

'Report,' snapped Antony.

The messenger took a breath, and Antony reined in his temper. The man had clearly been in battle. He had a purple swelling over one eye and carried his left arm gingerly across his body. His face and armour were grimed with congealed blood, and he looked exhausted, barely able to stand. Antony pursed his lips and gestured to a stool.

'Do you need to sit?'

'Thank you, sir,' said the messenger. 'I can stand.'

Antony nodded. 'Go on.'

'We caught Commius not long after dawn. He was riding east. He did not seem in a particular hurry. Volusenus suspected that Commius did not realise there had been a survivor from his attack, and so had not expected such a swift response.'

'You engaged him?'

'We tried. But he fled. Their mounts are fast, and they know the countryside better than us. Volusenus urged us to ever greater speeds, but not everyone could keep up with him. Some of our horses went lame, or just lacked pace. But the prefect would not give up, sir, not when Commius was in his sights. He carried on, and when we caught Commius, Volusenus had less than half the men who had set out with him.

'It was what Commius had wanted all along. He had reinforcements waiting for him. He must have known there was a survivor of the previous attack, and that an expedition would be sent out. He stretched our forces out, and then with a cry that he would avenge the injury done to him, he wheeled and charged us, his cavalry close behind.

'When the prefect saw how badly outnumbered he was, he ordered a retreat, but it was too late. Commius himself caught Volusenus and stabbed him with his spear, so it went straight through the prefect's thigh.'

Antony's heart stuttered, and he swallowed before trusting himself to speak.

'Volusenus lives?'

'When I left him, sir, yes, he was still alive, though for how long I couldn't say. It was a grievous wound.'

'What happened after that?'

'We saw Volusenus was injured, sir, and we rallied. We spun our horses and charged, and by now some of our stragglers had caught up with us. The Gauls hadn't expected us to be so bold, and we fought like demons, though I say it myself, sir, to protect the prefect. We routed those bastards, begging your pardon, sir, and drove them off like a herd of pigs. The victory was ours.'

Antony smiled thinly. 'You did well, soldier. And Commius?'

'Escaped, I'm sorry to say, sir. His horse was as fast as any I've seen, and none of us could match its speed. And our second-in-command ordered us not to pursue too far, lest we be ambushed again.'

'He did the right thing,' said Antony, though his guts clenched at the thought of the infuriating barbarian getting away again. Commius would be back, more supplies would be lost, more Romans would die. Almost as bad, Labienus would mock his rival's failure. And Caesar would be unhappy. He might even question his decision to have given Antony this command.

The messenger seemed to notice Antony's dissatisfaction and said encouragingly, 'Don't worry, sir. We beat those long-haired bastards up pretty well. Commius won't be causing any more trouble with that lot.'

Maybe, thought Antony. But this was his land. How hard would it be for him to raise another force? To cause trouble all over again.

Antony continued to fret for the rest of the day, until the sentries reported that the cavalry detachment was in sight of the base. Antony hurried to the gates and waited for their arrival.

Volusenus lay in the back of one of the ox carts his men had commandeered to transport the wounded. His lips were a thin, pale line, his cheeks like chalk. His breathing was shallow and ragged. A bloodstained strip of rag acted as a makeshift bandage around his thigh.

Antony laid a hand tenderly on his cavalry prefect's head.

'You did well, Volusenus. You're a brave man.'

Volusenus grasped Antony's hand. 'I'm sorry that I let you down.'

'You did no such thing,' said Antony. 'It's I who should apologise. It should be me lying there.'

'No, sir,' said Volusenus. 'You entrusted me with leading the men. You honoured me. I'm grateful.'

'Sir,' said a *medicus* who had come running over. 'Let us take him to the *valetudinarium*. He needs treatment.'

'Of course,' said Antony, stepping back. In a low voice he said to the medicus, 'Will he live?'

The medicus shrugged. 'That's in the hands of Apollo. You should sacrifice on his behalf.'

Antony let the medicus and his orderlies transfer Volusenus to a stretcher and carry him away. Then he went in search of a seller of sacrificial animals, to make the finest offering to the gods of healing that he could.

–

Volusenus did survive. Antony didn't know whether it was the half a dozen pure white doves he had sacrificed, or the skills of the medicus, or just blind luck. He was just grateful he didn't have his prefect's death on his conscience. Men died in battle, but it would have greatly grieved Antony if his own weakness was the cause.

Volusenus' recovery was prolonged, and it was two weeks before he was even able to stand. He was fortunate, though, in both that he had not lost too much blood, and that the wound did not putrefy. He did not even lose his leg, and within a month was able to take up light duties once more.

In the meantime, Antony sent out scouts to try to track down Commius. He thought at first that the Atrebatian chief had fled back to Germania, but intelligence kept coming back to Antony that he had remained in the area. Maybe his loss of the German cavalry had made him unwelcome there. If so, it may be that the Gaul was running out of options, running out of allies, and running out of places to hide.

Antony was practising his sword work with a *gladius* on the training ground when the sentries reported riders approaching, bearing an olive branch. Soon he was informed they were emissaries from Commius, and he ordered them to be admitted. He received them in his headquarters wearing his battle dress, still grimy and sweaty from his training, seated on a *curule* chair, Volusenus standing behind him.

The delegation consisted of half a dozen warriors and nobles from the Atrebates, their long hair, grey or blond, oiled and combed, moustaches shaped, their clothing fine. Commius, Antony noted, was not among them – he had met the Atrebatian chief more than once when they had been on the same side in Britannia. He motioned for them to speak, and an elder – grizzled, bent, walking with the aid of a spear from which the point had been sawn off – stepped forward and bowed respectfully.

'Marcus Antonius, legate of the great Caesar, we come to parley for peace on behalf of our king, Commius.'

Antony let his gaze drift across each of the envoys deliberately, then returned to the spokesman.

'Your king does not seem to have graced us with his presence.'

The older Gaul looked at his colleagues uncomfortably, then back to Antony.

'Legate, may I speak openly and honestly?'

'It's an unusual proposition,' said Antony, 'but let's give it a try.'

The Gaul swallowed.

'Our king, Commius, fears the good faith of the Romans.'

Antony raised an eyebrow but said nothing, forcing the Gaul to continue.

'You are aware that he was summoned to a meeting by Caesar's second-in-command, Labienus himself. And that, trusting to the renowned sense of honour for which Caesar is known, he attended as requested, only for an attempt to be made on his life.'

Antony resisted looking at Volusenus, though he heard the cavalry officer's breathing quicken.

'I am aware of this unfortunate event.'

'Commius swore to the gods he would never meet with a Roman again, and he begs you not to force him to break this vow. He offers you peace on any terms you wish. He will stay where you order him. He will give up hostages. Our king, and the people of the Atrebates, have had enough of war, and wish to return to tending our cattle and raising our families.'

Antony stroked his fingers across the stubble on his chin, looking up at the nervous envoy thoughtfully. He let the moment of silence stretch.

Then he said, 'Very well. I judge that indeed Commius was wronged by Labienus.' He felt Volusenus stiffen behind him. 'And by Labienus alone. Caesar had no part in this plan, and the officers who attempted to carry it out were merely obeying orders, and so no dishonour attaches to them. So, I agree to your terms. You will swear on your gods and ours never again to raise arms against the Romans. You will provide us with hostages for your good behaviour. And Commius, together with a small group of followers that he may choose, will leave Gaul for Britannia, not to return.'

The Atrebatian spokesman looked at his fellow envoys, who hesitated, then nodded their assent.

'We agree to your terms, wise and merciful Antonius.'

And with that, Antony ended the war in Gaul.

December DCCIII AUC (December 51 BC), Northern Gaul

'You said what?' yelled Labienus, the scarlet of his face matching Caesar's cloak. Caesar sat in his chair, lounging on one elbow, looking on in amusement. Antony stood stiffly, his report to Caesar interrupted by the outburst.

'I said that I understood Commius' reluctance to meet Romans after he was previously wronged.' Even though Antony had softened his words and removed any reference to the direct blame he had laid on Labienus, Caesar's second-in-command was furious.

'You besmirch my good name,' he growled.

'The facts are as they are. Whether you acted with honour, with deceit, or with tactical cleverness is not for me to decide. But the Gauls took their own view of the matter, and it was an understandable one.'

Labienus whirled on Caesar. 'Are you going to accept this? He sullies your name, too.'

'I was very careful to ensure they knew that Caesar had no part in planning the assassination attempt on Commius,' said Antony.

'Assassination? I am not a common murderer. This is a war.'

'It *was* a war,' said Caesar, drily. 'Antonius appears to have decided it is over.'

Antony flushed and stayed quiet. Caesar gave a sardonic smile. 'I will ratify your decision, Antonius. There is no benefit to continuing hostilities now. I have removed the centuries-old threat to Rome from the Gaul, vastly expanded our territories and brought untold riches to the Roman treasury. After nearly a decade, it is high time to think about returning to Rome for a triumph and a second consulship.'

Antony bowed his head. 'Thank you for your confidence, Caesar.'

Labienus glowered at them both, then said through gritted teeth, 'Caesar, will you excuse me? I have duties to attend to.'

Caesar inclined his head, and Labienus stormed out with as much anger as he could display without crossing the line into outright insubordination. Caesar watched him go, then sighed.

'A fine tactician, but not always wise in his strategy.'

'Do you want me to keep an eye on him?' asked Antony, a little boldly. 'Is there any chance he would do something rash?'

Caesar let out a little laugh. 'Labineus? No, of course not. He is as loyal as a hound. I know the *optimates* are approaching him to turn him to their cause, but he is Caesarian through and through.'

'That is a relief, Caesar. I'm sorry if I overstepped the mark in my negotiations with Commius.'

'Perhaps a little. But I trusted you with the responsibility, so I should back your decisions.'

'Thank you, Caesar. What news from Rome?'

Caesar sighed and took a sip of water from a plain cup by his side.

'Politics, Antonius, and more politics. The optimates hate me for my successes. Cato opposes awarding me a triumph. Marcus Claudius Marcellus congratulates me and proposes that, since the war is over, I should disband my armies and become a private citizen. Of course, that would leave me vulnerable to prosecution on whatever false charges they could dream up. Meanwhile, Pompeius sits on the fence, loving being needed by the optimates for what they see as a defence against me, while handing me belated crumbs of support to attempt to keep me subordinate to him. He will not tolerate an equal, it seems. Do you know what he said when someone asked what he would do if I wished to be consul and retain my army?'

Antony dutifully shook his head.

'He replied, "Suppose that my son wants to attack me with a stick?"'

Antony's eyes widened. It was threatening behaviour from someone who, superficially at least, was still supposed to be Caesar's ally.

'They mean to ruin me, Antonius. But they will not find it so easy. Not while I have this.' Caesar laid his hand on the hilt of his sword, and Antony nodded approvingly.

'Nor while you have me by your side, Caesar,' he put in enthusiastically.

Caesar smiled indulgently, like a father proud of a son after some strong performance on the Field of Mars. 'You're a good man to have by me, Antonius. Unfortunately, though, we must part again.'

'Caesar?' said Antony, hopefully, always both anxious and excited when Caesar sent him away. Would it be a new command? A promotion? Or some trivial duty, a punishment for his presumption in negotiating on Caesar's behalf?

'It's back to Rome for you,' he said.

'Oh.' Antony felt a knot of disappointment in his guts. Not a punishment, but not a command either. Politics, he supposed.

'I need you to stand for election for tribune next year, so your term will begin from the beginning of the following year. I need protection from my enemies in the Senate, and a tribune's veto can provide that. Did you know they can change the law retrospectively, so that legal actions I took at the time can later be found to have been illegal?'

'What about this year coming?' asked Antony. 'And what about after my term? A tribune only holds office for a year.'

'Don't worry, this year is in hand. And in the year of your tribunate, I will legally be allowed to stand for consul, since ten years will have elapsed after my last one. Thereafter I can obtain a proconsulship, which will secure my immunity from prosecution for the foreseeable future.'

'Why not just stand for the next consulship? Pompeius didn't wait ten years.'

'Pompeius and the optimates broke the laws of the Republic they claim to uphold, by making him consul before his time. And sole consul at that! There is no such thing as a sole consul. It's like being a sole twin!'

Antony nodded, his mind ticking over. This wasn't the first time Caesar had sent him back to Rome to advance his political career. But previously, he was simply elected to the quaestorship, as was expected, with no specific task in mind. Now, he was going to Rome expressly to protect Caesar's interests, to keep him safe from his political enemies until he was able to legally protect himself.

'And your term as proconsul in Gaul ends the year you can once again become consul?' asked Antony, to clarify things in his own mind.

'That is correct. Pompeius mandated a five-year extension to my original five-year term. Although,' and here Caesar's voice became guarded, 'there are some who claim that the new five years started at the time of Pompeius' proclamation, not at the end of my current term. And it's true the wording isn't clear. These are the sort of tricks you will need to be alert for.'

Antony swallowed. Although he was a trained orator, he had little experience in the Senate, and he wondered if he was going to be in over his head, trying to counter the wiles of the likes of Cato and Cicero. He would much rather be facing barbarians wielding swords than senators brandishing scrolls. Caesar clearly read the doubts in Antony's face.

'Don't worry,' he said. 'I am not sending you into the arena alone. You will find plenty of friends in Rome to encourage and guide you. Maybe one or two closer than you expect. I'll say no more.'

Antony knew better than to press, though he had a good idea of the identity of at least one of the friends to whom Caesar was referring. His mind drifted back to Rome. To parties and plays, to his mother and brothers, to his infant daughter, little Antonia. To his wife. And to Fulvia.

He suddenly realised Caesar, contrary to what he had just said, was still speaking, and also that Caesar had realised he wasn't listening. Caesar shook his head. 'Get yourself to Rome, Antonius. And get yourself elected.'

Chapter I

It was Antony's second day back in Rome, and he was reclining on a couch in the garden room of the house that Fulvia and Curio shared. It was the same house on the Palatine, next door to Cicero, that had once belonged to the friend of Curio and Antony – and Fulvia's late husband – the rabble-rouser Clodius. Letters from Antony's brothers, Gaius and Lucius, and from Curio himself, had kept Antony informed about Curio's activities. He had continued spending money lavishly after the extravagant funeral games he had held for his father, partly in support of the public works he was sponsoring, but mainly to win over the mass of supporters who had followed Clodius, and who he now saw as his dowry, having married Clodius' widow. Antony had marvelled at Curio's expenses and bluntly asked where he was finding his funds. His friend had simply replied enigmatically that money worries were a thing of the past for him now. Antony wished the same applied to him. The debts he had accumulated in his younger days had been eye-watering, and were only going to increase as he at least partially footed the bill for his upcoming election campaign, even with Caesar taking the lion's share of the expenses upon himself.

Although on his arrival back in the capital the previous day, his first wish had been to visit his closest friend and his friend's new wife, the enchanting Fulvia, he knew his first duty was to his own family. He had visited his mother and brothers, and had been greeted with floods of tears, never-ending embraces and celebrations fit for Odysseus' homecoming. Next, he had returned to his own house. Antonia had greeted him warmly enough, with equal measures pleasure and reserve, as was proper in a Roman matron. Above all, though, Antony was delighted to meet his tiny daughter – whom his wife referred to by the dimunitive Toni, to distinguish from her own name – for the first time, and had spent hours playing with her and questioning her mother and her nursemaids about every aspect of her behaviour, progress and personality. He was gratified to know that she had taken her first steps a little earlier than most, but her speech was maybe a little behind her peers. Antony dandled her on his knee, marvelling at her perfect tiny features, experiencing all the emotions of fatherhood all over again.

Little Toni was not his first child, but two with Fadia had died before the age of three, and the third had died with its mother during the birth. The memory caused a lump to suddenly appear in Antony's throat, and he found it hard to swallow. He told himself he shouldn't get too attached to this one either, not until she was past five years at least, maybe not even until she had stopped birthing her own children. But that was easier said than done when you had such a perfect little creature in your lap.

That night he had made love to his wife. She had been unusually stiff and unresponsive. Maybe she would take some time to get used to his return; he had been away a long time, after all. And he was thinking about other women anyway. The whole exercise felt like a function that had to be performed, and he was relieved when it was over. Then he was able to look forward to seeing Curio and Fulvia.

Sitting near enough to Fulvia now that he could smell her delicate rose-scented perfume, every time he looked at his best friend's wife he got a little flutter in his abdomen. She was no beauty, though she was handsome enough. But the twinkle in her eyes, the upturn at either side of her mouth when she was teasing Antony, the soft laugh, all aroused feelings in him that he knew were wrong, but he refused to repress. He would not act on those feelings, and he doubted that Fulvia, much as his attraction to her appeared to be mutual, would respond if he did. She was a woman of strong morals, proud of her *dignitas* and *pietas*. It made him want her even more.

'I'm sorry I missed your wedding,' said Antony. 'Was it very expensive, Gaius?'

Curio chuckled at the crass question, but it was Fulvia who replied.

'Of course it was, Marcus. You know Gaius. He was hardly likely to let his nuptials go by without a wholly unnecessary extravagance.'

Antony smiled, while briefly indulging in the fantasy that it was he who had, as ritual demanded, pretended to take Fulvia from her mother's arms by force and carry her over the threshold of his house;

that it was his family that welcomed her with fire and water, that it was he who had broken a loaf of bread over her head. What a delight it must be to be married to Fulvia. Not, he suspected, that Curio truly appreciated it. He had probably abandoned Fulvia's bed in favour of some young actor already. What a waste. Although Curio hadn't admitted it, even to his closest friend, Antony strongly suspected that his marriage to Fulvia was a purely political act, to inherit Clodius' client base and his popularity among the masses. As tribune, he had already started to embark on populist projects such as a redistribution of land to the poor, a grain dole and a programme of road building.

They talked of Gaul, of married life, of the current form of the chariot racing teams, the state of the roads. Then the topic came round to politics. Antony wondered if Fulvia would take the opportunity to excuse herself and let the men talk, but she was every bit as engaged as Antony or Curio, and, if anything, better informed.

'So do you think Caesar will give up his command and return to Rome as a private citizen, so he can stand for election?' Fulvia asked Antony.

'Why should he?' shot back Antony. 'His term runs for at least another year. Surely he has done enough for Rome to be able to keep his army and celebrate a triumph, and stand for election as consul again without fear of prosecution?'

'Marcus Claudius Marcellus claims that the extension to Caesar's first term was purely to avoid him having to leave his province while it was still in open revolt. Since Alesia and the mopping-up actions afterwards, that is no longer the case, and Caesar should surrender his army, allow another proconsul to take over, and return home.'

Antony felt a surge of irritation. 'The Marcelli brothers have never hidden their hatred of Caesar. They even had a Gaul, with Latin rights from a colony that Caesar founded, flogged for no more reason than as a challenge to the *Lex Vatinia* that recognised the colony's rights as well as Caesar's Gallic command. They then had the temerity to send the poor soul to Caesar to show him his stripes.'

Fulvia had a slight upturn in one corner of her mouth, and Antony realised he was being baited.

'Well, it will all come to a head soon,' said Curio. 'Pompeius has said that he will allow a debate on Caesar's command to commence in a few days' time, on the Kalends of Martius.'

'And then what?' asked Antony. 'Will they strip him of the legions and his governorship? Can they do that legally?'

'I think you should attend the Senate on the first day of Martius.'

'The whole of Rome thinks you are still against Caesar,' said Antony. 'But that's not true, is it? What do you have planned?'

Curio gave an enigmatic smile. 'You will just have to wait and see, old friend.'

Kalendis Martiis DCCIV AUC (1 March 50 BC), Near Rome

The Senate meeting took place in a large temple dedicated to Apollo, just outside the city. Since Pompey carried *proconsular Imperium* for his governorship in Spain – to which he had not actually bothered to travel, leaving the governance of that province to his subordinates – he was not allowed inside the *pomerium*, Rome's sacred boundary, lest he forfeit his command. So the consuls, Lucius Aemilius Paullus and Gaius Claudius Marcellus had prescribed this conveniently located temple for the venue, so that the foremost citizen in Rome was able to attend. After all, nothing important could be decided without Pompey's approval anyway.

Benches had been set up in the *cella*, but even this large room was not enough to contain the whole august body of revered fathers, and so further seats had been arranged in the porch, with a few even spilling out onto the staircase leading up to the portico. Antony sat at the back, his view partly obscured by the Ionic marble columns, tall and slender and topped with scroll-like ornaments. Although the temple provided some shelter from the wind, it was midwinter, and some of the senators were pulling their togas tight and grumbling about the cold. Antony, having experienced the severity of a Gallic winter, found the temperature quite tolerable, and smirked to himself at the discomfort of the oldest of his colleagues. Despite having been elected to the Senate over two years before, he had spent most of that time with Caesar in Gaul, and so attending a Senate meeting as a fully fledged senator was still a novelty to him. His eyes surveyed row after row of serious, important men of every rank, from the lowly *quaestors* such as himself, to the tribunes who sat together in a cluster on the left, Curio numbering among them, all the way up to the two consuls seated on their curule chairs at the front. But one chair remained empty, and no attempt was made to begin the proceedings.

The senator seated next to Antony leaned in to speak to him.

'Caesar's going to learn a lesson today, don't you think?'

Antony turned and found himself face to face with Marcus Junius Brutus. The senator was relatively youthful, a couple of years older than Antony, and had a head of thick, slightly curled hair with a neatly trimmed beard. His nose was rather pronounced, his lips full, the overall impression being of a handsomeness bordering on the feminine, contrasting with Antony's manly good looks. Marcus Brutus, like his distant cousin Decimus, was another favourite of Caesar's, although, unlike the brave and skilled Decimus, Antony could not figure what Caesar saw in this one. Like Decimus, Marcus was rumoured to be Caesar's son, and the fact that his mother, Servilia, was Caesar's favourite mistress gave some credence to this, even if his date of birth made it unlikely. Still, Marcus Brutus must have felt ambivalent towards Caesar, given Caesar's relationship with his mother, not helped by the fact that Servilia was the half-sister of Caesar's most implacable enemy, Cato.

'You think so?' asked Antony, keeping his voice light. Brutus had largely refrained from taking sides in the stand-off between the optimates and Caesar. Despite this apparent lack of overt hostility to the Caesarian cause, Antony couldn't stand the man, ever since Brutus had proclaimed the murder of Antony's friend Clodius by Milo as being necessary for the welfare of the state.

'Of course. Marcellus is going to bring him down to size. Pompeius is going to permit it. And Curio is going to keep the other tribunes in line to make sure everything is voted into law. Everyone knows he is a devout anti-Caesarian, like his father. This is the beginning of the end for Caesar.'

'You sound like you would celebrate the fact?'

'I have other things on my mind, to be honest, Antonius. That precocious idiot Publius Cornelius Dolabella is trying my father-in-law, Appius Claudius Pulcher, for treason and electoral malpractice.' Antony was well aware of the identity of Brutus' father-in-law, who was the elder brother of his late friend Clodius, though at the opposite end of the political spectrum, being a diehard conservative. 'I am preparing his defence, and both Pompeius and the orator Quintus Hortensius Hortalus have agreed to speak on his behalf. It's just a shame Cicero is stuck in his province while politics is at a standstill here. He would have been even better than Hortensius.'

'I'm sure Hortensius would be delighted to hear your opinion of him as second best.'

Brutus shot Antony a sharp look, then relaxed when he saw from Antony's slight smile that his words were a joke, not a threat.

'In any case, this posturing between Caesar and Pompeius bores me. Let's just get Caesar back in Rome, let Cato prosecute him, and let due process sort out all this mess.'

Antony was about to reply when Pompey walked in. Spontaneous applause broke out, and Pompey waved and nodded his head in acknowledgement before taking his seat. Once he was settled and the hubbub had died down enough for him to be heard, Paullus rose and opened the proceedings with the prescribed prayers and the sacrifice of a white kid. The formalities aside, he ceded the floor to Marcellus, who leapt to his feet in his eagerness to speak.

'Thank you to my fellow consul, to the magistrates and senators of this house, and, of course, to Pompeius Magnus.'

Pompey inclined his head, a subtle smile of approval and acknowledgement on his lips.

'Gentlemen, the Kalends of Martius is the date from which this house decreed that discussion of the governorship of Gaul be permitted, a decree which Magnus himself has approved. That day is today, and so it falls to me to open the debate on this subject. Let me begin by giving the proconsul, Gaius Julius Caesar, all due respect and honour. His achievements in vanquishing our ancient enemy to the north have been stunning, and unequivocal proof of his strength and power when he is in command of a large number of our fine legions.'

There were nods and grunts of approval from all around the benches of senators, but Antony saw reservation and suspicion in their eyes, too. Marcellus was choosing his words carefully, and making sure that the senators didn't forget that a man who could lead his legions to defeat the vast country of Gaul could easily turn his attentions to Italy.

'But he has done the job so well, surely there is nothing left for him to achieve there. Even last year, my predecessor and cousin, Marcus Claudius Marcellus, asserted that since Caesar's victories were complete, and that all Gaul is pacified, Caesar should return home. Others thought he was premature. But now there can be no doubt that our legions are no longer needed in Gaul in such strength. Furthermore, it has been decreed that if the Senate chooses to do so, Caesar can be removed from his command from this date forward.'

Antony realised his teeth were gritted and his fist clenched, and he willed himself to relax. If the Senate voted for Caesar's recall, the proconsul would be faced with a simple but terrible choice. On the one hand, he could obey the command, lose his right to a triumph, become a private citizen and open himself to vexatious litigation, which at best would be humiliating and at worst could lead to his exile. On the other hand was war.

Marcellus continued his speech, skilfully praising Caesar while making sure everything he said underlined what a threat the proconsul was to the Republic. Antony felt increasingly helpless. As the most junior senator, a humble quaestor, he was not expected to give a lengthy speech, and his vote was one among hundreds. He wished he was facing Gauls in battle with a sword in his hand, rather than these ungrateful old men.

Eventually, Paullus decided that Marcellus had spoken enough, and gently persuaded him to conclude. Antony noticed that Paullus did not speak on behalf of the motion, but he gave each of the other senators in turn a chance to speak, as was required. Even though most just gave a brief comment on their approval or otherwise, it was a lengthy process to get the opinion of so many – especially since a few, like Cato, expounded at length on the evil of Caesar's actions since the beginning of his consulship. Antony's bladder had been filling steadily, still collecting the excess from the previous night's drinking, and he used the opportunity to sneak out and relieve himself. When he returned Cato was still droning on, but he wrapped up uncharacteristically quickly, for him. Presumably he knew he ran the risk of the proposal being talked out by a filibuster – a tactic he frequently used himself – if he went on too long.

When Paullus invited Brutus to speak, Antony's neighbour stood up and said simply, 'I have no comment on this matter, and trust to the judgement of the other revered fathers.'

Antony was called on next, and as he stood, he weighed up his options. He knew he was a skilled orator, and could give a passionate speech on Caesar's behalf. Maybe it would make little difference, but Caesar would hear that at least he had tried. But as he opened his mouth, he caught Curio's eye, and his friend gave a little shake of his head. Antony hesitated, then said, 'Like my friend Brutus here, I trust to the judgement of my colleagues.' He sat back down.

Paullus finished polling the very few senators who were junior to Antony – the quaestors elected in the last couple of years – and then announced that the motion to recall Caesar to Rome, and to immediately end his governorship of Gaul and his command of the legions, would be put to the vote in three days' time. There was a general murmur of approval, and the shuffling of chairs and benches as they prepared to disperse.

Then Curio stood, and spoke, in a loud voice that carried throughout the chamber, to the porch and beyond to the interested crowd gathered outside, a single word.

'Veto.'

Literally, *I forbid.*

There was a stunned silence that held for several heartbeats. Then chaos broke out. All the senators began shouting at once, a minority applauding, the majority jeering and yelling curses and insults. Antony sneaked a glance at Brutus, whose face, despite his professed lack of interest, wore an expression of pure shock. He turned to Antony.

'But... But... Curio detests Caesar. He spoke against him when he was campaigning to become elected tribune.'

Antony shrugged in an attempt to appear nonchalant, but he couldn't help grinning broadly.

'You knew, didn't you?' said Brutus in a suddenly accusatory tone. 'Caesar has paid Curio off. So now that he has a tribune's veto in his pocket, the Senate is powerless.'

'Didn't Caesar help you become elected *pontifex*?' asked Antony casually.

Brutus bristled. 'He may have given me some support, but that doesn't mean I am his slave, bought and paid for. I am my own man, and always will be. It seems the same cannot be said for Curio.'

Antony considered debating the matter further, but the din in the temple made conversation hard, and he couldn't see any value in arguing with this self-righteous idiot anyway.

Paullus eventually restored some degree of calm, and Curio demanded that he be allowed to address the meeting. Paullus gave him the floor, and Curio stepped forward to face the senators. The hubbub broke out again. Howls of derision, cries of 'turncoat' and 'traitor to the Republic' were hurled in his direction, but he stood calmly, and after a while the noise died down enough for him to be heard.

'Revered fathers, you may wonder why I have interposed my tribune's veto to this proposal. Certainly, I cannot disagree that there is some merit in the suggestion to reduce the burden on the state by reducing the number of legions in Gaul if they are no longer required. And I know that some of you also fear too much power concentrated in the hands of one man. Personally I have no concerns about Caesar's motives, but I was only six years old when Sulla died, and I know some of the older of my colleagues remember all too well what damage was done to the Republic by the Dictator.

'But Caesar is not the only man who holds power in Rome. In fact, another man is his equal in his influence, his territories and his legions. Pompeius Magnus here is governor of Spain, has numerous legions at his beck and call, and has the wealth and authority to set himself over all of us. Furthermore, he has shown himself willing to use unconstitutional methods, such as becoming sole consul, an unheard-of state of affairs. I have no more reason to doubt the good intentions of Magnus towards the Republic than I do those of Caesar. And yet, is it not absurd to ask one of two powerful men with the potential to set themselves up as a king to disarm, without asking the other?'

Antony looked at Pompey, whose face was slowly turning bright red. He looked as if he would explode when Curio described Caesar as his equal. Pompey believed himself the first man in Rome, and would brook no rivals.

'I therefore propose that both Caesar *and* Magnus lay down their commands at the same time. This will reassure the Senate, and the people of Rome, that neither is any threat to the Republic. What say you?'

Curio returned to his seat as the chamber erupted. If his veto had provoked an earth tremor, this was as if Vulcan had torn the ground in two. But Antony could tell that there was much more support for Curio than when he had blocked Marcellus' proposal. After all, most of the senators had no strong opinion on the matter, and just wanted peace. This was a perfect compromise. And Antony had to marvel at the genius of it. He didn't know if the idea was Curio's or had come direct from Caesar. Either way, Caesar would have known about it, and approved

– for it showed him to be a man of compromise, of moderation, a man prepared to give up power for the sake of peace. For Pompey to oppose this, as he must if he wished to remain pre-eminent in Rome, would cast him in the role of the unreasonable one, the one wishing to hold himself above his nominal equals.

Slowly, Pompey got to his feet, and at last the Senate quietened down to hear what the great man had to say. Pompey took a moment to compose himself, then spoke in a steady, clear voice.

'Like young Curio here, I have no doubt about Caesar's good intentions towards the Republic. As I know, you have no doubts about mine. I have proven myself a friend to the state on many occasions, not least by refusing the offer of dictatorship during the crisis two years ago, and instead taking the less powerful role of sole consul, and then only for as long as the situation required.

'And though Curio's proposal seems equitable, you will see that it is actually quite unfair for us to lay down our commands at the same time. My term of office is set to run for much longer than Caesar's, so the deal is unequal.

'Nevertheless, I have no desire to see Caesar inconvenienced. I propose that he give up his command on the Ides of November. He then needs to wait outside the pomerium for a mere six weeks while waiting to take office as consul, if he is fortunate enough to be elected again.'

Was this reasonable? Antony wondered. Would six weeks be long enough for Cato and Caesar's other enemies to bring a successful prosecution before he gained the legal protection of consul once more? It would be tight.

Curio clearly thought the proposition was too much of a risk. He stood up and said loudly, 'Veto!'

Pompey turned and glared at him. For a moment, Antony thought he would stride over to Curio and strike him in his fury. Instead, he threw his hands in the air and strode out.

And with that, the meeting was over. The senators stood, arguing, gesturing, pointing accusatory fingers, shouting into one another's faces. But it was all meaningless now Pompey had left. There would be no further debate. Slowly, the meeting broke up and the senators wandered away disconsolately, aware that on that day they had taken one step closer to a civil war.

Maius DCCIV AUC (May 50 BC), Rome

The best thing about watching a mime instead of a pantomime, which had recently become popular in Athens, thought Antony, was that the performers were allowed to be female and did not cover up their faces with masks – nor even, in many cases, their bodies with clothing. This meant that no matter how dull or ridiculous the play, there was usually something pleasant to rest the eyes upon.

As it happened, this play, by a rather witty equestrian called Decimus Laberius who was sitting in the audience laughing raucously at his own jokes, wasn't half bad. Antony rather admired the man who, despite his elevated rank, was happy to spend his time creating entertainment of the lowest form for the masses. His work was certainly popular with the audience, who were howling with laughter at the farcical tale involving a hilarious fool, a donkey, an implausible mix-up of identity between a master and his female slave, and an intervention by a Jupiter wearing an unnaturally proportioned phallus.

The play was being held in a marketplace, not far from the Forum, that had been cleared for the occasion. A wooden stage had been erected, and a few stools and benches placed near the front for the more important members of the audience, such as Antony and Curio. It was late afternoon and the dying sun was behind them, giving the scenery and the actors' faces a warm orange glow.

Antony noticed that Curio's attention was captured by the fool, who was an athletic young man, capable of acrobatic tumbles and pratfalls. Antony, though, could not take his eyes off the actress playing the slave. She had long, blonde hair, high, prominent cheekbones and full lips. She wore a simple white *stola* that on several occasions 'accidentally' fell off, to her feigned embarrassment and howls of delight from the audience, to reveal a curvaceous, voluptuous figure. Antony thought she had something of a Gallic heritage about her, and wondered if she was descended from slaves taken from Gaul in decades or even centuries past. More than her beauty, Antony was captivated by her performance, by turns virginal and flirtatious, in which she showed off her beautiful singing voice, sensual dancing and perfect comedic timing.

As soon as the show ended, the whole crowd stood and applauded furiously. Laberius went up on stage and bowed to accept their praise.

When he had taken his fill of plaudits, he descended, and Antony nudged Curio hard with his elbow.

'Come on, let's introduce ourselves.'

Curio did not need to be asked twice. As senators, they were already situated at the front of the audience, so it was easy for them to intercept Laberius. Antony took his arm gently but firmly.

'Decimus Laberius, what a triumph,' he said. 'What a gift you have.'

Laberius had the good grace to look humble, though his broad grin suggested he was in complete accord with Antony.

'You are very kind, Senator. And you, too, Tribune. Thank you for attending my humble show.'

'Perhaps you could introduce us to the cast?' suggested Curio, in a voice that implied it was more than a suggestion.

'Of course, of course. My *domus* is nearby. Shall we retire there for an impromptu gathering?'

'That would be most agreeable,' said Curio.

Laberius' home was not as sumptuous as that of a senator, he being merely of equestrian rank, but it was still a decent size, and soon the actors, actresses and some select invited guests were enjoying fine wines and small dishes brought round by Laberius' well-trained staff. He was obviously no stranger to entertaining, and Antony commented to Curio that their host had put on a decent spread. Curio nodded non-committally, then spotted the actor who had played the fool. He slapped Antony on the shoulder, grabbed a second cup of wine and set off to accost the young man. Antony watched him go, wondering what his marriage with Fulvia was like. For all their closeness, he had never had the courage to ask him for details, mainly for fear of planting images in his head of his best friend in bed with the woman he dreamed of at night. But maybe that was a rarity, given where Curio's true interests lay.

'Marcus Antonius, what a pleasure.'

Antony turned to see the round, ruddy face of Publius Volumnius Eutrapelus grinning broadly. Antony smiled and gave the man a rough hug.

'Eutrapelus, my old friend. Where have you been hiding?'

'Me? It's you who has spent all these years in foreign parts. I miss our adventures.'

Eutrapelus was a part of the hellraising circle that in Antony's youth had included Clodius and Curio, and they had shared a fair few cups of wine, drunken escapades, and even women over the years.

'As do I, old friend. But I think you are putting those times behind you. I hear you are making a name for yourself as a philosopher now.'

'Ha, it is so. But I never heard it said that philosophy and parties do not mix. The Symposia of Socrates himself involved copious quantities of wine, it's said. But what brings Marcus Antonius, hero of Alesia, beloved of Caesar, rising star in the Senate, to my friend Laberius' humble abode?'

'You know me. I'm not one to miss out on a party.'

'That will never change, I suspect.'

Antony cast his eyes around the room. Curio had his arm around the young actor and was deep in conversation with him. The actors who had played the master and Jupiter were talking to matronly noble women who fanned themselves and appeared shocked at their bawdy jokes and innuendos, while continuing to lap them up. But there was no sign of the actress who had captivated him in the show.

Then she walked in. She had changed into a long blue stola and now wore a gold necklace, dangling earrings and bejewelled rings on her fingers and toes. She had removed the stage make-up and had replaced it with something much subtler and more alluring. Antony's mouth became suddenly dry, while paradoxically his palms became clammy.

'Oh,' said Eutrapelus. 'You have noticed my Cytheris.'

'*Your* Cytheris?' asked Antony in surprise. 'In what way is she *your* Cytheris?'

In answer, Eutrapelus raised his hands and beckoned her over. Cytheris approached, her gait graceful as a swan on a lake. She nodded to Eutrapelus, then turned a smile on Antony that felt like a hundred midday suns. Her scent was delicate – sweet but not overpowering. Antony could feel his heart thumping in his chest.

'Antonius, may I introduce my former slave, Volumnia Cytheris. Cytheris, my dear, this is Marcus Antonius, senator and legate to Caesar.'

Cytheris extended her hand, her bare, smooth, pale-skinned arm protruding from beneath the folds of her stola. Antony took it and bowed his head to kiss it.

'It's an absolute pleasure, Antonius,' she said. Antony was surprised to note that the coarse, vulgar accent she had used while acting the slave had been replaced by a far more cultured tone. Everything about her overwhelmed Antony, and he found himself uncharacteristically lost for words.

'Don't worry,' said Eutrapelus. 'She has that effect on many people. Even on me, when I owned her. But she is too beautiful a bird to keep caged. It was one of the happiest and saddest days of my life when I freed her.'

'You have always been kind to me,' said Cytheris, 'and I will always be your freedwoman, in law and in my heart, no matter where life leads me.'

Eutrapelus patted her arm affectionately. 'Well, life has led you here to meet this handsome and powerful young man. I'll leave you to get acquainted.'

Antony was dimly aware that Eutrapelus was playing the part of matchmaker for a reason. As he had said, Antony's star was rising, and in the Roman system of favours and back-scratching, it was in the interests of Eutrapelus – who, like Laberius, was an equestrian – to have someone as powerful as Antony in his debt. He was aware, too, that this could easily be read as Eutrapelus pimping out a former slave who was still beholden to him, especially one who belonged to a profession that was widely considered to involve prostitution to a greater or lesser extent. But at that moment, all he could focus on were Cytheris' eyes, with an occasional glance down at her generous breasts.

'It's stuffy in here,' said Cytheris. 'Would you care to accompany me on a promenade?'

'It would be a delight.' Antony offered her his arm.

Cytheris took it, and he led her out into the cool evening air.

They wandered west, through the Forum, out to the Tiber, crossing over the Pons Fabricius to the Tiber Island. Her easy manner quickly calmed Antony, and he found his voice again, so they chatted the whole way, talking about everything and nothing. She had a good understanding of current politics, philosophy and history, and also had a quick wit and charming turn of phrase. Thoughts of Fulvia were pushed to the back of his mind, and the fact that he was married to Antonia did not even enter his consciousness. When they returned across the Pons Fabricius towards the city, they stopped and watched the boats on the river, the reflected moonlight shimmering on the surface. Antony turned towards Cytheris, put both his arms around her waist, pulled her close and kissed her lips. She responded, her warm, soft body pressing against him close, her tongue touching his tongue.

They parted after a moment that stretched for an eternity and at the same time was far too brief.

'The hour is getting late,' said Cytheris. 'I should return home. Would you be so kind as to escort me?'

Antony readily agreed, and when they reached her apartment, which was on the first floor of a well-maintained *insula* in a comfortable neighbourhood, she kissed him again, and said, 'Thank you for a wonderful evening. I hope we meet again. Goodnight.'

She disappeared inside without a backward glance. Antony stared at the door she had closed behind her, not quite sure what had just happened. It was an unusual feeling for him to be left alone at the end of an evening, and it was doubly surprising given Cytheris' profession. Antony had lain with a fair number of actresses in his life, and though he was careful to only select those he thought showed a genuine interest in him, he was aware that sleeping with noble and powerful patrons and friends of the owners of the theatres and theatrical troupes was expected as part of the job. And yet, he had the strange feeling that if Cytheris had invited him inside, he would have been somehow disappointed.

He shook his head. Cytheris was right: it was getting late. Could he find another party? But the desire for more entertainment had left him. He headed for home, his sense of smell still saturated by her perfume, his lips still carrying her taste, his head full of this amazing woman.

–

It was probably past midnight when Antony returned home. The porter opened the door, and called out in a loud voice, 'The master has returned.'

Antony looked at him in surprise. Why was he announcing his arrival in his own home, especially at this late hour when everyone should be asleep? He walked through the atrium and noticed that there were lamps lit in the *peristylium*, so he continued through into the garden.

Antonia was sitting on a stone bench, opposite a man whose back was towards Antony. Her legs were crossed and her hands were in her lap. The flickering lamplight illuminated a serene expression on her face. She rose to her feet, and stepped forward to greet him, kissing him on both cheeks.

'Darling, welcome home.'

The man she had been talking to stood and extended his hand.

'Antonius, good to see you.'

'Dolabella,' said Antony, smiling and shaking the offered hand firmly, looking down at him. Dolabella was a particularly short man, and slight, in stark contrast to Antony's build. He was the best part of a decade younger than Antony, much closer to his wife's age than Antony himself. Dolabella had therefore been too young to be part of Antony's social circle before he left for the East and Gaul, and Antony had only met him a couple of times. Strangely, though, his name had come up that evening, as the well-informed Cytheris was updating him on the various goings-on in the city, filling in the lacunae in his knowledge of the latest gossip that his mother, his brothers, Curio and Fulvia had left out.

Until that evening, Antony had only the vaguest awareness of Dolabella's existence, though he knew he was a friend of Caelius – whom he had never forgiven for spying for Cicero against his father-in-law in the Catilinarian conspiracy – which was reason enough in his mind to be suspicious of him. He hadn't known his wife knew him at all, although, being of similar age, he supposed they might have met at one function or another in the past. Cytheris had more detailed knowledge of Dolabella than many, since he was a good friend of her former master, Eutrapelus, and Dolabella had had a lot going on in his life in the first few months of the year, much of it in the public domain. What was less commonly talked about, at least in social circles of the nobility, was what his slaves thought of him. Cytheris had told Antony that Dolabella had a reputation for casual cruelty, and seemed to enjoy punishing his slaves personally, with whip or rod or his bare hands, for the most minor of transgressions or for no reason at all. Antony had put a protective arm around Cytheris at that point. Even though she had never belonged to Dolabella, and it seemed Eutrapelus had been good to her, it made him shudder to think of a defenceless woman like her in the hands of a rough master.

Antony looked between the young man and his wife, and let the silence stretch, waiting to see what they had to say for themselves. Both spoke at once.

'Dolabella just came by to—'

'I had no idea how late it was—'

They both stopped and looked at each other.

Antony smiled and spread his arms in a welcoming gesture. 'Not late at all, Dolabella. Please, be seated. I'll join you. If –' he tilted his head quizzically – 'I'm not intruding.'

'Of course not, no,' they both gushed, and Antonia moved up on her bench so her husband could sit beside her.

'Your wife and I were just reminiscing over some childhood memories,' said Dolabella. 'Our fathers knew each other, and we played together from time to time when we were young.'

'I didn't know that.' Antony turned to Antonia, who was nodding in eager agreement.

'Yes, just chatting about our childhood,' she said earnestly. She was really quite attractive, Antony thought. He wondered why he felt so little for her. Was it because he didn't really choose her? Because marriage had been forced on him by Caesar, and his mother had selected the most appropriate candidate? Or was it just because there was so little about her? He thought of the women he had been drawn to – Clodia, Fadia, Fulvia, and now Cytheris. All very different, but all brimming with personality, with life. Antonia, for all her superficial beauty, just didn't stir any emotion within him.

Anything apart from jealousy, that was. She was still married to him, after all, and whatever his feelings towards her, she belonged to him. He fought down his irritation and kept his voice even and light.

'You've been busy lately, I hear, Dolabella,' he said. 'Commiserations on your divorce.'

Dolabella stiffened. His wife had left him a couple of months previously. She had not given a reason, but perhaps he had demonstrated the same cruelty to her that he showed his slaves. Of course, since she was a member of the aristocratic Fabian family, Dolabella would never have left a visible mark on her, but Antony knew that men such as he could be vicious in private while appearing to be upstanding citizens in public.

'Not every marriage is a happy one,' said Dolabella pointedly, not needing to look over to Antonia to make his point.

'True,' said Antony. 'Maybe your engagement to Tullia will be more felicitous.'

Now Dolabella looked shocked, and Antonia seemed to grow a little paler.

'How do you know about that?'

'This is Rome, young man,' said Antony, hoping he sounded patronising. 'One day, you will learn there are no secrets in this city.'

Cytheris had, in fact, told him that Cicero's wife Terentia was pushing for the match for their once widowed and once divorced daughter, although Eutrapelus, who often corresponded with Cicero, thought the orator was not so keen. But with news taking around two months to get to Cilicia and back, Cicero was too remote to have much influence on the matter.

'You're engaged?' asked Antonia, staring at Dolabella, her voice accusatory. Then she seemed to remember the presence of her husband. 'Congratulations,' she said, and forced a smile.

For a moment it crossed Antony's mind that Antonia had been unfaithful to him, here in his own house. He forced himself to confront the possibility. But he thought it unlikely. Their evening may not have been entirely appropriate, but Antony could not believe that they would be so blatant, with so many of his loyal servants in the household who would report back to him. Nor did he believe Antonia capable of such a betrayal. Still, he would have to keep an eye on them. But it seemed his mention of Dolabella's engagement had cooled Antonia's ardour in any case.

'And then, of course, there is your prosecution. Bad luck on that one.'

It had just been announced that the trial Brutus had mentioned to Antony – the prosecution of his father-in-law Appius Claudius Pulcher by Dolabella – had concluded, with the former censor and consul being fully acquitted. Given he had Brutus, Pompey and Hortensius – once the foremost orator in Rome, before Cicero had taken that accolade – testifying on his behalf, it had always been a hopeless cause. Sometimes, though, vexatious prosecutions were brought purely to raise the political profile of the prosecutor, regardless of the merits of the case, and Antony suspected this had been Dolabella's motivation all along.

The younger man shrugged. 'These things happen. But whatever the outcome, at least the trial will be remembered.'

'As an object lesson to budding jurists?' asked Antony with a smirk.

'No,' said Dolabella. 'As Hortensius' last ever trial.'

'He has retired?'

'No, he's dead. Keeled over in the street just this morning.'

Cytheris hadn't mentioned that. But he hadn't let the conversation stay on politics all night, so maybe he should take some of the blame for that.

'Well,' said Antony, taken aback. It seemed that Quintus Hortensius Hortalus had been around forever, having fought in the Social War forty years prior, and been a permanent fixture on the political and judicial scene since then, though lately he had spent most of his spare time breeding ornamental fish. He had caused a minor scandal by – at the age of nearly sixty – asking to marry Cato's twenty-year-old daughter, who was already married. Cato, wishing for closer ties to the orator, instead divorced his own second wife and allowed Hortensius to marry her instead, though she was only around twenty-five at the time. And now he was gone.

A thought occurred to Antony. 'Wasn't Hortensius an augur?'

Dolabella looked confused at the question. 'I... believe so.'

'Interesting.' And an idea took form in Antony's mind.

–

'Do you actually know anything about augury?' asked Curio, as they stood at the edge of the wide expanse of the *Campus Martius*, watching the long lines of tribal members casting their votes.

'I know that being elected to the college of augurs is one of the most sought after and prestigious posts in the Republic,' said Antony. 'I know that augurs have the right to adjourn and overturn elections and court rulings. And most importantly, I know they have a right to participate in all the state festivals and banquets.'

Curio shook his head. 'You can only overturn rulings if you observe signs that are not propitious. Do you know how to look for those signs?'

'I'll pick it up as I go along. How hard can it be?'

Antony doubted that few of the sixteen priests in the college of augurs really knew what they were doing, or even believed in all the superstitions associated with the position. It had long been a political post – one of great, if soft, power. And Antony was a well-educated man. He knew that augury involved the reading of signs largely related to the heavens, such as lightning and the flight of birds, as well as the feeding patterns of Mars' sacred chickens. He knew that augurs had, over the centuries, developed ways to ensure that the ship of state was not paralysed by the omens constantly surrounding them, such as avoiding looking for them or carefully choosing a time when the observations would be made. He knew, too, that most of the masses of the city believed in the superstitions absolutely, and that as a man of the people, he would have to appear to share their beliefs. Not that he completely dismissed them himself. He had a just-in-case attitude to the gods, happy to give them their dues on the off chance they existed. Many soldiers shared his pragmatism.

The voting procedure was lengthy, and Antony wearied of standing for such a long time, though he knew he had no choice. He sipped watered wine and shuffled from foot to foot, acknowledging clients and supporters offering him their best wishes with his best humour.

'Thanks for being here,' Antony said to Curio.

'Where else would I be?'

Antony was truly grateful for Curio's support. He had thrown all his power behind Antony's bid for the priesthood, marshalling all of Clodius' mob, whom Curio had inherited when he married Fulvia, to campaign on his behalf. Caesar, too, had given his full backing when Antony had informed him of his plan. He promised Antony an open purse to spend as he saw fit, canvassed vigorously on his behalf, and even sent soldiers and Gallic citizens to Rome to swell the ranks of the voters. It was just as well. It had been a bruising campaign, far worse than his election to the Senate as a quaestor, which was little more than a formality for one of his rank. Now he was seen as a limb of Caesar, and the optimates desperately wanted to avoid that man increasing his already vast power in any way.

The optimates' candidate was Lucius Domitius Ahenobarbus, a former consul. He was also Cato's brother-in-law, and his political views aligned completely with Cato's ultraconservatism. He was generally considered, by reason of his age, experience and support from the Senate, to be the clear favourite in this contest against the young upstart Antony, a lowly quaestor. Domitius had sworn to have Caesar's command in Gaul terminated several years earlier when he was campaigning for consul, but lost the election when Pompey's and Crassus' soldiers drove him from the Campus Martius. When he finally did get elected consul, Pompey's and Caesar's power was too great for him to move against them. Now, of course, with Pompey and Caesar no longer on friendly terms, Domitius had allied himself firmly with Pompey, who was also supporting his election. The optimates had done everything they could to damage Antony's reputation, bribing the electorate against him, publicly condemning his character, as well as warning of the threat to the state from Caesar's power that his election would augment. Antony had spent the last weeks making speech after speech in support of his candidacy up and down Italy. In his favour, too, was that Domitius already held a priesthood, and to have two was unheard of. He hoped that was enough.

As the vote neared its end, Antony felt a rising tension inside. Whatever else happened in his political career, this could be the making of him. A lifelong sinecure that brought prestige and influence would go a long way to solving his ongoing financial worries. And it would increase his standing even further in Caesar's eyes. He thought with satisfaction of the bitterness Labienus would surely feel at his further advancement.

The presiding magistrate mounted a platform and announced that the voting was concluded. Antony and Curio made their way forward and climbed onto the platform beside the magistrate, Cato and Domitius doing likewise. The crowds roared in favour of their candidates, and Antony could not tell who was getting the most cheers. Domitius wore a smug look on his face. Cato shot Antony a dagger glare. Curio squeezed his friend's arm.

The magistrate raised his arms for quiet. When the noise had died down sufficiently for him to be heard, he called out in a deep voice that carried well, 'The tribes of Rome have voted, and their decision has been made. The position of augur vacated by the late and much lamented Quintus Hortensius Hortalus, orator of renown, quaestor in the six hundred and seventh-third year since the founding of the city, *aedile* in the six hundred and seventy-ninth year since the founding of the city, *praetor* in the six hundred and eighty-second year since the founding of the city, consul in the—'

'Get on with it,' someone yelled, and Antony, who felt he was about to shake the magistrate, such was his suspense, smiled inwardly.

The magistrate looked irritated by the interruption, but continued smoothly, 'I hereby announce that the new augur will be Marcus Antonius.'

Antony's first sensation was profound relief, that he had not been humiliated, that he had not lost. This was quickly followed by a surge of excitement from deep in his belly that erupted from his throat in a triumphant cry. The crowd erupted into roars of delight and anger – an even split. The decision must have been very close.

Curio hugged Antony tight, and yelled in his ear, 'You're important now, old friend. I always knew you would be.'

Domitius stalked over to Antony, face like a storm cloud pent up with thunder and lightning. Grudgingly he held out a hand. 'I should congratulate you,' he said, 'though the words stick in my throat.'

Antony shook the offered hand. 'Very gracious of you, Domitius.' He was wondering what else to say when Cato physically thrust Domitius aside. As usual, he was barefoot and wearing a toga with no under-tunic, half his puny chest on display, puffed out in righteous indignation.

'You are the scum of the earth,' he said in a tone of barely repressed fury. Droplets of spittle flew out as he spoke, making Antony wrinkle his nose in distaste. Cato didn't seem to notice, and continued his rant, thrusting a finger close into Antony's face. 'You do the bidding of Caesar like you are his slave. Worse, his *catamite*. Every bit of power that Caesar grabs for himself, every ally of his that advances himself with Caesar's funds, brings Caesar closer to what he really wants – to be the first man in Rome, another Sulla, even a king!'

Antony shook his head. Caesar didn't want to be king. No one wanted to be king. Not of Rome, at least. It was an archaic and obsolete title. Far more *auctoritas* and *dignitas* could be garnered by a man taking the top jobs in the Republic and being acknowledged foremost among his peers, as Marius, Sulla and, until recently, Pompey had been. But then, he had always doubted how firm Cato's grip on reality was. Looking at him now, his dress inspired by statues of the ancestors, raging and frothing, Antony thought he was a short step away from standing naked on a rock in the desert, beard to his genitals, yelling prophecies at the vultures.

It would have been easy for Antony to argue back, to even take up violence against the self-righteous prig. No one who had witnessed Cato's provocation would condemn Antony for striking him. But his mood was too good to be spoiled by this ass.

'Cato, my friend, are you quite all right? You have gone red. I think maybe standing in the sun for too long has got to your head.'

Curio grinned, and those of the crowd near enough to hear the exchange laughed loudly. Cato blustered, even made to grab at Antony, uneven as that contest would have been. Domitius intervened, putting his arms around Cato and guiding him away.

'Come on, friend. Caesar's bribery and coercion has stolen this priesthood from me, but there is nothing we can do about that. We will have to find other ways to foil that man's rapacious ambitions.'

Reluctantly, Cato allowed himself to be led away. Antony turned to the crowd and gave them a short speech in his favoured Asiatic style, full of dramatic gestures, emotion and word play. It was fitting, since it had been Hortensius' favourite style, in contrast to Cicero's more simplistic Attic style, and Antony made sure to appease both the crowd and the shade of his predecessor by lavishing praise on the deceased orator and fish-fancier.

When he was finished, he left the Campus Martius with Curio, their entourages of slaves and bodyguards parting the admiring crowds to allow them to pass unimpeded.

'We celebrate tonight?' asked Curio.

'Of course,' said Antony, 'once I have written to Caesar with the good news.'

'Perhaps you would care to dine at my house?'

'Thank you. You know I never pass up a chance to spend time in the company of your beloved.'

Curio laughed. Although Antony had never expressed it, he was sure his friend knew his feelings towards his wife, but equally knew that Antony would never betray him, and nor would Fulvia.

'And you will bring your own delightful wife?' asked Curio, and Antony could tell he was hoping the answer would be no. It was, in fact, tempting to bring Antonia along just so he could keep an eye on her, but he had had a word with his most trusted household slaves to report back to him any suspicious or improper behaviour on her part, and so it was not really necessary. Besides, he had a much more agreeable companion in mind.

'No, I had thought to bring Cytheris.'

Curio stopped walking and looked at Antony, one eyebrow raised.

'You don't object?' asked Antony.

'Certainly not,' said Curio, then laughed. 'But many would. I'm just picturing Cato's face if, in the unlikely event you were invited to dine with him, you turned up at his house with an actress on your arm. I honestly believe he would faint in shock.'

Antony smiled, but it was a weak smile. His friend was more liberal in regards to associating with the lowest classes, the *infamia* who had lost certain citizen privileges because of their careers, like prostitutes and actors. Curio certainly had spent plenty of time around practitioners of both those professions. But it bothered Antony that people might think less of Cytheris – who he was becoming increasingly fond of – because of her position in society. It had been the same with his first wife Fadia, the daughter of a freedman.

He shook the feelings off. The political reality was that he did have to be careful about his reputation if he wanted to continue to advance. Becoming elected augur was a fantastic and fortuitous prize, but the real reason he was in Rome was to become tribune, and after this defeat, the optimates would be straining every sinew to make sure that Antony and Caesar's other preferred candidates did not succeed. Because, as Curio had shown, the power of the Tribune's veto could paralyse the Senate, and if Caesar could control the tribunate for one year, the calendar would have advanced enough that he could stand for consul before surrendering his army.

'Come on,' said Antony. 'Let's find a tavern for a decent drink before we go home.'

Chapter II

News spread around Rome the way a fire did. It caught in one corner of the city, then spread from house to house, street to street, bringing with it uproar and chaos. So it was on that day, when a messenger arrived from Syria to say that the Parthians were preparing to invade. The Parthians had become Rome's most feared enemy since, within the space of a few years, Caesar's brilliance had eliminated the Gallic threat to the north while Crassus' incompetence had vastly increased the danger from the East.

A meeting of the Senate was hastily convened to discuss what should be done; the venue once again was the temple of Apollo outside the pomerium, to allow Pompey to attend. Antony had to admit that it was reasonable that Pompey have his say as the commander of one of the two largest bodies of men in the Empire, and also one with considerable experience of fighting in the East. Antony was no stranger to the Eastern borders himself and, but for Pompey's interference, might have been part of poor exiled Gabinius' planned expedition into Parthia.

The details were vague, but it seemed that the Parthians had been raiding Syria for a few months, and then followed up with an assault on Antioch, which was being held off by Gaius Cassius Longinus, the survivor of Parthia. The senators muttered in disquiet. Some of the oldest members clearly remembered the surprise attack by Mithridates of Pontus on a number of Roman cities in Western Anatolia, that resulted in the massacre of some eighty thousand civilian men, women and children. Rome had had little trust for the peoples of the East since that day. An invasion by Parthia, while too far away to be a direct threat to Rome, could mean the loss of Roman territory in Syria and Asia – and, if they were really ambitious, might even threaten Egypt, source of a lot of the grain that kept Rome fed.

So there was a rare but genuine consensus that something must be done. What that something was, however, was more controversial. Some argued that Pompey, who really should have been in Spain, should immediately travel east with whatever forces could be mustered, to take command of the situation. Others asserted it must be Caesar who went east – he was no longer needed in Gaul, and had a battle-hardened army ready to smash the Parthian threat. But Pompey and the optimates were unwilling to extend Caesar's command in this way, or to allow him the glory of yet more victories. Defeating both Gaul and Parthia would without doubt eclipse anything that Pompey had done, and make Caesar the foremost general in Rome. Yet the optimates would not countenance sending Pompey east, since that would leave Rome at the mercy of Caesar.

Someone, for want of at least making some progress, suggested that Pompey and Caesar both contribute a legion from their armies and send them to Rome in preparation for an expedition against Parthia. The proposal was broadly welcomed, but before it was put to a vote, there was a moment of hesitation, when all looked to Curio to see if he would interpose his veto.

Curio stood, and seemed to enjoy holding the Senate's rapt attention for a long moment. Then he said, 'I support this even-handed motion, as I am sure would Caesar if he stood before you today.'

There was a massive sigh of relief, as if the whole room had been holding its breath. The motion was put to a vote and was passed with overwhelming support. Paullus declared that an official message be sent to Caesar, demanding that he surrender his Fourteenth Legion. Paullus then addressed Pompey.

'Magnus, which legion will you be donating to this expedition?'

Pompey stood up, looked around the room, and with a slight smile on his lips, said in a clear voice, 'The First.'

There was a moment's pause, then an outcry, half the house calling Pompey a cheat, half of them laughing uproariously. Brutus, who was again sitting beside Antony, looked at him in confusion. 'What's the problem with the First?'

Antony pursed his lips in irritation, then said in a tight voice, 'Pompeius lent that legion to Caesar three years ago to help with an uprising in Gaul. It is still numbered among Caesar's forces.'

'But it belongs to Pompeius. What is the problem?'

Antony didn't reply. Brutus was right. In theory, the legions did not belong to either Pompey or Caesar, but to the Republic. In practice, they tended to give their allegiance to their general, especially ones as legendary as Pompey and Caesar. But for Pompey to choose to weaken Caesar by demanding back the legion he had lent him, so that he lost no legions and Caesar lost two, was at best a sign of his mistrust of Caesar, and at worst, outright bad faith. Antony thought it probable that Caesar would obey the command. To refuse would put Caesar at odds with the Republic and push him closer to war – a war that Caesar still hoped to avoid. Antony, having spent the last few months watching Caesar's enemies from up close, was much less confident that this was possible. War, he was beginning to feel, was becoming inevitable.

Quintilis DCCIV AUC (June 50 BC), Rome

The speech had gone rather well, Antony thought, as he stood on the Rostra in the Forum, arms raised to receive the applause of the crowd. Curio had been coaching him on matters of electioneering, including telling the masses what they wanted to hear, and Antony's talent for oratory hammered the message home. That message could easily be summarised: Caesar good, Pompey bad. He added more nuanced arguments for those educated enough to understand and interested enough to care, such as Caesar's earnest desire to contest the election for consul within the terms of the law, in contrast to Pompey's unconstitutional behaviour in assuming a sole consulship. But really what the crowd wanted to hear was that when Caesar returned to Rome, he would distribute the vast riches he had accumulated in Gaul back to the city in the form of games, building works and lavish gifts to all and sundry. And for this to happen, they must elect Antony tribune, to protect Caesar's interests from those in the Senate who would harm him.

He descended from the Rostra into the Forum to walk among the people, followed by a decent-sized entourage of his clients and most devoted followers. Men pressed in on him to shake his hand, and women reached out to touch his specially whitened toga – the *toga candida* that showed he was a candidate for office – to receive the blessing of the city's newest priest. For a moment, he thought of the young boy he had once been, hearing the news of his father's death and facing grief and destitution. Or the adolescent, forced to stand by helplessly while Cicero ordered the execution of this stepfather. How far he had come!

His *nomenclator*, always close in attendance on occasions such as this, whispered into Antony's ear the names of the men who approached him, so Antony could greet them like old friends. He doled out generous amounts of cash, promised favours, and widely distributed free tickets to a gladiatorial contest that Curio had helped him organise.

There was a commotion near the edge of the Forum, and Antony, surrounded by the crowds, could not at first see what was happening. Soon it became clear – a large mob of Pompey's supporters, veterans and thugs, pushed their way towards Antony, shouting abuse and pushing the crowd aside, kicking and punching any who were too slow to move. Antony felt a moment of alarm. He was unarmed, and though he had his most loyal clients at his back, they, too, were weaponless, and they were mostly older equestrians who had never seen military service and would be of little use in a fight.

Then another noise attracted his attention. From the opposite side of the Forum, a section of the crowd suddenly pulled back the folds of their cloaks to reveal clubs and rods. With a yell, they charged forward, the rest of the crowd scattering out of the way. Antony braced himself. He was too hemmed in to run. There was nothing he could do but face this two-pronged attack and pray their instructions were to beat him, not kill him.

But the men with clubs flew straight past Antony and started laying into Pompey's men. A huge brawl broke out: dozens of men on both sides, wrestling, punching, biting, breaking limbs and skulls. Pompey's men were tough, but they had no weapons, and soon were in retreat across the rapidly emptying Forum, disappearing off in the direction of the *Subura*. The victors of the brawl were not sated, however, and took their clubs to the market stalls at the Forum edges, and to statues and ornaments, smashing them to pieces with loud cries of 'Down with Pompeius!' and 'Antonius for tribune!'

Antony's slaves formed a protective ring around him now, and led the bemused candidate away from the trouble, leaving the riot to burn itself out on its own.

Not clear what had happened, Antony needed the counsel of his closest friend, and so made his way to Curio's house on the Palatine.

When he arrived, Fulvia greeted him, and told him Curio had been in Campania, but she expected him back that afternoon. Antony wondered whether to return later, but Fulvia would have none of it.

'You look exhausted, Antonius, and dare I say it, a little pale? Come and sit with me, and take some wine and food and tell me about your campaign.'

Antony needed little encouragement to spend time with Fulvia, so he gladly accepted. The sun was beating down, and he was grateful for the watered wine chilled with the luxury of a little ice, imported at great expense from the heights of the Alps, as well as for the fanning of the slaves. They sat in the shade, and Antony let his eyes wander over the woman he craved but could never have.

Fulvia noticed the direction of his gaze and smiled knowingly. Antony looked hastily away, taking a sip of his wine to cover his embarrassment.

Fulvia asked some perceptive questions about the election, and Antony found himself drawn into a deep conversation about canvassing tactics, almost forgetting that he was talking to – and taking advice from – a woman about politics, something that was firmly a male domain. He could never have a conversation like this with Antonia, he thought. Cytheris, on the other hand, could have held her own in this discussion. She did not have Fulvia's level of education, nor her lifelong exposure to society's elites, though lately she had been moving in those circles. But she was sharp, naturally bright and a quick learner. Like Fulvia, Cytheris was someone he could talk to for hours about any topic under the heavens. It struck him suddenly that he was becoming rather fond of Cytheris, and was greatly looking forward to seeing her again later.

'You didn't tell me about your speech in the Forum today,' said Fulvia eventually. 'How was it?'

'Odd,' said Antony. 'There was an incident.'

'Oh? Tell me more.'

Antony relayed how Pompey's veterans had attempted to disrupt his meeting, but that another group of men had countered them – apparently his own supporters, though he had no prior knowledge of them.

'Ah,' said Fulvia, looking down into her lap.

'What?' asked Antony, a sudden realisation creeping over him.

'That may have been my doing.'

'Is that right?' said Antony, tightly.

Fulvia took an olive from a plate held ready by a nearby slave, chewed it, then delicately spat the stone out into the slave's hand.

'You aren't naive,' she said. 'Elections in Rome aren't fair. They aren't a demonstration of the will of the people. Rome is not a democracy like Athens once was. The results are unbalanced from the start, with the votes of the elites counting for more than the commoners, and with huge blocs voting the way their patrons dictate. Then there is the bribery, the extortion, the ballot box stuffing, the violence. It's only if these factors are balanced on both sides that a candidate is elected based on his own merits.'

'Of course I know all this,' said Antony. 'And so you, what – hired a mob?'

'Not I. Curio,' said Fulvia. 'But it was my suggestion.' She looked Antony straight in the eye. He looked away and shook his head.

'I want to be elected on my own terms, because of my own auctoritas and dignitas.'

Fulvia leaned forward and put a hand on Antony's knee.

'Marcus, the common people love you. Caesar loves you. Curio loves you. I…'

He looked up.

'I,' she continued, 'have a great admiration for your achievements. Quaestor, legate, now augur. And the tribunate will be yours, too. You just have to play the game. Not by the rules. By the way others play it.'

Antony sighed. She was right, of course, as usual. There was a name for people who played fair in Roman elections – losers.

'I suppose I should be thanking you both instead of grumbling, then.'

'That would be appropriate. Curio's mob saved you from a beating today. Or worse.'

'I should beef up my own bodyguard,' mused Antony, and he thought about drafting in a few veterans who had served with him in Syria and Gaul.

The guard dog barked, and Antony heard the front door open, footsteps in the vestibule. Curio came straight through to the peristylium, throwing off his travelling cloak and kicking off his dusty sandals, replacing them with clogs a slave hastily set out for him. He strode over to Fulvia and gave her a warm embrace and a small kiss, then turned to Antony.

'Marcus! What a pleasure to be welcomed home by my two favourite people in the world.'

Antony hugged him, careful not to squeeze too hard. Despite Curio having a few years on him, Antony had quickly outgrown him in their adolescent years, and in his twenties had become twice as broad as his old friend.

'I've got a bone to pick with you,' he said. 'You could at least have told me you were hiring a mob on my behalf.'

Curio waved it away.

'Don't be ungrateful, Marcus. It's not like you. Anyway, I have something much more important to talk about.'

'Oh?'

'I've just come back from paying my respects to Pompeius. I wanted to meet with him, to try to find some sort of middle ground with Caesar.'

'How is the grumpy old bastard?' asked Antony.

'That's the thing,' said Curio. 'He's dying!'

September DCCIV AUC (September 50 BC), Cisalpine Gaul

For most of that month, Pompey's life hung in the balance. The physicians declared he had a severe fever, and though they purged and bled him, they shook their heads gloomily when asked if he would survive. The citizens of Rome and all Italy publicly beseeched the gods to heal the great man. The sellers of temple animals made vast profits as they sold out time and again to people making sacrifices to Apollo Iatros, to Aesculapius and to Jupiter Optimus Maximus. Small groups of people muttered in taverns and marketplaces about what a disaster would befall Rome if her greatest general died, leaving the city defenceless against all enemies, internal and external.

So when it was announced that Pompey had, in fact, made a full recovery, the city erupted in spontaneous celebration. Plays were performed, more sacrifices made, and a vast crowd trekked to Pompey's countryside villa to greet him and show him how much he was loved. Pompey, of course, lapped up the adulation, and Antony was sure that he would take the adoration of the masses as proof of his pre-eminence, and his lack of need to continue to be on good terms with Caesar. After all, if he could command such loyalty in Rome, who could possibly assail his position?

The day of the elections for the ten tribunes of the plebs came. Antony had been quietly confident. The augury had been a long shot, but like the quaestorship, he was not expected to have too much difficulty gaining the tribunate, and he was duly elected, along with another of Caesar's supporters. Quintus Cassius Longinus was the cousin of Gaius Cassius Longinus, who was currently keeping the Parthians at bay in Syria without the assistance of the two legions the Senate had allocated to the campaign, which were still being held in Italy by Pompey.

After a single evening of heavy celebration with Curio and a night of passion with Cytheris, who was now his regular and sole lover, Antony travelled north up the Via Aemilia, hungover and sleep-deprived but nevertheless, very content.

Caesar had based himself in Mutina in Cisalpine Gaul, the province situated nearest Italy, south of the Alps. He had travelled there initially to campaign for Antony's election as augur, and then had decided to remain there, since it was conveniently close to Rome, to receive news and send instructions. The city was flourishing, lively, clean and lavishly decorated with flowers, despite being besieged only a generation earlier.

Antony located the sumptuous palace that Caesar had requisitioned as his headquarters and announced himself to the guards. Caesar himself came out to greet him with open arms, stepping forward to embrace him and kiss him on both cheeks.

'Marcus, my boy, you have caught the sun. The weather is more agreeable in Rome than Gaul, I take it?'

'It's a hot summer, Caesar, that's for sure. It's nice to get away from it for a few days.'

A palace steward arranged for Antony's bags to be taken to his quarters, and his horse and slaves to be accommodated. He was given the opportunity to wash away the grime of the road in the private palace baths before dressing for a formal dinner with Caesar.

Antony, of course, was not the only guest. Quintus Cassius Longinus had travelled up on the night of the election, and so had arrived half a day before Antony. He was pleased to find Decimus Brutus and Trebonius also present. Both were still serving as legates with Caesar, and they greeted him like old friends. Not so welcome was Labienus, who looked as if he was chewing something sour when he shook Antony's hand.

Caesar affected not to notice, but Antony saw that a slight frown crossed his face at Labienus' discourtesy.

'It's a great pleasure to welcome Antonius and Cassius here, and I thank you both for making the long journey. Let's start the evening with a toast. Friends, please raise your cups in honour of our two newest tribunes, Marcus Antonius and Quintus Cassius Longinus.'

Everyone around the table raised their cups and drank deeply. Decimus Brutus and Trebonius slapped their hands on the table, and Trebonius gave Antony a playful punch in the arm.

'Well done,' he said. 'I'm jealous, all the exciting things you are getting up to in Rome, while we sit around babysitting a defeated nation and waiting for the Senate to wake up and give Caesar his due recognition.'

'Quite,' said Caesar. 'But these things can't be rushed. I can legally stand for consul next year, and that is what I intend to do. And now we have Antonius and Cassius here to keep the Senate in line, there should be nothing to stop a peaceful transition into my new consulship, and thence to my next governorship.'

Antony and Quintus Cassius exchanged a glance.

'You don't agree?' asked Caesar.

'Proconsul,' said Cassius carefully, 'it's been a long time since you were in Rome. You don't know what the mood is like there.'

'Then enlighten me.'

Cassius looked beseechingly at Antony, who gave him a shooting glare.

'Antonius?'

Antony inhaled, then let out a calming breath through his nose. Caesar wasn't one of those leaders who flew into a fury at the messenger when he received bad news, but it was never enjoyable telling a superior something they didn't want to hear.

'Rome is a city divided, Caesar. Pompeius is still beloved of the masses, even more so since his near fatal illness. The Senate cling to him as their best hope of stopping you. You have many supporters in Rome, but the most influential belong to the optimates. Domitius, Scipio, Cato... especially Cato!'

'Yes, they control the Senate,' said Caesar. 'And if they had their way, they would vote to strip me of my command and send a new governor in my stead. But even if the term of my command expires, I will remain legally in charge here until the Senate votes for my replacement. And as long as the tribunes continue to veto any discussion of a new governor for Gaul, my position is safe.'

'Providing the Senate doesn't resort to other measures,' said Cassius.

Caesar cocked his head to one side. 'Other measures?'

'You know how things ended for the Gracchi.'

'You're right,' said Caesar. 'You both have bodyguards, I take it?'

Antony and Cassius nodded.

'Double them. I can't have my plans ruined by a stray assassin's blade just because you didn't hire decent protection. Oh, and have two food tasters check your food for poison, not just one.'

'Yes, Caesar.'

'And Cassius, what is the latest news from Syria? How fares your cousin?'

'Gaius is holding out, sir, but sorely pressed, at least the last we heard. And it isn't helped that Bibulus undermines him at every opportunity.'

Bibulus, who had been co-consul with Caesar, was the governor of Syria, but Gaius Cassius was the military tactician who was holding the Parthians back, though Bibulus was constantly trying to claim credit for his junior's actions.

'Do you think we will need to send legions east?'

'Perhaps,' said Quintus Cassius.

'I would dearly love that command,' said Caesar wistfully. 'I hope the need for action has not come too early for me. I would hate to see Pompeius getting all the glory.'

'They won't be sending Pompeius anywhere,' said Antony. 'Look at how scared they were when he became ill. They think he is the only thing keeping you from marching your legions straight into the Forum.'

'Where have they got this notion from?' said Caesar, irritation creeping into his voice. 'Am I not honourable? Am I not merciful?'

Most of the time, thought Antony, remembering the siege of Uxellodunum, where the rebellious Gauls had, rather than being slaughtered, simply had their hands cut off. Was that mercy? Kinder than outright slaughter, Antony supposed, though he wondered if many of those men and their families, unable to work, would simply starve to death in the winter.

'Your honour and mercy are without bounds,' said Antony. 'But the Senate twists every word you speak and every action you take into the ugliest shapes.'

Caesar nodded thoughtfully. 'Thank you, both of you. Now tell me, how are your families? Antonius, how is your lovely wife and daughter?'

'They are well, thank you for asking.'

'And you, Cassius – surely it's about time you found a decent match?'

'I'm still open to offers, Caesar, but I'm in no hurry.'

The conversation drifted into matters of politics, history, philosophy and gossip. Of the latter, Antony was able to supply – with Cytheris his source – that Cato was once again seeing his ex-wife Marcia, whom he had divorced and married off to Hortensius for political gain. Now Hortensius was dead, Marcia had inherited his vast fortune, and if, as was speculated, she intended to remarry Cato, he would become a very rich man indeed.

Caesar shook his head at this with a rueful smile. 'For one who dedicates his life to morality, he has a strange sense of ethics.'

The evening drew to an end, with Antony feeling pleasantly full and mildly drunk, but not enough to make a fool of himself. Caesar thanked Quintus Cassius and Antony again for their loyal service.

'Just remember,' he said, 'you can interpose your veto at any stage before a vote is actually taken, but not afterwards. Make sure that at least one of you is present at every Senate meeting – and preferably both. You never know when my governorship may be tabled for discussion unannounced. And if they attempt to replace me, or terminate my command, you know what to do.'

Antony and Quintus Cassius nodded their understanding. Caesar embraced them both, and bid them all a goodnight. Antony waited for his patron to leave, then turned to the others.

'Are there any good taverns in Mutina still open?'

'I'm sure we can get them to open their doors for us,' said Trebonius.

Decimus and Quintus Cassius laughed, and said they could manage another drink or two. Only Labienus declined, saying he was tired, and left them.

'He really hates me, doesn't he?' said Antony to Trebonius.

'Do you wonder? He has been Caesar's second-in-command for his entire Gallic campaign. Then you burst on to the scene right at the end, and all anyone can talk about is Caesar's new favourite, Marcus Antonius, hero of Alesia, legate, augur, tribune. But don't let it worry you. Labienus is a cantankerous bugger, but he is sound.'

Antony nodded, but the doubts persisted. He shook them away. 'Come on, let's see if you can still drink like you used to.'

November DCCIV AUC (November 50 BC), Rome

There was something arresting in the expression the sculptor had created for the crouching man sharpening a knife on a whetstone. He looked up with something pitiful, apologetic in his eyes. Antony couldn't tear his gaze away. Cytheris snaked an arm around his waist and pulled him close.

'What is he thinking?' asked Antony rhetorically, not expecting a reply.

'You don't know?' Cytheris seemed surprised.

'No. You do?'

'Yes. He is sharpening the knife so it can be used on Marsyas.'

Antony thought for a moment, recalling the myth. Marsyas was the Satyr who had challenged Apollo to a musical contest. When the Muses judged Apollo the winner, Marsyas was flayed alive for his hubris in challenging a god, and his skin was used as a winesack. For some reason, Antony thought of Pompey and Caesar. But which one was Marsyas and which was Apollo? He turned and gave Cytheris a kiss on the cheek.

'Your education would shame most of the men in the Senate.'

'I wouldn't presume to demonstrate it to them. They are too delicate to allow themselves to feel inferior to a woman.'

'And I'm not?'

She laughed as if the question was absurd. He held her tighter and they continued their stroll through the Gardens of Lucullus, the beautiful, verdant area laid out to the north of the city by the late general turned art collector and horticulturist. It truly felt as if they were in an oasis of peace away from the noise, the bustle and the smells of the city. Although they had been opened to the public after Lucullus died, patrolling guards kept away the riff-raff: the homeless, the prostitutes, the street-sellers, and anyone who looked so poorly dressed they might detract from the dignity of the haven. As a consequence, they were able to stroll in peace with only infrequent encounters with other walkers.

But then Antony saw a couple approaching along a narrow path that wended between two lines of bushes delicately coiffured into the shapes of nymphs.

'Oh, shit.'

Cytheris looked up and smiled. 'Here's a nice surprise for you.'

'Marcus Brutus,' said Antony, shaking his hand when they reached each other. 'And Claudia. Congratulations on your father's acquittal.'

Brutus' wife gave Antony a small nod of thanks.

'Antonius,' said Brutus. 'Congratulations on your tribunate. And who is your delightful companion?'

Antony stood a little taller and looked Brutus straight in the eye. 'This is Volumnia.'

'Volumnia? The freedwoman of Eutrapelus? The actress? What do they call her...? Cytheris, isn't it?'

'I didn't know you were a fan of the mime, Brutus.'

'Oh, sometimes a bit of lowbrow entertainment cleanses the palate between Aeschylus and Euripides.'

Antony felt Cytheris stiffen at his side.

'And how fares your master, Caesar?'

Now it was Antony's turn to take umbrage. Although it was undeniable that Antony was Caesar's follower, to label him 'master' gave their relationship more than a hint of slave and owner, something reprehensible to a man of Antony's rank. He felt his fists clench involuntarily, but then Cytheris gave his arm a subtle squeeze, and he forced himself to relax.

'He looked well, last time I saw him. Fighting fit, in fact.'

Brutus frowned. 'No one wants war, Antonius.'

'Do they not, Brutus? I think there are many among the optimates who are spoiling for exactly that. A chance to put Caesar in his place. Little men who feel threatened by greatness.'

Brutus sighed. 'Maybe you are right. But Cicero has left his province and is making his way back to Rome. His eloquence and moderation will reconcile the factions. I'm sure of it.'

'You have more confidence than me,' said Antony. 'Cicero will do whatever makes him appear most statesmanlike, while trying to ensure he doesn't endanger his skin by backing a loser.'

Brutus looked away, not rising to the bait. 'A beautiful evening, is it not? Lucullus really did wonders with this place. What a legacy he has left to the people.'

'To some of the people,' said Cytheris. 'The rich ones.'

Brutus glanced at her, then back at Antony as if she hadn't spoken. 'I will leave you to your evening. No doubt I will see you in the Senate before too long. Farewell, Antonius. All the best to your wife.' The last was said with emphasis and a glance at the beautiful woman by Antony's side. 'Farewell, Cytheris.'

'Farewell, Brutus,' said Cytheris. 'And it was a pleasure to meet you, Claudia.'

Claudia whitened, as if shocked she had been addressed by someone so lowly. She stuttered out a reply. 'A-and you, Volumnia.' Then she gripped her husband's arm and all but dragged him away.

'Little prick,' muttered Antony. 'I'm sorry about him.'

'Are you ashamed to be seen with me?' asked Cytheris.

He turned to look at her in surprise.

'Why do you say that?'

'You called me Volumnia.'

'It's your official name. It shows you have some standing in society, that you are free.'

'It shows that I was once a slave, and I am still bound to my former master.'

'You prefer to be called Cytheris? The name that marks you as an actress?'

'Frankly, yes. For that is what I am. It is my profession and I am good at it.'

'Yes, but—'

'You take me for private dinners with trusted friends. We take romantic walks in secluded areas of the city, but if we have to cross busier areas, you pull your head up, and continually glance around furtively, like you are committing a crime.'

'I do not,' protested Antony, but he knew she was right. 'Listen. I have a position to keep up now I have been elected tribune and augur.

My power comes not only from my offices, but from my reputation. If I do not have respect, I cannot protect Caesar's interests, or my own.'

'I see,' said Cytheris. 'I understand. I am an embarrassment to you.'

'Not at all!' He reached for her, to hold her, reassure her, but she pulled back.

'Would you take me home, please, Marcus? I feel suddenly very weary.'

Antony escorted her back to her apartment in silence. When they reached her door, she did not invite him in, but bade him goodnight, turning her cheek when he leaned in to kiss her. Antony stared at the door for some time after it had closed behind her, wondering what had just happened – what he had done wrong. Eventually, he shook his head, and made for Curio's house. Maybe he or Fulvia would have some advice for him. And if not, he could at least make a decent dent in their wine cellar.

Kalendis Decembribus DCCIV AUC (1 December 50 BC), Rome

It had been a whole *nundinum* since Antony had last seen Cytheris. He had called on her several times, but had been coldly informed by her maidservant that she was indisposed, out, or unavailable. Curio had been no help, just commenting 'Women!' and rolling his eyes. And Fulvia had been strangely reticent to get involved, stating that Antony's love affairs were his own business, and if he chose to get himself into such complex situations, it was up to him to get himself out of them.

Thoughts of Cytheris and Fulvia were distracting him as he sat in the Senate meeting. The morning was chilly, warning of the approach of winter, but the hot air emanating from the animated, argumentative senators more than compensated. This meeting had been arranged in the Curia Cornelia, the Senate house that had been quickly rebuilt by Sulla's son Faustus to replace the one burnt down by the rioters at Clodius' funeral. As it was right next to the Forum, it was convenient for most of the senators, especially the older ones, who did not want to travel too far if they could avoid it. It meant that Pompey could not attend, since the building was within the pomerium, which was a little surprising. But Antony supposed that the optimates knew Pompey's mind well enough to be able to vote without consulting him directly, and since the sole topic of debate once more was Caesar's command, nothing of interest was likely to occur. Antony wondered what had happened to all the other business of state that was usually conducted in Senate meetings – the laws, the treasury, the reports from the provinces. It seemed that the Republic was hamstrung by this stand-off between Caesar and the optimates.

Antony had managed to avoid sitting next to Marcus Brutus this time, and as a tribune-elect decided he could push himself forward a bit further, finding a gap in a bench among the Caesarian faction. As usual, Lucius Aemilius Paullus opened the debate and then handed over to Gaius Claudius Marcellus. And, as usual, Marcellus proposed that the Senate force Caesar to lay down his arms, resign his governorship and present himself in Rome. The anti-Caesarians roared their support, but overall the Senate was less enthusiastic. Antony detected a weariness with the situation. While the Senate was paralysed by vetoes, the elected magistrates could not be allocated roles, particularly the lucrative governorships of foreign provinces which they craved – and in many cases needed – in order to pay off the debts they had incurred getting elected in the first place. Two separate votes were proposed: that Caesar lay down his arms, and that Pompey lay down his arms. It was clear that the Senate was swaying towards a vote in favour of the former and against the latter, but Curio vetoed both, to much predictable anger.

However, when he stood up and renewed his proposal that both Caesar and Pompey lay down their arms simultaneously, there was a good deal more support than for Marcellus' bill. When Paullus opened up the debate to the other senators, some of the moderates expressed the opinion that Caesar was more of a Republican than Pompey, and others that it would not be prudent to dismiss Pompey's forces before Caesar had disarmed.

Then it was Antony's turn to speak. He got to his feet, and looked around the ranks of the revered fathers, some faces encouraging, some twisted in anger. His heart pounded and he felt himself shrink a little under the glare of their scrutiny. Then he remembered his oratorical training. He took a deep breath, and spoke. And quickly he found he was enjoying himself, as the whole Senate's attention was fixed on him. He used all the rhetorical flourishes at his disposal as he declaimed in his ostentatious, wordy style, painting a picture of Caesar as a friend of the Republic, a hero Rome needed to protect its interests at home and abroad. When he sat, the jeers from the optimates were drowned out by a swell of adulation from the rest of the Senate, and he felt his chest puff out in pride at the reception.

Paullus called a vote, and when all had had their say, three hundred and seventy senators had cast their votes in favour of Curio's proposal, against only twenty-two of Caesar's most diehard enemies – the likes of Cato, Scipio, Domitius Ahenobarbus and Bibulus. Marcellus stood and said in a tone of unrestrained anger, 'The Senate is dismissed. You have won. Take Caesar as your master.'

The Senate erupted in an outpouring of delight. Among the throng of old men hugging one another, shouting and dancing in pure joy and relief, Antony caught sight of Marcellus, surrounded by other leading anti-Caesarians, exuding waves of fury. Then Curio was with Antony, hugging him, leading him outside to the waiting crowds. There, Curio announced the result, and more joy broke out. Antony and Curio walked through the masses, soaking up the adulation, while the common people scattered flowers over them in sincere thanks that they had averted war. Antony accepted hugs, kisses, blessings and gifts, feeling as if he had just won a battle and was being honoured by his men. The sensation was almost as gratifying. Almost.

Then a loud voice broke through the noise. At first it was indistinct, but as the people turned to find out what was being said, the cacophony died down, and the words reached Antony.

'The Senate is reconvened,' cried Marcellus. 'An emergency has arisen. The Senate is reconvened. Return to your seats!'

Antony's eyes found Curio's, and they exchanged confused glances. They made their way back into the temple, a sensation of anxiety creeping up Antony's spine.

When some semblance of order had been restored, Marcellus stood in front of the confused senators with a sombre expression on his face.

'Revered fathers, I have just received grave news. Caesar has crossed the Alps with his legions, and even as we speak, he is marching on Rome.'

The collective gasp from the senators was like a rush of wind. No one had expected this. Of course, it was one of Caesar's great strategic skills – doing the unexpected, catching everyone off guard. If Caesar had genuinely decided that the Senate would never negotiate in good faith, it was a cunning move.

But it wasn't the impression Antony had taken away from his last meeting with Caesar. He had wanted Antony to take over from Curio as one of the tribunes, so he could continue down a political and diplomatic route. Nothing had changed since that meeting to provoke such a change in strategy.

Then Antony saw Marcellus' expression: smug satisfaction. Cato, too, was trying to hide a smile. And then it became obvious.

Antony pushed his way through the senators, who were on their feet in complete uproar, until he reached his friend.

'Curio, Curio. You have to speak up. It's not true.'

Curio, who had been looking as stunned as anyone, turned to Antony and took him by the shoulders.

'Speak up!' he yelled over the cacophony. 'What did you say?'

'Look at Marcellus' face. He's lying. You need to tell them.'

Curio turned, and saw what Antony had seen. He nodded resolutely, clapped Antony on the back and fought his way to the front of the chamber. There he leapt onto a table and cried at the top of his voice, 'Colleagues! Friends!'

Slowly the senators became aware that Curio was trying to make himself heard, and turned to him in desperation, hoping that he had something of comfort to tell them.

'Revered fathers,' he said, still almost shouting over the jeers, especially from those who saw him as Caesar's servant. 'Listen to me. It's a lie. That man is lying to you.' He pointed an accusatory finger at Marcellus, who just sat, shaking his head sadly, his previous smugness masked now with a stern expression.

'Caesar is not marching on Gaul. He would have informed me – he would have informed Antonius. He is still trying to pursue a peaceful resolution to this. And we have peace in our grasp. The votes you just cast ensure it.'

Marcellus stood up now, and Curio gave way, waiting to see how he would defend himself.

'Senators, I don't know if Curio is simply a naive and well-meaning follower of the would-be tyrant, or if he, too, is bent on committing treason.' Boos and jeers at the defamation Marcellus had cast on Curio were matched evenly by the cheers of agreement. 'But my information is true. Caesar is marching towards Rome, while we mill around like frightened sheep. I therefore propose a vote. Caesar must be declared a public enemy, and the two legions which were previously in Gaul must be led by Pompeius in defence of the city, our family, our homes.'

The senators were genuinely confused now, not knowing who to believe, fear and anger driving their actions. Marcellus raised his hands and called for a vote on the proposition, and Curio immediately cried out 'Veto!'

Marcellus glared at him, then turned back to the senators and said, 'If I am prevented by the vote of the Senate from taking steps for public safety, I will take such steps on my own responsibility as consul.'

'You can't do that,' shouted Curio in disbelief. 'The tribune's veto is inviolable. This is not in your power.'

'Senators, I am going straightaway to Pompeius, to command him in the name of the Senate to defend the city. Let all who truly love the Republic change their togas for an appropriate dress for the circumstances, and accompany me.'

And with that, a slave passed him a different toga – scruffy, dirty, darkened: the dress of someone of poorer social standing, and a well understood symbol of political protest. Several of the optimates had come prepared in the same way, and changed into filthy rags, which meant in Cato's case, since he wore no under-tunic, that the whole Senate got to see his skinny naked body in its entirety. Antony looked around at the other senators, who seemed largely impressed by this display of piety, amazed they were not reacting to how pre-planned the entire affair was.

Marcellus led the senators who wished to follow him, which was almost all of the house, north towards Pompey's suburban villa on the Campus Martius, just outside the pomerium. Antony tagged along behind, determined to find out Marcellus' intentions, so he could at least report back to Caesar, even if he couldn't stop him. Curio, as a sitting tribune, had power only within the city, and his sacred person was no longer inviolable if he went outside the pomerium, so he retreated to his house, taking with him a hefty bodyguard, to await the outcome.

Pompey had clearly been forewarned of their approach, and awaited them in the spacious gardens in front of his villa. Marcellus marched straight up to him and drew a gleaming, highly polished gladius from beneath his toga. Pompey watched him, unflinching, through narrowed eyes, while Marcellus knelt down and presented the sword to him, hilt first.

In a clear, ringing voice, Marcellus declared, 'On behalf of the Senate, which is prevented from acting for the good of the state, I order you to take command over all the legions in Italy, and any others that you wish to raise. You are to advance against Caesar. You are to defend the Republic.'

A hush fell over the watching senators and the crowd of curious onlookers who had accompanied them. Pompey let his gaze wander over the expectant faces.

Gods, don't let him do it, Antony thought. Remind him he was Caesar's friend, his son-in-law. Let him be the great man he once was, accept peace, put the welfare of the Republic above his need to be loved and admired more than anyone else.

But he knew his prayer would not be answered. This was all pre-ordained, a theatrical play written by Marcellus and Cato and Pompey days before, rehearsed thoroughly, now being performed in all its glory for its audience today.

Pompey seemed to let out an extended sigh. He said in a sad voice, 'If there be no better way.'

Then he picked the sword up and thrust it into the air, while the senators and the gathered crowd cheered their joy and their relief, and Pompey bathed in the glow from the adulation.

Chapter III

That Marcellus' announcement of Caesar's attack was a blatant lie was emphasised when Pompey, instead of taking his legions north to intercept Caesar's line of advance, marched them south into Campania for training and further recruitment. When Antony confronted some of the more moderate senators who had backed Marcellus with this argument, they mostly just shrugged, looked a little abashed, and muttered something unconvincing about Caesar being scared away by the steps the consuls and the Senate had taken. Antony and Curio had sent messengers to Caesar to inform him of the actions of Marcellus and his colleagues, and a few days later, they received visits from Aulus Hirtius and Lucius Cornelius Balbus, two of Caesar's trusted senior officers. They told them that Caesar still wished for peace but was ready for war, and gave them more instructions for negotiations with Pompey, the Senate and the optimates. Antony enquired whether they were going to visit Pompey and take Caesar's message to him directly, but they said they had no orders for that. Antony wondered if this was an unusual tactical mistake by Caesar – Pompey would surely take offence if Caesar's envoys snubbed him.

Five days before the Ides of December, Curio's tribunate expired. Concerned for his safety now his person was no longer sacrosanct in law, he bade goodbye to Antony and Fulvia and rode north to Caesar. The next day, Antony was himself invested in the office of tribune of the plebs.

It was a momentous event for him personally, and to be able to see the admiring expressions of his brothers and the look of pride on his mother's face was the cherry on the honeycake. But the uncertainty of the future was never far from his thoughts. Part of him felt a frisson of anticipation at the prospect of fighting by Caesar's side against Pompey for supremacy in Rome. What a clash of Titans it would be. But he also feared for his loved ones: his family, Fulvia, and of course, Cytheris, though she was still refusing to see him.

The *contio* – the speech he made to those gathered in the Forum on the day of his tribunate – was naturally partisan, but somewhat subdued. He had urged that the two legions in Italy that he considered Pompey had cheated from Caesar be sent to Syria, as had been intended, and also that Pompey should be stripped of the command of the new legions he was currently recruiting. A contio had no force in law and did not lead to a vote, but was a useful way of whipping up public opinion among the middle ranks and the masses. But when he walked among his friends and clients, more than one asked why he had not taken the opportunity to attack Pompey personally. He had brushed the queries aside, but the hint of accusations of cowardice in their voices stung. Did they think he was afraid of that pompous fool?

Was he?

Antony had grown up on tales of Pompey's exploits as a general, a statesman, the first among equals in the highly competitive hierarchy of the Roman nobility. It was inevitable that there would be some degree of respect and awe in his assessment of the great man. Did Pompey actually have some sort of hold over Antony, that he wasn't even consciously aware of?

These concerns nagged at Antony over the next few days, and all the while, more and more hostile signals came from Pompey's camp and the optimates.

So, on the twelfth day before the *Kalends of Januarius*, when Antony mounted the Rostra to deliver another contio to a large crowd of senators, equestrians and lower ranks who were gathered in the Forum to hear him, a contrary, defiant voice bubbled up from within him, demanding to be heard. He looked out over the expectant faces, all waiting anxiously to hear what the de facto spokesman of Caesar had to say. They were in the middle of the midwinter Saturnalia festival, when slaves were given banquets served by their masters, gifts were exchanged, colourful clothes were worn, and everyone gambled, overate and drank too much. Yet those gathered today did not look drunk or nauseous or exhausted from an excess of parties. The fear that hung over Rome like the rain-filled clouds that he recalled perpetually covered Britannia had clearly put people off celebrating.

It was so unnecessary. Caesar's demands were completely reasonable. He had shown himself to be one of Rome's greatest ever generals, and he deserved to be praised to the gods, awarded his triumph, and allowed to stand for election to consul as was his right, without fear of small, petty men trying to drag him down with vexatious legislation.

Antony gritted his teeth, clenched his fists. His brow furrowed. He crossed his arms in front of him, and stared out over the crowd, who sensed his anger, and fell silent.

'I come here today to speak to you of peace. And of those who oppose it.'

No response, but rapt attention.

'My commander and friend, Caesar, has proposed compromise after compromise that ensure both the security of the Republic and the preservation of his own dignity. Time after time, his proposals have been rejected. And by whom? By you, the people of Rome? No. You do not show disrespect to a hero of this city, a man who has removed a centuries-old threat to the empire, eliminated it for all eternity. You do not quarrel among yourselves like wild dogs fighting over scraps, desperate for a governorship here, a magistracy there, but uniting against the lion in their midst to make sure no one can appear superior to them. You do not drag the Republic towards war for the sake of your own pride and fear.'

A few shakes of the head, mutters of agreement.

'So who does these things? We know their names. Cato. Bibulus. Marcellus. Ahenobarbus. Scipio. Scared little boys, frightened of being made to feel less important, terrified of anyone else showing them what true greatness is – something they can never achieve. But these cowards would be nothing if they were not allied to another. You know the one I talk of.

'Pompeius, the so-called Great.'

The faces in the crowd looked at one another. So-called? This was getting interesting.

'Three centuries ago, Alexander of Macedon conquered the whole of the Eastern world. A man of undoubted genius, undefeated in battle. Who gave him the title Magnus – the Great? We did – we Romans, many years after his death, in acknowledgement of his supreme ability, his achievements and his legacy.

'And who awarded Pompeius the title Great? Why, he took it for himself, while still a young man, for his so-called victories over fellow Romans! Though others called him the adolescent butcher, for the atrocities he carried out against his fellow citizens.

'Yes, this is the calibre of the man who now threatens the peace, who, by reason of his own fear of a rival, will tear down the very Republic rather than acknowledge Caesar as an equal, let alone his superior.'

The crowd, already large, was swelling now, as word spread that this speech was different, that Antony was attacking the darling of the Republic.

Antony continued, his deep voice booming out over the Forum, demanding the attention of his audience. He was animated now, waving his arms, jabbing his finger, appealing to the heavens as he drew on every trick of his rhetorical training. He criticised Pompey's record. He damned Pompey's character. He cursed his bad faith in his betrayal of Caesar's friendship. He listed Pompey's achievements and tore them down, one by one.

'Who defeated Spartacus? Crassus. Who took the credit? Pompeius. Who defeated Mithridates? Lucullus. Who took the credit?' He put his hand to his ear and the crowd yelled out, 'Pompeius,' as they revelled in this iconoclastic invective.

'Who is scared of Caesar taking his rightful place as one of the consuls, and yet two years ago illegally took the position of sole consul, and used it to condemn citizens to death or exile without trial?'

'Pompeius!'

'Who was awarded the governorship of Spain, but instead of going there and fighting for the Republic, as Caesar has done for ten years in Gaul, has sat on his fat backside in his villa in Italy while his underlings and his legions fight and die on foreign soil in his name?'

'Pompeius!'

'Who wants war?'

'Pompeius!'

He had them – he knew it. Now to show them there was an alternative.

'And tell me... who has won victory after victory against an ancient enemy? Who has ensured the security of Italy's northern borders for all time? Who has sent untold amounts of gold, silver and slaves into Rome? And in return, who is it that asks only for his constitutional rights to a triumph and to stand for election as consul once more?'

'Caesar! Caesar! Caesar!'

Antony joined in the chanting with the crowd, whipping it up to a frenzied crescendo, and Caesar's name reverberated from the Forum and throughout Rome. He wondered if Pompey, relaxing in his villa to the north, could hear it. He hoped so.

When the chanting showed signs of peaking and receding, he held up his arms to be heard once more.

'When you leave here, and talk to your friends and your families, just remember these two things. Pompeius wants war. Caesar does not want war. But he does not fear it.'

And with that, he descended from the Rostra and into the crowd, accepting their adulation with the same satisfaction he got from the praise he received from his men after a victorious battle.

Maybe the thrill of politics *could* match the thrill of war, he thought.

He made his way slowly through the crowd, and out of the Forum. When he was clear, he looked around, the feeling of elation still ringing inside him. He thought about going home, but that felt like such an anticlimax. He thought about summoning some of his friends for a bout of drinking, but he wasn't sure they would appreciate what he had just achieved.

So, instead, with a few slaves in tow, he made his way up the Palatine to see Fulvia.

Kalendis Ianuariis DCCV AUC (1 January 49 BC), Rome

It was reassuring to have Curio's stolid, politically experienced presence beside him as Antony stood in front of the gathered Senate. Not that he had much fear of speaking to them now. After his contio in the Forum a few days previously, he had greatly increased his self-confidence before an audience, even one as august as the one he faced now. Word of his attack on Pompey had spread quickly, aided by the fact that, as was customary, he had provided a written copy, so his speech could be circulated throughout the city and the whole of Italy.

Curio had returned from Gaul just the day before, and they had made it known to the consuls that they wished to address the Senate.

The consuls had reluctantly agreed and had summoned a meeting. The senators waited expectantly for Antony to begin.

'Revered fathers,' he said, his voice even and firm. 'My predecessor in the sacred post of Tribune of the Plebs, Gaius Scribonius Curio, returned to Rome yesterday with news from the Governor of Gaul.'

Murmurs of interest rippled through the Senate. Antony focused his stare on a few faces in turn – some friendly, like Quintus Cassius, some neutral, like Brutus, some overtly hostile, like Cato. Then he drew out a rolled scroll from the folds of his toga.

'I have with me a letter from Gaius Julius Caesar, which he wishes read before the house.'

An outcry immediately broke out.

'Stop him!' shouted Bibulus. 'It's a declaration of war!'

'Let him speak, by all the gods,' cried Cassius. 'It is his right!'

Jostling broke out on the benches as senators who wished to hear Caesar's word tried to quieten those who were determined not to let the letter be read. Scipio rose from his seat, stalked towards Antony, and tried to grab the scroll out of his grasp. Antony moved the letter out of his reach and gave Scipio a firm shove in his chest that sent the furious senator stumbling backwards.

'Revered fathers,' he called out. 'I demand my *tribunician* right to be heard.'

'No,' said Gaius Claudius Marcellus, one of the new consuls, and cousin of the Marcellus who had been consul the previous year. He marched forward and stood directly in front of Antony, facing into the chamber. 'The letter will not be read. This meeting is dismissed.'

There was more outcry – an equal mix of outrage and support. Marcellus turned to leave.

Antony leapt onto a bench and shouted in a voice that cut through all the chaos, 'If you will not hear Caesar's words, I will take them to the people.'

The skirmishing senators turned to him, hushing down. Marcellus stopped and looked back.

'How will it be if the people hear that Caesar's peace proposal will not even be heard by this house? Do you think they will treat you kindly? Are you prepared for the consequences if the mob takes up arms against you?'

Antony wondered if the threat was too much, too populist. It was just the sort of thing that Clodius would have done. But Clodius had got results.

'Let him be heard,' said Lucius Cornelius Lentulus Crus, the other new consul. 'We can decide on the value of his words once they have been read out.'

Marcellus glared at him, then returned to his curule chair. 'So be it, Lentulus, but it is on your head. Antonius, read the letter.'

Antony remained standing on the bench, from where he could dominate the floor with his elevation as well as his physical presence and powerful voice. He held the scroll out in front of him, and declaimed loudly in a bombastic style. It was a lengthy letter, but Antony kept the senators in rapt attention.

Caesar started by outlining his many achievements on behalf of the Republic, the posts he had held, the enemies he had vanquished, the riches he had returned to the city. Then he declared that it was his dearest wish for peace, and that he was prepared to lay down his arms at the same time as Pompey. This got the usual reaction from the partisans of both sides – cheers from Caesarians and jeers from Pompeians – with the neutrals largely in favour. But when Antony spoke Caesar's next words, the senators quietened.

'If, though,' he read, 'Pompeius does not relinquish his command, then not only will I keep my own legions, but I will come with all speed to defend the Republic and my own honour.'

The senators looked at one another as the words struck home. For the first time, Caesar had threatened to march on Rome, to seize the city by force. Those old enough to remember the bloodbaths that had ensued when Sulla and Marius had brought soldiers into the capital shuddered. Then another cacophony of shouts broke out, and it was some time before enough order was restored for Antony to finish the letter: more assurances from Caesar of his wish for peace, but of his readiness to defend the Republic.

As soon as Antony had finished, Scipio rose, and without preamble, proposed a vote that Caesar dismiss his army or be considered an enemy of the state. The words were barely out of his mouth before both Antony and Cassius had cried out 'Veto!' Scipio cursed them and sat back down, folding his arms angrily. Then Lentulus stood and proposed a debate on the use of the tribunician veto. When Antony vetoed this debate as well, the meeting degenerated into a free-for-all of accusation and counter-accusation.

In exasperation, Marcellus declared the meeting adjourned, dismissing the senators with an announcement that Pompey, who had been having couriers bring him news of the meeting at his villa outside the pomerium, required all senators to attend him that evening. To Antony, it felt like a command from a father to a group of naughty children, summoning them for a lecture on their behaviour. He was tempted not to attend, from an instinct of contrariness at having someone tell him what to do, but he knew that Caesar would expect him to go and report back.

He found he was suddenly hungry and tired, and he left the senate house and headed home, accompanied by his ever-expanding entourage of slaves, clients, well-wishers and supplicants. When he was home, he asked one of his personal slaves to fetch him food and wine, then went to see Antonia, who was sitting in a *cubiculum* teaching their young daughter, also called Antonia and nicknamed Toni, how to spin wool. He watched them for a brief while with affection, particularly for the young girl. He wondered again why he felt so little physical interest in his wife. She was certainly beautiful, more so than Fulvia, who he still pined over. Maybe it was because he hadn't chosen her for himself. Maybe it was her insipid personality. Maybe it was something to do with his suspicions about her fidelity.

A slave appeared, bearing a silver tray on which were balanced a bronze cup of wine and a plate of meaty pastries. His entrance alerted mother and daughter to his presence. His wife seemed startled, and Antony thought he caught a flash of guilt on her face, as if she had been caught doing something she shouldn't. His daughter beamed at the sight of him and ran over to throw her arms around his waist. He picked her up and threw her into the air so she giggled and screamed, before catching her and gently setting her down. Antonia stood, smoothed down her stola, then stepped forward to give him a chaste kiss on the cheek. He couldn't remember the last time he had taken her to bed. There seemed no desire for such things on either side.

He embraced her dispassionately, tousled his daughter's hair, then told them he was going for a nap. Little Toni pouted her disappointment, but Antonia nodded, and Antony was sure she seemed relieved that he wasn't inflicting his presence on her any further. He went to his bedchamber, lay down, and within moments was asleep and dreaming of Cytheris.

–

Antony didn't stay at Pompey's meeting for long. The proconsul was haranguing the gathered revered fathers like a head steward appraising the performance of the household slaves. Some were praised for their diligence in standing up for the Republic against Caesar's aggression, while others were chastised for their lack of backbone or outright disloyalty. After a short while of this, Antony, Cassius and Curio ostentatiously walked out, making sure their exit was noted by all.

They had a few drinks standing at the street-facing bar of a tavern, then the young actor whom Curio had been chatting up recommended a play for them. They agreed it would take their minds off the stresses of the current political situation, and Curio's new friend led them, drinks still in hand, to the nearby plaza where it was being staged. It was an Atellan farce, a traditional masked, semi-improvised comedy that, provided the actors were skilled enough, was guaranteed to have the audience in stitches, and this was no exception. They took the best seats in the front row, which, of course, made them the butt of some of the jokes, which Curio and Antony took in good part. Cassius, though, was not such a good sport; after one of the actors let out a loud and very smelly fart in his face, Antony's co-tribune stormed out in disgust, which sent Antony and Curio, as well as most of the crowd, off into howls of laughter.

But while the play took Antony's mind off the looming clouds of war, it sent his thoughts towards Cytheris, and the first time he had seen her performing. Soon the wistful longing became a compulsion, and he clapped Curio on the back and left him with the actor, who he now had an arm around. Weaving slightly from the wine in his belly, he made his way to Cytheris' apartment, climbed the exterior steps to the first floor and hammered on the door.

'Who is it?' came her voice from inside, and the sound of it quickened Antony's pulse.

'Marcus. I need to see you.'

'Go away,' she shouted.

'Please, Cytheris.' He pounded his fist on the wall, hard enough that the frame shook and some plaster came loose.

'Stop that,' came Cytheris' voice. Antony continued to knock and she called out, 'Fine, just wait a moment.'

There was some shuffling from inside, then the door opened a crack. Antony could see half of Cytheris' beautiful face through the gap.

'What do you want?' she demanded, her voice a hiss.

'Cytheris, I miss you. I'm sorry if I offended you. Please forgive me.'

'Marcus, now isn't the time. You're drunk and—'

'I may have to leave Rome soon. I may be in danger.'

Cytheris paused, opened her mouth to say something.

A man's voice came from within the apartment.

'Will you tell whoever it is to get lost, Cytheris? Otherwise I'll be letting Eutrapelus know how disrespectfully you treat his friends.'

Cytheris' eyes went wide. Antony stared at her, eyes narrowing, suddenly feeling his pulse pounding in his temples while his guts twisted into tight knots.

'Marcus, don't—'

'Get out of the way, Cytheris,' he growled. She saw his expression and stepped hastily back.

Antony kicked the door so hard that it nearly came off its hinges. He strode into the dimly lit apartment, marching through the vestibule into the comfortable atrium. Reclining on a couch was a skinny-chested man with spindly legs and a wispy grey beard. He was naked and shiny with oil. Antony glanced at Cytheris, who was fully clothed in an alluring, full-length stola, which she was trying to avoid touching with her greasy hands. Well, if the evening's entertainment was intended to go further than a massage, that clearly hadn't happened yet, and nor would it now Antony had arrived.

'You,' gasped the man. 'You're Marcus Antonius.'

Antony looked down at him, breathing hard through clenched teeth, fists balled. His anger was boiling over, and he could no longer restrain himself. He took a step forward.

Cytheris grabbed his arm, held it tight. He glared at her, saw the imploring look she was giving him. He turned back to the naked man.

'Get out,' he said, his voice low, back in control.

The man stood hastily and moved towards the corner where his tunic, cloak and shoes lay in a heap. Antony blocked his path. 'Out,' he said. 'Now.'

'But...' The man looked longingly at his clothing, then back into Antony's face. He swallowed, bowed his head and then hurried out, naked, into the night.

Antony watched him go, then turned to Cytheris. Her arms were folded under her bust, her lips were a thin line, and her stare was like a needle pinning him to the spot.

'What were you doing with him?' demanded Antony.

Cytheris cocked her head on one side, her look implying it was a stupid question.

'But why?' Antony asked, hating the imploring tone that had entered his voice. 'Why him?'

'Because my master demanded it,' said Cytheris, voice full of resentment.

'Your master? You are free.'

'I am a freedwoman, not a free woman, Marcus. You know the difference. I still owe a duty of obedience to the man who set me free.'

'Eutrapelus? Well, yes, there is some degree of obligation for a freedman or freedwoman to show loyalty to their former owners, but no more than my clients owe me. I could not demand the daughter of one of my clients sell her body, like a common—'

He broke off, seeing her face twist, moisture pooling in her lower lids, overflowing. The anger drained instantly, and he stepped forward and wrapped his arms around her. She held on to him and sobbed into his shoulder. When the convulsions died down, she stepped back. Her face was a mess of snot and tears, and Antony searched around for something to clean her. He found a silk cloth and used it to gently wipe her face, doing his best to tidy the smeared kohl and rouge.

'There. Beauty restored,' he said.

Cytheris let out a little laugh. 'Gallant of you to say so, though I'm sure I still look frightful.'

'Never.' He looked down at his shoes, swallowed. 'Cytheris, I'm sorry. For tonight. And... before.'

Cytheris sat on the couch and patted it for Antony to sit next to her. When he did so, she put her arm around his waist and moved close.

'I do understand. Being a freedwoman is bad enough. A small step up from being a slave. But I am worse than that. I am a mime. An actress. In the eyes of the law and society, I am *infamis*. I belong among the ranks of undertakers, executioners, gladiators and prostitutes. I cannot vote. I cannot testify in court. I can be beaten like a slave if someone sees fit to punish me. You know what happened in the trial of Gnaeus Plancius?'

Antony tried to recall the case a few years prior.

'Bribery, wasn't it? He was acquitted.'

Cytheris nodded. 'During the trial, he was accused of taking part in the gang rape of a young mime from Atina. Cicero said that this was a privilege, allowed to youths at those sort of games. He said it was a tribute to his client's propriety as a youth that the only accusation against him was for an act that he was permitted to commit. The brutal violation of a young woman of my station is not only allowed by law, you see, but held up as an example of good behaviour.'

'I know what Cicero is like,' said Antony. 'He will argue any proposition to win a case.'

'But this is what Rome thinks of me... of the likes of me. Even if I accrue wealth and socialise with elites like you, to believe myself better than the whore who plies her trade under the arches is just self-deception.'

Antony put a finger under her chin and turned her face to his. Then he kissed her, long, slow, taking his time, making sure he showed her the depth of his feelings. He felt her thaw, melt into him. He kissed her neck, her décolletage. He gently undressed her, laid her back on the couch, and made love to her with exquisite tenderness.

Afterwards they lay together, cuddled up tight, Antony cradling her head and stroking her hair. Abruptly she sat up, propping herself on one elbow.

'Marcus. When you were asking to come in... You said you were in danger?' Her eyes were suddenly wide with concern.

'It's nothing.'

'Tell me,' she demanded.

Antony sighed. 'I know you have some knowledge of what happens in the Senate, but maybe you aren't aware of how bad things have become. We are reaching a crisis point. Neither Caesar nor Pompeius will back down. We are close to war.'

Cytheris shivered and moved closer to him again. 'And you are a target?'

'I'm Caesar's highest ranking representative in Rome. Tribune and augur. Pompeius and the anti-Caesarians in the Senate might decide they want me out of the way. It would be easily achieved. They could arrest me on some trumped-up charge, if they were hypocritical enough to ignore the constitutional sanctity of tribune. Or they could have me assassinated. Both techniques have been used often enough in the past to remove political opponents.'

'What will you do?'

'I am bound to Caesar's standard. If Caesar is defeated, in the Senate or in battle, then I am lost. So I must defend his interests as best I can, both through honour and self-interest. Soon, though, I fear discussions will be at an end, and I may have to flee without warning.'

'You should prepare yourself,' said Cytheris. 'Make sure you have a disguise and some transport ready, should it come to that.'

Antony nodded. 'You're right, I hadn't really planned for the eventuality. But if war comes and I have to run to Caesar, and he loses, it is likely my life will be forfeit. It's why I wanted to say goodbye. Maybe I'm being foolish. I don't know if you have real feelings for me, or if I was just another mark that Eutrapelus told you to seduce, for his own advancement.'

He looked at her with a mix of hope and trepidation. She looked down and his heart sank.

'I will not lie to you, Marcus. Eutrapelus asked me to seduce you at that party.'

'I see,' he said.

'But after that first evening, when you treated me so well, I began to... to fall—'

Antony pressed a finger to her lips.

'Don't say it. Not until this situation is resolved. Don't make declarations to someone whose life may be numbered in days.'

She looked into his eyes. 'It's because of my feelings that I pushed you away. I'm used to being the dirty secret, the excitement for the respectable nobleman. But when you behaved the same, when you told me I could damage your reputation, then I felt...' She swallowed, looked away. 'I felt worthless.'

'Cytheris,' he said, taking her hand, 'I promise you this. If I live through what is to come, all Rome will see what you mean to me.'

She trembled, but the earnestness in Antony's gaze left her in no doubt of his sincerity. She kissed him, fierce and passionate this time. They made love again and again, more times than he had thought he was capable of. When dawn came, he kissed her gently goodbye. She clung to him for a long moment, then sighed, let him go, and turned away.

ante diem viii Idus Ianuarias DCCV AUC (6 January 49 BC), just outside Rome

Antony took the cup of wine that the slave passed him, and peered into it suspiciously. He looked at Cicero, reclining opposite him, who himself had just accepted a cup of wine from the slave.

'That's a beautiful vessel,' said Antony. 'May I see?'

Cicero looked down at the silver cup in his hand, shrugged and passed it to Antony. It was embossed with a Greek mythological scene – Leda's seduction by Zeus in the guise of a swan. Antony spent some time admiring it, then said, 'I like this cup. If I may, I will drink from this one.'

He passed his own cup to Cicero, who took it, instantly understanding Antony's suspicion. The orator frowned, then ostentatiously took a long drink from the cup Antony had passed him, before setting it down by his side and glaring at Antony.

Antony took a deep drink himself, then lay back and plucked some grapes, still on the stem, from a platter beside him. He spat the pips into his hand and wiped them on the couch, enjoying the look of distaste on Cicero's face. Of course, they were in Pompey's villa, so the petty action did Cicero no actual harm, but Antony had little respect for Pompey either. His gaze was caught by the expensive gold necklace Cicero wore, and the ruby- and emerald-encrusted rings on his fingers, and he recalled what Cytheris had told him.

'Defending the reprehensible is still paying well, I see,' he said. 'How is Gnaeus Plancius, by the way?'

Cicero ignored the question.

'What brings you here, Antonius?' he asked. 'I have been back from my province for only two days, I am still tired from my journey, and I have a thousand matters to attend to.'

'Thank you so much for seeing me in such trying circumstances, then,' said Antony. 'Though to be frank, it was Curio's insistence that I come to see you, rather than my own volition.'

'Then we both owe Curio a debt,' said Cicero, his tone making it clear it was not a debt of gratitude.

'Indeed,' said Antony. 'But to come to the point. Caesar still sees you as a neutral in this argument between him and Pompeius.' He tried by expression and tone to convey his own scepticism of Cicero's neutrality. 'He has sent word of another proposal for peace, and he wishes you to convey it to Pompeius and argue in its favour with all your customary aplomb.'

Cicero raised one eyebrow. 'Let's hear it, then.'

'Caesar says that he will surrender all but two of his legions if he is allowed to stand *in absentia* for the next consular election.'

Cicero sat back and looked at Antony with calculation.

'Just two legions? It's an interesting proposal.'

'It is against my advice, I have to say. But Caesar really does want a peaceful solution. He feels two legions will be enough to protect his interests, while ensuring he is no threat to Rome.'

'Pompeius is at home,' said Cicero. 'Why don't we take Caesar's proposal to him directly?'

'I fear Pompeius is not my biggest supporter after the speeches I have given recently.'

'Ah yes, he did complain about that to me. How did he put it? "How will Caesar behave if he gets control of the state when his weak, worthless quaestor dares to speak like this?"'

Antony's jaw clenched involuntarily, and he forced himself to relax.

'He referred to me as quaestor? He has been away from the Senate too long – he forgets my highest rank.'

'Perhaps,' said Cicero. Antony knew that the insult – failing to acknowledge his ranks of tribune and augur was deliberate, a greater slur than the weak and worthless jibes.

'Nevertheless, why don't you run along with Caesar's proposal to the Great One, and see if he is prepared to see sense?'

It was Cicero's turn to bridle, and Antony watched him physically bite back a retort. He was sure that Cicero also genuinely desired peace and, much as he disliked and mistrusted him, he expected his innate cowardice in the face of conflict would impel him to argue Caesar's proposal convincingly. Cicero stood and turned on his heel, gathering his toga about him and marching off in search of Pompey.

He was gone for some time, and Antony became listless and bored. He got up and paced the extensive atrium, admiring the trophies on display that Pompey had brought back from his victories in Spain and the East – a rhinoceros head, a jewelled dagger, a silver statuette of Apollo on a marble stand. He accosted a passing slave and asked him irritably for more wine, then berated him when he was slow returning. He drank deeply, noting that it was a mid-quality vintage, likely one of the poorest offerings from Pompey's cellar. He downed it nevertheless, feeling the warmth ease his frustrations a little.

Eventually Cicero returned, and motioned to Antony to be seated once more. Antony took a couch and leaned forward, his elbows on his knees.

'Well? What did he say?'

Cicero shook his head. 'He said no.'

Antony sighed. Part of him was irritated by Pompey's obstinacy, and saddened by the thought of the destruction and death the coming conflict would cause. But he had to admit, if only to himself, that he was excited by the thought of riding into battle by Caesar's side once more, and winning not just glory in a foreign land, but ultimate power in the Empire for his commander, with Antony himself in the position of his deputy.

'The problem,' said Cicero, puncturing Antony's fantasising, 'is that the main strength available to Pompeius is the two legions that Caesar sent him. He doubts their loyalty should it come to a fight. But I think I can persuade him to accept, if Caesar agrees to divest himself of all but a single legion.'

Antony considered this. There was no time to put the counter-proposal to Caesar himself. He could take it to Curio and Cassius, but ultimately Antony was Caesar's mouthpiece in Rome, and the decision was his. How easy it would be to reject the offer – to provoke war, to ride to Caesar and return with an army to crush the likes of Pompey and Cicero and Cato.

'That would be acceptable,' he found himself saying.

Cicero leapt up and shook Antony's hand vigorously, clapping him on the back and smiling broadly.

'This is wonderful,' he said. 'I knew that you and Caesar would see reason. This means peace, you know. Caesar is no threat to Rome with one legion, but he has strength enough to defend his rights until he gets elected consul.'

Antony nodded, smiling despite himself. It was good news. So why did he feel so deflated?

'I will take the news of the agreement to Curio and Cassius, and send word to Caesar at once.'

'As the man who was awarded the title Father of the Fatherland, I thank you on behalf of all Rome.'

Antony tried not to sneer. The gall of the man, still living off the glory of the minor revolt he'd squashed with undue force and illegality. He wondered what his stepfather, executed by this odious little man, would have thought if he could see Antony now, and he felt ashamed. But it was done, and it was the right thing, for Caesar and for Rome.

Antony gave a curt nod and took his leave.

ante diem vii Idus Ianuarias DCCV AUC (7 January 49 BC), Rome

When the Senate met in the Curia the next day, neither Pompey nor Cicero were present. Neither could cross Rome's sacred boundary – Pompey because he would have to give up his proconsular power, Cicero because he would have to forfeit his right to the triumph he had been angling for after some minor military success in Cilicia. The consuls could, of course, have convened the meeting in Pompey's villa by the Campus Martius with little inconvenience, as they had previously, but Antony quickly found out that the leading optimates had no wish for the two most respected men in Rome to have their say.

Lentulus rose first, and the senators, who all knew Caesar and Pompey were on the verge of a compromise, waited in silence.

'Revered fathers,' he said in a firm voice. 'There has been talk of Caesar giving up all but one of his legions, giving up all of Gaul and holding only Illyricum as a province. There has been talk of support from Pompeius for his proposals. There has been talk of allowing Caesar to stand for consul in absentia, long after he should by law have laid down his arms and presented himself as a private citizen in Rome.'

There were nods and mutters of agreement and approval.

'Well, I say this to you… No!' The last word was a roar. 'Caesar is a citizen of the Republic. No matter what great deeds he has done in barbarian lands, he is subject to the laws of the Senate and People of Rome.'

A large section of the senators – the optimates, all huddled together – cried out their support.

Cato demanded to be heard, and Lentulus gave him the floor.

'Pompeius tells us that all he has to do is stamp his feet, and all Italy will rise to support him. He tells us that if Caesar disobeys him, he would beat him with a stick as if he were his son. So what is the cowardly capitulation he confronts us with now? Only a few days ago, he was exhorting us all to stiffen our sinews, to gird our loins, to prepare to fight for the Republic. And now he wishes to let Caesar break all laws and customs and stand for a consulship while still holding the imperium of a proconsul. He should be standing before us in irons, answering for his crimes!'

The shouts of support were mixed with jeers and insults as the pro-Caesarians found their voices. Cato was forced to sit down again, but Scipio took his place, reiterating his opposition to any middle ground, and arguing that Caesar was forcing war upon them, and it was war he should have.

Antony looked at Curio and Cassius, who were watching the proceedings with an increasing pallor.

'They were never going to allow peace,' he said to Curio. 'They hate Caesar so much they would put his downfall above the welfare of the Republic they claim to defend.'

Curio nodded.

'It's getting ugly in here. Do you think there will be violence?'

Antony shrugged. At that moment, he would have relished a fight, even though he was unarmed.

Lentulus stood again, calling for calm, and speaking when he could finally be heard.

'Our Republic is in peril, from a man more dangerous than Catilina, than Sulla or Marius, or even Hannibal. I propose we vote on a *senatus consultum ultimum*.'

An audible gasp went around the chamber. It was a decree of a state of emergency, rarely invoked. Most recently, it had been used to squash the conspiracy of Catilina and the disorder engendered by the rivalry between Milo and Clodius. The recriminations from the decisions taken under those acts of law by Cicero and Pompey were still reverberating to that day.

Cassius opened his mouth to veto, but Antony put a restraining hand on his arm.

'Wait. Let's hear the wording. We just need to veto before the vote.'

'I propose that this house decrees the *senatus consultum ultimum*, and that we call on the consuls, praetors, tribunes and all the proconsuls near the city to ensure that the Republic comes to no harm.'

'It's a declaration of war against Caesar,' hissed Curio. 'Stop them.'

Chaos was breaking out in the Senate; old men were making threatening gestures, jostling and shoving one another, screaming spittle-flecked invective in one another's faces. Antony called out his veto, but he was unable to be heard. He pushed his way forward, using his bulk to thrust the senators out of the way. Hands tried to pull him back; nails from clutching fingers gouged his forearms and tore his toga. He pressed on, aiming for the space where the consuls sat, so he could get the Senate's attention and interpose his veto. He locked eyes with Lentulus, who saw the imposing figure bearing down on him, and backed away in fright. Antony clenched his fists, ready to fight for his right to be heard if necessary.

Then something smashed into the back of his head and sent him sprawling forwards. He lay on the floor for a moment, stunned, then slowly rose to his feet, shaking his head, looking for all the world like an angry bull. He turned to see a suddenly very scared-looking Marcellus holding the broken remains of one of the curule chairs. Antony balled his fists and shouted a curse.

'You son of a whore! I'm going to kill you.'

He stepped forward, but a firm hand pressed into his chest.

'Marcus,' said Curio urgently, restraining his friend. 'The Forum is filling with Pompeius' soldiers. We have to get out of here.'

Marcellus, seeing he was no longer in immediate danger, recovered some nerve and said defiantly, 'Yes, leave, you traitors. Run back to your master like the dogs you are.'

Lentulus stepped up beside him and said more formally, 'Antonius, Curio, Cassius, you must leave the city. As you are clearly intent on obstructing the legitimate business of the Senate, this house can no longer guarantee your safety.'

Antony gaped at him. It was a stunning declaration. The person of a tribune was inviolate, a sanctity as old as the office, reaffirmed by Sulla. To threaten violence against a tribune was sacrilege, not far in impiety from deflowering a Vestal Virgin.

Antony pointed at the consuls with a trembling finger.

'You hypocrites!' he cried out, turning slowly so his stare took in the whole of the Senate, who had stopped their brawling to watch this momentous event play out. 'All of you! You claim to protect the *mos maiorum*, our ancestral customs, you say you value the Republic above your lives. And yet as soon as it suits you, you break one of the Republic's oldest, most important laws, the sacrosanctity of the Tribune of the Plebs. Have you forgotten that to harm a Tribune of the Plebs or interfere with his right to veto is a crime punishable by death?'

Marcellus seemed to flinch at this, but Lentulus stood firm.

'I have made no threats and done you no harm,' said Lentulus. 'I have merely warned you that you are in danger.'

'Marcus,' said Curio urgently, 'we have to go.'

Antony hesitated, torn between further defiance and the need to escape with his life. He took two more swift steps forward, and Lentulus and Marcellus flinched backwards as if he was about to strike them.

'Remember, I am an augur as well as a tribune. And I foresee that your actions today will lead you to death.'

A mutter went around the Senate chamber, and many of the senators made signs to ward off evil. Superstition was as rife in the upper classes as the lower, though they tried to hide the fact. Nor were Lentulus and Marcellus immune to the fear that a curse or prophecy could engender. Satisfied that he had struck home, Antony allowed himself to be dragged away by Curio. Cassius was waiting for them at the steps leading down into the Forum, and when Antony reached him, he could see why he had paused.

The Curia was ringed with legionaries, armed and armoured. They stood at attention, polished armour reflecting the low sun, gladii sheathed but *pila* held at their sides, pointing at the sky. There was no obvious exit. Antony suddenly felt naked and vulnerable, with only his toga and under-tunic to turn a sword or spear thrust, and no weapon to strike back.

He took a breath and advanced on the line of soldiers. Curio and Cassius followed behind with trepidation. He approached the officer supervising one section of the line.

'Centurion,' he greeted him.

'Tribune,' replied the centurion stiffly.

'That's "Legate" to you,' snapped Antony.

'Sorry, sir... I mean... Legate.'

'Better. Now, what's the meaning of this?'

'Orders, sir. Pompeius told us to surround the Curia and not let anyone leave.'

'I see. And you know that as a Tribune of the People, any who impedes my work or harms me will be sentenced to death?'

The centurion – clearly a veteran nearing his discharge, from his scars and the grizzled tufts of hair protruding from under his helmet – shifted from foot to foot uncomfortably, but did not move aside.

'My orders come from Pompeius Magnus, Trib— Legate.'

'Which legion are you from?'

'The First, Legate.'

'One of the legions that Caesar sent to Pompeius to defend Rome against the Parthians. How is your war against them going, Centurion?'

The centurion looked even more uncomfortable, stuttered, but could not articulate a reply.

'You were at Alesia, weren't you? We fought together.' Antony turned to the *optio* by his side, who looked as if he was trying to sink into the flagstones. 'You... I know you. I broke bread with you in your *contubernium* during the siege.'

'You did, Legate. Ate our food and treated us as comrades.'

'Comrades we are, and always will be. Bonds forged in battle cannot be broken – isn't that so?'

'Yes, Legate. That is so.'

Antony turned his attention back to the centurion. The officer was a large man, but Antony's physique dominated him nonetheless. He looked him right in the eyes and said, 'Stand aside, Centurion.'

The centurion seemed to wilt. He took a step to one side, opening up a gap in the line. Antony gave him a nod, and walked through. As he passed, the centurion said, 'Go with the blessings of Mars, Legate.'

Curio and Cassius hurried through in Antony's wake, and they walked briskly out of the Forum along the Vicus Tuscum. There was a commotion behind them, shouts, and Antony glanced back. A senior centurion was berating the officer who had let them pass, pointing at Antony and shouting orders. A dozen legionaries saluted briskly and broke into a trot, heading in their direction.

'Run,' cried Antony. The three men started to sprint, Antony easily able to outdistance the other two, but checking his pace to allow the less fit men to keep up with him.

'Where are we going?' gasped Cassius.

'Just follow me,' said Antony. 'And don't look back.'

The Vicus Tuscum led to the *forum boarium*, the old cattle market that had become an area of bustling commerce, situated near the docks. Antony threaded his way through the curious market-goers, construction workers, warehouse labourers and dockers. He heard the soldiers behind yelling for the citizens to make way. The fit young legionaries were faster than Curio and Cassius, and Antony glanced back to see with frustration that they were gaining on them. It would have been easy to leave his friends to their own devices, but the thought never crossed his mind.

'Keep going!' he urged. 'There's a warehouse by the docks where timber is being unloaded. You can't miss it. I'll delay them. Go!'

Cassius and Curio ran on, and Antony turned to face his pursuers, casting about him for a weapon. A trestle table nearby was piled high with copper and bronze pots and pans. He stepped up to it and tipped it over, a massive crash reverberating around the marketplace as the kitchenware hit the cobbles.

'What are you doing?' cried the merchant, but Antony ignored him. He grabbed one of the table legs, and, chest heaving, wrenched it free. The soldiers were nearly on him, but they came to an abrupt halt as they found themselves confronted by Antony's imposing bulk, patting his improvised club threateningly.

'Come with us, sir,' said the optio leading the men. 'You are under arrest by orders of Pompeius Magnus.'

'He has no authority over me,' said Antony. 'You know this.'

'That is not for us to question, sir. Now please, put down your weapon. We don't wish to hurt you.'

'Come and take it from me,' snarled Antony. The optio looked at his comrades, then unsheathed his gladius and took a step forward. Antony advanced on him in two quick steps. The optio raised his sword in a panic, and Antony smashed it aside, using the weight of his club and all his strength to send the sword skittering away. Then he brought the club back hard against the side of the optio's shin. There was a crunch of bone, and the optio went down with a cry.

'Who's next?' cried Antony, brandishing the club wildly.

The legionaries looked at one another, trying to find the courage to attack this man – not only an inviolate tribune, not only their former comrade in arms, but a huge, fearsome beast of a warrior who would undoubtedly do them some serious damage before they could restrain him.

'I think you should be on your way, sir,' said one of them. 'We need to attend to the optio. But don't tarry. More will be coming.'

Antony growled, his blood up, relishing the idea of wading into combat against the legionaries. But his rationality reasserted itself. He gave them a nod, and ran off in pursuit of Curio and Cassius, through the stunned crowd.

They had reached the warehouse just ahead of him, and were now standing, looking around in confusion.

'What now?' asked Curio.

Antony reached down behind a crate and fished out some tunics, soiled and torn, little more than rags.

'Put these on.'

Cassius looked at them with distaste, a sneer on his face as he held them up between finger and thumb, as if they would pollute him.

'Are you serious?'

'Just do it,' said Curio. 'Unless you want to go back out there and face down the soldiers.'

They hurriedly shrugged off their togas and fine woollen tunics and donned the rags, taking on the appearance of slaves or paupers, provided no one looked too closely.

'Follow me,' Antony said when they were dressed. He led them out of a small door in the back of the warehouse, and they exited onto the Forum, shuffling along with their heads down like reluctant slave workers. An ox cart was waiting for them, a tarpaulin covering the contents. The driver seated at the front gave Antony a nod and gestured with his whip to the back. Antony lifted the tarpaulin and helped Cassius and Curio in, then hopped up beside them and pulled the tarpaulin over them. Darkness descended, and with it a claustrophobic, warm atmosphere, heavily scented with the smell of cabbages.

'This is outrageous,' complained Cassius, but Curio slapped his arm and put a finger to his lips.

'Quiet,' he hissed. 'Unless you want a spear in you.'

Cassius clamped his mouth shut, and Antony thumped the front of the cart twice with his fist. There was a crack of the whip, a jerk as the oxen took up the strain on the yoke, and the cart trundled forward.

It was a short distance to the Pons Aemilius across the Tiber. Antony peered out from under the tarpaulin and saw the river. Then the cart came to a sudden halt. He hastily pulled the tarpaulin back down as he heard a soldier's voice.

'You. What have you got in the cart?'

'Cabbages,' said the driver.

'Why are you taking cabbages out of Rome? Surely you should be taking them the other way, from the farm to the market.'

Antony cursed the driver's stupidity. He didn't know the man – his steward had procured his services – and he wished now he had taken a more active role in the recruitment process.

'No one wanted them,' said the driver, unconvincingly.

'Show me,' said the soldier.

There was a moment's pause, then some mumbled conversation, then the clinking of some coins.

'You may pass,' said the soldier, and the cart began to move again. Antony let out a breath of relief. It had always been possible that the driver would keep the money he had been given for bribes, and Antony thanked the gods for the man's probity... or fear of punishment.

The cart rolled across the Pons Aemilius and out on the Via Aemilia. Once they were well clear of the city, Antony threw the tarpaulin back and took some deep breaths of the clean country air. Curio looked grim, and Cassius looked as if he was about to vomit.

Antony glanced back at the city, wondering when and under what circumstances he would see it again. Then he turned his face to the north.

Towards Gaul.

And Caesar.

Chapter IV

ante diem iv Idus Ianuarias DCCV AUC (10 January 49 BC), Ravenna

Ravenna was a small town in Cisalpine Gaul – the part of the province on the Italian side of the Alps – situated on the coast of the Mare Adriaticum. Although it had been accepted into the Roman Republic forty years previously, it lay just north of the border of Roman Italia proper, and so remained within the borders of Caesar's proconsular province. Caesar had been waiting here for some months, ostensibly to support Antony's election to the tribunate, though more likely, Antony conceded privately, to be in a position to keep a close eye on events in Rome. He was accompanied by just a single legion, the rest of his forces still stationed on the far side of the Alps so as not to appear too threatening to Pompey and the anti-Caesarian Senate faction. To Antony's mind, this, if nothing else, showed that Caesar was sincere in his wish to resolve the dispute by peaceful means. If he had aggression at the front of his mind, his entire battle-hardened force would have been drawn up along the border, ready to march.

Ravenna itself was an odd little place, situated in an extensive marshy lagoon, its houses built on earthen piles that made small islands. It would be a hard place to conquer, Antony thought, but a miserable place to live, with all the biting flies and pestilence that marshes brought. Caesar had obviously felt the same, and set up his legionary encampment on drier ground a little way out of the town.

Antony rode into the camp on the morning of the fourth day before the Ides of January, tired and saddle-sore, accompanied by Curio, who looked as if he could barely stay in the saddle, and Cassius, who had not stopped grumbling since they left Rome. They had made excellent time, swapping to fast horses as soon as they were out of sight of the city, and changing the mounts at way stations whenever the beasts started to flag. They had rested little, despite Cassius' protestations, and

Antony realised they must have looked a strange sight to the legionary guards – grimy from the road, bleary-eyed and dressed in rags. But the sentries had instantly recognised Antony, and he was quickly conveyed to the *principium*, where Caesar, who had been informed of their arrival, awaited them.

Antony straightened his back, ignoring his chafing thighs, and with Curio and Cassius in tow, he entered Caesar's quarters.

Caesar was standing behind a table stacked neatly with scrolls and papyrus documents, with Labienus and Trebonius either side of him. As soon as Antony entered, Caesar broke off his conversation with Labienus and strode over to him, throwing his arms around him and embracing him like a long-lost son. Then he stood back, put his hands on Antony's shoulders and regarded him with a beam on his face that Antony could rarely recall seeing.

'My boy, it gladdens my heart to see you. What good service you have done me! And of course, you, Curio and Cassius.' He shook their hands vigorously. Then he noticed the scratches on Antony's forearms. He turned him and saw there was matted blood on the back of his head that had dribbled down and stained his tunic.

'What harm has been done to you, Antonius?'

Antony looked grave. 'I have news that will distress you, Caesar.'

Caesar addressed a couple of hovering orderlies. 'Fetch a medicus to attend to the tribune. And fetch bread and wine. These men are exhausted. Antonius, Curio, Cassius, please sit. Then you can tell me all.'

Folding chairs were fetched and they all sat, Antony gratefully sinking into a linen seat. Caesar listened intently with an expression of increasing anger as Antony related the events in Rome since the beginning of the year when the new consuls took office. When he got to the point where he had been attacked and they had to flee for their lives, Caesar jumped to his feet.

'This is an outrage. They dare to lay hands on a tribune? Have they no honour? Do they not know shame?'

Curio interjected at this point. 'It is a tragedy, Caesar. Cicero himself told me that Pompeius had accepted your peace offer. But the optimates have no desire for peace. With Cicero and Pompeius unable to attend the Senate meeting, the optimates engineered a coup. They will not let you keep your armies, nor your imperium. They will not allow you to stand for consul again. They will bring prosecutions against you as soon as you are a private citizen, and they will make sure of guilty verdicts by bribery and extortion. They will tear up every tradition of the Republic they purport to love in their campaign against you. They fear you, and they will not stop until you are completely destroyed.'

Caesar looked from Curio to Antony and Cassius, who both nodded their agreement.

'Curio's assessment is correct, Caesar,' said Cassius. 'The hatred of you and any who support you from the optimates is profound.'

Caesar put his hands on the table, bowed his head and sighed.

'Pompeius, you fool. Why have you thrown your lot in with these short-sighted idiots? Were you so unwilling to share the glory of your position with me that we must bring our lands to war once more? If only Crassus had survived...'

He looked up, and Antony could see genuine anguish in his eyes. 'He was my friend, and my beloved daughter's husband. But he has made his choice. And I must make mine.'

He turned to Labienus. 'Have the legion drawn up outside immediately. I will address them shortly.'

The medicus came in with a bucket of water, a sponge and a bag full of medical instruments and bandages. He approached Antony, but Caesar held up a hand.

'Antonius, I think our men need to see what has been done to you. Can you wait for your wounds to be attended, just a little longer?'

Antony smiled grimly. 'These injuries are mere gnat bites,' he said. 'I can bear them as long as you need.'

Caesar gave an approving nod. 'Come.'

He led Antony and Cassius out to the parade ground, where the Thirteenth Gemina Legion was drawn up in all its pomp. Recruited in Gaul early in Caesar's command of the province, it had taken part in battles against the Nervians, as well as Gergovia and Alesia. The pride of their achievements and their love of their commander shone from the eyes of each and every one of them. Caesar mounted a small wooden platform that had been brought up for his address, and beckoned Antony and Cassius up to join him.

'Men of the Thirteenth, most loyal of my comrades, I stand before you today as a man wronged. My enemies in the Senate have struck blow after blow against me. They have attempted to have me replaced as your commander—' Jeers and boos broke out at this. 'They have tried to deny me my right to stand for a second consulship. They have set our struggles, our injuries and losses, our glorious achievements on behalf of the Republic, at nothing, while they sit in their expensive houses, drink fine wine and banquet on oysters and sows' udders.'

More shouts of disapproval came from the arrayed legionaries, and Caesar let them have their voice before continuing.

'My friend, my brother, Pompeius Magnus, has been led astray and corrupted by the self-styled optimates of the Senate, through jealousy and a desire to take away my credit, though he has always supported my honour and dignity in the past. But now, a new precedent has been set by these vipers. In the past, it was necessary for force of arms to restore and affirm the veto of the tribunes. Now armed force has been used to take it away. Even Sulla, who stripped all other power from the tribunes, left them the right of free intervention, and Pompeius restored the privileges that Sulla removed. Yet look what the ignominious wretches in the Senate and their soldiers have done to the sacrosanct, inviolate persons of our tribunes.'

Caesar ushered Antony forward, and he stood before the legionaries, still dressed in bloodied slave rags, turning this way and that so they could all see the injuries inflicted on him. The howls from the legionaries reached a new crescendo of outrage. Antony felt like a performer on stage, and was distracted for a moment by thoughts of Cytheris. But Caesar's powerful voice broke over his reverie.

'And further, they have decreed the *senatus consultum ultimum*, for which there is no precedent in these circumstances.

'I have been your commander for nine years, and under my leadership your efforts have brought fortune and riches to Rome. You have fought countless successful battles and pacified the whole of Gaul and Germania. I call on you now to protect my reputation and dignity against those enemies that wish me harm. Will you stand with me?'

The roars of approval were deafening now. Caesar stood, basking in the adulation of his men, and Antony, standing on his right side, soaked up the reflected glory. *This* was command, he thought. *This* was power. And this was better than any speech in the Senate, no matter how well received. Nothing could compare to this feeling.

Caesar held his arms up to be heard again.

'Comrades, friends, you have my gratitude, though I never for a moment doubted your courage or loyalty. Now go, and prepare for the struggle to come, in which we will free the Republic from the unworthy men who hold it in their grasp.'

He descended from the dais and headed back to his headquarters, Antony and Cassius following. Inside, Curio, Trebonius and Labienus were waiting to receive them. They all applauded, though Antony noted that Labienus was a little less enthusiastic than the others.

'That went rather well, I thought,' said Caesar.

'It was magnificent,' said Trebonius.

'You have them in your palm, Caesar,' said Curio.

'Well done,' said Labienus.

'Thank you, all, for your praise and your efforts on my behalf. But I must pay tribute to one man above all others, without whom my position would be far worse. Marcus Antonius has protected my interests in Rome with courage and conviction, no matter the risk to his personal safety and his own interests. He has been elected to the augurate and the tribunate in the face of intense hostility. He has had physical injury inflicted on him in my service. Antonius, you truly deserve to be at my side.'

Antony beamed, and mumbled his thanks.

'We march tonight. Make your preparations. For my part, I am going to take a bath. Farewell.'

Caesar left them, and Curio came over to clap Antony on his back and congratulate him. Curio and Cassius had worked hard on Caesar's behalf, too, but Curio seemed to take nothing but pleasure in the praise credited to his best friend, and Cassius would surely admit that Antony had been the senior of the two of them in the tribunate, taking a lead on everything to do with Caesar's case. Trebonius, too, seemed happy for his friend and comrade-in-arms.

But Labienus, widely acknowledged as Caesar's most able lieutenant, steadfast by his side throughout his long campaign in Gaul, and responsible in his own right for some of Rome's most famous victories in the province, had an expression like a thundercloud. Antony returned his stare calmly, but he knew that Labienus was mortally insulted. Had Caesar made a rare tactical blunder in overlooking his longstanding deputy?

Antony mentally shrugged. If so, it was all to his own benefit.

'I'm going to get out of these filthy clothes and have them burned,' he said. 'Then I'm going to have the medicus attend to my wounds and get myself a good rub down to knead out the knots and kinks from the road.'

He took his leave, stomach churning in excitement. After more than a year of politics, he was heading back into battle.

ante diem iv Idus Ianuarias DCCV AUC (night of 10 January 49 BC), the Rubicon river

'Is that it?' asked Antony.

Caesar smiled. 'You crossed it on the way north just yesterday.'

'Yes, but it's so insignificant I didn't notice it.'

Caesar had moved with his customary alacrity, setting out with the Thirteenth Legion as soon as it was ready to move. They had marched at double time, reaching the river Rubicon in darkness, deliberately timed to conceal the legion's movements from prying eyes. Now that they were on the Rubicon's bank, Antony was distinctly unimpressed. It was little more than a stream, with a kind of ruddy colour to its water that he could make out in the moonlight, which gave it its name.

Caesar was seated in a carriage, comfortable but not ornate, and Antony was back in the saddle again, riding alongside. Others of Caesar's most intimate circle were close by – Cassius, Curio, Trebonius. Labienus was notably absent. Antony presumed he was sulking with the rearguard.

The legion had halted behind Caesar, and waited expectantly. Caesar got out of his carriage and gazed out across the tiny river, standing in Gaul, looking out into Italy.

'If I do not do this thing,' he said in a clear voice, so all around could hear him, 'then it will be the start of a great evil for me. Yet if I continue, what an evil for all mankind.'

Antony looked at him in surprise. The mighty Caesar, the unperturbable genius who planned everything with precision and always acted with supreme confidence and decisiveness, was having second thoughts? Antony looked around at his comrades, who were equally taken aback. No one else replied, so he spoke up.

'Caesar, this is not your doing. This is not your choice. This situation has been forced upon you. Maybe people will see you taking your army across the Rubicon, in contravention of the laws, as a declaration of war on the Senate. But in truth, with their decree, the Senate has already declared war on you.'

Caesar nodded, and gave a half-smile. Then he said, 'So be it. Let the die be cast.'

It was a popular saying among gamblers, and spoken by another, it might concern the men, who always preferred a sure thing to a gamble when it came to battle. But this was Caesar, the favourite of Fortuna, his luck legendary. His words filtered back to the legionaries, who took it up as a slogan to be repeated like a battle cry.

Caesar ascended into the carriage once more and ordered the driver to advance. The order to march was sent back to the *primus pilus centurion*, the most senior centurion of the first cohort, and the legionaries set off, following their commander as he led them into rebellion. The Rubicon was spanned by a low wooden bridge to accommodate wheeled transport, but the river was low and fordable at this point, so Antony rode his mount into the water, and escorted Caesar across. He made sure the proconsul reached Italy first, then pulled up beside him.

'So, here we are, Marcus. Where will this path lead us, I wonder?'

'To Rome,' Antony replied simply.

Caesar laughed. 'Sometimes you come across as a learned student of history and philosophy and a skilled orator and politician. Sometimes you seem a simple soldier.'

'It's possible to be both, I think.'

'Quite so. Very well. Forward.'

The single legion continued into Italy, aiming for its first objective, the town of Ariminum. Dawn broke, the sun rising into an orangey sky punctuated with high wispy clouds, and with it the town came into view. It was a venerable *colonia*, founded by the Romans a couple of centuries previously, and had a history of supporting Roman leaders associated with the people, such as Gaius Marius. As they neared, Antony enquired if they should arrange the legion into battle formation, but Caesar waved the idea away carelessly. When he could see the city walls more clearly, he understood why. The gates were already open.

Antony gave Caesar a sideways glance, but the proconsul had a smug, satisfied look on his face, so he decided not to enquire further. When they reached the gates, half a cohort of legionaries bearing the standard of the Thirteenth was waiting for them, and they came to attention as Caesar approached.

'Well done, boys,' he said. 'Any trouble?'

'None at all,' said the senior centurion. 'A bit of cash and a flash of some steel and they were falling over themselves to get ready to welcome you.'

Caesar had sent an advanced force to take the town, Antony realised. He must have dispatched them as soon as Antony had arrived with news of the Senate's decree. He thought back to the crossing of the Rubicon a short time ago. Caesar's doubts and reluctance were all a show. From the moment he had found out the Senate had declared war against him, he had acted with his characteristic speed and decisiveness. That he was trusting to his luck was still true, but he had the ability and self-confidence to make sure the dice were loaded in his favour. And he had known that perception was going to be important in the war of words that would surely come. Showing he had doubts about tipping the Empire into war was his way of making sure the moderates and neutrals could support him with an easier conscience.

Caesar entered the forum in his carriage, where he was met by the town's officials, who formally surrendered the town to him. He quickly set about making sure his men had rest and food, and he established a temporary headquarters for himself.

Antony took the opportunity to requisition a billet, taking over a nice domus that had been abandoned by a fleeing supporter of Pompey. It was strange to be unaccompanied by his household slaves. Even when he was fighting in Gaul, he had always had some of his personal servants around to attend to his needs, but his hurried flight from Rome had left him without domestic help. He needn't have worried, though. Caesar allocated some of his own slaves to make sure Antony had everything he needed, and not long after arriving in the town, he had bathed, dined, drunk well and was fast asleep.

ante diem iii Idus Ianuarias DCCV AUC (11 January 49 BC), Ariminum

Antony was woken later that day, partly refreshed by a few hours' sleep, by a messenger from Caesar, summoning him to a meeting. When he arrived, armed and armoured and ready for battle, he was greeted by two pieces of unwelcome news. The first was that Marcus Caelius Rufus had decided to join Caesar's cause.

As they waited for Caesar's arrival, Antony sidled up to Caelius. He had never liked the slimy young man. He was Cicero's protegé, which was bad enough, but Antony was sure he had spied for Cicero during the conspiracy of Catilina that had led to the execution of Antony's stepfather. More than that, he had been the lover of Clodia, the exquisitely beautiful and sophisticated lady for whom Antony had fostered his own deep but unrequited love as a youngster. He had never been able to work out what she saw in Caelius, but their affair had gone horribly wrong, ending in a court case and accusations of attempted poisoning.

'What are you doing here?' Antony asked, without first offering a greeting.

'Choosing the winning cause,' said Caelius simply.

'Not the just one?'

Caelius shrugged. 'These things are subjective. But I have little doubt that Caesar will emerge from this struggle the victor, and I have no intention of siding with the losers, no matter how noble they claim their motives to be.'

'Not many in Rome agree with your assessment of Caesar's odds.'

'Maybe not. But Rome is full of fools. What do you think his chances are?'

Antony considered for a moment. 'I would never bet against Caesar.'

'Well,' said Caelius. 'There we are.'

'Just a word of warning, though,' said Antony. 'If I hear even the slightest whisper that you are spying for Cicero or Pompeius, I will personally break your neck.'

Caelius swallowed. It was clear that Antony had both the strength and the will to do just that.

'I am not here to spy, Antonius. You have my word.'

Antony thought about saying more, but at that moment Caesar swept in, dressed in his armour and his distinctive scarlet cloak. He gestured to them to be seated, and they all settled themselves onto the stools, chairs and benches that had been put out for them. Antony looked around at the rest of the war council: Curio, Cassius, Trebonius, Caelius, Decimus Brutus and the legate, poet and noted intellectual, Gaius Asinius Pollio. One seat, though, remained empty.

'Where is Labienus?' asked Caesar.

Curio and Cassius looked bemused, but Trebonius and Pollio exchanged anxious glances. It was Trebonius, the more senior of the two, who spoke up.

'I have troubling news, Proconsul. Labienus has deserted to the enemy camp.'

Caesar's expression did not change. Antony couldn't imagine what a personal blow to him it was to have his second-in-command of so many years abandon him at this most extreme moment of crisis. Still, for Antony, it was a blessing. There could be no doubt now who Caesar's lieutenant was. Antony had just become the second most powerful man in the Caesarian faction. It was hard to take in. So much had happened since he had left Syria and joined Caesar in Gaul. Quaestor. Legate. Augur. Tribune. And now this. Whatever this was.

Caesar shrugged and kept his voice even.

'Make sure to have his baggage and his treasures sent on to him. Now, to business. We have just one legion, but a large force on the far side of the Alps that is hurrying rapidly to our aid. Pompeius has been raising troops in Italy, but he has only two veteran legions, the First and Fifteenth – the ones he took from me on the false pretext that he was going to invade Parthia. He will be wary of their loyalty, but will still be confident in his strength and will have assumed that I would wait for reinforcements before taking action. I think most of you here know me better.

'Speed and surprise are our friends. Our forces will proceed down the peninsula and advance on Rome. If we are quick enough, we will have the city, the Senate and the treasury in our hands. Therefore, Antonius, you will take five cohorts and take control of Arretium and the Via Cassia. I will also send a cohort each into Pisaurum, Fanum and Ancona, and the remaining two cohorts will stay with me while I raise further levies and wait for news of the response in Rome.'

Antony wondered if Caesar had intended to give him the command of half of the entire force available to him, or whether that appointment was supposed to go to Labienus. Much as he knew he was brave and strong in battle, he did not have Labienus' experience in command.

'Thank you for your faith, Caesar,' said Antony. 'I won't let you down.'

Caesar regarded him steadily for a moment, then nodded. 'I'm pleased to hear it. I had this morning a deputation from your cousin.'

'Lucius Caesar?'

'The same. He is following Pompeius, unfortunately, though his father, your uncle, remains loyal to me. He brought a message from Pompeius to the effect that they would grant my wish for a consulship if I abandon Ariminum, disband my armies and return to Gaul. However, he stated that his decision would have to be ratified by the Senate, and he did not offer to disband his own forces. This is clearly unacceptable. I consequently sent young Lucius back to Pompeius with a message informing him that I decline his terms.'

Caesar looked around his subordinates slowly, to see if there were any who disagreed or wished to challenge his decision. There were no gainsayers. Caesar gave a small, satisfied nod.

'Now, to other items of business.'

Antony found his attention wandering as Caesar discussed the finer points of supplies, available manpower, marching distances and recruitment strategies. Soon, he would be sword in hand once more, assaulting a fortified town, just like he had in Syria, Judaea and Egypt. Soon he would have that fire in his belly as he faced down his enemy with the strength of his own right hand.

Februarius DCCV AUC (February 49 BC), Picenum

Unfortunately, Arretium did not prove to be the glorious battle Antony had been hoping for. The walled town threw its gates open for him at his approach, and greeted him and his men like long-lost friends rather than marauding invaders. Antony wasted little time there, leaving a garrison and marching the rest of his men back to link up with Caesar at Ancona. He learned there that Curio had been dispatched with two cohorts to take control of Iguvium, whose townsfolk wanted to join Caesar, but were being prevented by a Pompeian supporter with *propraetorian* status and five newly recruited cohorts. As at Arretium, there had been no resistance. The *propraetor* had fled and the green troops deserted. Caesar continued south, entering Auximum and capturing the garrison, many of whom joined him.

Town after town threw their gates open to Caesar. These walled bulwarks against Gallic barbarians welcomed this new invader from the north with open arms. Even Cingulum, which had been founded and fortified at considerable expense by the deserter Labienus, came over to Caesar's cause, supplying soldiers and promising to follow his commands to the best of their abilities.

Caesar's Twelfth Legion now caught up with him, considerably augmenting his forces. They continued on the Via Asculum, which was hastily abandoned on Caesar's approach by Lentulus Spinther, the man who had held Antony's stepfather prisoner before his execution, and whose brother, Lentulus Crus, was the current consul who had been so instrumental in provoking this crisis.

It was at Corfinium that they encountered their first real resistance. Domitius Ahenobarbus held the city, and had no intention of surrendering it. The man who had lost to Antony in the election for augur had been appointed by the Senate to succeed Caesar as governor of Transalpine Gaul after the declaration of the *senatus consultum ultimum*.

When they came in sight of Corfinium, scouts reported to Caesar that a large detachment of Pompeian troops, five cohorts strong, were attempting to break down the bridge over the river Aternus that protected the city. Antony's ears pricked up at this, and he pushed himself forward.

Caesar was muttering curses. 'This could hold us up considerably. And delay will be fatal for our cause.'

'Proconsul, with your permission, I will lead a unit to take the bridge,' said Antony eagerly. This sounded like a chance for real action at last.

'Very well,' said Caesar. 'Take out a dozen cavalry *turmae* to engage them immediately, with three cohorts of infantry to follow as soon as possible. Save that bridge. Go!'

Antony saluted and rushed out, his soul singing. Within moments he was mounted and leading three hundred auxiliary cavalrymen at a canter in the direction of the city, while behind him a military tribune and some senior centurions rounded up the infantry to march double time to back them up.

It was not a long ride to the bridge, and the horses still had plenty of wind when they crested a hill and saw the valley of the Aternus below them. Antony called a halt and let the unit form up. Legionaries were scurrying around the bridge across the river, but they seemed not to have done any significant damage. Maybe they had a lack of skilled engineers. Caesar's men would have made short work of the structure, Antony knew.

He spent a few moments fixing in his mind the enemy strength and positions, as well as the lie of the land. Then, once the men were in position, he drew his spatha and roared out the order to charge.

The cavalry thundered down the hill, and it was only now that the Pompeian legionaries saw the danger they were in. There was an immediate response, but it was disorganised, panicked. Some legionaries ran across the bridge towards the safety of the walled city, which quickly became jammed with panicking soldiers. Others were ordered into a defensive line, three deep, the front line with shields to the fore, the second and third lines with shields raised against missile attack. But the hastily formed line was gappy and in poor order. Antony suspected these were recent levies, with no battle experience and little training.

With Antony in the front, they hit the defensive line in a wedge and split it like a melon cleaved by an axe. The Pompeian legionaries scattered, bowled aside by the momentum of the heavy mounts. Antony slashed down left and right with his spatha, metal biting into shields, mail, flesh. In the heat of the battle, it barely occurred to him that these enemy soldiers had once been his allies, his friends.

Then they were through the line and in its rear. Antony gave the order for a tight wheel, and his highly disciplined cavalry followed him, turning like the expert chariot drivers at the end of a lap of the Circus Maximus. The rear line of the Pompeians presented their spears, but the return charge broke them apart a second time.

Antony's cavalry galloped clear of the Pompeians, a few desultory javelins hurled ineffectually after them. When they were out of range, he ordered a halt and drew his men back up in formation. The Pompeians were reorganising, too, and many of those who had attempted to flee to the city were being forced back to reinforce their colleagues by the shouts and threats of furious, red-faced centurions. Although poor in quality, they were large in number, and Antony weighed up whether to engage them again. But all work had stopped on the bridge, and Antony knew that his infantry would soon arrive.

He looked around at his own men. Their casualties were light, but some of the horses had blood running down their flanks, and some of the men had taken spear wounds. Half a dozen were dead, and a dozen were too wounded to take any further part in the battle.

Nevertheless, when Antony ordered another charge, his men did not hesitate, and were on his shoulder the moment he kicked his horse into motion. This time, though, the charge was not completed. Just as they came within missile range, Antony gave the order to turn and retreat. The legionaries wasted a volley of javelins hurled at the backs of his cavalry. And the effect was as Antony had hoped. The Pompeians remained in line, and ignored their work to destroy the bridge. Now all he needed to do was have his men in position to charge if they showed any sign of turning back to the city. If the defenders broke their defensive formation, the cavalry would crush them.

It was less than an hour before Antony's infantry reinforcements arrived, and as they marched down the hill to join the cavalry, the dismay from the defenders was palpable, even at a distance. Antony now organised them into a much more conventional assault, his three cohorts advancing steadily until they were in range, exchanging a volley of javelins, then charging the last dozen yards so they could smash, shields first, into the enemy front line.

The Caesarian cohorts were outnumbered, but these were men of the Thirteenth, the toughest of the tough, forged and honed through years of combat in Gaul. What's more, the Pompeians had no cavalry, and when the Pompeian legionaries were engaged, pinned in position and fighting for their lives, Antony led another cavalry charge into their flank.

It was too much. The Pompeians broke and fled. They streamed back towards the city, fighting one another in their haste to get back to the safety of the walls. Those who could see they would not make it surrendered, and Antony took them under guard. No doubt Caesar would incorporate them into his own legions. He harassed the retreating soldiers, but did not press too hard, unwilling to risk his men's lives further in the cause of a battle already won. Instead, he waited until the bridge was clear, then occupied it. He ordered the engineers among the cohorts to assess the damage and make it good, and waited for Caesar to arrive.

The proconsul rode up at the head of his army a couple of hours later, and greeted Antony with a nod and a perfunctory word of congratulations. He then led his men across the bridge up to the city walls.

Unlike the other fortified towns they had encountered on their march south, the gates of Corfinium remained firmly closed. No one from the city came out to negotiate. Caesar shrugged and set about besieging the city, building defensive works around his camp and organising provisions to be gathered from neighbouring towns.

The next day, Caesar informed Antony that he had received a deputation from the nearby town of Sulmo, the people of whom wanted to support the proconsul, but were being prevented by a Pompeian senator called Quintus Lucretius and a local dignitary named Attius, who commanded seven cohorts. Antony was dispatched with five cohorts to bring the town over and, excited by the prospect of another battle, he set off in high spirits.

It was only a seven-mile march, and they arrived before noon, his five cohorts resplendent in the sunlight, standards waving at the front of each century. As soon as the townsfolk saw the approaching legionaries, they threw the gates open, which gave Antony mixed feelings at gaining a victory without any action.

When he reached the gates, two figures dressed in formal togas stood on the parapets, looking down. He halted and called up.

'Lucretius and Attius, I presume. I am here to accept your surrender.'

'Never!' called one. 'I am Quintus Lucretius, I am a senator of the Republic, and I will die for it.' And with that, he hurled himself from the walls. They were about thirty feet high, and it took only a heartbeat before he hit the ground with a crunch of bones. The body moved feebly for a brief moment, then was still.

Attius peered over the edge, then stepped back. He hesitated, then shuffled forward.

'You don't have to do this,' shouted Antony. 'You can surrender with honour.'

Attius looked down at him, uncertainty and terror in his face. Then a brick beneath him came loose and his foot slid out. He scrabbled for balance, then tipped forward. He turned, clutched at the defences, and grabbed a crenellation. He dangled precariously, feet swinging in the breeze, crying out for help.

Antony grabbed six legionaries and ordered them to the base of the wall with their shields raised above their heads.

'Brace yourselves,' he said, just as Attius lost his grip. His scream was cut short as the breath was knocked from him when he impacted the shields. The men beneath collapsed in a heap, groaning and cursing. Others rushed over to help them up. One legionary had a broken arm, another a broken collarbone, and all were bruised and decidedly unhappy. Attius, though, was brought over to Antony, limping, dazed, but alive. He dropped to his knees and looked up at Antony.

'I plead for mercy.'

'That is for Caesar to decide,' said Antony. 'See to his injuries,' he ordered his men, 'then bind him.'

Later, the same day Antony had set out, he led Attius and seven new cohorts back to Caesar.

Februarius DCCV AUC (February 49 BC), Corfinium

Caesar did indeed pardon Attius, and released him with no more harm than he had inflicted on himself. Caesar incorporated the new cohorts into his growing army, and after three days of the siege, the Eighth Legion arrived from Gaul, together with new levies from Gaul and more cavalry donated by the king of Noricum, swelling his ranks even further. Caesar set up a second camp on the far side of the town, and put Curio in charge of it.

Antony later found out that Pompey had instructed Domitius to abandon Corfinium and head south to meet up with the rest of the senatorial forces, but he had refused to accept Pompey's authority, and instead had written to him imploring him to bring his legions north to his relief. Caesar's siege works now made it impossible to obey Pompey's orders and Pompey clearly had no inclination to send men to attempt to bolster a hopeless position.

Nevertheless, Domitius told his men that Pompey was on his way, and prepared to make a secret escape with Lentulus Spinther and a few other friends. But his men discovered his treachery and, one night a week into the siege, a deputation from the city came to Caesar, saying they were prepared to open the gates and surrender Domitius to him. Caesar, however, was wary of sending his men into the town at night for fear of an orgy of pillage and looting. So he sent the deputation back and set up a ring around the city, men stationed within touching distance of each other, so none could escape.

As dawn approached, Lentulus Spinther called for parley with Caesar, and when Caesar agreed, his own men brought him into

Caesar's presence. As soon as he saw Caesar, Lentulus threw himself to his knees and began to beg for his life, his voice broken by sobs as he reminded Caesar of past friendship and favours that Caesar had previously bestowed on him. Antony couldn't keep a contemptuous sneer off his face at this display. Nor was Caesar overly impressed, and he interrupted him.

'I didn't leave Gaul with the intention of harming anyone,' he said. 'I am merely protecting myself, defending the rights of the tribunes, and freeing the Republic from domination by a tiny clique of self-interested senators.'

The relief was clearly visible on Lentulus' face. He asked to return to the town to organise the surrender, and Caesar granted him permission.

As the sun rose, the gates opened, and several senators, including Domitius and Lentulus, and a large number of *equites* and councillors were brought to him. Caesar's soldiers hurled abuse, and even some excrement, in their direction, but Caesar ordered they should not be harmed. When they were before him, he commented archly, 'I note that I have received no thanks for all I have done for you. Nevertheless, you are free to go.'

The senators looked at one another in surprise. It was that simple?

The local councillors presented Caesar with six million *sestertii* that Domitius had brought with him from the treasury in Rome, but he returned it to Domitius, stating that he had not brought his army into Italy for financial rewards. Then he dismissed his surrendered enemies, and took the oath of allegiance from their legionaries, before giving the order to prepare to continue their march south.

ante diem vii Idus Martias DCCV AUC (9 March 49 BC), Brundisium

Caesar followed Pompey to the port of Brundisium, situated at the heel of the boot that represented the Italian peninsula. By the time he arrived, he had three veteran legions, the Eighth, the Twelfth and the Thirteenth, plus three newly recruited legions, while Pompey had only two. Antony wondered what the senators in the Pompeian camp now made of their leader's boast that he merely had to stamp his foot and all over Italy, soldiers would rise from the ground.

Caesar immediately began to besiege the city, and at the same time began construction of two breakwaters made of earth and rafts that would cut off the harbour. Messengers flew back and forth between the two camps, carrying overtures of peace and proposals for treaties, but whatever the appetite to cease hostilities, there was no trust on either side to permit it.

Antony found the subsequent days of inactivity supremely frustrating. Caesar was firmly in charge of every aspect of the siege, so Antony had no real strategic role, and skirmishes between the two sides were few and far between, so he didn't even get an opportunity to draw his sword in anger.

Caesar was receiving intelligence from people within the town, and one night, eight days into the siege, he got the message that Pompey was embarking his forces for evacuation. Caesar immediately prepared his men to assault the walls of the city with their scaling ladders, but the spies warned him of trenches and spikes that Pompey had prepared in defence. He halted the assault, and instead led his men around the city walls to the harbour. Here, Pompey's men were well into the process of embarkation onto the big fleet at his disposal. Caesar did what he could, using skiffs and dinghies to capture two ships that had collided with the breakwaters. But then he had to watch in impotence, Antony fuming by his side, as Pompey sailed east with his men, his fleet and the bulk of the Senate.

When Pompey's ships were out of sight, Caesar turned away.

'We will build our own fleet in due course and pursue him,' he said to Antony. 'But first we must return to Rome.'

Antony cast a final glance out across the Mare Adriaticum, across which Pompey had fled, abandoning Italy to his enemy. Hannibal was considered Rome's greatest enemy and one of the most skilled generals of all time, Antony reflected. Yet he had marauded up and down Italy for ten years without ever conquering Rome. Caesar, who had set out with just a single legion, had conquered the entire peninsula in just three months.

Chapter V

Rome was a city subdued and cowed when Antony arrived. Caesar had sent him on ahead to convene a meeting of the Senate on his authority as tribune, but even before Antony reached the capital, word had arrived that Caesar was on his way with his legions. The city's business had ground to a halt. The streets, usually choked with pack animals and carts and city-dwellers going about their daily routines, were all but deserted. The markets were empty, the shop fronts shuttered. Dogs, pigs and chickens rooted around in the mud for morsels to eat, enjoying the unusual space afforded by the absence of the humans.

Antony's first port of call was to his mother, Julia, and his elder brother, Gaius – Lucius being away, annoyingly stuck serving as a propraetor in Asia under a Pompeian governor. Gaius cried out with happiness as Antony strolled in, saddle-sore and grimy from the road. He hugged him and pressed him for every detail he could give them about Caesar's advance through Italy and his brother's part in it. His mother, much more reserved, hushed them and shooed them aside, then gave Antony a gentle embrace. She summoned slaves to bring Antony refreshments, a change of clothes and a bowl to wash his feet, and Antony let himself be pampered, sighing in pleasure at the comforts of home after three months in the field.

'How are my wife and daughter?' he asked after some time, realising that maybe he should have enquired after them a little sooner.

Gaius made an odd expression that Antony did not miss. He was about to ask what the matter was when his mother put in smoothly, 'They are well. Your daughter is growing by the day.'

Antony fixed his brother with a glare. 'Is there something I should know?'

Gaius opened his mouth, but Julia gave him a withering stare and he closed it again.

'The usual gossips have been at it again,' she said. 'There is nothing with which you need to concern yourself.'

'What are they saying?' asked Antony, but Julia would not be drawn.

Antonia's greeting was pleasant enough, though he felt her stiffen when he kissed her. His daughter, little Toni, let out a squeal of delight when she saw him and rushed over, wobbling dangerously on her tiny legs. He bent down and tossed her into the air, catching her and hugging her tight, smiling, glad that at least his daughter was pleased to see him.

He dined with Antonia and his daughter. His wife had provided a lavish feast for his return, and he reflected she must be happy that, at least for the time being, their money worries were over. When dinner was over, Antonia instructed their daughter's nanny to take the little girl to bed, despite her protests. When the screams of outrage had faded, Antonia asked if Antony would like to accompany her to the bedroom. Her eyes were demurely lowered, and her cheeks were flushed red.

Antony looked at her properly for the first time that night. She was still very pretty in his estimation, and it had certainly been way too long since he had had a woman – since he had fled Rome the opportunity had just not presented itself. But something was holding him back.

'I have business to attend to tonight,' he said, trying to put some regret into his voice. He couldn't help but notice that she seemed to be hiding a sense of relief, offending him even further. He stood abruptly, gave Antonia a chaste kiss on the cheek and took his leave.

He did, in fact, have somewhere he wanted to be that night, although calling it 'business' was a stretch. He wandered through the quiet streets, escorted by a couple of bodyguards, and soon found his way to the apartment of Cytheris.

Kalendis Aprilibus DCCV AUC (1 April 49 BC), Rome

The meeting was convened in a temple outside the pomerium. Caesar was still forbidden to cross the sacred boundary, as he was a proconsul, and so remained outside until he could be elected consul once more. The irony – that the man who had illegally brought his army into Italy was now choosing which laws to obey – was lost on no one, but Antony knew it was important to try to maintain at least a semblance of legality, hence the necessity for senatorial support.

The rump Senate that Antony had managed to gather looked pathetically small, and he could see the disappointment in Caesar's face when he stood to address it. The bulk of the senators had left Rome with Pompey, who had made it known that he would consider any who remained behind to be in Caesar's camp. Still, there had been a number who had remained in Italy, waiting to see the outcome of the war, and some of those had returned to Rome to present themselves to Caesar. Caesar's father-in-law Lucius Piso, Lucius Volcacius Tullus, Marcus Aemilius Lepidus and his brother Lucius Aemilius Paullus and Servius Sulpicius Rufus, all nominally neutral, attended the meeting, as did Caesar's supporters such as Antony's uncle Lucius Julius Caesar and the ancient former consul, Publius Servilius Vatus Isauricus, who was now in his mid-eighties.

But the Senate that met that day was decidedly lacking in both numbers and senior senators, particularly those that had previously been consuls. Cicero – though Antony hated to admit it, still one of the most respected and influential of all the senators – had chosen not to follow Pompey. However, he had decided to remain at his country estate rather than obey Caesar's summons, a snub to Caesar that Antony could see rankled.

Antony brought the meeting to order, and gave way to Caesar. There followed a prolonged diatribe of condemnation of his enemies, self-justification and demand for loyalty, that quickly lost Antony's attention. Instead, his mind drifted back to the last two wonderful nights he had spent with Cytheris. Her reaction to his return had been in complete contrast to that of Antonia – full of genuine pleasure at the sight of him, followed swiftly by genuine passion. He had got precious little sleep since his return to Rome because of the beautiful actress, and he realised he was going to struggle to stay awake if Caesar droned on too long.

Caesar was determined to take every opportunity to lecture his captive audience, however, and soon Antony had to take to discreetly plucking at his pubic hairs beneath his toga to stop himself from drifting off. Eventually the proceedings were livened by a vote on a measure of Caesar's to send peace emissaries to Pompey, which was easily agreed. After that, a number of other measures were proposed and passed, although one tribune, Lucius Caecilius Metellus – who had previously been sympathetic to Caesar – now became obstructive, vetoing seemingly innocuous propositions for no apparent reason. When Antony tried to catch his eye, he looked away. It was obvious to Antony that he had been bought by Pompey, just as Caesar had bought Curio.

At first, this presented no real problem in the Senate meeting. If a proposition was vetoed, it could be retabled in a different formulation. But the vetos became more frequent, until even trivial proposals were being prevented from passing. Caesar, exasperated, ordered Antony to close the meeting.

Metellus was to prove even more troublesome, however, when Caesar ordered his men to take possession of the treasury, kept in the Temple of Saturn in the Forum. The Pompeians had fled in such a hurry that they had left most of the treasury behind, having time only to lock the doors and take the key with them. When Caesar, still outside the pomerium, ordered the doors broken down, Metellus stood in front of them.

'I interpose the sacred body of the tribune,' he stated, and his inviolate person prevented Caesar's soldiers from carrying out their orders. When word of this was brought to Caesar, he finally lost his temper.

'Tell him that we are at war, and war is not a time for the freedoms of peace. And if he resists, tell him I have given orders for his execution.'

Even Caesar's closest adherents gawped at this. The whole *casus belli* had been based on the optimates' blatant disregard of the tribune's sanctity, and now Caesar was hypocritically threatening the exact same. It made Antony realise just how much stress Caesar must be under, for all his outward stoicism. After all, as he had implied at the Rubicon, he was gambling with not only his life but, more importantly, his reputation.

Fortunately, Metellus took the threat seriously without it having to be carried out, and the treasury was duly looted of the vast funds that Caesar needed to pay his men and ensure their loyalty. He also took the reserves that were kept in case the city was ever besieged again by the Gauls, on the grounds that he had removed all possibility of future threat from that direction. Then, maybe realising he may be going too far, he softened his attitude to Metellus, stating that for one of his renowned clemency, it was harder to threaten death than it would have been to carry it out.

But after just seven days camped outside Rome, Caesar had had enough. Pompey was in the East with the Senate, though the bulk of his legions were in Spain. The Caesarian Senate was proving ineffective, and carried little authority. And Caesar had little further to gain from remaining in Italy, while Pompey grew his strength in the rich Eastern provinces.

Accordingly, he issued a raft of orders. Marcus Aemilius Lepidus, who had the rank of praetor, was given charge of Rome. Curio was to take an army to Sicily and North Africa to secure the grain supply, and Dolabella was to command the fleet in the Mare Adriaticum. Surprisingly, Antony's brother Gaius, a newly fledged senator, was promoted to governor of Illyricum and tasked with guarding Rome's north-east border despite his complete lack of political and military experience. It concerned Antony that his younger brother was being given such responsibility – he hadn't followed Antony into the legions and had shown little interest in advancing himself.

Caesar himself was to take his main forces north through Gaul into Spain, taking with him Decimus Brutus, Trebonius and Quintus Cassius, in order, as he said, to deal with the army with no general, before turning against the general with no army. It was a sensible move in Antony's eyes. Heading east before dealing with Spain would leave Italy vulnerable to a counter-invasion, and Caesar was too canny to allow that to happen.

The big surprise, to Antony and to most others, came at the end. Antony was to be given a propraetorian rank, and put in charge of all Italy.

He stared at Caesar in dismay. He did not dare to contradict him publicly, especially in his current intense and intolerant mood, but as soon as he got him alone, he made his protests known.

'Caesar, I want to come with you. You know my value is on the battlefield. I'm not a civil administrator.'

Caesar did not show any sign of anger at this questioning of his orders, and was happy to mollify Antony.

'Marcus, you come from an illustrious family. You hold political rank – augur and tribune. I need someone with that level of authority and nobility to command the Senate. What's more, you have proven your loyalty, and I trust you. I do not make any decision, but especially one as important as this, lightly or frivolously. I'm expecting you to keep the peace in Italy, but prepare for my return so we can take the war to Pompeius. You will need to build a fleet and recruit an army. You will need to administer our homelands firmly but fairly. You will need to keep the legions I leave behind loyal and in good spirits. I know you can do all these things. Do you believe it, too?'

Antony nodded. 'Yes, Caesar. If this is your wish, I will do as you command.'

And so, Antony, standing next to Lepidus, watched Caesar march north, and with a sudden heady rush of pride and terror, realised that he was now the most powerful man in Italy.

Aprilis DCCV AUC (April 49 BC), Rome

Antony knocked on Cytheris' apartment door, feeling as nervous as a young suitor calling on his first crush. It was stupid. Cytheris had accepted him back, and they had re-consummated their relationship on numerous occasions during the few days in which he had been back in Rome. But always he saw that reserve in her eyes: the knowledge that she was illicit – not exactly a secret, but neither openly acknowledged.

Her slave opened the door, but rather than accept the invitation to enter, Antony told the young lad to ask his mistress to come to him. After an excruciatingly long time – partly the compulsory application of make-up and perfume and the delicate hairstyling, but partly, he suspected, just to show him she could make him wait for as long as she desired – she emerged.

Antony's breath caught. She was radiant.

'If you stood alongside the three goddesses, Paris would surely choose you,' he said, then winced inwardly. He was clearly spending too much time with poets.

But Cytheris bestowed a soft smile that showed her even white teeth, and he knew from the way that her eyes crinkled at the corners that she was genuinely pleased.

'Tribune Antonius, to what do I owe this pleasure?'

Antony took her hand and looked into her eyes earnestly.

'Cytheris, our love has been too long in the shadows. I have been a coward, fearful of what others might think or say, fearful of how what we have may affect my reputation, my career. But, my sweet, no longer.

I am propraetor in command of all Italy. My word is law. It is time for you to step out of the shadows, and into the light beside me.'

He stopped, his mouth drying up. He had prepared and rehearsed this little speech incessantly, and now it just sounded trite and insincere in his ears. He looked at his feet. This was ridiculous. He had faced down Gauls, Britons and Judaeans on the battlefield; he had spoken in front of a hostile Senate; he had loved dozens of women. He looked back up into her face.

Tears were flowing down her cheeks, rivulets of kohl making dark tracks. He stepped forward swiftly and embraced her, and she grabbed him and sobbed into his shoulder.

After the initial emotion had subsided, she hurried back into her apartment, and emerged a few moments later with her make-up back in place. She took his hand and stared earnestly at him, her gaze switching from one eye to another, still seeming to expect his words to be a lie, or a joke. He squeezed her in a way he hoped conveyed reassurance.

'Marcus, are you sure? Society will say—'

Antony stopped her with a wave of his hand. 'Society answers to me now.'

She swallowed. 'Marcus, you have no idea what your words mean to me. I am infamis. I am beholden to my former master, I am at the whim of powerful men, and yet respectable people look down on me, sneer at me, cross the street to avoid me.' Her voice became choked.

'No longer. Now, come with me, I have something to show you.'

He led her down the apartment steps to the front of the insula. She turned the corner and stopped dead at the sight that confronted her.

A train of carriages occupied the street, and they were filled with friends of hers – actors and actresses, mimes and poets and artists. *Lictors*, the bodyguards of consuls and other officials, flanked the train, standing stiffly in formal pose. At the front was a war chariot in the British style, and it was yoked to two fine dun stallions whose manes had been plaited to make them look like lions.

'We tried real lions,' said Antony, 'but they kept eating the drivers.'

Cytheris looked at him, and he smiled to show he was joking.

'Marcus, what is all this?'

'My duties are going to take me all around Italy. I depart today. I want to travel in style, and I want you by my side.'

Her breathing was shallow, her face pale, but her eyes were sparkling.

'Oh, and may I formally introduce my mother?'

Julia dismounted from the rearmost carriage, helped down by her own personal slave.

'Mother, this is Volumnia Cytheris, my… companion.'

Julia was fully aware of her son's relationship with Cytheris, and Antony had spoken to her of his intentions to make it public. She had vociferously argued against the move, but when she realised he would not be gainsaid, she bowed to the inevitable.

'Mother is coming with us on our Italian tour, I'm afraid. My brothers are serving now, and she gets lonely. I hope you don't mind.'

Cytheris still seemed overwhelmed. 'Of course I don't mind.' She bowed low before Julia. 'Mistress, it is an honour.'

Antony's mother patted Cytheris' hand affectionately. 'Julia is fine, my dear. Now, I will take my place in the carriage at the rear. I'm not a talented performer like you, and I don't want to be centre stage.'

Antony looked at his mother to see if there were any hidden barbs in her words, but he detected none. 'As you wish, Mother. If you are fully prepared, we will depart.'

The entourage, led by Antony and Cytheris in their chariot pulled by lionesque horses, surrounded by burly lictors, full of chattering, singing, laughing artists, with the noble matron bringing up the rear in full dignity, made its way out of the city, watched by a gawping, fascinated, stunned crowd.

ante diem v Nonas Maias DCCV AUC (3 May 49 BC), Misenum

Antony knew he should have been exhausted, but he could not recall a time in his life when he had had so much energy. As he progressed through the Italian countryside, his mornings were spent visiting local troops, giving rallying speeches, recruiting new levies and training with the men. His afternoons were reluctantly given over to hearing local disputes, though he was sure his lack of interest in such trivia was obvious. His evenings were spent partying with the actors and poets, drinking, dancing and extemporising bad poetry. And his nights were spent making love with Cytheris. He presumed he must have fitted some sleep in from time to time, though he wasn't sure exactly when.

Caesar had given him a number of tasks in his rule of Italy while the proconsul was in Spain. He was to grow and ready the army for the next phase of the war, build a fleet, stabilise the economy, keep the peace, and make sure the senators who had not followed Pompey stayed in Italy and remained loyal to Caesar, or at least not actively opposed. It was a daunting list for the most veteran of governors, and Antony's experience of civil administration was virtually nil.

His approach, then, was to prioritise what he thought was most important to Caesar's cause, and this meant the army. Consequently, he spent much more time with soldiers than politicians, and became progressively more popular with the troops as he became less popular with the senators. His hedonistic lifestyle and his flagrant relationship with Cytheris reinforced the feelings of both those groups, the soldiers believing his choice of companion and his drinking and partying showed he was one of them, while to the senators it demonstrated the opposite. But, despite the obvious disapproval of the elites, and gentle advice from his noble friends and family, Antony would not be dissuaded from his relationship. He could not recall ever having been this happy in the company of a woman, not even in the early, responsibility-free days with Fadia.

But the biggest thorn in his side was Cicero. Curio had met the orator when he was on the way to take up his command in Sicily, and had reported back to Antony that Cicero was considering leaving to join Pompey. Of all the senators left in Italy, Cicero was by far the most influential, and what's more, he was a man for whom Caesar himself showed a great deal of love and respect. But Antony couldn't stand him.

Reluctantly, he had written to Cicero before he left Rome, gritting his teeth as he poured out insincerities onto the page. 'Had I not been very attached to you, much more so than you think, I would not have been alarmed by a rumour which is being spread about...' It had made the bile rise in his throat. 'I cannot believe you are about to go abroad, considering what love you hold for Dolabella and your beloved Tullia.' Antony had nothing against Cicero's daughter Tullia, though she was an insipid little mouse of a thing. She was entirely unsuited, though, to her dissolute husband, whose profligate infidelities put Antony's own to shame, and who treated his wife with ill-disguised contempt.

'I want to convince you that no one is more dear to me than you, except Caesar himself,' he had lied. He finished by exhorting Cicero not to commit himself to Pompey, nor to flee from Caesar, who held him in the highest standing.

Cicero had replied that he had nothing against Caesar, that he would be with Pompey if he had, and he was conscious that Dolabella – his son-in-law – was with Caesar. But he said that he wished to leave the country and reside in Malta, so as to remain neutral in the struggle. Antony knew this meant that Cicero was too cowardly to take a stand and choose a side, for fear of ending up with the loser. Caesar was clearly dominant at this moment, but only a fool would underestimate Pompey, with all the riches and strength of the East at his disposal.

Antony replied that he who wished to stay neutral should remain in Italy, since to leave would suggest they had taken sides. But he shifted the responsibility for forbidding Cicero from going abroad to Caesar – who had instructed that none of the senators should leave Italy – and told him to send his supplications to Caesar directly.

Antony reached Misenum, not far from Cicero's estate in Tusculum, at the beginning of May. He arranged for his entourage to be accommodated by the local dignitaries, not without some grumbling at having to put up actors and other undesirables in their luxurious homes. He spent the morning on sword drills with his men, which always helped sluice away his hangover, took a light lunch, and then steeled himself to receive the inevitable regional deputations.

He was not so crass as to have Cytheris at his side during these meetings, but that was due to her sex, not her status. He would not have had Antonia – or even his mother – present, for fear it would seem he was relying on the advice of women. Cytheris took herself off to enjoy the local baths while Antony granted a hearing to adjudicate a dispute about the border between the estates of two local councillors. It was frustrating to be occupied with such trivia and he forced them to come to the point swiftly, then gave a peremptory, and probably arbitrary, judgement.

The freedman organising his diary announced the next deputation was a group of fourteen local officials from Neapolis and Cumae. Antony thought for a moment. Both those towns had refused to support Caesar at the start of his campaign, and in fact had sent him defiant and insulting messages.

'Tell them I need to have a shit and a bath,' he said. 'They can come back tomorrow.'

With that, he rose from his chair and went to do exactly as he had said.

He found Cytheris relaxing in the pool of the private villa they had requisitioned for their stay, and he stripped off and slid into the warm water alongside her. She ordered the slaves to fetch them both wine, and they relaxed together, eyes closed, enjoying each other's company in peace. Then Antony sighed and heaved himself up onto the side of the pool.

'I need to see Cicero,' he said.

Cytheris wrinkled her nose in distaste at the idea.

'But you hate him.'

'That's true. But Caesar needs him.'

'And will your visiting him be enough to persuade him to stay in Italy?'

Antony considered this. It was a good point. For all his dislike of Cicero, he hadn't spent much time wondering if the feeling was mutual.

'Curio did tell me that Cicero said some rather dismissive things about me when he last saw him.'

'Such as?'

'He wasn't specific. I know his hatred of Clodius spilled over to all of Clodius' friends, who include me. But that was a long time ago.'

'And how long ago did he execute your stepfather?'

'Good point.' Antony took a thoughtful sip of his wine.

'So, you hate him, he hates you. Do you think it will be a productive meeting?'

'It seems unlikely,' conceded Antony, 'although I can use my propraetorian imperium to order him to stay where he is.'

'You can do that just as well by letter.'

Antony gave Cytheris an appraising look. 'And what do you have against Cicero?' It was obvious she disliked him, too.

She shrugged. 'Just that I know what he thinks of the likes of me.'

He felt a sudden surge of anger, that anyone could bear unkind feelings towards this woman that he loved – this beautiful, intelligent, witty, talented individual. Loved? Yes.

'I love you,' he said.

Cytheris looked shocked, then said the words back to him. They kissed, long and slow, and then made love in the pool.

A few days later, Antony left for Capua without seeing Cicero.

And a month after that, reportedly furious at Antony's snub, Cicero embarked on a boat he had had waiting for him, and sailed away to join Pompey.

November DCCV AUC (November 49 BC), Rome

Awaiting Caesar's arrival in Rome, Antony reflected on his performance as propraetor of Italy. Despite losing Cicero and a few other senators to Pompey, he thought he had done rather well. He had kept peace in the peninsula, and kept the legions fed, paid and loyal, which was more than Caesar himself had achieved, having had to put down a revolt by the Ninth in Cisalpine Gaul as he returned from Spain, going as far as threatening decimation and disbanding the entire legion. He had levied a large number of legionaries to augment Caesar's forces, and trained them hard to make them useful. He had made good progress on increasing the size of Caesar's fleet to enable him to take the war east. And he had travelled the length and breadth of Italy, promoting Caesar's cause, raising funds, and liberally doling out judicial rulings and administrative decisions.

The news from the west was consistently encouraging. Massilia on the southern coast of Gaul had rebelled against Caesar under the recently pardoned and released Domitius Ahenobarbus. A long siege caused some delay, but Caesar had left Trebonius in charge, assisted by the fleet in the capable hands of Decimus Brutus. Antony had sent Caesar the Eighth, Twelfth and Thirteenth legions to make up the reduction in Caesar's forces due to the men he had left behind to enforce the siege, and in just over a month Caesar defeated the three Pompeian legates and took control of all Spain. He left Quintus Cassius Longinus in charge with four legions, composed mainly of those legionaries who had just surrendered to him, and returned to Massilia in time to take the city's capitulation. Despite the disloyalty of the Massiliots, Caesar inflicted no retribution, and allowed no pillaging, much to the disgust of his own men. Domitius Ahenobarbus escaped by ship to join Pompey.

Less encouraging was the situation in the Adriatic. Dolabella, Cicero's son-in-law – and Antony's friend – had been defeated in a sea battle. Antony had reluctantly reinforced him with ships drawn from the new fleet he was constructing, commanded by Quintus Hortensius, son of the orator to whose position as augur Antony had been elected. He also sent Dolabella three legions that were supposed to be protecting the Italian coast, including one under his brother Gaius. Unfortunately, Pompey had been able to commandeer a large number of vessels from the trade centres in the East, and Dolabella was defeated again, with Gaius being captured along with fifteen vital cohorts. Not only was it a personal tragedy for Antony, but it was a disaster for Caesar's cause, with the land route to Greece in Pompeian hands, and the sea dominated by Pompey's larger navy. Antony wondered if Caesar would have to delay his invasion of the East, or even wait for Pompey to come to him in Italy.

But the very worst news came from Africa.

Antony had received regular dispatches from Curio. As early as April, Curio had reached Sicily and expelled Cato from the island without a fight, securing Rome's grain supply. In the month of Sextilis he had set sail from Sicily to Africa, held with two legions by Publius Attius Varus, who had been sent there by Pompey at the outbreak of hostilities. Varus had also forged an alliance with the Numidian king, Juba. As well as having family ties to Pompey, Juba disliked Curio, who had proposed while tribune that Numidia should be made into a Roman province.

Antony had deep misgivings about Curio's command, given his complete lack of military experience. In many ways it would have made more sense if their positions had been reversed – that Antony would have gone to Africa and Curio governed Italy – but Antony couldn't really complain, since by appointing him to the propraetorial position, Caesar had made it clear that Antony was his deputy, his second-in-command. And the first letter Antony received after Curio arrived in Africa told of a great victory at Utica, where his men had defeated a contingent of Numidian cavalry and taken possession of the supplies from Varus' docked fleet.

But the next letter that arrived from Africa was not from Curio, but from one of his legates, Gaius Asinius Pollio. Antony received the letter while reclining in his peristylium with Cytheris by his side. He read with increasing dismay, and as Cytheris noticed the change in him, she drew close and put an arm around him.

'Marcus, what is it?'

Antony didn't reply, reading rapidly the news of the disaster as it had unfolded. Curio had besieged Utica, where Varus was holed up and on the verge of surrender, but had to lift the siege when he learned that King Juba was marching to the city's relief. He retreated to his base on the coast, where he planned to wait for reinforcements. But then Curio received intelligence that actually Juba was over a hundred miles away, and what they had observed was only a small force of Numidians. Curio had rapidly marched out and his cavalry had overrun the Numidian camp. Overjoyed by his success, he had marched on, leaving part of his exhausted cavalry behind. He found the retreating Numidians and chased them. But it was a trap.

Juba was, in fact, nearby, and sent large numbers of infantry and cavalry against Curio. Initially the Romans under Curio fought well, but heat, thirst and exhaustion soon began to tell, while the Numidians were constantly reinforced. Curio's legates begged him to flee, but he said stoically he would not be able to look Caesar in the eye and tell him he had lost his army. He went to the fore, sword in hand, and was cut down.

Antony let out a gasp, and Cytheris squeezed him tightly. 'It can't be true,' he whispered. 'He can't be gone.'

Antony forced himself to read on, though his eyes were blurred with tears.

Pollio and a precious few others had escaped. Most of Curio's legionaries had surrendered, and Varus had given his word they would not be harmed. Juba had had other ideas, though, and with the exception of a few senators, he executed every last man. Curio's head, he had placed on a spike and had paraded in front of him.

Antony let the letter fall from his fingers.

Curio, his best friend since their childhood, was dead.

And it was his job to tell Fulvia that, once again, she was a widow.

December DCCV AUC (December 49 BC), Rome

By the time Caesar returned to Rome, he was Dictator. It had proved legally problematic to make him consul in the absence of the other consuls, so Lepidus had pushed through a vote to have Caesar elected to the ancient emergency position. It was an unsettling development for the populace. The role of Dictator had an honourable past, with notables such as Cincinnatus, who had left his farm to take up the role and defend Rome against the invading Aequi, then returned to his farm once the crisis was past. Or Fabius Maximus Cunctator, who had successfully held off the rampant Hannibal after his crushing victory over the Romans at Lake Trasimene. But there had only been one other Dictator in the last hundred and fifty years – the infamous Sulla, who had used his powers to indulge in an orgy of violence, particularly directed against the upper classes. That Caesar had so far shown great clemency gave some reassurance, but it was still an anxious city that turned out to greet him.

Caesar summoned the *comitia centuriata* and had them declare him consul for the following year, bypassing the need for an election, with his colleague being the innocuous Publius Servilius Vatia Isauricus. Hasty elections were then held for the other major posts, and since all the pro-Pompeians had fled, the positions were filled by necessity, as well as design, by Caesar adherents: Cicero's protegé Marcus Caelius was made the Praetor Peregrinus, with responsibility for foreigners in the city; Gaius Trebonius was made Urban Praetor to replace Lepidus, who was sent as proconsul to Spain; Decimus Junius Brutus was made proconsul of Cisalpine Gaul. Antony himself was not given a new magistracy, but had his tribunicial and propraetorian imperium extended, and was once again made a legate in Caesar's army.

Caesar was largely pleased with Antony's performance in his absence, particularly with the size of the fleet he had gathered, though it was still far too small to transport Caesar's entire army. He was less happy with the senatorial defections to Pompey, especially that of Cicero, but Antony came away from his first meeting with the new Dictator with the impression that Caesar thought he had done a good job.

Caesar held the dictatorship for only eleven days, during which he passed a number of laws, such as a restructuring of the debt problem that was threatening to overwhelm the economy. A number of exiles, including Aulus Gabinius, Antony's old mentor, and Antonius Hybrida, Antony's uncle and father-in-law, were pardoned and recalled in order to swell the ranks of the Senate with pro-Caesarians of consular rank. He then resigned the position and ordered Antony to be ready to leave for the East.

Antony toured the houses of friends and family to say his goodbyes. His mother did her best to be stoical, but Antony could tell that she was terribly worried that all three of her sons were involved in the war, although at least the imprisoned Gaius was – for the moment – out of danger. She would be lonely, too. She had devoted herself to her sons after the death of her second husband, which had been decreed by Cicero, and had not taken another. Now her sons were gone, too, although at least her brother Lucius Julius Caesar was remaining in Rome to help maintain Caesar's political interests. His farewell to his wife, Antonia, was stiff and formal, and his daughter Toni, though sorry to see him leaving, was too young to understand the uncertain length of his departure or the danger he would be in. His parting with Cytheris was emotional, full of declarations of love and fidelity and repeated assurances that he would return safely to her.

But it was the meeting with Fulvia that had proven the most difficult. He had been seeing less of her since his relationship with Cytheris had blossomed, but when, the previous month, he had taken the news of Curio's death to her, all the old feelings had come flooding back. Her marriage to Curio had not been passionate, born largely out of Curio's desire to inherit her previous husband Clodius' popular following, but they had nevertheless grown close. Fulvia had tried to be brave, but the terrible blow of a second widowhood was too much, and she had collapsed into his arms. They had spent the rest of the night talking, reminiscing about Curio – about Clodius, too. Antony retold stories of their childhood escapades, though Fulvia probably knew them by heart, and they celebrated Curio's full life with laughter and tears.

Now, on the eve of his departure to war, Antony sat with her and tried to bring her out of her sombre mood.

'I can't lose you, too,' she said, holding his hand tight.

'Why would you lose me? You know my prowess in battle.'

'Prowess is no defence against the whims of the gods. The shades of Hector and Achilles could testify to that.'

'But I will be fighting beside Caesar. Not only is he a far superior general to Pompeius, he is luckier, too. Nothing will go wrong.'

Fulvia shook her head and bit her lip, saying nothing. Antony took her in his arms and held her close, caressing her hair with his hand as he cradled her. She started to sob silently against him, and Antony let her release her grief and fear.

He wasn't being untruthful to her, not in his mind, by giving her false reassurance. He was supremely confident in his own abilities, and those of Caesar. But he had to concede the role fortune and divine caprice could play in battle. And he resolved to do his best to come home – to Fulvia, to Cytheris, to his mother and his daughter – not only alive, but victorious.

Chapter VI

Januarius DCCVI AUC (January 48 BC), Brundisium

As soon as Caesar arrived at Brundisium at the beginning of January, he embarked and sailed for Epirus. The Pompeians were caught completely by surprise, having believed he would never attempt a crossing with the worst of the winter storms on their way. Unfortunately, he only had enough transports for half his forces, so he had left Antony behind in charge of the other half, with instructions to bring them over as soon as the fleet returned for the second journey.

Ever efficient in logistical matters, Antony had the legions under his command drawn up and ready to embark on the appointed day. He stood on the docks with Aulus Gabinius, his friend and former commander, and another of his officers, Quintus Fufius Calenus, gazing out expectantly to sea. It was about eighty miles to the coast of Epirus, well beyond the horizon, and Antony knew that from his position at sea level he would only be able to see the masts of the returning fleet when they were a few miles away. Still, surely they should be in sight by now?

Calenus couldn't stand still, and began to pace. Gabinius was outwardly calm, but Antony suspected his friend was hiding his anxiety, just as he himself was.

One of the legionaries, situated atop a lookout post, spotted the ship – a *trireme* – first, and called out to Antony. It was still some time before it was visible to Antony, with his lower elevation and older eyes.

'Just one ship?' Antony commented. 'Where is the rest of the fleet?'

The truth became clear with agonising slowness. Another of Caesar's ships came into view, then a third – these last two being transports – but no more, and as they approached the harbour, it became clear that they had been in a serious fight. Masts were splintered, sails tattered, and there were scorch marks on the decks.

As soon as the first ship had docked, Antony ran up the gangplank, not waiting for the captain to come ashore to report. There was a pervading smell of smoke, and groans from injured sailors mingled with the lapping waves and calling gulls.

The captain presented himself to Antony with a salute.

'What happened?' demanded Antony.

The captain looked deflated, defeated, but he met Antony's gaze with a steady eye and a straight back.

'It was Bibulus.'

Bibulus, the former co-consul with Caesar and one of his most embittered enemies, was the admiral of Pompeius's fleet.

'Go on.'

The captain took a breath, then gave his report. 'We landed and disembarked without any problems. But when it was time for us to return, Bibulus had been alerted. He summoned his full fleet and intercepted us. Half the transports were captured, the other half were set on fire. The crews were burned alive on board. We could hear... smell...'

He paused for a moment and swallowed. Antony waited, sympathetic but anxious to hear the rest.

'We three ships are all that escaped. We fled before the wind, and rowed until our lungs burst, and we managed to outpace Bibulus' pursuit ships. They broke off a few miles back. Presumably they have blockaded Caesar now.'

'And no doubt they will do the same to us,' said Antony. 'See to your wounded and get the shipwrights working on repairs. Then get some rest. You have done your best.'

The captain nodded disconsolately and set about giving orders.

At least Caesar had disembarked his men before the destruction of his fleet. But he had only half of his forces with him, and now found himself outnumbered and blockaded. He needed Antony and his men. But what could Antony do without ships?

Februarius DCCVI AUC (February 48 BC), Brundisium

Antony looked out across the harbour to the small island a few hundred yards off the shore. Dozens of enemy warships were docked there, and more patrolled further afield. The blockading fleet, commanded by Bibulus' deputy, Lucius Scribonius Libo, had appeared off the coast of Brundisium a few hours after the survivors of Bibulus' ambush had docked, and had taken control of the harbour island. Antony had discovered that the island had no water, and had stationed his superior land forces along the coast, to prevent Libo's ships from landing on the mainland and replenishing their supplies. But it was taking longer than he had hoped to dislodge the stubborn Pompeian, and in the meantime he was receiving increasingly demanding and angry messages from Caesar, who was hemmed in by Bibulus' blockade and Pompey's army, which was twice the size of Caesar's.

Aulus Gabinius joined him.

'Caesar needs you, Marcus,' he said.

'You think I don't know that?' snapped back Antony, irked at the comment, and the informal way that his old mentor – but current subordinate – had addressed him. He quickly regretted his tone. 'How long can they hold out without water anyway?'

'The question,' replied Gabinius, 'is not how long they can hold out, but whether they can hold out longer than Caesar.'

Antony pursed his lips. 'We need to try something else. What do you think of this idea?'

And together, he and Gabinius formulated a plan.

Martius DCCVI AUC (March 48 BC), Brundisium

Antony had ordered the rapid construction of new ships, with every available shipwright, every carpenter and sailmaker and vast numbers of free workers and slaves drafted in. It would take far too long to build enough ships to outnumber the Pompeians, but at least it redressed the balance somewhat. One difficulty, however, was making sure the ships were seaworthy after their construction, given that they were trapped in the harbour. Consequently, new ships had to run the blockade for their sea trials.

That morning there was a low cloud and a light drizzle, but the wind, though fresh, was not too strong. Antony watched from the water's edge as two brand new triremes slipped their moorings and sailed slowly out to the edge of the harbour. The triple banks of oars rose and fell in good order, especially considering the inexperience of the newly drafted crews, and Antony observed in satisfaction the progress of the two vessels.

But Libo had seen them venturing out, too. Seeing a chance to reduce his enemy's fleet even further, he ordered four *quadriremes* from the island against Antony's new ships. The triremes were too far away to be able to hear any warnings from the shore, and Antony sent a silent prayer to Neptune that the ships' captains would see the threat and respond accordingly.

Soon, the triremes began to turn back towards the harbour. But they were slow, some of the oars pulled by the green rowers clashing and hindering the manoeuvring capability. The quadriremes advanced rapidly, and by the time the triremes were pointing in the direction of safety, the quadriremes were almost within bowshot. Seeing their prizes within grasp, they redoubled their efforts, sailing further and further into the harbour itself.

Antony watched anxiously, biting his lip.

Then, when he was sure the quadriremes were fully committed, he sprang his trap.

He had stripped the skiffs and small boats from the ships of his fleet and hidden them, under cover of darkness, along the mainland shore opposite the island. At his signal, sixty boats packed with veteran legionaries rowed out towards the large enemy ships.

The quadriremes immediately saw the danger, and as the little boats approached, their archers loosed their arrows. But Antony had protected the boats with wicker screens that absorbed most of the incoming missiles.

Now the quadriremes abandoned their pursuit and turned sharply, oars slashing through the waves in an attempt to escape the boats that swarmed towards them like hornets from a disturbed nest. Three ships completed their turns, and though Antony's boats came close enough to exchange javelin volleys with them, they made it back to the open water and the haven of the island.

The most advanced quadrireme was not so lucky, however. Before it had completed its turn, the boats were upon it, tossing up grappling hooks to anchor the boats to the ship and allow the legionaries to clamber up the sides. Antony watched impotently from the shore, close enough to see the hand-to-hand combat on the deck, and slowly, yard by yard, to see his men force the Pompeian sailors and marines back.

Before long, the Pompeian crew knelt and offered up their weapons in surrender, and a great cheer erupted from the legionaries on the ship, echoed back by the men who had gathered along the shores in Brundisium to watch the outcome.

It was a rare victory for Antony, and he mingled among the men, making sure he wrung from the success every drop of benefit to their morale. He knew, though, that it was far from sufficient to break the blockade.

He wandered back to his headquarters with Gabinius, trying to enjoy the moment while knowing the victory was hollow. He invited Gabinius to stay for dinner and ordered wine brought for them both. A slave brought cups and poured for them, but Antony had barely taken a sip before a centurion appeared with despatches from Rome.

Antony opened them with a sigh, then frowned as he read the contents.

'What is it?' asked Gabinius.

'It's that stupid boy Caelius. Cicero's pet.'

'What's he done now?'

Antony read on, then gave Gabinius a summary. 'It seems like he was trying to be the new darling of the masses. He proposed that the payment of all debts should be deferred for six years, with no interest accruing in the meantime. It's not really in his remit as Praetor Peregrinus, and Trebonius and Isauricus opposed them. He whipped up a mob that assaulted Trebonius, so the Senate passed the *senatus consultum ultimum* and debarred him from office. He's teamed up with that murderer Milo, and they are in open revolt in the south of Italy.'

Gabinius laughed. 'I never did trust that little weasel. I wouldn't lose too much sleep over it. Caelius has precious little popular support, and everyone hates Milo.'

And as it turned out, Gabinius was quite right. Within a month, Antony had received word that Milo had been killed by a stone thrown from the wall of a city he was besieging; Caelius was captured by the Gallic and Spanish cavalry he was trying to bribe to rebel, and executed.

Milo, the murderer of Antony's friend Clodius, and Caelius, whom Antony was sure had spied for Cicero, leading to his stepfather's execution, were both dead.

Antony shed no tears.

ante diem iv Idus Apriles DCCVI AUC (10 April 48 BC), Brundisium

Eventually it was thirst, not defeat, that drove Libo's fleet off the island in Brundisium harbour. But that did not mean the blockade was completely lifted. Libo still possessed greatly superior numbers in ships, and Antony agonised over the next step. It was midwinter now, and the storms in the Mare Adriaticum were frequently violent, but there were intermittent fine days where he was tempted to embark his army and set sail. But if he did so, and was caught by Libo, Caesar could lose half his army, which would inevitably lead to his defeat. On the other side of the coin, Caesar may be hard-pressed and on the verge of being overwhelmed by Pompey, if not already vanquished. Antony had not heard from him for some time, presumably because Bibulus' corresponding blockade on the other side of the sea was preventing messages getting out.

So the entire success or failure of Caesar's venture depended on what Antony did next. But Antony could not decide on the best course of action.

Gabinius was no help. He laid out the pros and cons of action and inaction, but said that ultimately Antony was in charge, and it was up to him.

Antony watched the sun rise that morning, racked by doubts and indecision. It looked to be a fine day, and the omens for success had been good. The seasoned sailors among his men told him the weather was likely to hold for the rest of the day, but they suspected storms would be coming in soon. Antony thought back to the Rubicon, and all of Caesar's actions since. The general was always decisive, always certain what to do, even if the outcome was unknown.

'Let the die be cast,' Antony muttered.

'What was that?' asked Gabinius.

Antony took a deep breath.

'Give the order to embark. Four legions and eight hundred cavalry. We sail immediately.'

Gabinius gave him a steady look, nodded, then went to make the arrangements.

Before the first ship was ready to sail, a small boat put into the harbour, bearing a legionary with a message from Caesar. The man informed Antony that they had managed to sneak past the Pompeian blockade, and bore the news that Pompey's admiral Bibulus had recently died of illness and exhaustion. More importantly, he bore letters from Caesar for Antony, Gabinius and Calenus. Antony broke the seal and read rapidly, then handed his letter to Gabinius, who swapped it with his own. Both were the same, and they presumed Calenus had also received similar words.

Caesar was ordering them to embark at the next opportunity, whatever the threat. If Antony did not carry out the order, Gabinius was to overrule him and do so, and if Gabinius refused, Calenus was to give the command.

Antony was dismayed. For the first time, Caesar had shown a lack of faith in him. Did he think him a coward? A traitor? Antony just hoped that it would be reported back that he had decided to set sail before receiving Caesar's ultimatum.

It was late afternoon, and he was in a grim mood when he finally embarked, and set sail from the harbour of Brundisium on the lead ship. But his mood soon lifted when he looked back and saw the fleet behind him: transports and warships packed with men, horses, supplies and weaponry. He was sailing to war, with the largest force he had yet commanded at his back. And what's more, there was no sign of Libo, and they had the entire long winter night to make the crossing unobserved.

The wind was strong, but southerly, so although they made good speed, when they reached the coast of Epirus, they were pushed north. Pompey held Dyrrhachium, with Caesar camped to the south of that port. But between the strong winds and the blockading Pompeian ships, it was impossible for Antony to land in Caesar's vicinity. His entire fleet sailed up the coast of Epirus in the direction of Macedonia, first past Caesar's army, then past Pompey's army and the fleet.

The warships of the Rhodian fleet at Dyrrhachium, under Gaius Coponius, immediately put to sea to pursue Antony's smaller naval force. Antony's transports were more heavily reliant on the wind than the oar-powered Rhodian triremes and quadriremes, and he ordered his flagship captain to find a suitable place to put ashore as soon as possible.

Then the wind dropped.

Antony looked back in despair as his fleet became more strung out, the slowest sailing vessels being left behind as his oared ships ploughed on. The Rhodians, already quicker than most of Antony's ships, closed rapidly, their brutal rams slicing through the waves. Antony looked at the sails of his own transports, slack in the calm, and at the ships that bore the burden of Caesar's hopes for success. Despair and impotent rage filled his heart. They were going to be caught. Maybe a few of his fastest ships would make landfall, but far too few to make a difference to Caesar's cause. He cried out prayers to the Anemoi, the wind-gods – especially Notos, the god of the south wind.

Whether his prayers were answered by Notos or Fortuna, a strong southerly wind suddenly sprang up again. The sails filled and the ships seemed to leap forward through the waves. Now the Rhodians were at a disadvantage, relying primarily on their tiring oarsmen, while the forceful wind whisked Antony's ships north. Two of the slowest ships did not accelerate fast enough, and were overtaken by the Rhodians. In desperation they veered off, and ran aground. Antony could just make out one of the ships surrendering and being overwhelmed – he later found out that all the legionaries were immediately executed. The veterans of the other ship, maybe seeing the fate of their fellows, or maybe being made of sterner stuff, fought their way ashore and eventually made it through to Caesar's lines.

But now Antony had another problem. The strong wind was bearing him further and further north, away from Caesar's position. And the Rhodians were still pursuing. If the wind dropped again, they would be caught. He summoned the flagship captain.

'Where is the nearest harbour?'

'That would be Nymphaeum,' he said. 'But that's no good to us.'

'Why not?'

'It has no protection from a southerly wind. You risk the destruction of the fleet from the weather.'

Antony took only a moment to consider. He remembered the near disaster that Caesar had twice suffered in Britannia when storms wrecked his ships. But the ships themselves were now of lesser import-ance than getting his men ashore. It was the infantry and cavalry that would make the difference in this fight, if he could just get them to join up with Caesar.

'Do it,' he said. 'Take us into Nympheaeum.'

The captain protested, but Antony stood firm, and huffing and puffing, the captain gave the orders to enter the small harbour.

The Rhodians were not far behind them when they began to dock, and Antony realised that they were still far from out of danger. If the Rhodians closed on them while they were disembarking, they could sow chaos, ramming the stationary transports, setting fire to the ships with fire arrows, boarding the smaller vessels and putting their crews to the sword. How much damage would they do before Antony's men were safely ashore? How much of his strength would he lose? A quarter? A half?

And then the wind changed again. Antony's ships were in the harbour, but disorganised, trying to manoeuvre against the breeze to put themselves in position to land. The Rhodians were bearing down on them at full speed when gusts of near gale strength slashed them from the south-west. The Rhodians were blown completely off course, and as Antony stared in disbelief, most of the Rhodian fleet, including all sixteen of the larger warships, crashed into the rocky coast to the south of the harbour and were smashed into a mess of shattered beams, broken masts and splintered oars.

Antony offered a prayer of thanks to Fortuna and the Anemoi. He had no idea whether this was divine intervention, or the luck of Caesar playing its role again, but he was prudent enough to show gratitude to the gods when it was due.

With the threat of the enemy fleet removed, and panic among the ships quelled, the disembarkation proceeded in a much more orderly fashion, and before long Antony was able to walk down a gangplank and set foot on the Macedonian shore. Soon he had messengers despatched to Caesar with news of his arrival, and parties gathering up supplies and survivors from the wrecked Pompeian ships. As soon as the rest of his men were in marching order – or, at least, the closest they could come to it after a long turbulent sea crossing – he set off for the nearby stronghold of Lissus, leaving orders for the transports to return to Italy to fetch the remainder of the Caesarian forces as soon as the disembarkation was complete. The Pompeian commander of Lissus fled at their approach, and the citizens of the town welcomed Antony and his men with palm branches and garlands.

That night, Antony slept on a fine feather mattress in a plush house into which he had been invited by the local town council leader. He was given his choice of beautiful Greek slaves to warm his bed, but whether it was loyalty to Cytheris, exhaustion, or the remnants of seasickness, he decided to spend the night alone. Within moments of lying down, he was fast asleep.

Aprilis DCCVI AUC (April 48 BC), Dyrrhachium

Antony allowed his men only the briefest of rests at Lissus, and was on the march before dawn. Word soon reached him from his scouts that both Pompey and Caesar were racing north to meet him. He forced his men at double pace southwards, desperate to reach Caesar's army before Pompey caught up with him. Antony's legions would considerably swell Caesar's strength, but would be nowhere near enough to resist Pompey's might on their own.

He nearly met with disaster, for Pompey had in fact moved quickly and set up an ambush on his line of march. But Antony's efficient scouts warned him of the trap, and he ordered his men to halt and dig in while they waited for Caesar. Caesar arrived the next day, and Pompey, now finding himself trapped between the two armies, withdrew.

Antony was sure there were tears in Caesar's eyes when they met, though undoubtedly the great general would have flatly denied it. He did embrace his deputy and poured fulsome praise on him for his efforts in bringing the reinforcements. It seemed that Caesar's doubts about him had been comprehensively dispelled.

Caesar now had the biggest army in Epirus, but he quickly gave up this advantage. To Antony's surprise, he sent one legion away to Thessaly and Aetolia, and two under Gnaeus Domitius Calvinus to Macedonia, to secure the corn supply and to act as a blocking force against Scipio, who was bringing two veteran legions from the East to reinforce Pompey.

With Pompey refusing to engage in open battle, Caesar decided upon a lightning strike against Dyrrhachium. The port was the capital of Illyricum, and the main depot and source of supplies for Pompey's army. Caesar's swiftness of offensive had taken Pompey by surprise twice already – once on crossing the Rubicon with a single legion, once crossing the Mare Adriaticum in the face of the winter storms. Taking Pompey's main supply base would be a similarly audacious victory.

Although Caesar took a circuitous route to the port in an attempt to deceive Pompey as to his true target, Pompey's scouts soon divined his intentions, and the two armies raced to reach Dyrrhachium first. It was Caesar who won the race, but he arrived before Dyrrhachium with a fortified city to his fore and Pompey's army at his back.

Caesar called a council of war, and laid out the options to his senior officers. Pompey would not offer open battle. Caesar could withdraw, perhaps to confront Scipio in Macedonia, or to go north into Illyricum, which was of little strategic importance. In either case, Pompey's army would be harassing his rear. Or he could dig in at Dyrrhachium and settle down for a lengthy siege.

'Speed and surprise have been your greatest weapons since the Rubicon,' said Antony. 'We should go east and defeat Scipio, ensure our supplies, then return to Pompeius and deal with him.'

Publius Cornelius Sulla, nephew of the old tyrant, disagreed.

'If you abandon your defences, you risk being trapped between the armies of Pompeius and Scipio.'

Caesar looked down at the map on his table, his brows furrowed, for a long, long while.

Then he said, 'We will besiege Dyrrhachium.'

But for the first time ever, Antony saw doubt in his eyes.

Chapter VII

The two armies continued to dig in as winter turned to spring. Caesar, vastly experienced in siege warfare after his time in Britannia and Gaul, ordered his men to build a seventeen-mile network of fortifications to encircle Pompey, starve him out and force his men to surrender. But Pompey was no Vercingetorix, and this was no Alesia. Pompey was encamped on a hill known locally as Petra, with good access to the Bay of Dyrrhachium, and although he could not access the port directly, a constant influx of small boats came in to the bay, bringing Pompey vital supplies while Caesar's own stores dwindled alarmingly. Caesar could do nothing about this, but he did order his men to dam all the rivers and streams in the area, so that Pompey was deprived of fresh water.

Although there were no mass engagements between the two sides, skirmishes constantly broke out as they attempted to disrupt the construction work of the enemy. Antony was commanding the Ninth Legion – the same legion that had narrowly escaped decimation when they'd recently mutinied against Caesar in Placentia. Caesar's treatment of them then – threatening to disband them all and already addressing them as civilians – had transformed them into the most fanatical of his men, and Antony enjoyed fraternising with them.

That afternoon, he was eating some lunch with the men of a century who were off duty and relaxing. He broke a loaf and chewed, then frowned at the taste and texture.

'What in the name of Fornax is this shit?'

The legionaries looked abashed. 'There isn't enough corn to bake bread anymore, Legate. But some of the men found these roots growing in the valleys. The locals call it *chara*. If you grind it and mix it with milk, it makes a decent flour.'

Antony swallowed and took another bite. The flavour was unusual, but it wasn't bitter, and it quietened a growling stomach.

'How long have you been eating this for?'

'A couple of days, Legate.'

'No illness? No diarrhoea, vomiting, blindness, fits, sudden delusions that you are a god?'

'No, Legate.'

Antony nodded and took another bite.

Just then, a messenger, a fresh-faced young legionary, came rushing up to him, halted, saluted and stood at breathless attention.

'What is it?'

'Sir, there's trouble.'

'Go on.'

'Pompeius is assaulting the hill.'

Antony threw down his food and strode over to a low mound that afforded him a view of his men's position. They had been fortifying a hill at the south-east of Caesar's lines, which would give them a strong defensive position. Antony squinted, using his hand to give him some shade against the sun shining directly into his eyes. He saw immediately that the detachment – a large number of cohorts of the Ninth – was under heavy attack. Archers and slingers surrounded them, loosing arrows and slingshots at the Caesarian legionaries, and light infantry had brought up *ballistae* to harass the men and smash the fortifications. The legionaries were forced to abandon the work on their defences just so they could protect themselves from the assault.

Antony thought for a moment. Caesar himself had selected this position to reinforce. His men could hold, but for how long?

'Go straight to Caesar and inform him of the situation,' he said to the messenger. Then he summoned one of his tribunes and ordered them to form up the reserves.

It was not long before Caesar arrived, galloping up on horseback, scarlet cloak flowing in the wind behind him. He dismounted, tossed his reins to an orderly, and snapped at Antony to report. Antony outlined the position as he saw it, and Caesar looked out at his men, exposed on the hill and under heavy attack.

'They are too exposed,' he said. 'How long do you think they can hold for?'

'You know the Ninth, Caesar. They will hold for as long as you command.'

Caesar nodded. 'Good. We'll get them out of there in due course. But not before we have arranged a surprise for Pompeius.'

He ordered wicker screens brought up to conceal the reserves that Antony had assembled, and then had the legionaries dig a wide trench filled with spikes and caltrops. He positioned slingers to the sides, and when this was complete, he sent a signal for the men to withdraw.

In fairly good order, with shields raised, the detachment of the Ninth slowly retreated down the hill, back towards the defences Caesar had prepared. But the Pompeians saw this as evidence that their enemy was on the verge of breaking, and began to press their attack, their infantry charging forward. The Caesarians crossed carefully back over the trench in the positions their men indicated for them, but the Pompeians were close on their heels, and when they reached the defences, they simply threw the wicker screens over the trench to enable them to cross easily.

'Consul, they are going to be overrun,' said Antony earnestly. 'Let me take the reserves up.'

Caesar watched for a moment longer, then nodded.

'Very well.'

Antony ordered his *bucinator* to sound the trumpet signal to advance. Antony drew his gladius and, leading from the front, he charged up the hill to the relief of his men. As soon as they were in range, he ordered an abrupt halt and a volley of javelins. They arced upwards and then descended like hail into the Pompeian ranks, causing their charge to falter. Then Antony yelled for the advance once again.

The reserves of the Ninth reached their retreating comrades, who had maintained their formation. With exquisite discipline, the with-drawing legionaries slipped through the friendly ranks, then turned and formed up behind them. The Pompeians were almost on them when Antony ordered his men to charge. Pointing his sword straight at the enemy, he sprinted up the hill. His muscular legs ate up the ground, so that the legionaries either side struggled to keep up. He hit the enemy line a heartbeat before his men.

The legionary opposite him was battered backwards as the boss of Antony's shield smashed into his face, breaking his jaw and smashing out his teeth. Antony immediately had to parry with his gladius a sword thrust from the opponent to his right, while using his shield to push the man on his left backwards. Then the rest of the Ninth caught up with him, and the Pompeian line crumpled at the impact as the charging veterans crashed into them. Many of the Pompeians turned and ran for their rear, but this meant them retreating over the defences they had just crossed, hindering their flight. The Ninth took advantage to inflict as much damage as possible, stabbing unprotected backs and slashing hamstrings. The Pompeians broke, completely routed, and the Ninth roared in victory and pursued.

Antony halted, panting, giving his men free rein to indulge their battle frenzy. But before long they neared the Pompeian defensive lines, and would soon be in range of the enemy artillery and slings and arrows. Reluctantly, he had the order for withdrawal sounded.

To their credit, the Ninth obeyed in an instant, reforming their ranks and slowly returning, the front row always facing the enemy as the rear ranks ran back, then turned and set their shields so the front rank could leapfrog them.

Antony returned to Caesar with a gory sword and blood streaked across his face.

'Well done, Legate.'

For a moment, Antony wondered whether he had done anything deserving of praise. Killing fellow Romans didn't feel particularly honourable or praiseworthy. Nevertheless, they were the enemy.

Antony's grim thoughts were disturbed when one of the soldiers that he had been eating with just before the battle passed them, laughing.

'What's so funny, Legionary?' called out Caesar.

The legionary saw who had spoken and came to attention.

'Sorry, Caesar, I didn't mean to—'

'Just tell me the joke, man.'

'Well, it's just… When we halted, one of the Pompeians shouted out that we would be starving to death soon. So I tossed him one of our chara loaves. You should have seen the look on his face, Caesar.'

'Chara loaves?'

Antony explained what the men had discovered.

And for the first time in many days, he saw Caesar smile.

'Antonius, make sure the word is passed around that this root is good to eat, and where to find it. This could make the difference between holding out until the cornfields ripen, or starving.'

Then Caesar strode away to give another part of the line his attention.

Kalendis Quintilis DCCVI AUC (1 July 48 BC), Dyrrhachium

On the night of the first day of Quintilis, they advanced from Caesar's camp at the north of their defences under the cover of darkness. Antony led the Ninth as usual. Somewhere ahead, Caesar was with his beloved Tenth. Deserters from Dyrrhachium had told them that sympathisers within the port would throw the gates open as soon as Caesar approached. It was too good an opportunity to miss. Taking Dyrrhachium would be a massive prestige blow to Pompey, while hugely augmenting Caesar's immediate supplies and giving him access to the extensive docks. They might even capture a large portion of Pompey's fleet if they were swift enough.

A wide causeway linked the tip of the peninsula on which Dyrrhachium was situated to the mainland, near Caesar's camp. To the south was the bay; to the north were inland lakes and marshes. They advanced in as complete a silence as several thousand armoured men could manage. Caesar's Tenth was fully across, and Antony, with the leading century of the Ninth, was the first of his legion to step off the causeway. The walls of the city loomed up out of the darkness. He felt a surge of excitement. They were nearly there.

A whooshing sound like a great wind was the first warning of the attack. Then a rain of arrows descended out of the dark sky. Yells of fear and screams of pain and anguish broke out all around. Beside Antony, a man staggered back with an arrow in his shoulder, and another crumpled silently, struck in the temple by a slingshot.

'Shields up!' yelled Antony, entirely unnecessarily, since all the legionaries were already in the process of raising their shields to defend themselves from the deadly barrage. 'Close up. *Testudo!*'

The men capable of doing so shuffled together, forming the traditional tortoise defensive formation with each side covered. The missile attack continued, and some penetrated through the defensive shell to pierce flesh or break bone, but most of the arrows and slingshots bounced off harmlessly or lodged in the shields. Antony peered out, trying to work out the direction of the attack. There was only the merest hint of dawn in the east, so it was difficult to make out anything in the gloom, but as far as he could tell, they were being attacked on three sides. Not only were the walls of the city lined with archers and slingers, but arrows were also coming in from the marshy areas to the north, and when he turned south, he could make out a large number of ships that Pompey had brought up.

It was a well-sprung ambush. The intelligence from the city had clearly been fake, and Pompey had lured Caesar into a deadly trap. Antony pulled his shield back in place and thought hard. They could not advance against the city while being attacked from both flanks, and besides, they were not really equipped for an opposed assault on the fortification, having been expecting to enter through the front gates. But they could not reach the ships that stood offshore and attacked them with impunity, and charging into the marshes at night, against an unseen enemy with who knew what defences, was tantamount to suicide.

They had to retreat. But Caesar and the Tenth were ahead, trapped by the Pompeians, and unable to withdraw with the Ninth so close behind.

'First century, prepare to advance,' Antony called out. 'The rest of the legion retreat back across the causeway at best pace in testudo formation.'

With the mutual protection of the First century of the First cohort of the Ninth, they pushed forward to make contact with the rearguard of the Tenth, who were hunkered down, attempting to weather the storm. Antony gave orders for the rearmost cohorts of the Tenth to begin their withdrawal, and he pressed on with his century in search of Caesar.

He found his commander sheltering beneath the closely packed shields of his bodyguards. He shuffled forward, flinching as an arrow penetrated the shield above him, the tip coming to rest an inch from his cheekbone.

'Caesar,' he called out, and, crawling on hands and knees, reached his side.

Caesar slapped him on the shoulder.

'What's your assessment, Marcus? What have you seen?'

'Ships to the south. Large numbers of enemy infantry to the north, and I think on the south coast, too. And I can see the city gates remain closed.'

'Betrayed, Marcus. Curse their lying souls.'

Antony didn't bother to point out that Caesar had taken control of many cities in his career by deception and treachery, rather than by all-out assault. It was good tactics, and Pompey was proving that he was still a great general.

'The Ninth are withdrawing in defensive formation,' he said. 'And I have had your rearmost echelons begin to make their way back across the causeway.'

Caesar nodded.

'I approve, Marcus, though make sure not to exceed your authority in future.'

'Yes, Caesar. What are your orders?'

'We have no choice. Let's get our men back to safety.'

The command was circulated and the Tenth Legion, with Antony's century embedded within, began to make its way back east across the causeway.

Abruptly the missile barrage halted. Antony and Caesar exchanged glances. It seemed unlikely the Pompeians had run out of ammunition.

Then a great cry reached them, assailing them from north, south and west, and out of the twilight came charging hundreds of Pompeian legionaries.

'Shields front,' called out Caesar. 'Brace.'

The legionaries on both flanks thrust their shields into the wet earth to provide some resistance when the wave hit, and put their shoulders against them. Behind, their comrades pressed against them. They held their collective breath, then had it knocked out of them as the enemy legionary charge hit.

Then they were fighting for their lives, hacking, stabbing and shoving their attackers back.

Caesar issued orders for the men to retreat, and with every ounce of discipline and bravery they could muster, the Tenth Legion fought its way back over the causeway, step by bloody step.

The first rays of the sun emerged over the hills, and with it they could see the extent of the forces they faced. A dozen warships lay just offshore to the south, and Antony estimated there were thousands of legionaries surrounding them. To the east, on the far side of the causeway, the Ninth Legion were holding off a determined attempt to cut off their escape, and he was pleased to see they were fighting with bravery and discipline. He was aware, though, that, huge as the numbers against them were, this was a long way from being Pompey's full strength. He had a brief moment to wonder where the rest of Pompey's legions were, before he was once again fighting for his life, his sword thrusting out again and again, his powerful frame helping to ram his comrades through the enemy lines and back towards safety.

By the time they made it back to their own lines, the sun was high in the sky. The Pompeians were beaten off, with heavy losses on both sides. As they re-entered the Caesarian camp, they were greeted by Publius Cornelius Sulla, who had been left in charge of the encampment and the reserves. His face was haggard and pale.

'Caesar, are you injured?' he asked, voice full of anxiety.

Antony glanced at Caesar and saw his helmet, his armour, his bare forearms and his face were all streaked with congealed blood. Antony realised he must have looked the same.

'No, I have no injuries,' said Caesar, voice steady despite the fatigue he must have been feeling.

'I'm relieved to see you back, Caesar,' said Sulla. 'I must inform you that we have repelled a strong attack by Pompeius' forces.'

Caesar seemed to pale a bit at this, but patted his arm reassuringly. Antony was amazed. Pompey had pulled off a beautiful attack, combining misinformation, ambush and perfect timing to assault Caesar on multiple fronts. He felt completely foolish for ever having doubted Pompey's generalship.

'Well done, Legate. Let's tour the defences while you give me your report.'

Antony went with them as Sulla showed them three points where Pompey had attacked. In one fort, defended by a single cohort, Sulla had brought two legions up and easily repulsed the attack. He had even had the opportunity to pursue the Pompeians, who were fleeing in disorder, but had pulled his men back into defence.

'Quite right,' said Caesar. 'You are a legate. A decision to press an attack like that rightly belongs to your commander.' He gave Antony a pointed look, who had the good grace to at least appear suitably admonished.

They visited another fort that had resisted the attackers, who seemed to have been rather half-hearted, and did not press too hard. But the third fort was a different matter.

Antony looked around at the defences and the defenders, stunned. The woodwork was in every place splintered and shattered. Every patch of ground was stained with blood. Every single defender bore at least one wound. Sulla explained that for the entire battle, three cohorts had held off an entire legion, three times their strength. He presented to Caesar the six centurions who had kept their men from breaking. Four of them had bandages and patches over ruined eyes.

A huge mound of arrows that had been fired into the fort had been gathered. The centurions proudly displayed them to Caesar, pointing out that there were three hundred bundles, each comprising a hundred arrows. Then the senior centurion showed him the shield of a junior centurion called Scaeva. It bore over a hundred holes.

Even Caesar could not help but be impressed by this. In a loud voice, so all around could hear, he praised all the defenders, promising to double their wages and their allowances of corn, clothing and food. The announcement of the increased food rations got the biggest cheer. Then he singled out Scaeva for further praise, promoting him to a senior centurion of the first rank and rewarding him with the fabulous sum of two hundred thousand sestertii.

The battered, bruised and bleeding centurion seemed to find this hard to take in, and could barely stutter out his thanks. Antony led the men in cheering for Scaeva's bravery and good fortune.

Then Caesar made his way back to his tent. He dismissed everyone except Antony, and when the two of them were alone, he slumped into his chair. Antony thought he looked exhausted, and he poured him a strong cup of wine. Caesar waved it away.

'We held, Marcus,' he said.

'We did, Caesar.'

'We were lucky. Pompeius nearly had us.'

'Your genius has always been leavened with fortune, Caesar.'

Caesar closed his eyes wearily. After a few moments, Antony realised he had fallen asleep. He slipped quietly out of the tent.

They had survived a near disaster. They had tasted defeat by the walls of Dyrrhachium, but had gained a victory in the Caesarian camp. Ironically, both Caesar – who had led the attack on Dyrrhachium – and

Pompey – who had led the attack on the camp – had been defeated that day, each by his opponent's subordinates. It was hard to tell who had emerged from the mess in the stronger position.

But time was against Caesar. The single legion he had sent to delay Scipio could not hold him forever. Soon, Pompey would be reinforced, and Caesar's double siege of Dyrrhachium and Pompey would be endangered. Did Caesar think he could repeat Alesia? Repel an attack from outside his defences while maintaining the siege kept within? The circumstances were wholly different. Pompey may be short of water, but he wasn't starving, like Vercingetorix. Nor were his men undisciplined barbarians. And, Antony was now starting to believe, maybe Caesar's enemy did indeed equal him in strategic and tactical genius.

Antony returned to his own tent, tired and sore, and summoned one of his personal slaves to feed, bathe and massage him. But restoring his bodily strength was not enough. His mind had become heavy with doubt.

ante diem vii Idus Quintilas DCCVI AUC (9 July 48 BC), Dyrrhachium

The two sides settled back into their siege routines. Caesar was everywhere, praising, cajoling, admonishing... whatever was needed to raise morale. The men were clearly shaken, but his strength of personality reassured everywhere he went. Antony, too, did his bit, mingling with his men and assuring them of victory if they would just hold. It was remarkable that through all the hardships of the siege, no significant desertions from Caesar's camp occurred.

By contrast, a steady stream of deserters from Pompey's camp brought news that morale there was at breaking point. Hemmed in by Caesar's defences, the Pompeians were suffering from a lack of fodder for the beasts, thirst, overcrowding, and its inevitable sequel, disease, with reports of an outbreak of typhus.

The engineers and carpenters brought the fortifications back up to their previous strength and beyond as the days passed. The walls consisted of strong forts with palisades and ditches linking them together, the fifteen-feet-high defences reinforced with boulders and blocks from the quarries, from city walls and from the homes of the local Greeks.

But even after all this time, they were not fully complete. Since the previous ambush, Caesar had begun to worry about the prospect of Pompey using his fleet to attack from the sea. He had therefore ordered the construction of a double wall to the south, where his defences met the shore, with a fifteen-foot ditch and two earthen ramparts. It was a prudent measure, but there was only so much manpower to go around, especially with all the repair work necessitated by the recent attack, on top of the routine maintenance of seventeen miles of fortifications.

And before they were finished, Roucillus and Egus deserted to Pompey.

The two brothers were the sons of a Gallic chieftain and had fought with courage in Gaul. Caesar had even, surprisingly, made them senators during his short reign as Dictator. But they had been caught embezzling funds, claiming pay for non-existent cavalry. Caesar had been lenient with them, chastising them in private and warning them of their future conduct, but their offences were common knowledge, and they were subjected to constant abuse and mockery from the men. So, one evening, they slipped through the lines with their bodyguards, a large sum of cash and a large number of horses, and defected to Pompey.

Caesar was furious, not only at the insult, but also because they were senior enough to know everything about the Caesarian defences – the fortifications, the timetables of the sentries, even the conscientiousness of the officers in charge of the watch at different forts. But he could do nothing apart from double the sentries and press on with the construction work, hoping it would be completed in time.

It wasn't.

Antony was just waking up, in the process of splashing some water on his face from a bowl and thinking about using the commode, when the messenger rushed in.

'Legate, an attack, from the sea.'

Antony pulled on his armour while he listened to the full report. As Caesar had feared, just before dawn, Pompey had launched an attack on the south-westernmost defences with six legions. As the sun rose, he had brought in a second strong force of light infantry by sea between the half-finished defences.

Antony summoned his tribunes and leading centurions and quickly informed them of the situation, then ordered them to form up every available man. He paced up and down in frustration while he waited, though the disciplined legionaries of the Ninth and Tenth were swift to respond. As soon as they were ready, he led them out at a fast march.

Antony's camp, the headquarters of the Ninth, was at the south-east corner of Caesar's lines, and Pompey's attack from the sea was in the south-west corner, some two miles from Antony's position. They covered the ground rapidly, but by the time they arrived, the situation was already a disaster.

It was hard to make out the details among the chaos of the battle. As far as Antony could tell, the initial defences had been overwhelmed, and the reinforcements from the nearest camp were on the verge of fleeing. Pompey's men were assaulting the camp and there was a stream of men fleeing back towards Antony's position.

'Set the signal fires,' Antony commanded, and one of the centurions hurried off to light the fire that would send a smoke signal to Caesar to inform him of the emergency.

'Now follow me!'

Leading the charge, Antony sprinted towards the enemy front line. He was vastly outnumbered. The twelve cohorts he had brought up numbered around five thousand men, with another few thousand who had been present at the start of the attack and were now milling around in panic. The sight of Antony's legionaries charging forward, screaming out their battle cry, stiffened the resolve of the struggling defenders, and for the most part they faced forwards again and joined the charge.

The unexpected appearance of Antony, and his unhesitating attack, stopped the Pompeian advance. His tough veterans unleashed a volley of javelins and then smashed into the Pompeian front line, which was hastily reorganising itself to receive the charge. Metal clashed on metal. Shields splintered. Cries of pain, anger and despair resounded all around.

Antony was in the thick of the action, fighting like a legionary – step forward, thrust, twist, step forward again. Their initial assault, concentrated in the centre of Pompey's lines, forced the enemy legionaries back, away from the vulnerable camp. But the superior numbers against them soon began to tell. With some difficulty, Antony extricated himself from the front line so he could take stock of the situation and issue orders. The ability to manoeuvre was limited in the spaces between the defences, but Pompey still threatened to outflank him on both sides. He could do nothing, though, but exhort his men to hold on, and wait for Caesar to arrive with further reinforcements.

It was the best part of an hour before Caesar finally appeared. An hour of brutal, attritional warfare, both sides fatiguing, Antony giving ground against the superior numbers, but his men battling over every inch lost. It was with profound relief that he heard the signal trumpets. Caesar had gathered thirty-three cohorts, which at full strength would number around fifteen thousand men, but after the losses from a long siege, were only at around two-thirds of that strength. Still, it was enough to bolster Antony's men, and the combined Caesarian army fought the Pompeian attack to a standstill.

Antony found Caesar, surrounded by bodyguards, a short way back from the front line, and reported the situation to him as best he could. They had held the camp, but Pompey had punched a gaping hole in Caesar's defences, and now had access to a much wider area in which they could forage and receive supplies.

With the fighting in a lull, Caesar ordered a new fort to be hastily thrown together to provide defences against Pompey's new position. Then scouts came up with reports that Pompey had occupied an old camp of Caesar's that he had abandoned when he had altered the front lines.

'We need to regain the initiative,' said Caesar. 'Marcus, leave two cohorts along our front and have them spread out to make it look like we have a full force there. Then bring the Ninth with me.'

Caesar led the men on an indirect route towards the old encampment, hoping to surprise the Pompeian legion that was flying its standard there. Antony marched with the Ninth, who were in good spirits, despite being badly mauled. They reached the camp without being spotted by Pompey, and Caesar immediately launched an attack on the left, taking the defenders by surprise, and forcing them off the ramparts.

The gate was blocked by a large hedgehog defence – a wooden barrier studded with vicious spikes – and Antony saw the fighting there was intense, with the Pompeians defending vigorously. Soon, though, the hedgehog was smashed apart, and the Caesarian legions rushed into the fort with a roar and began to massacre the Pompeians sheltered within.

Antony observed from the rear, where Caesar had placed him with some reserves. It looked like Caesar's plan had paid off, he thought with satisfaction. He had lost contact with the other wing of Caesar's army, though, which had been probing the defences to the right, with all of the Caesarian cavalry. But this didn't seem to matter too much, as Caesar was on the verge of forcing the Pompeians out of the rear gate of the fort.

And then Pompey arrived. He had hastily assembled five legions and a large number of cavalry. The cavalry made straight for the right wing, and soon after, Caesarian cavalry came charging back in disarray. Following behind them came an ever-increasing flood of fleeing infantry. The Ninth Legion on the left saw their comrades on the right fleeing, and panic rapidly spread through their ranks. With the legion they were fighting still to their fore, and Pompey's new legions coming up behind, they feared they would be trapped, and they broke.

Antony immediately moved his reserves forward to prevent a rout, but it was hopeless. Even with Caesar present, shouting and haranguing his men, the chaos was absolute. Every man fought for his own life, against the enemy, against his own side, giving in to the animalistic panic to get away. Antony fought his way towards Caesar, who was standing with just a couple of bodyguards, shouting in impotent rage at his men's cowardice.

A standard-bearer, his bearskin head-covering flapping behind him, rushed past Caesar, his terror blinding him to the presence of his general. Caesar stepped in front of him, hand out.

'Halt. You are a *signifer* of the Ninth. Turn and do your duty.'

The signifer stopped and stared at Caesar for the briefest moment, then pulled his standard back and, with a cry, prepared to thrust the sharp butt into Caesar's torso. Antony cried out a warning, but was too far away to stop it. The standard thrust out.

Then Caesar's bodyguard hacked downwards against the signifer with all his might. His gladius bit all the way through the man's upper arm, and the standard, still clutched in the signifer's severed limb, fell to the ground. The man dropped to his knees, clutching the spurting stump. Antony doubted he would survive the injury, but didn't care.

He reached Caesar's side.

'You can do nothing more. We need to get you to safety.'

Caesar seemed numbed, stunned by the sudden reverse, his men's cowardice, and the attempt on his life. He let Antony and his body-guards lead him off the battlefield. Antony found them horses, and together they cantered back to their own lines.

'It's over,' said Caesar when they dismounted. 'Pompeius has every advantage now. He just has to continue his attack, and we cannot resist.'

Antony tried to think of words of encouragement, but none came. He didn't have Caesar's experience, but even he could tell when a position was lost.

Now they just had to await the arrival of Pompey, bearing the executioner's axe.

ante diem vi Idus Quintilas DCCVI AUC (10 July 48 BC), Dyrrhachium

But Pompey did not come. For reasons Antony could not comprehend, he called off the attack. It was certainly not due to sentiments of mercy. Word came to them from deserters that Labienus had rounded up the Caesarian prisoners, paraded them in front of his men, insulted them, and then executed them all. Was Pompey concerned he was overcommitting? Or was he just scared of Caesar, terrified that his opponent was in fact the better general? Had this all been a plot to lure the bulk of his forces into a trap?

Whatever the reasoning, Caesar was able to bring the majority of his men back to safety behind his defences. As soon as the wounded had been taken to the hospital station, and the rest of the legionaries had returned to their units, he sent word to withdraw the garrisons from the forts, and to assemble the entire army so he could address them.

'Loyal soldiers of Rome,' he called out in his clear tones. His voice carried far, and was relayed by centurions even further, so every man could hear every word. 'By the favour of Fortuna, we took Italy without bloodshed. We pacified both Spanish provinces despite their belligerent soldiers and experienced leaders. We control all the provinces needed to supply us with grain. And we have been lucky enough to cross from Italy when the enemy fleets infested the waters. But sometimes, we must look to our own efforts rather than simply trusting always to fortune. This reverse is not my doing. I gave you the opportunity to fight on good ground, I took the enemy camp, and I drove them out.

Whether it was your nervousness or a mistake, or just bad luck, the victory was snatched from our grasp. So I require you to make good on this damage with your courage. If you do so, our loss will become our success, as after Gergovia, and those who are afraid will clamour to offer themselves for the fight.'

Cheers resounded around the gathered soldiers, and Antony joined in, a full-throated roar. But, though he understood that Caesar could not admit an error to the rank and file, he wondered if the general was really so self-assured.

Caesar went on to demote some standard-bearers who had fled the battle – a truly light punishment – and he left the men cheering his name and vowing to restore the damage to their reputation.

Caesar then gathered his legates and tribunes around, and received reports of the casualty list.

In all, he had lost nearly a thousand legionaries, thirty-two tribunes and centurions, together with their standards, as well as a handful of men of equestrian and senatorial rank. He received the death toll in silence, then gave orders to prepare to break camp.

Some of the legates and tribunes protested that they should take the fight straight back to Pompey, but Caesar shook his head.

'Our men are injured and demoralised, and our corn supplies are too low. Pompeius has improved his position and worsened ours. We have nothing to gain by prolonging this siege. We will depart tonight under cover of darkness. The baggage train and the wounded will go first, with a legion to protect them. When they have a head start, all but two legions will go after them, marching light. In the morning the last two legions will sound the trumpet horns that wake the camp, so Pompeius thinks we are still there. Then they will strike camp and follow with all speed. We will make sure we are far gone before Pompeius realises.'

'Where will we go?'

'South to Apollonia, then east. We need to get away from the sea, where Pompeius dominates us with his fleet. And we can meet up with Calvinus' two legions to make good our losses.'

The officers bowed and left Caesar's tent, but Caesar indicated Antony should stay behind.

When they were alone, he sighed and sat heavily. He looked crushed. He reached for a cup of wine and his hand trembled. It was the first time Antony had seen him beaten. He had joined him in Gaul just after his most crushing defeat at Gergovia, and so his first experience of Caesar's leadership was his greatest triumph at Alesia.

'I should never have besieged Pompeius here,' he said, his voice flat. Antony didn't reply. It was not his place to criticise Caesar, and even if it was, what use would it be? What was done was done.

'I thought I could repeat Alesia, but Pompeius had too many advantages.'

'We can regroup, Caesar,' said Antony, trying to sound reassuring. 'The men are behind you, every one.'

'Apart from those treacherous Gauls,' said Caesar bitterly. 'It would have been better if I had them beaten to death.'

Antony had to agree here, but simply said, 'That's just hindsight. And your clemency is winning you far more support than harsh punishments ever did. The men are furious with Labienus. Not only do they think him a traitor, but now he has executed the prisoners, a murderer, too. If he is ever captured, he would do well to fall on his sword before the men get their hands on him.'

Caesar gave a wry smile.

'Clemency has its place in war and politics, this is true. But there is a time for harshness as well. I think the men need to see that side of me before too long.'

That sounded ominous, Antony thought.

Caesar dismissed him, and he went away to make preparations for their departure. He doubted he would be getting much sleep any time soon.

ante diem iv Idus Quintilas DCCVI AUC (12 July 48 BC), Gomphi

Caesar's army managed to extricate itself from the siege with the minimum of fuss. As Caesar had hoped, Pompey had not discovered the departure until it was too late, and the slower Caesarian units were already far away. Although he harassed Caesar's rearguard with cavalry, this was little more than a gnat bite, and soon he gave up the pursuit.

Caesar resupplied at the town of Apollonia, then marched south-east along the valleys of the rivers Aous and Drino. At Aeginium, Caesar's legions were reinforced by Calvinus, and it was here that Caesar learned that after Pompey had given up his pursuit, he had turned east and attempted to surprise Calvinus. Fortunately, Calvinus was warned of the danger, and he had been able to slip away and head south to join Caesar. From here, the augmented army travelled south. The villages and towns along the way were largely welcoming, but Antony detected a certain reticence that had not been there previously. They were not so forthcoming with supplies, and fresh levies were sparse, as if the men of military age had made themselves scarce when they heard of Caesar's approach. Antony supposed word had got around of their defeat, and it put the local settlements in a difficult position. Did they aid the general with the large army on their doorstep, or refuse to co-operate for fear of punishment from the general who was far away, but likely to be the ultimate victor?

But it wasn't until they reached the town of Gomphi that they encountered their first real resistance. Gomphi was the first fortified settlement in Thessaly that a traveller from Epirus would meet. It was of strategic importance, guarding the passes into the plains of Thessaly, and for this reason had been involved in a major battle in the past, when the Romans had taken it during the Second Macedonian War against Philip V.

A few months previously, the town had sent messages of goodwill and support to Caesar. But when he rode up to the town, he found the gates firmly shut against him.

He sent an envoy to the walls to demand the town was opened to his men. Androsthenes, the ruler of Thessaly, came to the ramparts himself and told the envoy to inform Caesar that he had declared for Pompey, and that he had sent messengers to Scipio and Pompey to come to his relief.

When the envoy delivered this reply to Caesar, his face turned the colour of his cloak.

'They think to defy me? Gaius Julius Caesar, who is descended from Venus?' His voice was shaking with anger, and all Caesar's officers quailed, unused to seeing their leader let fury rule him to such an extent.

'I will teach them what folly it is to stand against me,' he roared. 'Take the town, and put it to fire and sword. Gomphi will be a lesson to all!'

Caesar's men needed no encouragement. Let off the leash after a prolonged siege and a humiliating defeat, determined to prove their courage, they rushed the town walls with siege towers and scaling ladders. Antony took no part in the assault – he was clearly not needed – and within hours the walls had been taken and the gates flung open. Caesar ordered his men into the town, and told them they could do as they wished.

The legions cheered their approval and rushed in, shields and packs abandoned, only taking swords and daggers to do their work.

Antony entered after the first wave of legionaries had gone past, and wandered disconsolately around. Everywhere he looked there was chaos and suffering. No one was spared. Old men, women and children were dragged into the street and hacked to death. Shops and houses were looted and set alight. Temples and fine mansions were plundered, legionaries emerging with arms full of gold and silver – coins, plates, cups, necklaces.

He saw a finely dressed old woman having her fingers sliced off so two legionaries could steal her rings, though she was still alive. He saw a white-haired man curled up in the dust while two soldiers took it in turns to kick him to death. He saw a woman held down and raped by several soldiers in turn, while she howled and reached towards the body of her dead infant son nearby.

It sickened him.

This was not war. This was not honourable. It was butchery.

Antony had not witnessed scenes like this before, despite all the battles he had been in. He had, in fact, prevented exactly such a situation when Ptolemy Auletes had ordered the massacre of the citizens of Pelusium. He felt a resentment towards Caesar building inside him. He knew that Caesar could rationalise this brutality – claim it was good for the battered morale of the men, and that it acted as a warning to any other settlements that defied him. But Antony couldn't help wondering if the man who prided himself on his self-control was letting the anger at the humiliation of his defeat dictate his actions.

Antony admired Caesar, respected him, even loved him. But that didn't mean he was blind to his faults.

He decided he had seen enough, and strode back out of the town towards the camp of the Ninth

Chapter VIII

Antony's stomach gave a clearly audible growl. Caesar gave him a disdainful glare, and Antony spread his hands in apology. But he couldn't help it. He was hungry. Of course, as Caesar's most senior commander, he could have demanded extra rations, even luxuries that were not available to the other officers. But that was not his way. More often than not, he dined with the men, eating the same as them – the quality and the quantity. Antony was an energetic man with a big build to maintain, and he was sure he was becoming gaunt. The crops were ripening in the fields, but they were not yet ready for harvest, and the supplies looted from the cities they had marched through on the way were nearly gone.

Caesar was, in fact, discussing the supply problem with his generals, which just made Antony even more hungry.

'Even foraging at night to avoid Pompeius' cavalry, we have almost completely exhausted this area. Pompeius, by contrast, is supplied from all around, by road, by ship, and from the strongholds to the east. He knows we can't maintain this stand-off indefinitely.'

They had arrived in Thessaly a few days previously and encamped on the plain near the city of Pharsalus, taking control of the bridge over the river Enipeus. Pompeius, who had been marching south to intercept Caesar, secured the supply route from Larisa and camped a mile to the west, on a hill on the northern edge of the plain.

Every day, Caesar had offered battle to Pompey, drawing his troops up in battle formation, where they stood in the heat of the day, hurling insults at the Pompeians, who remained behind their fortifications. But he could not risk an uphill attack on Pompey's fortified position, and if Pompey wouldn't come out to fight, it was a stalemate.

'So we are going to break camp?' asked Calvinus. Since bringing his legions to join up with Caesar, Gnaeus Domitius Calvinus had taken up position among the most senior commanders, along with Publius Cornelius Sulla and Antony.

'Just so,' said Caesar. 'We are going to break camp and prepare to march north-east to Scotussa, and then onwards to resupply and recruit more men. And we are going to do it slowly, carefully, in broad daylight, and in full view of Pompeius.'

Antony frowned. Caesar usually moved swiftly and under cover of darkness, to take his enemy by surprise. An army on the march, its camp broken down, laden with packs and wagon, was highly vulnerable.

'But, Caesar...' he began.

'What's more,' said Caesar. 'I have sent some trusted men over to Pompeius' camp, claiming to be deserters and informing him of our plan to move today.'

Realisation broke over Antony, and he grinned.

'If he doesn't come out to fight on those terms, it will look like he is scared of defeat.'

'Prudence turns to cowardice,' agreed Sulla, nodding.

'And we shall be ready,' said Caesar. 'If he decides to fight, we will be more prepared than he expects. And if he decides not to... Well, the fools of the Senate who pull his strings might decide he is not the leader they thought he was, and think one of them could do better. Certainly his allies in the East will have serious doubts about their allegiances.'

Antony could picture the scenes in Pompey's camp: Cicero whingeing; Scipio blustering; Labienus slandering Caesar's generalship and fighting strength, and no doubt having choice words about Antony, too. He smiled inwardly. Surely Pompey would rather fight than endure those old women any longer.

'Now,' said Caesar, gesturing to a large map unrolled on his table. 'If Pompeius offers battle, this is our plan.'

–

Antony was in command of the Eighth and Ninth legions, but they had been so badly mauled at Dyrrhachium, they amounted to little more than a single full-strength legion. They were champing at the bit, however, desperate to avenge the dishonour of that defeat. Experienced veterans all, they had been tempered in battle after battle under Caesar, and feared no one. Antony, too, was supremely confident, though part of him knew they were facing severe odds. The Caesarian infantry numbered just over twenty thousand, against Pompeian forces double that size. But it was in cavalry that Pompey truly dominated, with their spies estimating around seven thousand horse to Caesar's one thousand. There were veterans of the disaster at Carrhae on both sides of this conflict, who had witnessed how cavalry superiority could be used to destroy an army composed predominantly of infantry. Antony himself had commanded cavalry to great effect in Syria and Britannia. Still, overall, Pompey's army was an inexperienced mishmash of legionaries and light infantry, and you only had to look at Alexander or Hannibal to realise that discipline, experience and great generalship could overcome numerical superiority.

The men were pulling up the stakes that made the palisade around their camp, extracting the nails that held the wooden buildings together, stuffing their backpacks with their kit, all in good humour, enjoying the unusually relaxed pace of their labours. Antony stood with Caesar, who was looking west towards Pompey's camp intently, eyes narrowed. The sun was only just over the horizon, and it cast long shadows in the direction of the enemy, but illuminated the foothills where Pompey was stationed in an orange glow.

'Anything?' he asked Antony.

Antony squinted, striving to make out any detail at that distance.

'I think... maybe. Yes. They are marching out.'

Caesar nodded. 'Now we will see if they will just array themselves in defensive formation on the slope once more, or if they will seize this opportunity to force a result. It would be much to Pompeius' advantage if he could defeat me in Greece and avoid a war on Italian soil.'

He turned to Antony. 'You know the victor of this conflict will be greater than Sulla ever was. Unlimited power is at stake here.'

Antony nodded, and a chill went down his spine. He wasn't sure if it was excitement or trepidation at that thought. He looked out towards Pompey's position again.

'They are at the bottom of the slope,' he said. 'They aren't stopping. They are marching onto the plain.'

Caesar's lips pressed together in a tight smile.

'Let battle commence.'

–

The Pompeian army was drawn up in the classic triple line formation: eleven legions, with Pompey and Domitius Ahenobarbus on the left, Scipio in the centre and Labienus in charge of the cavalry and auxiliary archers. Antony was in command of Caesar's left wing, his Eighth and Ninth legions' flanks protected by the river Enipeus to his left, and Calvinus' legionaries to the right. Sulla nominally commanded Caesar's right wing, though Caesar was in real command there, since he had chosen to position himself opposite Pompey.

Antony was conscious that he had been given the most responsible task that Caesar could bestow – to ensure the weak Caesarian left held, no matter what. But he also knew that most of the action would be on the right, where Pompey's overwhelmingly superior cavalry forces were arrayed, ready to chase off Caesar's cavalry, then roll up the Caesarian right flank.

This was to be the largest battle that had ever been fought between two Italian forces. Moreover, Caesar's legions were drawn almost exclusively from Italy, Gaul and Greece, but Pompey had forces drawn from a multitude of nations – Thrace, Cilicia, Syria, Phoenicia, Judaea, Cappadocia and Armenia, among others. It was truly a war involving the whole world, Antony thought.

Antony waited behind his men, mounted on a restless bay mare. Caesar's generals had been given strict instructions not to charge until Caesar himself gave the order by means of a flag signal. Antony looked to his right. Caesar was clearly visible, sitting astride a leggy grey, his scarlet cloak flapping gently in the light breeze.

In front of him, Antony looked out over a sight that had struck terror into millions of barbarian hearts over the centuries: a Roman army, drawn up in full battle array, ready to charge. And yet this time, Roman opposed Roman. They were armed and armoured the same – *pilum*, *pugio*, gladius, shield, armour and helmet. They were positioned identically, as if they faced a mirror. Each side counted friends, cousins, brothers among the enemy.

Caesar rode the length of the front line, loudly encouraging his men. Given that the legions were stretched out across a couple of miles of the plain, he had to repeat his speech multiple times. Antony suspected that Caesar's throat must have been sore by the time he reached the left flank by the river where Antony was stationed, but their commander's voice still rung clearly. He reminded them that he had earnestly sought peace, and never desired bloodshed. He thanked his men for all the service they had done for him, and exhorted them to one last effort on his behalf, and on behalf of justice, of Rome and of its people. Cheers followed him like the swell of waves on the ocean, rising and falling as he passed.

Then a silence fell, unlike any Antony had ever experienced before a battle. Was each man reflecting on the enormity of what the day would bring, a battle that would decide the fate of the Republic, the Empire, the world? Or were they thinking about acquitting themselves honourably, of being strong for the comrades by their sides, about surviving the fight and returning to their homes and families?

Three crows flew overhead, their caws startling in the profound quiet. Antony wondered if they were a good or bad omen, then chuckled, because, as an augur, he was supposed to know. He really should learn something about that job, he thought.

The sun moved higher in the sky, and neither side made a move. Then, far to the right, a small group of around a hundred men charged out from the Caesarian lines. Antony later learned they were led by a centurion named Crastinus, who had sworn to earn Caesar's thanks, alive or dead. They quickly covered the distance between the two armies and bit deeply into the Pompeian front. Crastinus was felled with a sword thrust that entered his mouth, the tip penetrating the back of his neck. Caesar made sure to show his gratitude, and praised the brave man after the battle.

Antony never found out whether Crastinus had charged without orders, or whether Caesar had commanded him to make the first move. It seemed strange to order such a small body of men forward alone. But soon after this first skirmish, Caesar raised the flag, and trumpets blared out. Antony called to his centurions to order the advance, and with a roar, gladii thumping against shields to set up a din designed to inspire friend and terrify foe, the Caesarian front line broke into a run.

It was normal practice in battle for infantry to advance to receive a charge. It was simple physics, which Antony was familiar with both from his studies in Greece and his experience in the field. If a moving object hits a stationary object, the stationary object will be knocked back. If two objects of similar weight and speed moving in opposite directions collide, then their momentums will be cancelled out. And yet, Pompey's men did not move. Antony had a moment to wonder at the tactic. Did Pompey believe it would be easier to receive the initial javelin barrage with stationary ranks? Did he hope that Caesar's men would be too tired to fight, having run twice the distance expected?

But Caesar's men were veterans, full of guile and experience. The centurions, of their own accord, called a halt. The men had covered half the distance to Pompey's army, sprinting in full armour and roaring with all their might. Now, panting heavily, just out of missile range, they reformed their lines and regained their breath.

More moments passed. Antony's horse shifted from foot to foot, sensing the tension, rider and mount both anxious to be pressing on. Antony bit his lip, waiting for the order to continue the advance. Both sides were committed now. Neither could retreat, since turning their unprotected backs on their opponents would invite a massacre.

The flag went up once more; trumpets blared again. The legionaries, sweaty from exertion and fear, but with their wind recovered, charged once more. As soon as they were in range, the centurions yelled orders to unleash the javelins, and the front rank heaved the missiles into the air, so they arced down into the waiting Pompeians. The closed shields of the Pompeian legionaries did indeed blunt the worst of the damage of that first volley, but Roman javelins were built with soft necks, so they bent on impact. This meant that they were useless for the enemy to throw back, but also that when they lodged in a target, they were hard to remove. Many of the Pompeians had to discard their shields, which were now weighed down by the javelins, just as the Caesarian charge reached them.

Antony, seated on horseback, was afforded a perfect view of the first clash, though he could only watch in frustration and wave his sword in encouragement. The initial impact had indeed pushed the Pompeians back a short distance, but since they had double the number of the Caesarians, their rear ranks were able to brace the front, and push forward. Now, Pompey's superior numbers in infantry should have made a difference, but arrayed in defensive formation as they were, their full strength could not be brought to bear. The fighting quickly settled into a contest of shoving and stabbing, each side trying to force the other to give ground. It seemed a stalemate was beginning to develop, which might only be broken when one side was too exhausted to continue.

Antony rode up and down beside his men, well within missile range, often ducking slingshots or fending off arrows with his shield. More than once he led small groups of reserves into the affray to block up a breach, and his cavalry sword was soon dripping red. He tried not to think about the fact that it was the blood of Roman legionaries that coated his weapon, rather than that of barbarians. He consoled himself with the strong belief that he was fighting for justice against the conservatives who were persecuting his friend and commander.

Clouds of dust rose up from the dry earth, stinging the eyes and throat. Antony could taste the dirt on his tongue. The noise was deafening. And yet, above the shouts of anger, the cries of agony, an even louder sound echoed across the plain. Antony looked to the right, and through the haze saw that Pompey had ordered his cavalry forward, with his full complement of archers behind. Caesar's vastly outnumbered mounted forces bravely rode to meet them, but were quickly brushed aside. Caesar's right became vulnerable. A cavalry charge into the unprotected flank could quickly lead to a rout that would spread like a fire throughout the whole army. It was on this outcome – a certainty provided by his overwhelming superiority in horse – that Pompey had rested all his hopes.

But Caesar had known this was his greatest weakness, and had planned accordingly. He had withdrawn a cohort from each legion and stationed them behind his cavalry. It was an old trick, taking advantage of the fact that foot soldiers would be hidden by the height of the mounted troops. So when the Caesarian cavalry gave way, the Pompeians, scenting glory and victory, split into squadrons to surround the exposed Caesarian flank. That was when Caesar gave the order for his hidden reserve of infantry to advance. They charged into the Pompeian cavalry, stabbing their spears up into the faces of the riders, as they had been trained.

This was the pivotal moment. Antony had known what Caesar had prepared, but even Caesar had not been fully confident in the outcome. Would the surprise of the Pompeian cavalry being confronted by their worst nightmare – a body of spearmen – be enough to turn the battle? Or would they have the courage, training and experience to withdraw in good order, regroup, and strike again?

Antony tried to make out what was happening on that far-off flank, but his own men were beginning to waver. Their initial efforts had been heroic, but they were showing clear signs of exhaustion. They were slower to raise their swords to parry, their ripostes with their shields were weaker, and they began to give ground. Antony looked behind him, where Caesar still held a third line of infantry in reserve. Should he order it forward? But he had no authority to do so, and Caesar had given strict instructions that it should only advance on his command.

A short distance from him, a legionary stumbled, went down, and his assailant, no longer opposed, stabbed sideways into the armpit of the fallen soldier's neighbour. A breach began to open up, and the Pompeians pushed forward.

Without pausing for thought, Antony spurred his horse forward into the gap, smashing the Pompeian infantry back, slashing down to the left and right. His mounted bodyguards followed him, and they drove a wedge into the Pompeian front rank, which halted their advance and momentarily pushed them back.

But now Antony was exposed, surrounded on three sides by enemy infantry. He wheeled – a skilful manoeuvre in the chaos and crush of the battle – and thrust his way back towards the safety of his own lines. His bodyguards carved a path out before him. One fell, dragged by his foot from his mount, and was immediately set upon by the Pompeian infantry, who stabbed and hacked at his prostrate body. The rest made it back with Antony behind the front line of their own legionaries. The soldiers of the Eighth and Ninth, granted that brief respite, were able to close the gap and reform their front line. The stabbing and shoving recommenced, but Antony knew they couldn't hold out much longer.

He looked desperately to the north, to the right flank. To his immense relief, he saw that the Pompeian cavalry was in full flight. Unable to hold against the unexpected onslaught of Caesar's specially trained anti-horse infantry, they had turned and fled the field towards the hills, harried by more Caesarian troops whom Caesar had hidden, ready to ambush them in their retreat and ensure they would not return to the fight.

And now, Pompey's entire force of archers and slingers, who had been following their cavalry, were exposed and unprotected. The heavily armoured Caesarian legionaries, exultant from having chased off the Pompeian horse, fell upon the light missile infantry, and massacred it. Suddenly, Pompey's two main advantages – his cavalry and his missile troops – had been nullified. He still held an advantage in manpower in terms of numbers of legionaries still on the field, but the initiative was now entirely with Caesar. Even as Antony's legions on Caesar's left were starting to give way, Caesar personally led the reserves of the third line in a charge against Pompey's vulnerable left flank. His well-trained men, who had fought side by side for years under the same commander, responded without hesitation. Pompey's hotch-potch multinational army could not be brought to bear with the same alacrity. Nor, with the river on Pompey's right, and Antony's legions still holding, could Pompey organise a counter-attack on Caesar's left flank.

The rout began in Pompey's rear. The allied forces who had joined him from beyond the borders of the Empire, to get into the good books of the likely winner of the civil war, could see the way the battle was swinging, and could see no reason to continue to support a losing cause. When the rear echelons of Pompey's legionaries saw the threat to the flank and the flight of the reserves, they, too, turned and ran, easily able to extricate themselves from a battle they had not yet fully engaged in.

The front ranks of the Pompeian legions did not give up so easily. They were Roman legionaries, after all, with many veterans among them, some of whom had even served with Caesar in Gaul. In fact, while the Pompeian left was crumbling, the right was still advancing, and Antony and his legions remained hard-pressed until at last the collapse reached them.

Then it was Antony's turn to advance, shouting at his men to press the advantage as the opposing ranks tried to withdraw, first in good order, but soon in panicked flight.

It took just a handful of heartbeats for Antony's battle to turn from a desperate struggle to survive into a complete victory. One moment, he was slashing around him, nostrils filled with blood, sweat and dust, sword arm burning with fatigue; the next, he was sitting on his mount, panting, as the Pompeians streamed away to the west, some throwing off their armour and jumping into the river to escape.

Antony looked around him. His men were in no state, physical or mental, to pursue the enemy. Everywhere his gaze fell, he saw men lying, prone, supine, propped on one elbow, exhausted, injured, dead. The midday sun beat down and stinging sweat trickled down his spine. Flies buzzed around sightless eyes and open wounds, settling to sup or lay eggs. Antony slumped in his saddle, one hand gripping tightly on to one of the four saddle horns so he didn't slide out of his seat.

It was a strange kind of victory. Should he exult over the hundreds of dead Romans all around? Were they compatriots or enemies? He had fought alongside many of Pompey's men in Gaul and Syria. His attention was drawn to a legionary on his knees: a man of the Eighth, clutching the body of another legionary, who was still holding a shield decorated with the colours of one of Pompey's legions. Antony supposed they had been comrades, friends, or even family. He shook his head and prepared to organise his men into parties to care for the wounded, gather supplies, prepare defences.

The sound of pounding hooves getting nearer made him look round. Charging towards him was Caesar on his white stallion, scarlet cloak flapping behind him in the breeze.

'Antonius, what are you doing?' he said, pulling his horse up abruptly beside Antony.

'Looking after the men, Caesar,' replied Antony, confused.

'Get them up and moving. We have won the battle, but if we press forward, we will win the war. Get your legions back in order and pursue the enemy to their camp. They still outnumber us, and they must not be allowed time to regroup.'

Antony looked at his spent men. He squared his shoulders. 'As you command, Caesar.'

Caesar didn't stop to check that Antony was going to do as he was told. He dug his heels into his horse's flanks and galloped back down the line, shouting orders as he went. Antony summoned his tribunes and senior centurions – or at least those who were still alive and walking.

He couldn't help but admire the resilience of these tough veterans. Bleeding, bruised and worn-out, they helped one another to their feet and shuffled back into formation. Antony rode out in front of them, and led them at a steady march west. There was no complaining, and some of them even struck up a loud, tuneless song:

Caesar ploughed the lands of Gaul, and Nicomedes ploughed our Caesar,
Caesar is now triumphing, the same man who ploughed the Gauls,
No triumph for Nicomedes, though, who ploughed our Caesar.

Antony couldn't suppress a smile. Nicomedes was the old king of Bithynia who was rumoured to have taken a youthful Caesar as a lover. Antony knew that Caesar detested this kind of soldier humour, but accepted it was good for morale. For his part, Antony enjoyed it, and didn't care what the men said about him, as long as they loved him and obeyed him.

It was a bare half-mile from the battlefield to Pompey's camp, and the whole of Caesar's army descended on the fortification like a giant wave. Though the encampment was well built, as Roman field tactics dictated – situated on a hill, with ramparts and ditches and other formidable defences – the defenders were shattered, demoralised and hopeless. Many had discarded their weapons and shields in their haste to flee, and were now defenceless and toothless.

Caesar made no attempt to encircle or besiege the camp. The full force of his legions charged up the hill and smashed into the palisade with the force of Vulcan's hammer. Any Pompeians who showed their heads on the rampart were immediately struck down by a storm of javelins. Scaling ladders were tossed against the walls, and it was the work of moments for the Caesarian legions to storm into the camp and throw the gates open.

There was still some resistance, and the auxiliaries fought particularly hard, maybe believing – correctly, as it turned out – that they were less likely to be spared than Pompey's Roman legionaries. But the majority, as soon as the walls were breached, fled for the hills behind the camp. Any who still fought were cut down where they stood.

Once the camp was secured, Caesar summoned Antony, Calvinus and Sulla to meet with him. Antony looked around at the site of what for the last few days had been Pompey's stronghold. There was much more luxurious accommodation than was normal for a marching camp. Artificial arbours had been created, and many of the largest tents were laid with artificial turf and decked with large amounts of silver plate. No doubt the self-important senators had demanded the best quarters, and all the amenities and comforts they were used to in their villas in Italy.

The tents and wooden buildings had already been decorated with ivy and laurel, so confident had the Pompeians been that victory would be theirs. Antony could only imagine how difficult it had been for

Pompey, dealing with the likes of Cicero, Scipio, Domitius Ahenobarbus, Lentulus Crus and Marcus Claudius Marcellus. He had had
enough problems of his own with them during his time as tribune,
and he was sure they made no less troublesome allies than they did
enemies.

Caesar's three leading generals waited for his orders. But the great
commander seemed uncharacteristically lost for words. His face was
expressionless, but his eyes darted around. He seemed to be unable to
take in all the destruction he had caused, and at the same time stunned
by the ridiculous extravagance the Pompeian leadership had indulged
in while his own army had starved. Antony wondered if he was also
looking for someone specific among the bodies. Marcus Junius Brutus,
Caesar's lover's son, had been with Pompey, and Caesar was surely
worried for his safety.

Eventually Caesar let out a long sigh and said, 'They would have it
so. They brought me to such a pass that I, Gaius Julius Caesar, after
being victorious in the greatest of wars, would, had I disbanded my
armies, have been condemned in their courts.'

Antony nodded gravely, but could find no words that would console
his commander and friend.

'It is done,' said Caesar. 'Tonight we will feast at the expense of
Pompeius. But before then, we must finish the task. Make sure there is
no looting until we have repaired the fortifications. Sulla, organise the
defences, bring me lists of the casualties, and make sure the wounded
of both sides are treated. Calvinus, you will come with me with four
legions to cut off their retreat. Antonius, take the Gallic cavalry and seek
out any stragglers. Roman legionaries are to be given the opportunity
to surrender and join us. Foreign auxiliaries may be slaughtered at will.'

'Yes, Caesar,' said Antony. 'And what of the senatorial leadership?'

'You know my views. Everyone gets one chance. Any who surrender
and throw themselves on my mercy will be spared, provided they have
not abused my clemency in the past.'

'And if they have previously surrendered and then reneged on
previous promises not to oppose you?'

Caesar pursed his lips. 'Then do as you must.'

'And Pompeius?'

Caesar's face darkened, and he pointed a finger at Antony that shook
with barely repressed emotion.

'Gnaeus Pompeius Magnus is not to be harmed.'

–

Riding down and massacring defeated fugitives was a dirty job, thought Antony, but it had to be done. There had been no sign of Pompey. Pompeian survivors reported that he had fled the battle as soon as it was clear he had lost, entered the camp and shut himself in his tent to await the outcome. When the Caesarian legions had started their assault on the camp, he had immediately disguised himself in plain clothes and fled. And while Pompey remained at large, the war was not really over. If he could escape to the east, he could raise a new army and threaten Caesar once more. Pompey had made mistakes that day, and Caesar had tactically bested him. But he was still an experienced and great strategist, and there was no guarantee that if there was a rematch between Caesar and Pompey, that the outcome would be the same.

So it was necessary for Pompey's forces to be reduced as much as possible, and that meant destroying the remnants of his army before it could regroup. It was not difficult work, but nor was there any glory in it. Occasionally small groups of Pompeians would make a stand, but most were unarmed and too fatigued to put up much resistance. Others kept running in blind panic until a spear or sword thrust into their backs brought them down. Some just fell to their knees, weeping, begging for mercy or stoically accepting their fate. As Caesar had instructed, the legionaries were taken prisoner. The foreign auxiliaries were cut down on the spot.

Antony had come across several men of equestrian or senatorial rank, alone or accompanied by small entourages of bodyguards and slaves bearing their most precious treasures. To a man, they had thrown themselves at Antony's feet and begged forgiveness. He couldn't help but enjoy the immense feeling of power, to hold the lives of these important noblemen in his hand. But he had spared them all, sending them under guard to Caesar.

Then he encountered Lucius Domitius Ahenobarbus.

Domitius had been a thorn in Caesar's side for over a decade, and was firmly aligned with the highly conservative views of his brother-in-law, Cato. He had attempted to deprive Caesar of his command in Gaul seven years earlier, and in fact had been appointed by the Senate as the new Gallic governor on the very day that Caesar had crossed the Rubicon. Domitius had been one of the most active in the Senatorial faction to oppose Caesar, the only one to resist him in Italy when he had initially refused to surrender Corfinium, and then fighting at Massilia despite Caesar's previous clemency. He must have known that he would not be forgiven twice.

Domitius also bore a personal enmity towards Antony, who had defeated him against the odds in the election to become augur on the death of Hortensius. So when, making his way west on horseback along the foothills with a dozen bodyguards and slaves, he realised it was Antony pursuing him, he turned towards him, a twisted snarl on his face, and drew his sword.

Antony had split his men to maximise the ground they could cover, but made sure each unit was big enough to crush any expected resistance with ease; of course, being mounted, they could retreat if they unexpectedly came across a superior force. Still, Antony had a hundred horse at his back, and Domitius had no hope of victory or escape. So when he dug his heels into his horse's flanks and charged at Antony with a roar, his sole aim must have been to kill Antony before he himself was cut down.

Antony growled at his men to hold back and urged his own mount on, drawing his spatha as his horse leapt forward at the touch of his spurs. The two senators, years of hatred enraging them both, raced towards each other. Domitius leaned forward in his saddle, one hand gripping a supporting horn, the other holding his outstretched sword, aimed directly at Antony's chest. Antony kept his gaze fixed on Domitius' eyes, watching for a move, a feint. But Domitius had no such guile. He had had no significant military service before the civil war, and was unskilled in martial ways. Moreover, even in his prime, he would have been no match for Antony physically, and he was actually two decades older.

So when the two riders met, and Domitius swung his sword at Antony in a frenzied rage, Antony merely batted the stroke away with his shield and then, as they passed, slashed at Domitius' horse's hamstrings. The beast gave a pitiful whinny and its hindquarters collapsed, tipping Domitius sideways. He sprawled face first in the dust, sword flying from his grip.

Antony jumped lightly from his saddle and walked slowly over to where Domitius was scrabbling for his lost weapon. He waited for his opponent to rearm himself and get to his feet. Domitius confronted him. He had a ruddy graze down one cheek and a cut above his eye from his fall. He breathed heavily, flecks of spittle flying out from between his gritted teeth.

'You don't scare me, Antonius,' he snarled.

'Then you are either very stupid or very brave,' replied Antony. 'I suspect, in fact, that you are both.'

Domitius lunged forward, swinging his sword downwards and sideways from above his shoulder. But he was wielding an infantryman's gladius, a stabbing weapon. It did not have the reach to be swung like a cavalry sword, and Antony easily sidestepped, using his shield to safely guide the blow to one side. Domitius tried again, with no better skill or luck. On the third attempt, Antony parried with his longer sword, then thrust the iron boss of his shield into Domitius' face. He felt, rather than heard, reverberating through the iron framework, the crunch of cartilage and the splintering of teeth. Domitius, face bloody and eyes wide with shock, toppled on to his backside, where he sat like a stunned toddler.

'Surrender,' said Antony. 'Caesar was merciful to you once. There is a slim chance he will be so again, but it is better than no chance at all.'

Domitius struggled to his feet and stood swaying, dazed. Then he raised his sword over his head and rushed at Antony again.

Antony simply pushed his spatha forward, and with the long reach of his sword increased by his own long arms, the tip of his blade bit into Domitius' guts before he had chance to strike. He looked down at the iron protruding from just under his ribs, then stared at Antony and, with hatred emanating from him, took another step forward, and another, the blade penetrating him deeper and deeper. He came face to face with Antony, so that Antony could smell the sweet wine he had drunk before the battle, no doubt toasting victory. He opened his mouth to spit out a curse, but only blood poured forth.

Then he slid off the blade, like tender steak falling off a knife, and lay still, head to one side, sightless eyes glaring into the distance.

Antony looked down at the fallen senator for a long moment, then picked him up and carefully placed him over the back of his own horse.

Then, holding the reins, he led his mount with its grim burden back to Caesar's camp.

ante diem iv Idus Sextilis DCCVI AUC (10 August 48 BC), Pharsalus

Dawn the next day saw the end of the final resistance of Pompey's army. Surrounded on a hilltop, unfortified, cut off from water and leaderless, their position was clearly hopeless. Caesar gave orders for them to descend and throw down their weapons, and they eagerly obeyed. Row upon row of Roman legionaries knelt before him with hands stretched upwards in supplication as they begged for their lives. Caesar walked among them and spoke in a gentle voice, assuring them that he knew they had been misled, that they were only doing their duty towards Pompey, but that Pompey had fled and they must now swear an oath to him. Some of the Pompeian legionaries and centurions he recognised from their time in Gaul, and he acknowledged their previous good service and hoped he could rely on them once more. They all stammered their gratitude at his mercy and promised to serve him loyally from that day on.

Caesar had looked disapproving when Antony returned with the body of Domitius, but Antony assured him that he had given Domitius every opportunity to surrender, and reminded Caesar that he had already pardoned him once. Caesar grudgingly accepted Antony's explanation, though he commented that it was a mark against his renowned clement nature.

As it turned out, Domitius was the only person of high rank to die at Pharsalus. Caesar's losses had been light, as was often the case in pitched battles, where most of the damage was inflicted on the defeated, fleeing side. The Pompeian casualties amounted to around fifteen thousand, with over twenty thousand captured, along with one hundred and eighty military standards and nine legion eagles.

A number of Pompey's senior commanders escaped. Pompey and his sons had disappeared east. Lentulus Crus, Lentulus Spinther and Labienus were unaccounted for, and were presumed to be intending to fight on.

But not all of Pompey's adherents were keen to continue the fight. After two days of rest and numerous sacrifices given in thanks to the gods, conducted by Caesar as *Pontifex Maximus* and ably assisted by Antony in his role as augur, Caesar led his army to the nearby city of Larisa, to which Pompey had initially fled. It was here that he received a letter from Marcus Junius Brutus, informing him that he had survived by fleeing from the camp during the battle and making his way to Larisa overnight by way of some difficult to cross marshland.

The relief in Caesar's expression was visible to all when he read this letter, and though Antony did not think Marcus Brutus was Caesar's son – he actually thought that Decimus was the more likely Brutus to be Caesar's illegitmate offspring – he could see how Caesar's evident love for the young man had given rise to the rumours. When Marcus Brutus, by invitation, presented himself to Caesar, Caesar embraced him, and both of them wept like reunited lovers.

While Caesar and his men rested and continued their thanksgivings and their honouring of the dead, scouts were sent out to track down the senior Pompeians. In the meantime, Caesar took long walks with Brutus, sounding him out about the mood in the enemy camp, and Pompey's likely next steps. Antony could not help but feel some jealousy at the way Caesar treated Brutus. Antony had stayed by his side throughout, no matter what the hardship, the odds or the personal danger. Brutus had actively opposed him, and was being treated like a confidant and favourite.

After a few days, the scouts reported back with accurate locations of the main Pompeians. Pompey was heading towards Syria with Lentulus Crus and Lentulus Spinther, as well as his younger son Sextus. Scipio had gone west towards allied coastal cities, with intelligence suggesting he was planning to meet up with Cato, who had not been present at Pharsalus, in Corcyra. Pompey's elder son, Gnaeus, was on his way to Spain, and to Caesar's great irritation, it seemed that Labienus had survived the battle and was accompanying him. Cicero, by contrast, was in Dyrrhachium in a slough of despondency, busying himself with sending apologies and requests for forgiveness to Caesar, while writing to his correspondents about the incompetence with which Pompey had managed the war.

Caesar now had to decide whether to pursue Scipio with the remnants of the army, or try to chase down Pompey. He summoned Sulla and Antony and informed them brusquely of Pompeian movements and what he had decided.

'I will head east. There is no general but Pompeius among the Senatorial faction with the skill to oppose me. While he remains at large, my position will always be under threat. So I will follow him to Asia Minor and Syria and prevent him rebuilding his army. Maybe, if I can talk to him, there is still the chance for a reconciliation. We loved each other once, and he was deeply attached to my daughter. I can only hope that we can resolve our differences, for our own sakes and the good of Rome.

'Sulla, I want you to go west and clear out any resistance in Greece, especially on the coast. I want the sea route between Italy and Greece to be open to my forces whenever I need it.'

Antony bit the inside of his lip.

'And what of Italy – of Rome? There are still large Republican armies in existence, not least those under Cato. What if there is an invasion of Italy? And what of unrest in the city in your absence?'

'That's where you come in, Marcus.'

Antony had a sudden, familiar sinking feeling. He thought he knew what was coming. Caesar was going to war and sending him off to an administrative role once more.

'You want me to resume my tribunate with Imperium to command Italy?'

'Not quite,' said Caesar. 'Yes, you are going to Italy, where you will take command. Isauricus is currently my co-consul, but he is entirely unsuited to organise a military defence of the peninsula. That will be your job. You are to take the surplus legions, make sure there are land and pensions for those that can be disbanded, prepare to defend Italy against any threat, and ensure that order is maintained.'

'Yes, Caesar. On what authority?'

'You are to inform the Senate of Rome that I am to be made Dictator for the period of one year. And that you are to be my Master of Horse.'

Antony took a breath. Previously, Caesar had only been Dictator for a few days, as a way of ensuring the elections could take place. Now, he was taking power for himself, for a whole year, with Antony as his deputy. And he would be absent from Rome for an indefinite period while he continued the war against Pompey and the Senatorial faction.

That left Antony as the highest authority in the Empire. Supreme, uncontested, immune from all laws. And though it gave him a pang of guilt to entertain the thought, if Caesar should fall in battle, the entire Empire would be his!

Chapter IX

Antony arrived in Rome in early October, accompanied by a large army: those victorious soldiers from Pharsalus who Caesar had thought either necessary to keep control in Italy, or surplus to his require-ments and eligible for pensioning off. He left the bulk of them stationed in barracks outside the pomerium, but entered Rome in full armour, a sword strapped around his waist, escorted by half a cohort of veteran legionaries. Crowds lined his route, waving laurel branches and throwing flowers into his path. But when he focused on individuals in the throng, he could see their smiles were strained, forced, and that there was an anxiety behind their eyes. He knew why. Caesar had won, and he and his representatives now had a free hand to do as they wished. Would Caesar's renowned clemency prevail, or was it all a sham to achieve his objectives? Would he now turn into another Sulla? Would the massacres now begin?

If Antony had been of a mind to reassure them, he would have entered the city as tradition and law demanded – in civilian dress, unarmed, with all his soldiers left outside the pomerium. But he had a city to rule in Caesar's absence. Despite Caesar's trust in him, he felt profoundly unqualified. Who was he, after all, but a capable military commander? Son of the failure Antonius Creticus, the man of chalk. Stepson of the traitor Lentulus. A man who had never held higher office than tribune was now meant to rule a city that had proven hard to control by even the most powerful men over the last half-century.

So, he had decided to play to his strengths. Show the city that he was, first and foremost, a soldier, and it was as a soldier that he would keep order and rule in Caesar's stead.

Cytheris sat by his side in their carriage as they processed towards the Forum, uncharacteristically quiet. She had been waiting for him when he had docked in Brundisium, and the sight of her had filled him with joy. He hadn't realised quite how much he had missed her until he actually had her in his arms. They had spent a magical evening ensconced together in the villa of a Pompey supporter that he had commandeered, raiding the wine cellar and kitchens and making full use of the chefs and masseuses, the bathing facilities, the gardens and, of course, the luxurious master bedroom. Her evident delight at their reunion was infectious, and their sedate journey through Italy had been like a romantic holiday, if it was possible to ignore the legions tramping along in their wake.

But now she seemed uncomfortable, out of place. Antony squeezed her knee in reassurance, and she gave him a half-smile. He rarely considered her position in society – it just didn't concern him in the normal course of events. Now, however, he could see that she feared the opprobrium of the crowds, that she, an actress, lowest of the low, should be parading before them like a queen. Antony felt his chest puff out of its own accord, his jaw tighten. She may be an actress, but she was his queen, and Rome had better get used to the fact.

Still, he had duties to perform, and once they reached the Forum, he helped her alight from the carriage and dispatched her to her home with a small escort of soldiers, who looked delighted to be tasked with looking after this stunning woman.

Antony marched up the steps of the Curia, head held high, hand hanging loose by the pommel of his sword. He reminded himself that he was there by right. He was the grandson of Marcus Antonius, the orator. He was a tribune and an augur. He was the chosen deputy of Gaius Julius Caesar, now indisputably the most powerful man in the Republic. His uncharacteristic self-doubt suppressed, he strode into the Senate house.

The full Senate had been instructed to assemble by messengers he had sent ahead, and they had dutifully turned up. There were many Caesarian supporters among their ranks, and no Pompeians, who had all fled, either with Pompey or at the news of his defeat. However, there were a sizeable number of neutrals on the benches. While Pompey had declared that any who were not with him were against him, Caesar had taken the opposite position, and said that any who were not against him were with him. This allowed the neutrals to stay in Rome, reasonably reassured they were not in danger from Caesar's vengeance, and in turn it had allowed him to maintain a larger Senate to give credence to his legitimacy.

So all of the senators stood and applauded when he entered, though some more enthusiastically than others. Publius Servilius Vatia Isauricus, Caesar's co-consul, rose from his curule chair, and embraced Antony firmly.

'It's good to see you,' he said with sincerity. Isauricus was a staunch ally of Caesar, and one whose life would undoubtedly have been forfeit if it had been Pompey returning to the city, victorious.

'The same,' said Antony. 'You have done a fine job of keeping things together in Caesar's absence.'

Isauricus had, in fact, suffered a tawdry time. Marcus Caelius, agitating for the cancellation of debts, had set up a magistrate's chair next to Antony's old comrade-in-arms, Gaius Trebonius, who, as urban praetor, was responsible for debt, and offered to hear anyone who felt cheated by Trebonius. Repeatedly provoked until his patience broke, Isauricus had gone to him with lictors who were carrying axes in their *fasces* – the bundles of wood which were carried by the magistrates' bodyguards to deal out corporal punishment to miscreants, and which only contained axes in times of serious danger.

After a heated argument, Isauricus had drawn out one of the axes and smashed Caelius' chair. Caelius had simply had the chair repaired, and mocked Isauricus with it. Eventually, though, he had been driven from the city and had begun an armed rebellion with Clodius' exiled murderer, Milo. Both had been killed, and Antony was pleased he would not have to deal with the little snake himself.

Antony turned to the senators and waved his arms to hush them and bid them sit, which they did after a seemly display of reluctance to cease their applause. He saw Trebonius in the front rank and gave him an affectionate smile, then cleared his throat to speak, fortified by the presence of his friend.

Antony was a good orator, though Cicero mocked his bombastic style. He addressed the Senate in a loud, clear voice.

'Conscript Fathers, thank you for assembling today, and for hearing me. I bring greetings from the consul, Gaius Julius Caesar. You are no doubt aware already of his famous victory in Thessaly over the rebel forces under Gnaeus Pompeius.'

Some of the senators exchanged glances at his use of the word 'rebel' to describe the most senior members of the Senate, who had largely supported Pompey, and also his dropping of Pompey's honorific, Magnus. Both were deliberate.

'I bring you, too, a request from Caesar. He is in pursuit of Pompeius and the remnants of his forces, and he needs extraordinary powers to ensure the peace and safety of the state. He therefore asks that you make him Dictator for a period of one year.'

This caused murmurs of surprise around the chamber. The maximum term of a dictatorship was six months, with the holder expected to lay down his command as soon as whatever crisis he had been appointed to overcome was resolved. But they all knew that this was no request, and when, after minimal debate, Isauricus put the proposal to the vote, there was an overwhelming majority in favour, with no tribune imposing a veto.

When the vote had passed, Antony stood again.

'Now we must turn to the matter of the Master of Horse.'

The Master of Horse was no longer a cavalry position, but was the official title of the Dictator's deputy, who could wield every bit of authority as if he was Dictator himself if the Dictator was absent.

'Caesar has kindly proposed that the position of Master of Horse should be undertaken by me.'

There was no surprise at this announcement. Why else would Caesar have sent Antony to Rome to propose these measures?

'The term of office for Master of Horse is also to be one year.'

There was further general approval, but one section of the Senate muttered disapprovingly, shaking their heads.

Antony turned to Isauricus in surprise. Isauricus looked equally taken back, spreading his hands and shrugging in lieu of explanation.

'Is there a problem?' asked Antony belligerently.

Gaius Claudius Marcellus, the consul of two years previously, who had done so much to provoke the civil war, but then – unlike his brother and cousin – had decided to watch from the sidelines rather than take part, got slowly to his feet.

'The college of augurs object.'

Antony realised now that the group of men that Marcellus was speaking for were all augurs. He should have noticed the connection, as an augur himself, but he had to concede he had spent precious little time attending to his priestly duties or attending meetings of the college. He wondered if that was the reason the augurs were now being obstructive. Maybe it was revenge for his lack of dedication to his duties.

'What do you object to specifically?' he asked. 'That I be Master of Horse?'

'Not at all,' said Marcellus. 'But it is against tradition that a Master of Horse serve for more than six months.'

'But you have just voted Caesar the dictatorship for a year,' said Antony, exasperated. 'That is against tradition, too!'

'I think we can all agree that Caesar is an exception,' said Marcellus.

Antony turned to Isauricus in helpless appeal. Isauricus got to his feet.

'I am an augur myself,' said the consul, 'and this objection is patently absurd. To appoint a Dictator for a year and not to afford his deputy the same courtesy is ridiculous. I demand you withdraw your objection.'

The augurs conferred among themselves, some raising their voices as they discussed the situation forcefully. But eventually, Marcellus rose again, and said, 'For the sake of peace within the Republic, we withdraw our objections.'

Isauricus quickly called a vote and Antony was elected Master of Horse for a year, albeit with a smaller majority than Caesar.

And so, with Caesar absent, Antony once again became the sole ruler of Italy. But unlike the previous occasion, when he had simply held an imperium to run things without an official role beyond his tribunate, he was officially the deputy to the Dictator, in command in Caesar's absence. He had immunity from prosecution for any and all deeds. He could make laws, appoint and remove magistrates, confiscate property, condemn citizens to death without trial. With the legal position of Master of Horse, and the legions to back him up, he had absolute, unchecked power.

Unbidden, an image of himself as an eleven-year-old boy, receiving the news of his father's defeat and ignominious death came into his mind. He wondered what that young boy would think of the man he had become. Roars of sycophantic cheering broke out from all around the Senate house and from the large crowd that had been listening outside the chamber. He pulled himself to his full height, thrust his chest out, and soaked it up.

November DCCVI AUC (November 48 BC), Rome

The month of November had been ridiculously busy for Antony, but with his new powers he had no problem asserting his will. His main issue was his lack of experience in running a city and an empire. This felt different from his previous stint in charge, when Caesar had granted him imperium to rule Italy. Then, he had been entirely focused on preparing for war, something he was temperamentally suited for. Now, he was tasked with returning the city to peace. That meant becoming involved with matters as diverse as the sacrifice of the October Horse, planning the Plebeian games, ensuring the adequacy of corn imports, and approving urgent repair works to the sewers and aqueducts.

He also had the political side of life to attend to. Though there were few out-and-out Pompeian supporters in Italy who had not already benefited from Caesar's clemency, there were many neutrals who had not declared a side, even after Antony's arrival in the city hot on the heels of the news of Pompey's defeat at Pharsalus. After all, Pompey still lived, and he had many powerful allies. For many, the war was not yet decided.

And then Antony had his personal affairs to attend to: visiting old friends – both for pleasure and to shore up their political support; spending time with his mother, Julia, and his wife and daughter, the two Antonias, as well as catching up with Fulvia. But most of his free time was spent with Cytheris, and at parties. Many, many parties. The elite social set fell over itself in its anxiety to have the first man in Rome in attendance at their banquets and soirees, but he was just as happy, if not more so, at the raucous weddings and after-show bacchanals of his actor friends.

It was with drooping eyelids, a familiar headache and some nausea, that he received the courier that morning, but he came fully alert when he saw Caesar's seal on the scroll that he was handed. He broke it and read hurriedly. It was dated about twenty days previously.

Idibus Octobribus, anno DCCVI ab urbe condita, Alexandria
To Marcus Antonius, Magister Equitum,
From Gaius Julius Caesar, Dictator

Greetings. I write to inform you of events in Egypt, subsequent to the great battle. Pompeius fled to the island of Lesbos, then to Cyprus. From there he made his way to Pelusium, his attention seeming to be to take control of the wealth of Egypt in order to continue the war against me. However, Egypt is in the middle of its own struggle, between the boy Ptolemy XIII and the queen Cleopatra VII, who, in the strange Egyptian way, are both siblings and spouses. It seems that Ptolemy desired to gain my good graces, and when Pompeius landed on Egyptian soil, he was immediately killed by a Roman soldier, in full view of his wife Cornelia, who was on a ship just off the shore. When I arrived in Egypt, his head was presented to me as some sort of trophy. I wept bitterly at the demise of my old friend. The murderer was a Roman military tribune who had been stationed there as one of the so-called Gabinian mercenaries, ever since Aulus Gabinius and yourself restored Ptolemy XII to the throne there. I have demanded he be punished, but he is currently in hiding and eluding justice.

I will need to remain in Egypt for some time. The winds are against our fleet leaving for the time being, and in any case I have demanded the repayment of a ten-million-denarius debt that Ptolemy XII owed me. Further, the country is in chaos, and it is important that I resolve this war so that it has a favourable account for both Rome and our own cause, given the importance of Egypt in terms of wealth and grain supplies.

I have complete faith in your prudent and moderate rule of Rome in my absence. Ensure that the grain supply is maintained, the economy is stable, the citizens are quiescent and the solders are content.

Farewell.

Antony stood and paced the room. Pompeius dead? Then the war really was over. Or was it? He had received word that Cato, Scipio and Labienus had reached Africa, and were raising forces in alliance with King Juba to continue the struggle. But there could be no real doubt that Caesar was now completely dominant. And Antony was his sole representative in Italy.

He called for his slaves to bring his military uniform and sword, and made his way to the Rostra, composing a speech in his head. As he stood on the ancient ship's prows, reminiscent of the atrium in Pompey's old villa that Antony had owned, symbolic of the great man's stunning victory over the pirates, he looked down over the expectant crowd. What note to strike? Triumph and scorn seemed out of place at this moment, and he considered how the dignified Caesar would have spoken of his former friend.

'Citizens of Rome, my brothers and my friends. Today I bring you the terrible news of the death of Pompeius Magnus.'

Despite the fact that the majority of ordinary Romans were firm adherents to Caesar's cause, even more so since his victory at Pharsalus, a deep groan echoed around the Forum. Pompey had been greatly admired and loved by the common people, too, and there was no harm in praising him, in letting the masses mourn him, now he was no longer a threat.

'The list of Pompeius' achievements are lengthy. His skill as a general, his leadership of his country in times of crisis, are undoubted. Let us not dishonour his legacy with remembrance of his misguided latter days, when he was led astray by the self-interests of a traitorous clique within the Senate. Let us forget that their actions led him to defeat, betrayal, and murder in a distant land. Let us instead give thanks for one of the greatest Romans to have ever lived, for everything he did for our city and its Empire. Let us lift up prayers, sing songs of praise, and make sacrifices in the honour of the shade of Gnaeus Pompeius Magnus.'

The cheers resounding around the Forum reassured Antony that he had struck the right note.

ante diem vi Kalendas Martias DCCVII AUC (24 February 47 BC), Rome

The *Regifugium* was the first day of the year by the archaic form of reckoning, although everyone knew it was not quite as simple as that. In the times of the kings, the month of March marked the first month of the ten-month year, and only later were January and February added, hence the seventh month of the Republican calendar was Quintilis and the twelfth month December. But traditionally February only had twenty-three days, with five extra so-called intercalary days being added by the priests trying to keep the calendar matching the seasons. So the twenty-third day of February was the last day of the year, marked by the *Terminalia* festival, making the twenty-fourth day of February the first day of the new year, although technically that was actually the first day of March. At least, it was something like that, Antony thought, although he was sure most people simply pretended to understand the complexities of the calendar, past and present. What was certain was that it had been a long time since the months of the year bore any relationship to the seasons, which meant planning anything, from planting crops to a military campaign, involved careful calculation.

These were the only dates in the calendar where two major and ancient festivals fell on consecutive days. Antony needed little excuse for a party anyway, but the Terminalia was a decent affair that involved sacrifices to Jupiter Terminalis, the god of boundaries. Antony had attended the ceremony at the sixth milestone on the road to Laurentum, which pitiful distance had once marked the boundary of all Roman territory. He had then gone to a play with Cytheris and had got very drunk at the after-show party. It was noon when the pair of them crawled out of bed, only to start the festivities again, this time in honour of the expulsion of the last king from Rome by an ancestor of Marcus and Decimus Brutus. The celebrations seemed particularly exuberant this year, and Antony couldn't help wonder if there was a fear among the populace that they would soon have a new king.

That evening, he attended a private party hosted by a very rich equestrian who was anxious to get on his good side, and there he encountered Dolabella. He had seen the young man increasingly frequently over the last few months, at social and political occasions, and had found himself warming to him, despite his initial misgivings. Dolabella was charming, witty, sharp-minded and handsome, and Antony had come to realise that he lacked a friend who was both like-minded and a peer. He enjoyed the company of Cytheris' circle – the actors, dancers, mimes and musicians – but since the deaths of Clodius and Curio, he had had no one of his own rank with whom he could let his hair down.

Dolabella filled this hole, and they had become roaringly drunk together on more than one occasion, recreating Antony's adolescent nocturnal exploits, with copious quantities of wine and music, gambling, petty vandalism, and the gentle bullying of helpless drunks they encountered on the streets.

That evening Dolabella was in a more serious mood, turning to his favourite topic of debt reform. Antony indulged him, knowing that before long he would tire of the subject and they could get on with the more important business of heavy drinking.

'It's unsustainable, Marcus,' Dolabella was saying, his sentences coherent even if the individual words were slurred.

'You don't need to preach to me about debt,' replied Antony, also quite drunk, though he had to consume around twice as much wine as Dolabella for it to have the same effect. 'I still owe a good deal myself. The difference is that now my creditors don't press me for repayment – they know I'm good for it.'

'Maybe the best solution is to die in debt. That's the only way you can get away with repaying debt permanently. Just like poor old Gabinius.'

Antony looked up sharply.

'What happened to Gabinius?'

'Oh, sorry, Marcus. I forgot you two were close once. The news just arrived today from Illyricum. He was attacked by Dalmatians and Pompeians under Marcus Octavius, but managed to beat them off.'

'I knew of this, of course, but I hadn't heard of his death. He was killed in battle?'

'No, an illness, I heard. It can be terribly unhealthy in those foreign parts.'

Antony shook his head. Dolabella had seen no action nor travelled extensively, apart from being present at Pharsalus, where he had played no important role. Antony had travelled the length and breadth of the Empire with the legions, and prided himself on his knowledge of the farthest lands.

'Poor Gabinius. Never really fulfilled his potential.'

Dolabella raised his cup. 'To the shade of dear departed Aulus Gabinius.'

Antony clinked his cup against Dolabella's, spilling some of the liquid.

'Aulus.'

They both drunk deeply, and Antony dribbled wine down his chin. Both he and Dolabella sported neatly trimmed beards, which were now sticky with food and liquid, and they had grown their hair long in the latest fashion among the youth – though, unlike Dolabella, Antony could not really count himself one of their number anymore.

'Did you ever screw Lollia, his wife?' asked Dolabella.

Antony looked up, shocked. 'Of course not. Aulus was my friend.'

Dolabella shrugged. 'Well, Caesar did. And Catilina.'

'I know, but still…' He looked at Dolabella with a sudden suspicion. 'Did you?'

'No, no. A bit too old for me. Not that I haven't dabbled in the more mature woman from time to time. There are a few senators' wives who have taken a shine to me.'

Antony suddenly recalled how Dolabella was friends with his own wife, Antonia, but suppressed the unpleasant images that came to his mind. She had assured him there was no impropriety between them, and he was confident there was nothing untoward going on.

'Anyway, you've been around a bit yourself, haven't you?'

Antony smiled and inclined his head. He felt it didn't hurt to have a reputation as successful with women, even those already taken. It had certainly done Caesar no harm. And it was true that Antony had had his fair share of dalliances with married women, some of them with important husbands. He took particular pleasure in cuckolding Pompeian supporters, but recently he had indulged in this pastime less and less. His affections were fully consumed with Cytheris, and she didn't like him playing with others. He felt the same, and despite her profession and obligations to her former master, she had forsworn other men. Eutrapelus had been perfectly happy with this arrangement, given the access it gave him to the foremost man in Rome, and as well as indulging Cytheris extravagantly, Antony had made sure some of his wealth flowed towards Eutrapelus to keep him sweet. In fact, all of Antony's family, friends and clients benefitted from the largesse that his good fortune allowed, as well as a host of sycophants and chancers.

Cytheris came to join them, sitting on Antony's lap and draping her arm around him. He kissed her deeply, a long, sloppy kiss with lots of lip, tongue and saliva. Dolabella laughed.

'I'll leave you two soppy doves to it. Anyway, I've just spotted Porcia over there, and she seems to be distinctly lacking in male company.'

Antony laughed out loud. Porcia was Cato's daughter and Bibulus' widow. She was a potentially advantageous match for someone, with her family connections and wealth, but at that politically charged time, with the Pompeian cause that her father and husband had so vigorously supported seemingly dead, no one of rank and ambition would consider a marriage offer.

'Good luck. Go gentle with her. She can't help her relatives.'

An odd look came into Dolabella's eyes. 'Gentle?' Then he clapped Antony on the shoulder, bowed to Cytheris and headed towards Porcia like a wolf towards an injured rabbit.

'I don't trust him,' said Cytheris quietly.

Antony looked at her in surprise. It was unusual for her to express an opinion. Maybe it was her upbringing as a slave; maybe she felt, even now, it wasn't her place. Antony wished, in fact, that she would contribute more when he was musing about the weighty matters that were always on his shoulders. Whether it was adjudicating legal cases, hearing the complaints of pensioned veterans, attempting to stabilise the economy, or allocate military resources to keep the borders of the Empire safe from barbarians while dealing with the revolts of Pompey's sympathisers that kept popping up like the Hydra heads, he was constantly besieged by demands for decisions. It was a position he was in no way prepared for. He was a soldier, a brave and strong fighter and a gifted tactician. Running an empire was a completely different matter, and he had few that he could rely on for counsel.

One exception to this was Fulvia. She, at least, was a constant friend and a wise head. But then he realised with sudden guilt that he had not visited her for at least a month. Between his duties as Master of Horse and his hard partying with Cytheris and their actor friends, he had made little time for her. He resolved to call on her the very next day.

'Dolabella is harmless,' said Antony. 'But he has some ambitions, like every young nobleman, and he is gaining in popularity with the masses, like Clodius and Curio did. It's to my benefit to keep him on my side. Besides, I like him.'

Cytheris closed his mouth, and Antony regretted shutting her down without exploring her opinion further. But before he could find a way to draw her back into the conversation, she kissed him again, and whispered an enticing suggestion in his ear, and he forgot all about Dolabella, Fulvia, Caesar and his duties.

Iunius DCCVII AUC (June 47 BC), Rome

The mid-morning sun beat down relentlessly, an exceptional heat for late spring. Antony had been awake for less than an hour, most of which time he had spent sitting on the latrine with his head in his hands. His slaves had quietly and respectfully washed him, combed and oiled his beard and hair, and helped him into his toga – it was too hot for his usual military uniform, though he still strapped on his sword. His servants were well used to his delicate state most mornings, and were remarkably skilled at preparing him for the day with the minimum of discomfort.

The previous night had been particularly raucous. The occasion had been the wedding of one of Cytheris' closest friends, the mime Hippias. It had been a wonderful feast, all the more so since Antony had generously subsidised the costs, with delicacies from all across the empire – exotic fruits, shellfish on ice, flamingo pasties, sow's udders – as well as the finest Falernian and Campanian wines. An army of dancing girls and boys, cymbal and flute players, mimes and acrobats had entertained the guests, who were largely drawn from the lower classes and had never experienced such luxury. The notable exception was Decimus Laberius, the witty equestrian, who had written a mime especially for the occasion, which was performed by Cytheris herself alongside Antony's friend Sergius, another mime. Antony could not recall a superior evening for sheer fun.

The festivities had still been going when Antony, feeling like a failure, had taken his leave after dawn. Cytheris had retired to the sumptuous town house he had purchased for her, and he had grabbed a couple of hours' sleep before being gently awoken and informed that a throng of people were requesting he come to the Forum for a hearing.

Now he was suffering. He had refused all food his slaves had proffered for breakfast, even the traditional deep-fried canary that was supposed to be a wonderful hangover cure, taking only a few sips of very well-watered wine. His head was throbbing as if a Gaul were smashing it with an axe, and his stomach was roiling as if he was on a storm-tossed ship. He knew that he was still very drunk, and he forced himself to concentrate on the words of the equestrian who stood before his gilded magistrate's throne in the Forum, declaiming in a loud but highly monotonous voice.

'And furthermore, Magistrate, there are some who say we should go beyond even Caesar's decision to remit all interest on debts incurred during the recent conflicts, and that we should forgive the capital on every debt. Can you imagine the chaos that would cause? You are aware, I'm sure, how many loans are secured against properties. If the debt is forgiven, who owns the property? It will bankrupt many respectable citizens, and then they will be in debt themselves. Where does it end?'

Antony leaned forward, opened his mouth, and vomited noisily into his lap. The folds of his toga caught most of the vomitus, but some of it splashed onto the ground and onto the shoes of the proclaiming equestrian, who jumped backwards with a cry of disgust.

Two of Antony's attendants stepped forward swiftly, using cloaks, hoods and scarves to mop up the chunky liquid and clean Antony's face. But by all the gods, that felt better.

Antony rose unsteadily to his feet, and spoke in a voice made hoarse by singing and laughing the night before. 'I apologise, but I seem to have been struck by an illness. I must take my leave.'

The queue of supplicants who had been awaiting their turn since before sunrise groaned and jeered. Antony waved a perfunctory apology and allowed himself to be assisted into his litter. His slaves pulled the curtains closed around him, and he sank back into the cushioned seats and allowed himself to be led back to his house.

Antonia greeted him coolly on his arrival, and he struggled for a moment to recall when he had last seen her. It had certainly been some days. He gave her a chaste kiss on the cheek. His daughter came running out of the garden, where she had been playing, and hugged him tight, almost making him vomit again.

'Daddy, will you come and play with my dolls?'

'Darling, your father is not feeling very well,' he said. 'Maybe later.'

The look of crushed disappointment on her face tugged at his heart, but he really needed a lie down, and he tousled her hair and dragged himself to his sleeping cubiculum. There he passed out, and remained in a dreamless sleep until dusk.

–

Antony was out and about the following day, dressed in his legate's uniform, gladius on one hip, pugio on the other. He was conscious that he should be feeling some embarrassment about his accident the previous day, but he was not one to dwell on it, nor to abase himself with humble apologies. Instead, he strode around the Forum, heard legal cases and gave an impromptu speech from the Rostra. He even found some time to attend a religious ceremony in his role as augur at the temple of Hercules, from whose son Anton the Antonius family claimed descent. Antony was perfectly happy to believe the truth of the assertion, given his own muscular physique.

Some wags teased him about the event, shouting sarcastic good wishes for his health as he passed, and even saying he should not be so mean with his money that he was eating spoiled meat. Antony took the ribbing with a good nature. Better to laugh about it than be angry, and he took heart that the common people were comfortable enough with him that they could behave in such a disrespectful manner. If they hated or feared him, they would not dare.

He spent the afternoon with little Toni, entertaining her with scary tales of mythical monsters, playing with her dolls, and engaging in some rough and tumble that had her shrieking in giggles. She was around five years of age now, and loved the attention from her father on the admittedly infrequent occasions she received it. It had taken her a short while to get over her initial fear of him, since he had become a near stranger to her during the almost two years since he had fled Rome to join Caesar. Though she was just a girl, he was genuinely fond of her – one of the few traits he had in common with Cicero, who doted on his Tullia, Dolabella's wife.

Antonia came to join them, sitting on a bench with her hands on her lap and an indulgent expression. Antony looked up at her and gave her a smile. She wasn't a bad sort really, he reflected. Pretty enough, inoffensive enough. Not for the first time, he wondered why he had so little real love for her. Maybe it was his fault. Maybe he was too negligent. He promised himself he would make more of an effort to spend time with his family, mother and daughter.

But not that day. He had an invitation to dine with Fulvia, a dear friend he feared he was also neglecting. Antonia didn't look particularly

Alex Gough

disappointed when he informed her he was dining elsewhere. Maybe she was used to it, or maybe she didn't care. It hurt his pride somewhat to consider that he, the great romantic, had a wife who didn't love him.

He was the only guest at Fulvia's house on the Palatine; she still lived in the home she had shared with Clodius. Cicero had moved back next door, having had the ground that Clodius had dedicated to Liberty deconsecrated, so he could rebuild the dwelling Clodius had had demolished during Cicero's exile. Antony had initially obstructed Cicero's return to Rome, partly because Caesar had forbidden any Pompeians not specifically forgiven from returning, and partly because he couldn't stand the man. In the end, Antony had relented and given in to his constant whining entreaties, though he had made it clear that he was making a singular exception to Caesar's edict in favour of Cicero, of whom Caesar was fond, emphasising to everyone that Cicero was renouncing his Pompeian ties by coming back to Rome.

He was shown to the peristylium, where Fulvia waited for him on one of two couches, the evening air cooler than the stifling heat of the day. She was wearing expensive but plain jewellery: gold necklace, silver rings and bracelets. Her fragrance was delicate, and her make-up light. Antony was suddenly conscious that he was overdressed: a purple and gold silk robe, every finger bearing a ring with a gemstone, a perfume that was eye-watering both in expense and physical effect. There was a twinkle of amusement in Fulvia's eyes when she rose to greet him, and when he embraced her and kissed her on both cheeks, she gave a little sneeze.

Antony grinned, abashed.

'I thought this was to be a larger affair. I didn't realise it was to be a little romantic dinner for two.'

Antony saw a sudden flash in Fulvia's eyes. Was it anger? Distress? As far as he knew, she had remained chaste, though nearly two years had passed since Curio's death, long beyond the prescribed ten-month period of mourning that was designed to ensure there was no doubt about paternity when the widow remarried.

He arranged himself on the couch, and allowed the slaves to serve him some simple plates – cheese, ham, bread and fruits, as well as some well-watered wine. He had to admit, his stomach appreciated the break from the rich and heavy food and drink he usually indulged in. It was testament to his energy that he hadn't put on any weight, still finding time to exercise with the soldiers on the Campus Martius most days.

'It's good to see you,' he said. 'How are you doing?'

'I'm well. I keep myself occupied with attending to running the household, weaving and spinning, attending to religious duties, writing letters, that sort of thing.'

Antony smiled. 'You may be a perfectly behaved noble widow, but I don't believe you are content taking on the role of a Cornelia.'

Cornelia was the daughter of the famous Scipio Africanus and mother of the demagogic tribunes Gaius and Tiberius Gracchus. She was a famously chaste and virtuous widow who supposedly kept herself out of her sons' politics, though who knows what strings she pulled behind closed doors.

Fulvia cocked her head to one side, and Antony noticed the fine line it made of her neck.

'Rumour has it that you spend a lot of time receiving Clodius' and Curio's clients.'

'My late husbands' followers are very generous in their attention to a poor widow like me.'

'I think you would have had my friends' ambitions if you had been born as one of our sex. I wonder what sort of a ruler of Rome you would make. A rabble-rouser, like Clodius? A conservative, like Cato or Cicero?'

Fulvia wrinkled her nose in distaste. 'Why not a great general, like Caesar?'

Now Antony laughed out loud. 'The legions would never be led by a woman. Nor, for that matter, would Rome.'

'And why not? It has happened before.'

'Not with any success.'

'Well, what about Caesar's new girlfriend, Cleopatra? She seems perfectly capable of commanding both a country and an army.'

Rome was buzzing with the gossip about Caesar and the Egyptian queen. It seemed that he had thoroughly fallen for her charms, for reasons Antony couldn't fathom.

'She did have the small matter of the most powerful man in the world to help her back onto the throne she lost to her brother-husband. I met her once, you know.'

'Yes, I know. You have told me before.'

'I'm not sure what has fascinated Caesar so much. She was an intelligent young thing, but not much to look at.'

'She has become a woman since then, I understand.'

'True. But I wish she would release Caesar from her embrace. Much as I enjoy being the supreme ruler of Rome and Italy, it does get a bit boring. Only today I heard the legions in Italy are grumbling about their rewards, and they have chased off the representatives I sent to negotiate with them. I'm going to have to travel south to see them in person. It's so tedious. I tell you, I'm ready to hand the reins back.'

'Don't be so unambitious,' snapped Fulvia, and Antony chuckled.

'See, there it is. The real Fulvia lurking such a tiny depth beneath the surface.'

She sat up, swinging her feet onto the floor, and leaned forwards, looking into Antony's face earnestly.

'Marcus, you need to understand, Caesar is not immortal. And the civil war is not yet won. Pompeius may be dead, but look who still opposes him – Scipio, Cato, Labienus, both of Pompeius' sons. They have vast resources and powerful allies. It is not a foregone conclusion that Caesar will ever return to Rome to enjoy the benefits of his victory. And even if he does, he is… what, fifty-two now? If an assassin's knife or a poisoned mushroom doesn't carry him away, age and illness one day will. You need to ensure that you are in a position of power when that day comes. If not, there will be many seeking vengeance on those associated with Caesar when he is no longer around to cow them.'

Antony leaned back, pursing his lips. He wasn't in the mood for a lecture on politics, and he found himself wishing he was spending the evening in the simple company of Cytheris. But Fulvia wasn't finished.

'And it isn't enough to assume you will inherit power from Caesar. Maybe he will name you as his heir, maybe he won't, but you need more than his legacy to be safe when he is gone. You need your own power base.'

Antony frowned. 'I have my clients…'

'Everyone has clients. But where you are patron to a few hundred important people, and to a number of small towns in Italy, Caesar is patron of whole countries, as was Pompeius when he lived. Nor do you have the wealth of Caesar or Pompeius – your spending power is due to your position allowing you to borrow heavily. If you lost your position, your creditors would demand repayment and you would be in exile in a month.'

Antony spread his hands. 'What would you have me do, Fulvia?' he asked in exasperation.

'There is another source of power in Rome, that doesn't depend on clients, or money, or even the army. Clodius showed Rome what could be achieved with the support of the common people. How far might he have gone, if it wasn't for that son of a whore, Milo? Curio, too, if he hadn't—'

She broke off, and Antony saw genuine emotion in her eyes. Given Curio's sexuality, his marriage to Fulvia had not been a conventional one, but she had managed to bear him a single son, now two years old – indisputably Curio's, both in looks and because Fulvia had been devoutly faithful to both her husbands – and Antony knew she had loved them both deeply.

He reached forward and squeezed her upper arm gently, and she laid her hand over his.

'What I'm saying, Marcus, is that you need to make moves to position yourself as the new Clodius. If you can bind the common people to you, it would give you a strength that would give even Caesar pause. And you need to do it before someone else does.'

'Someone else?'

'Dolabella.' And with that name, Fulvia's face grew dark. Antony looked into her eyes, puzzled.

'Dolabella is my friend. I know he has some ambition to be another Clodius – he even copied him with that whole patrician to plebeian adoption trick so he could become a tribune. But if he becomes popular and powerful, it will only enhance my position.'

'Dolabella is not your friend.' Fulvia looked down into her lap.

Antony put a finger under her chin and lifted it so she was looking into his face. Her eyes were wet with tears.

'Fulvia. What aren't you telling me?'

'I'm so sorry that it must be me to break this news. But it is better to come from me, rather than from an enemy wishing to taunt you.' She took a breath, straightened her back and said, 'Dolabella is carrying on an improper relationship with your wife.'

Antony went rigid. It was as if a bucket of cold water had been thrown over him, and he found it suddenly hard to breathe. A small part of him whispered, what does it matter? You don't love her. You have Cytheris. But that voice was swiftly drowned by the tsunami of rage that flooded over him. How dare she? How dare *he*? This was not about love, or faithfulness. It was entirely about injured pride and loss of face. Marcus Antonius, being cuckolded? And by a man he called 'friend', too. It would not stand.

He rose slowly to his feet, his nostrils flaring as he breathed heavily, the blood pounding in his temples.

'Marcus,' said Fulvia anxiously. 'You mustn't act impulsively.'

He didn't reply, simply staring at her, his fists clenching and unclenching. He realised suddenly that he hadn't attempted to deny the truth of her words. He knew there was no point. The attraction between Dolabella and Antonia was obvious, and besides, Fulvia would not lie to him.

'How did you find out?' he managed to say through gritted teeth.

Fulvia shook her head. 'Dolabella is hardly discreet. He is boasting openly to his friends that he is sleeping with the wife of the first man in Rome.'

'I'll kill him,' said Antony, and it was not an idle threat. At that moment he was prepared to march straight to wherever Dolabella was skulking and run him through. And he was immune from prosecution. He wheeled abruptly, calling for his sword, which he had unstrapped when he had entered Fulvia's house. Fulvia grabbed his arm.

'No, Marcus. Be smart. Think of what we have been talking about. Dolabella has been garnering the support of the people. If you murder him, you will lose them, and look how that worked out for Milo. You need to undermine him, make the mob turn against him. Once you have cut away his foundations, you can finish him.'

Antony took a deep breath and held it, then let it out slowly, partially restoring at least a semblance of calm.

'How will I do that?'

'There is a tribune who is opposing his debt reforms, correct?'

'Lucius Trebellius Fides. He has already tried to get me on side.'

'Then stay outwardly neutral in the argument, but secretly support Fides. Make sure Dolabella loses. Once he is out of favour with the people, you can step in and take his place.'

'Why would they change their loyalty to me, if I have not been actively supporting their cause?'

'I have an idea about that. But that is for another time.'

Antony looked at her quizzically, but another thought smashed into his awareness like a battering ram.

'Antonia,' he said, his voice little more than a whisper. 'What should I do with her?'

Fulvia put a hand to his face.

'You know what you must do, dear Marcus. Remember when Caesar said that his wife must be above suspicion? That applies just as much to your wife. It doesn't matter that neither Caesar nor you are faithful – no man cares about that. But your wife? The parentage of any children would be in question. And you would be a laughing stock. There is only one option.'

Antony swallowed. He knew Fulvia was right.

–

Fulvia had insisted Antony spend the night in one of her guest bedrooms. She knew him well, and if she had let him leave, he would most likely have indulged in a serious drinking spree that would have ended in him violently taking out his temper on someone, deserving or not.

So it was with a clear head that he made his way to his own house that morning. His slaves took his cloak and offered him food and wine, but he waved them away. Little Toni came running to see him as soon as she heard his voice, and he hugged her tight until she became fidgety and wriggled out of his grip.

His wife appeared, looking solemn and beautiful.

'Marcus, it's good to have you home. Are you staying?'

Antony gestured to his slaves. 'Leave us.' He knelt down to look into his daughter's eyes. 'Could you go and play in the peristylium. Your mother and I need to have a talk.'

'Yes, Father,' said Toni, and skipped away, her long, curly hair flapping behind her. Antony watched her go, feeling a solid lump in his throat that would not dissipate, no matter how hard he swallowed.

'Marcus,' said Antonia, when they were alone. 'What is it?'

'I'm divorcing you,' he said bluntly, without preamble. He had rehearsed the moment in his head over and over, and each time, it had given him a nasty vengeful thrill. Now, looking at her stricken face, watching her collapse backwards onto a bench, seeing the absolute dismay in her expression, he felt no pleasure. Even the thought of her and Dolabella together, in his own house, in his own bed, failed to raise his ire. Maybe he would have been more angry, if he had loved her better. But though he held her in no deep affection, neither had he ever had much antipathy towards her until he had found out about her infidelity. Watching a woman suffer was something he just couldn't abide, no matter what she had done. He wanted to step forward, to comfort her, to tell her not to worry, that everything would be fine.

But he imagined Fulvia standing beside him, snapping at him to be a man, to show he had a backbone. He remained where he was, stiff as a statue, keeping his face neutral, trying to show neither anger nor sorrow.

'Marcus,' she whispered. 'Why?'

Antony shook his head.

'You know very well why.'

Now Antonia lunged forward, grabbed his legs.

'Marcus, Marcus, please don't do this. Forgive me, I beg you. I never meant to hurt you. I was just so lonely.'

He looked down at her, requiring a force of will to stop himself placing his hand on her head and caressing her.

'I travel south on state matters this afternoon. I will be gone a few days. When I return, you will be gone from this house. Go back to your father on the isle of Kefalonia.'

'But, Marcus, what of our daughter?'

Antony looked up, and saw Toni peeping round the edge of the door, eyes wide. He stared at her, and for a moment he couldn't breathe. Traditionally, the children from a divorced marriage stayed with the father. Maybe he should keep her. She would be well looked after, would be given everything she needed, everything she desired.

Except her mother.

'You may take her with you,' he said. Then he pulled his leg sharply from Antonia's grasp, and strode from his house before they saw him break down into sobs.

Chapter X

Quintilis DCCVII AUC (July 47 BC), Camp of the Tenth Legion, south of Rome

The Ninth and Tenth legions had some legitimate complaints, in Antony's opinion. Caesar had sent them back to Italy with Antony, and Antony had settled them a little way out of the city. He sat in the *Principium* of the legionary camp of the Tenth, with a small group of senior centurions from both legions. He wore his military uniform, but was unarmed and unguarded. Despite the fact that the discontented legions had expelled Antony's envoys with threats of violence, he felt no fear at being in their midst without protection. He was Marcus Antonius, legate, and he had marched with them, eaten with them, slept beside them, and fought shoulder to shoulder with them.

And the centurions did indeed treat him with courtesy and respect. They gave him all the due of both his military rank and his position as Master of Horse; they saluted where appropriate and addressed him correctly. But they would not be moved on their demands.

This was his third day of negotiations. The air was hot and still, and he was becoming irritable. His latest offer of increased pension pay-offs on their discharge had been rejected again.

'Legate,' said the centurion who had been nominated as spokesman, 'you have to understand our position. We have served Caesar loyally for many years. Hundreds of us died fighting for him, and most of us bear scars from the battles. We were with him in Britannia, at Gergovia, at Alesia, at Pharsalus. And now we have been sent away to sit on our arses with nothing to do, while he takes an extended holiday in Egypt with that whore of a so-called queen.'

Antony narrowed his eyes.

'Be careful how you speak about Cleopatra,' he said. 'She is greatly favoured by Caesar. You wouldn't want word getting back to him of any disrespect.'

'I apologise, Legate. It's the frustration talking. But please realise, many of our number have served their allotted number of years, and are anxious for their discharge and the land grants that Caesar promised them. And the rest of us are still waiting for the bounties he swore would be ours. No offence, but what you have offered so far is a spit in the ocean compared to what we are owed.'

Antony sighed. The problem was that Caesar had left precious little in the treasury. Rome was in serious need of funds, and Antony had been doing his best to raise cash with taxation, fines, and confiscations of Pompeian properties. But Caesar had instructed him not to auction off the villas and townhouses until his return, and so the best Antony could do was to pay the legions their salaries and sprinkle donatives in their direction to attempt to keep them happy. His actions had staved off outright mutiny, but their demands had not gone away, and Antony couldn't blame them.

'Caesar will return soon and—'

'Legate, you are in charge in Italy in Caesar's absence. Why can't you settle our legitimate claims?'

'Centurion, I understand your position, but it isn't that simple.'

One of Antony's bodyguards, who had been waiting outside, entered.

'Apologies for the interruption, Magistrate. I have an urgent message from Rome.'

Antony held out his hand and looked at the scroll he was given. The seal was that of Lucius Caesar, his uncle, whom Antony had left in charge of the city while he was away. He opened the letter and read swiftly.

To Marcus Antonius, Master of Horse, from Lucius Caesar, Urban Praetor. Matters in Rome require your urgent attention and attendance. The Tribune Dolabella has proposed a bill of complete debt relief. He has argued with the Tribunes Asinius Pollio and Trebellius Fides in the Senate, and their rival supporters have clashed violently in the streets, which has sadly led to some fatalities. Fides and

Pollio have vetoed Dolabella's proposal, but in response he has gathered his supporters and barricaded himself in the Forum. Further, they have armed themselves, in direct contravention of your edict regarding the bearing of arms within the pomerium. The Senate has passed a senatus consultum ultimum authorising me to deal with him in whatever manner I deem necessary. But I regret to say that I lack sufficient men to dislodge him by force, and he refuses to listen to reason, or to negotiate in any way until the Senate has given in to his demands regarding debt.

I urge you to hurry back to Rome at your earliest convenience to assist me in this dangerous situation.

Antony let out a loud curse and threw the letter to the floor.

'What is it, Legate?' asked the centurion, concerned at Antony's outburst, despite the fact they were on opposite sides of the negotiating table.

'Problems in Rome,' said Antony bitterly. 'That flea-sized prick Dolabella is leading an uprising. I have to return to deal with it.' He fixed the centurion with an earnest stare. 'Listen, I hear your arguments and I sympathise. I will do what I can to ameliorate them, and intercede with Caesar when he returns, to get you what you deserve. But now I need something from you.'

The centurion frowned. 'What is that?'

'I have plenty enough loyal cohorts in the vicinity of Rome to deal with little Dolabella and his band of thugs and gladiators. But what I don't need is a full-scale mutiny behind me at the same time. Can I rely on you to make no moves, at least until Caesar returns?'

'And when might that be?'

'Honestly, I don't know. But he must return soon. Pompeius' successors are growing in strength, and if Caesar does not act, he will lose everything he has gained. And one thing we both know about Caesar – he is not foolish enough to let that happen.'

The centurion nodded. 'It's in no one's interests for Rome to be in anarchy, and there is no love for Dolabella among the legions. I will talk to the men and urge them to hold their grievances in check. But they won't be restrained for long. If Caesar's promises aren't honoured soon, by you, by Caesar, or by someone else, then I can't promise there won't be consequences.'

'I understand.' Antony rose and shook the centurion's hand firmly. 'Thank you. We will resume negotiations soon.'

Quintilis DCCVII AUC (July 47 BC), Rome

Antony descended on foot from the Capitoline hill, where he had left two cohorts of fully armed legionaries awaiting his commands. He wore full armour, pugio and scabbard on his hips, and he was accompanied by the twenty-four lictors allowed to a Dictator, all bearing their fasces wrapped around heavy axes.

The city was deserted, the shops shuttered, the temples locked. Even the Vestal Virgins had fled to the countryside.

Dolabella was waiting for him, standing on a pile of furniture so he could peer over the barricades his men had made out of wagons, shutters and pieces of masonry they had torn down. Antony looked up at him, not bothering to keep the sneer out of his expression. Even standing on such a height, he still seemed like a small man: thin-faced, skinny, completely lacking in stature compared to Antony.

'So, the chief magistrate deigns to bestow his presence upon us,' said Dolabella in a loud voice, allowing his followers to support him with sycophantic guffaws and jeers. 'You think your lictors are enough to dislodge us?'

'This has gone far enough,' said Antony. For all the pure hatred he felt towards this man he had called friend – whom he had supported and defended, and who had betrayed him in the worst way possible – he still wanted a peaceful solution to the stand-off. 'Come down. You know I have been behind you in your quest for debt reform.'

'We both know that has changed, Marcus.' The familiarity with which he used Antony's first name was completely inappropriate, but Antony did not rise to the bait. 'You may not have said so in public, but it is obvious you are putting your influence and money behind Fides and Pollio now. You are putting your personal feelings above the good of the Republic. Support me, and together we will rule Rome.'

'You seem to be forgetting that I already rule Rome. And I am doing you a courtesy by talking to you now.'

'Oh, a courtesy, is it? Nothing to do with the thousand or so armed men at my back.'

Antony did not even spare a glance for the hundreds of men behind Dolabella, brandishing clubs, axes and old swords.

'Tear down these barricades. Disperse your men. Come to speak before the Senate again. This city has had enough of anarchy and disorder, and I will not tolerate it.'

'*You* won't tolerate it. Our Master of Horse, Caesar's lackey, a man who has achieved nothing on his own merits. A man who can't even keep his own wife satisfied, so she has to look elsewhere for her pleasure.'

The men behind Dolabella roared their laughter and cried out their contempt for Antony. He stood, accepting it, the barricade preventing him from indulging in his deepest desire, which was to grab Dolabella and rip his arms and legs off with his bare hands. The words of Caesar after Pharsalus came to mind: 'They would have it so.' He took a breath, and said in as even a voice as he could manage, 'I've given you every chance, Dolabella. Beyond what you deserve.'

He turned on his heel and strode back up the Capitoline hill, his lictors hurrying to keep up, the catcalls and insults from Dolabella's thugs echoing behind him. He went straight to the senior centurion he had placed in command of the legionaries.

'Have your men fall in, and prepare to attack. They are lightly armed, but no doubt will have some stones and roof tiles, so approach in testudo formation to rip down the barricades. After that, let the men have their heads. Anyone opposing them, anyone holding a weapon – in fact, anyone behind the barriers in the Forum – is an enemy of Rome, and is to be treated as such, with no quarter.'

'Yes, Commander,' said the centurion without hesitation. He yelled out a series of commands which were picked up by the other ranks, and in moments the disciplined legionaries had formed up in full battle order. A trumpet blared, and they marched out, their hobnailed boots stomping on the cobbled streets in perfect unison, the sound of a thousand iron-shod feet echoing around the entire city. Antony followed close behind, mounted so he had a clear view of what was happening.

It was a trivial operation for men accustomed to assaulting hill forts in Gaul protected by ditches lined with stakes and ramparts bristling with archers and slingers. Although, as Antony had predicted, some pottery and bricks were hurled in the direction of the legionaries, they all bounced harmlessly off their raised shields. Under this protection, they swiftly tore down the barricades, using swords, axes, ropes tied to hooks, and even bare hands to smash or haul them apart. It took just moments for a way through to be cleared, but the senior centurion held his men in check until a wide enough gap had been made for an assault. Then he gave the command to attack, and with a roar, the legionaries charged against the civilians.

Some put up a respectable fight. There were gladiators and veterans among the protestors who knew how to handle a sword, and who had some bulk and fitness. But they were unarmoured, and fighting as individuals. The Roman army fought as a single unit, and it was as one unit that they pushed into the Forum, massacring everyone they encountered, whether they were standing to fight or turning to flee.

Antony dismounted and walked into the Forum behind the legionaries, stepping over bodies that numbered in the hundreds. Some were still moving weakly or crying for mercy and aid; most were still, exhibiting gaping wounds, entrails and amputations, with copious lakes of blood already beginning to congeal underfoot. A very few escaped, Dolabella among them. He was no fool, and Antony suspected he had known the outcome as soon as he had set eyes on the legionaries, and so had fled for his life.

The centurion approached Antony and saluted.

'Legate, we have some prisoners.' He indicated a group of men on their knees, hands bound behind them, guarded by a dozen legionaries who looked as if they had barely broken a sweat. 'What shall we do with them?'

Antony looked at the cowering, shaking men with contempt. He felt none of the mercy that was his usual characteristic in these situations.

'These men are traitors. And we have an old punishment for traitors in Rome, don't we?'

'Yes, sir, we do.'

'Very well, see it is carried out.'

Antony was determined to bear witness to the sentence he had imposed, and accompanied the centurion and the struggling prisoners as they were led up the Capitoline hill. Some of the prisoners were protesting their innocence; others were keeping quiet, waiting to see what their fate would be. As they were led to the south side of the hill, the realisation broke over them.

The Tarpeian rock had been used as a site for the punishment of treason since the time of the kings, five centuries before. It stood atop a steep cliff that towered about eighty feet above the rocky ground that bordered the street of the Yoke-Makers. It was such a byword for execution that anyone referring to 'The Rock' would be understood immediately.

Dolabella's thugs were as familiar with the place as any. They struggled, screamed, cried, wept. The battle-hardened legionaries, who had lived through years of death, pain and hardship in the field, had not the slightest compassion for these insurrectionists who had dared to attempt to take Rome from the hands of its rightful ruler – their beloved Antony, no less.

One by one, the prisoners were dragged to the top of the rock and, without ceremony or hesitation, thrust over the edge. Every single one let out a despairing scream that descended in volume before ending abruptly.

When they were all gone, Antony walked to the edge and peered over at the crumpled corpses far below.

A small doubt gnawed at him. Had he overreacted, because of his anger towards Dolabella? But he suppressed it. Caesar would not have tolerated this uprising, and would surely have responded in the same way.

Antony looked back down to the Forum, far below and behind him. The legionaries had already started the work of clearing the bodies, hauling them into carts to be returned to their families or buried in a mass grave outside the city.

'They would have it so,' whispered Antony. The wind swirled around the heights, carrying his words away.

September DCCVII AUC (September 47 BC), Rome

Antony was woken by a gentle knocking at his bedroom door. He opened his eyes, blinked at the bright light flooding in from the window that faced into the peristylium, then closed them again and rolled over. The knocking came again, more insistent. He tried to ignore it, but Cytheris shook his shoulder.

'Marcus, I don't think they are going away until you answer.'

He groaned and sat up, grasping his head in both hands and squeezing in a vain attempt to relieve the throbbing headache. Cytheris cuddled up next to him, her naked body close to his, and laid her head on his shoulder.

As soon as Antonia had vacated Antony's house and returned in disgrace to her father, Antony had moved Cytheris in. Previously, he had given her use of a nice town house on the Esquiline, but Antony's home was on another level of space and luxury. That said, it was far from the most expensive house in Rome, and soon after the news of Pompey's death arrived, Antony was eyeing up his vast suburban villa that was now lying vacant except for a staff of slaves that maintained it.

'Enter.' His voice was hoarse. He seemed to remember he had been singing a lot the night before. And his cheek felt swollen and bruised. Hadn't there been some sort of wrestling match?

The servant entered sheepishly, and averted his eyes from Cytheris' nudity.

'Master, a letter.'

Antony clucked his tongue in irritation.

'I receive many letters. Why are you disturbing me with this?'

'It's from Caesar, Master.'

That woke Antony up abruptly. Caesar's letters were infrequent – just often enough to keep Antony informed of his movements, though little of his plans. Antony knew, for example, both from Caesar and other connections in Caesar's camp, such as Hirtius and Calvinus, all about the crisis he had weathered in Alexandria. At the time Caesar had arrived in Alexandria, Ptolemy XIII was in charge in the city, but his sister-wife Cleopatra VII was with her army in Pelusium. When Caesar announced he was going to arbitrate in the conflict between them, Cleopatra, now twenty-one years of age, smuggled herself into his presence, and soon she was his mistress – much to Antony's surprise, still remembering the spotty, unattractive youth he had met years before – and partner, with Ptolemy placed under arrest and held prisoner in the palace, along with Cleopatra's younger sister Arsinoë and their youngest brother, another Ptolemy.

The Egyptians rebelled, and Caesar was besieged, badly outnumbered, lacking in fresh water, his ships blockaded by the Egyptian fleet. Arsinoë escaped and appointed her tutor to lead the army against Alexandria. Caesar led a surprise attack on the blockading Egyptian fleet and burnt a large number of their ships. This enabled the Thirty-Seventh Legion to land and greatly augment Caesar's strength. Caesar released Ptolemy after hearing pleas for peace from an Alexandrian deputation, but the fourteen-year-old, who had promised to bring the war to an end, promptly joined his sister Arsinoë and continued the conflict.

Several skirmishes and battles took place, including one in which Caesar and his men were cut off while they were on the long causeway to Pharos island called the Heptastadion, and had to swim to safety. Further reinforcements now arrived from Caesar's allies, including Antipater, Antony's old comrade from his own time in Egypt.

The matter was ended towards the end of March in the Battle of the Nile, in which a combined army of Caesar and Cleopatra crushed the Egyptians. Arsinoë was taken prisoner, and Ptolemy drowned trying to flee across the Nile. Cleopatra assumed the Egyptian throne, although she took her youngest brother, now Ptolemy XIV, as her husband and co-ruler.

After this battle, Antony heard nothing from Caesar for some time, though Hirtius wrote and informed him that Caesar had embarked on a lengthy and luxurious cruise down the Nile accompanied by Cleopatra, most of the army and four hundred ships. No reason was given for this excursion, and though there may have been a political angle to showing the country its new ruler and the support she enjoyed, it seemed that even Caesar needed a holiday sometimes.

But Caesar's break was disturbed by the news that Pharnaces, son and deposer of Mithridates the Great, the king who had been so troublesome to Rome over so many years, had rebelled, defeated Gnaeus Domitius Calvinus, and overrun a large part of Asia. The last Hirtius had heard was that Caesar was on his way to Asia via Judaea, with the Sixth Legion and Jewish allies led by Antipater.

Antony ripped open the letter and scanned it quickly. It was written in the hand of a scribe, but the style was unmistakably Caesar's.

> ante diem iii Nonas Sextilis anno DCCV ab urbe condita,
> Pontus
> To Marcus Antonius, Magister Equitum
> From Gaius Julius Caesar, Dictator

Greetings. I write to inform you of another victory. On hearing of the revolt of Pharnaces, I led my men and allies over land. Leaving Sextus Julius Caesar as governor of Syria, I sailed to Tarsus, where, incidentally, due to the intercession of Marcus Junius Brutus, I forgave Gaius Cassius for his opposition to me. With my legions, the legions of Calvinus and my Jewish allies, I met Pharnaces at a place called Zela.

I came, I saw, I conquered.

I shall return to Rome in October.

Farewell.

Antony read through the letter twice more. Though the brevity told him nothing of Caesar's mood, it was typical of his style.

'Marcus,' said Cytheris. 'What is it?'

'Caesar – he's on his way.'

Cytheris looked deep into his eyes, as if she was trying to read his thoughts.

'What does that mean? For you?'

Antony swallowed, a lump of anxiety suddenly materialising in the pit of his stomach.

'I don't know.'

October DCCVII AUC (October 47 BC), Rome

Caesar had received Antony with a cool politeness that concerned him, after all their time apart. Antony had given an extensive report of his official activities in Rome since he had arrived after Pharsalus, and though he had, of course, tried to cast his actions in their best light, he made sure to include both the good and the bad. He had watched Caesar's face for any reaction as he described his attack on Dolabella's thugs in the Forum, and the concerns of the restless legions in Capua. Caesar remained impassive, and Antony presumed he had already heard many others give their own versions of these events, as well as Antony's performance as Master of Horse. Cicero was back in Caesar's favour, and Antony doubted that old worm had anything good to say about him.

At the end of their meeting, Caesar had thanked him for his service, and dismissed him with a wave of his hand, picking up a scroll from a pile of letters and beginning to read before Antony had even left. He had wandered back home and spent the afternoon with Cytheris, feeling useless and unnecessary now Caesar was back in charge.

A few days later, Caesar had authorised the auction of the bulk of the confiscated Pompeian assets in Rome and Italy, in order to raise funds for the continuation of the war against the Pompeian holdouts. Antony had attended, and joined in eagerly. The glut of property suddenly appearing on the market depressed prices, but when Pompey's estates came up for sale, there were none in Rome who could afford them, valued as they were at around two hundred million sestertii. Antony himself still owed tens of millions of sestertii to various creditors, but nevertheless decided he would put in a bid. None opposed him, and so he gained ownership of all of Pompey's sumptuous estates for a knockdown price. Not that he had any intention of paying for it. He was Mark Antony, Master of Horse, Caesar's right-hand man. Who would be foolish enough to call in a debt on him?

Then news came through that the legions in Italy had finally run out of patience, and were marching north towards Rome to make their demands of Caesar in person. He rode out to meet them, and listened to their demands for him to honour his promises, and to allow them to retire – likely a bluff, because most of them were still keen to take part in further campaigns and accrue the rewards that came from them. Caesar spoke to them in a measured tone, shocking them by addressing them as citizens rather than soldiers, renewing his promises to reward them and casually acceding to their demand to be disbanded. Quickly the mood changed, and before long the legions were demanding to be reinstated and included in his upcoming campaign. Caesar reluctantly accepted, with the noted exception of his beloved Tenth, whom he was discharging because of their ingratitude. They actually went as far as begging to be decimated for their disobedience, as long as he would take them back. Caesar graciously let himself be persuaded, and announced there would be no executions. And just as easily as he had swept aside Pharnaces, he re-established the loyalty of the legions.

Antony was by his side at the next meeting of the Senate. His reception by the overwhelmingly pro-Caesarian senators was deafening, and it was some time before enough order was restored for Caesar to speak. He thanked them for their loyalty and steadfastness in his absence, and publicly acknowledged his appreciation of Antony for his service, which was received with only a polite smattering of applause.

'Now I have some announcements to make. Soon, though it pains me, I must depart, to continue the fight against those misguided senators who still continue stubbornly in their opposition to me. But the crisis that confronted the Republic is much lessened since our victory over the conservative forces, and with the sad demise of my friend Pompeius. I therefore tell you that today I am laying down my position as Dictator.'

Antony stiffened. Caesar hadn't warned him of this. With no Dictator, there was no Master of Horse. So what did that make Antony?

'My last act as Dictator will be to establish the magistracies going forward. Though there are only two months left, I will appoint as consuls for this year two men who have served me loyally as legates.'

Antony looked up hopefully.

'Quintus Fufius Calenus and Publius Vatinius are therefore appointed as consuls for this year.'

Well, thought Antony, it was just an honorary position for some of Caesar's more minor servants. They had no real power to do anything in the time left to them. Next year's magistrates would be much more important.

Caesar named ten praetors instead of the usual eight – all rewards for strong supporters – and then came to the matter of the consulship for the following year.

'I will take one of the positions of consul for myself, since I need the authority to conclude the war. For my co-consul I will take...'

Antony prepared to stand and shake Caesar's hand, and receive the acclamation of the Senate.

'Marcus Aemilius Lepidus.'

–

'How dare you do this to me?' Antony spat. They were alone in Caesar's private office. 'After all I have done for you?'

'Marcus, you have been loyal, but you are not the only person who has served me loyally,' said Caesar calmly. 'I must be even-handed, and reward others, too.'

'Yes, but you have given me nothing. Nothing!' Antony was shouting now, and Caesar's brows came together in a frown.

'Remember who you are talking to, Marcus.'

Antony tried to repress his anger, but it was too much.

'Who supported you in the Senate when they tried to strip you of your command? Who put his life in danger opposing the Republicans in your name? Who fought alongside you in Britannia and Alesia? Who relieved you at Dyrrhachium, and commanded a wing for you at Pharsalus? Who ruled Rome in your absence to the best of his ability, though the economy was shattered and the troops and populace were mutinous, while you took holidays on the Nile with your new lover! Me! I did all those things! And this is how you reward me?'

'Marcus Antonius, be quiet!' snapped Caesar, his voice not loud but firm, and brooking no argument. Antony closed his mouth, breathing hard, flaring his nostrils like an angry racehorse.

'It is true you have been of service to me. But your conduct in my absence has been less than praiseworthy. I desired of you to be my representative here, to act as a model ruler, who would give neither the Senate nor the people reason to fear my return.

'And what do you do? You parade around the city with your whore, Eutrapelus' freedwoman—'

'She isn't—'

'Do not interrupt me again, Antonius, or I swear I will have you strangled in the Tullianum, like your stepfather!'

If Caesar was trying to provoke Antony, he had succeeded beyond measure. First he'd slandered his beloved Cytheris, then his stepfather. Antony's fists opened and closed and Caesar watched his eyes calculatingly, waiting to see if he would strike him. Antony knew it would mean death to lay a hand on the Dictator, but it still took every ounce of his willpower to prevent him lunging and grabbing the skinny older man around the neck and choking an apology from him.

When Caesar was sure Antony had mastered himself, he continued.

'You parade around with your *whore*,' he said, emphasising the word this time. 'You gamble and drink with the dregs of society.'

Antony thought how ironic it was that Caesar positioned himself as a man of the people, when, as a patrician and a descendant of Venus herself, he held them in such contempt.

'You are unable to perform your public duties without vomiting. You show disrespect to the senators and equestrians whose goodwill we need. And you even set the army on the common people who were protesting in favour of debt reform – a subject I addressed the last time I was in Rome, I might remind you.'

'May I speak, Caesar?'

Caesar considered, then waved a hand in assent.

'Your measures regarding debt were neither one thing nor another, pleasing neither debtors nor creditors. I inherited an economy in complete disarray. But I had no authority to support a general cancellation of debt, much as it might have benefitted me personally. As for the rioters, I was authorised by a senatorial decree to put them down. Would you have tolerated such insurrection yourself?'

'I would not. But I would not have had to resort to such violence to end the matter. Which brings me to your handling of the mutiny by the Italian legions.'

'I kept them in check until your return. It was you who made them impossible promises – promises I see you have still not fulfilled.'

Now it was Caesar's turn to appear angry, his face darkening ominously, but Antony did not quail. Caesar may have been the most formidable, the strongest, the most capable man he had ever met, but Antony refused to fear him.

'They just needed a few words from me, and they are loyal once more. You, who boast of being loved by the legions, could not even manage that.'

'You only recovered their loyalty because they believe that as you are Rome's ruler, you have funds and campaigns to reward them that are not available to me.'

Caesar clearly did not like to hear this, but to argue against Antony's position could sound whiny, so he did not respond. He looked away, lost in thought for a moment. Then he looked back, and his features had softened.

'Listen, Marcus. It is true you have been a faithful ally. I might even count you a friend, if I believed I had friends. I gave you a difficult task, and though you have performed it less well than I'd hoped, Rome is still standing, and you are still loyal to me.

'I cannot give you rewards for your term as Master of the Horse, nor show you favour at this time. Neither the Senate nor the people would stand for it. But neither have I any wish to cast you aside. You may yet be of great aid to me, and I would be foolish to so casually discard someone who has proven so brave and loyal.

'I travel soon to Africa, to confront the optimates. You will stay behind, with no official office. While I am gone, I want you to mend your ways. Show me, show the Senate, show the people, that you are a man of substance, who can be trusted to hold positions of power and responsibility.'

'How am I to do that?'

'That is not for me to say, Marcus. Maybe your mother is best placed to offer you wisdom in this respect.'

The last person Antony wanted to talk to about his fall from grace and his dissolute lifestyle was his noble, upright, disapproving mother.

'And what will Dolabella's punishment be?'

'I see no need for punishment. I will take him to Africa to fight with me, so he is no danger in my absence.'

'But—'

'I am giving you a chance, Marcus. I strongly recommend you take it.'

Antony bit his lip. He knew that further discussion was futile. Caesar was not one for changing his mind without good reason, and Antony could think of no argument that would help.

'I will do my best, Caesar.'

'Glad to hear it. Oh, and Marcus, make sure you pay what you owe for Pompeius' villa. It is not appropriate that such a great man's possessions should be given away on the cheap.'

Antony nodded, thinking how impossible that would be. He walked out of Caesar's office, past guards who were standing straight as pila, fixed expressions trying in vain to appear as if they had heard nothing, and wondered who he could turn to for advice.

–

'I mean, who even is Marcus Aemilius Lepidus?' raged Antony. 'He is a nobody. A nothing.'

He had managed to work himself up again, recounting the conversation to Fulvia. She sat on a bench in the peristylium, listening without comment as he strode up and down, gesticulating wildly and occasionally thumping his fist into his palm, punching a pillar or kicking a statue.

When the storm of his anger had dissipated, Fulvia spoke up.

'When you came here tonight, you said you wanted my advice. Was it rather that you just needed someone to shout at?'

Antony slumped down on a couch, and ordered one of Fulvia's slaves to bring him wine.

'Make sure you water it well,' added Fulvia, and Antony glared at her. 'Let's start as we mean to go on, shall we?'

'What are you talking about?'

'Caesar wants you to mend your ways. That starts with moderating your way of living.'

'Are you serious? You want me to give up wine?'

'Of course not. I said moderate, not forgo. But there are other changes you could make that would please Caesar and the Senate.'

'Such as?'

'Stop chasing after their wives, for one.'

'I hardly ever do that these days. What else?'

'Stop associating with people they consider undesirable. Even the common free man on the street does not approve of consorting with actors and musicians.'

'Abandon my friends and my social life,' said Antony bitterly. 'Got it. What else?'

'Marry well.'

Antony looked at her sharply.

'Marry? Again? No chance. It was Caesar's idea that I marry Antonia, and look what that got me.'

'Respectability and a beautiful daughter.'

'But not love. And ultimately just shame and betrayal.'

'Then marry someone you care for.'

'You just said I had to stop consorting with actors and musicians. Besides, I cannot legally marry Cytheris – her profession prohibits her from marriage.'

'Is Cytheris really the only woman you have feelings for?'

'Of course,' said Antony. 'Apart from my mother, the only other woman I love is…'

He stopped. Fulvia was looking at him oddly, her face half hopeful, half anxious, as if she was ready to have her dreams fulfilled – or her worst fears realised.

'You.'

She smiled, a shy smile, embarrassed almost, so uncharacteristic of this strong, self-assured woman.

'But... W-we can't,' stuttered Antony. 'I mean. Could we?'

'Name me a single impediment.'

Antony ran through them in his mind. There was no legal reason they could not be wed. She was long past her period of mourning. Antony was divorced. She was of an appropriate rank.

'There are none,' he said.

'Then let me list you some advantages,' she said. 'I am fertile, and young enough to bear you more children. I am from a noble family. The Fulvii number many senators and consuls in their ancestors, and the patrician Sempronia *gens* of my mother needs no one to speak on behalf of its nobility and distinguished past. I am wealthy. I have inherited the powerful clientele of both Clodius and Curio, and they remain loyal to me personally, not least because of the children I bore them. Furthermore...'

Antony stepped forward, grabbed her by the shoulders and silenced her with a long, slow kiss. It was strange, a distant part of his mind considered, that he had known her and loved her for so very long, and yet this was the first kiss they had shared.

They held each other for a long time afterwards, close together in the glow of their embrace, silently willing the moment to last forever – this instant of acknowledgement of a love that was both new as a fresh-born foal, struggling to stand on its wobbly legs, and yet that felt as if it had been eternal.

Eventually they separated, and Fulvia looked down, unable to keep the broad grin from her face.

'You know, together, we will be a force to be reckoned with,' said Antony.

'I already was,' said Fulvia. 'You're just an added bonus.'

He laughed and they kissed again. Then she grew serious.

'We should start making arrangements for the ceremony as soon as possible. You must speak to your mother, though, before we make any announcements. And there is one other person you need to talk to.'

A sudden shock of realisation hit Antony, as if someone had thrown a bucket of water over his head. His face fell. Fulvia took his hand.

'I'm sorry, Marcus. But it is necessary.'

—

To Antony's relief, Cytheris was dignified in her response to the news. Maybe she had not expected to be treated any differently, given her position in society. When she was a slave, she had been used to being passed around from man to man with no say in who got to keep her company, to dine with her, dance with her, and slake his lusts on her body. When she became a freedwoman, her profession as mime meant she kept her position as infamis, unable to testify in court, subject to corporal punishment, forbidden from marrying a freeborn citizen. Maybe she had just expected that Antony would get bored with her and move on.

But that was not the case. Clumsily, Antony tried to assure her that his feelings had been genuine.

'I did not lie to you, Cytheris. I did love you. I love you still. But Caesar has made his position clear. I must renounce what he considers my hedonistic ways.'

'And I am just part of your hedonism,' said Cytheris flatly. 'I do understand, Marcus. You are a powerful man. You have hit a setback in your career and you must make sacrifices to continue to move upwards, to regain the respect of respectable people.'

Antony wanted to contradict her, but he could not. She was right. He was sacrificing her for his ambition. He could renounce any further participation in politics. He could step off the *cursus honorum*. He could spend the rest of his life drinking, having fun, making love to Cytheris.

But it wasn't enough. He wanted to show his worth – to Caesar, to the world.

To Fulvia.

'I am sorry, Cytheris. I will make sure you are properly taken care of. You will not want for anything.'

'Don't worry about me, Antonius. I used to be a slave. I have experienced far worse in my life than to be no longer required as a rich man's toy.'

Antony sighed.

'Stay here as long as you need, until you find somewhere to your liking. I will move in with my mother for the time being.'

He left her there in his atrium, so beautiful, so sensual, so much more than what the world thought of her, so much more than she thought of herself. He would miss her, so dreadfully. But worse, he knew his actions that day just reinforced her lowly self-opinion. And for all the power he had possessed, that he hoped in time to regain, and more, he felt completely unable to help her realise how wonderful she was, and he cursed the world, and his own failings, that made it so.

Chapter XI

The traditional Roman wedding was full of violent symbolism. The custom was for the bride to display fear and reluctance at the union, the implication being that she had been stolen from her family like the Sabine women. She was supposed to be torn from the hands of her mother or a close relative. She was supposed to lament on her way to the bridegroom's house, and her cries of pain at the loss of her virginity were supposed to echo from the bedchamber for all to hear.

Fulvia would have none of that. Though these rituals and behaviours were expected even when a woman was taking her third husband, she declared the whole thing to be nonsense.

'I have three children,' she said to Antony. 'Do you really expect me to play the virgin?'

Antony didn't have any strong opinions on the subject. This was also his third marriage, and he did not feel he was missing out on anything by skipping some of the more distasteful aspects of the ceremony. Still, much as this was a joining of two people who had cared for each other for a long time, it was also a political union. He wanted to ensure it was seen to be as traditional and legitimate as possible, to avoid any suggestions of impropriety, or disrespect to the *mos maiorum*, the customs of the ancestors. So he had insisted he perform the auguries to make sure the event was auspicious, that all the wedding guests wear the same clothes so the evil spirits could not identify the wedding couple, that Fulvia's veil was made from a garment worn by the *flaminica dialis*, the wife of the high priest of Jupiter. He ensured that she wore a tunic that she had woven herself – which had evoked some grumbling from Fulvia, who had little time for the traditional roles expected of a good Roman matron – and that her hair was dressed with the *hasta caelibaris*, a bent iron spear covered in flowers. When he had reminded her that this showed the dominance of the groom over the bride, she had just raised an eyebrow, which was enough to let him know her thoughts on that matter.

Then the party began.

It was a much more measured affair than Antony had become used to. As tradition dictated, the wedding party took place at the house of the bride's family. This was, in fact, the house Fulvia had shared with Clodius and then with Curio, since her father had died many years before, and her elderly mother Sempronia lived with her.

Fulvia kept an eye on how often Antony's wine cup was refilled, and the music and the dancing was less Bacchanalian than at the get-togethers of Antony's actor friends. The guests were largely drawn from the upper echelons of society – those of senatorial and equestrian rank – including, of course, as many of Antony's and Fulvia's relations, close or distant, as were in Rome at the time. Antony still managed to sneak in a couple of his less reputable friends, such as Sergius, the actor, and others who dabbled on the edges of disrespectability, as well as Eutrapelus, Cytheris' former master, and Decimus Laberius, the author of mimes of dubious artistic and cultural merit. Fulvia had not exactly approved of these additions to the guest list, but had not vetoed them, which had pleased Antony.

At one moment during the festivities, he had managed to talk to Sergius alone.

'How is Cytheris?' he asked in a low voice.

'You want the truth, Marcus?'

Antony wondered if he really did. Maybe a bland reassurance was all he was looking for. He mentally braced himself.

'I do.'

'She is distraught. I know she was calm and collected when you broke the news to her, but she has barely stopped crying since. She really loved you, you know.'

'And I loved her, too, friend. I still do. But...' He spread his hands and looked around.

Sergius nodded. 'You did what you had to. I understand. I think she does, too, really. It just doesn't make it easier.'

Fulvia appeared at his side.

'Are you attempting to turn my husband back to his old ways, Sergius?' she said, but there was a twinkle in her eye.

Sergius bowed. 'I have tried, mistress, but in vain. He is a changed man now, with the morals of Cato.'

'Gods, please don't wish that on me. I would rather be wed to a drunken philanderer than that prig.'

Sergius laughed and took his leave. Fulvia linked her arm through her husband's and put her head on his shoulder.

'Are you happy, Marcus?'

Antony stroked her hand affectionately.

'Yes,' he said. 'I really am.'

She sighed in contentment. 'So am I.'

The evening continued, and Antony had to admit that remaining in possession of his faculties allowed him to take pleasure in the more refined aspects of the event – poetry readings, dances and conversation with a variety of well-educated men and women. Not that there weren't also plenty of complete bores, simpering idiots and fake well-wishers trying to get advancement, even though it was public knowledge that he was currently out of favour. He had had to fend off a number of questions, subtle and not so subtle, about the reasons for his falling-out with Caesar. But he had no desire to discuss it, especially at his wedding.

Darkness fell, and the time came for the wedding procession. Antony went ahead to await Fulvia's arrival. She was escorted in a torchlit procession to the house on the Campus Martius, just west of the Capitoline hill, that had once belonged to Pompey, and Antony picked her up and carried her over the threshold. In the vestibule he set her back down and kissed her, to a huge cheer from the onlooking well-wishers. Then he pointedly closed the doors on them, and led her inside.

Antony had owned the house for a couple of months now, but he had not yet taken up residence, although he had previously toured the vast mansion in amazement. This was Fulvia's first visit to their new matrimonial home, and he was childishly excited to show her around. The house was situated within a vast estate that extended as far as Pompey's stone theatre, where the Senate met from time to time. The overall style was luxurious, but not to the point of bad taste.

They walked through the enormous vestibule, the far wall of which was decorated with the prows of ships that Pompey had captured in his successful campaigns against the pirates twenty years before. They were a painful reminder of the failure of Antony's own father against those same enemies, but Antony was not going to let that spoil his mood.

They continued through into the atrium and then around a sample of some of the wondrously decorated rooms. With the purchase of the house had come intricate tapestries, tasteful statues in brightly painted marble, and an extensive silver dining service.

'The wine cellar is intact, too,' said Antony. 'That in itself is worth the price I paid.'

'Paid?' said Fulvia.

'Fine – bid.' He didn't want to be reminded of the sum, cheap as it was, that Caesar had demanded he find to settle the auctioneer's bill.

They stood in one of the *triclinia* and looked around at the frescoes.

'How did Pompeius bring himself to dine in such a modest home?' said Antony, and Fulvia laughed.

'It's truly amazing,' she said. 'And this is where we live now?'

'It is.'

Fulvia nodded.

'We have been blessed, Marcus. What an opportunity we have, if we can just seize it. With your charisma and military prowess, and my clients, and let's not forget, my good sense, we have the potential to be the most formidable couple that Rome has ever known.'

Antony smiled at her indulgently. Thoughts of power and politics were far from his mind at that moment. He snaked an arm around her waist, pulled her close and kissed her gently.

'I think it's time I showed you the bedroom.'

ante diem xi Kalendas Octobres DCCVIII AUC (21 September 46 BC), Rome

Caesar returned to Rome towards the end of the month of Quintilis, after a successful campaign in Africa. News of his victory at the Battle of Thapsus in April had arrived in the city by May, and it seemed that his luck had once again held. The optimates were nominally commanded by Scipio, although Labienus was the real tactical genius responsible for the battle plans. They were also reinforced by King Juba of Numidia, who had been instrumental in the death of Curio, Antony's best friend and Fulvia's husband. Not only had Caesar been outnumbered, but he was also opposed by sixty war elephants, capable of destroying a front line and swinging a battle.

But many centuries had passed since Hannibal horrified Rome by bringing his elephants over the Alps. Tactics to deal with the enormous beasts had been refined over the years, so when Scipio's elephants on the right flank attacked, Caesar's archers targeted them, sending them fleeing back into their own lines and causing chaos. On the left flank, Caesar's legionaries simply stood aside to allow the elephants through, straight into an ambush of trained spearmen, who stabbed at their eyes and frightened them with trumpets. They, too, fled into their own men, turning the battle in Caesar's favour.

Scipio, Juba and Labienus survived the battle and fled, but Juba was killed and Scipio committed suicide after losing a naval battle. Cato had been stationed at Utica, and as the victorious Caesar advanced on his position, he, too, chose to kill himself, but his death was typical of the man in its melodrama. Having dismissed his family, friends and servants, he stabbed himself in the abdomen with a sword. However, as someone quite unused to battle, his blow was too feeble, and when his servants heard his cry, they rushed in to find him still alive, his guts exposed but intact. A surgeon sewed him shut, but when he recovered consciousness, he ripped apart the wound and tore at his entrails to ensure his death. Caesar's reaction to this was largely irritation that he did not have the pleasure of forgiving the proud man.

The Senate voted a ridiculous forty days of public holidays in Caesar's honour, consisting of public banquets, wild beast hunts and gladiatorial and athletic contests. Criminals were forced to fight to the death in staged re-creations of battles, and part of the Campus Martius was turned into an extensive lake to stage a mock naval engagement. Hundreds of lions and giraffes imported from Africa were slaughtered in public shows dedicated to the memory of Julia, Caesar's daughter and Pompey's wife. The recently completed Forum of Julius Caesar and Temple of Venus Genetrix were dedicated in formal ceremonies.

More importantly, Caesar was granted the position of Dictator for an unimaginable ten-year period, without any serious opposition. And possibly most importantly of all for his pride, the Senate allowed him to celebrate four triumphs. It was not proper to show pride in the defeat of fellow Romans, but Caesar was able to claim that he had defeated foreign foes, even in his civil war battles, because of the barbarian allies who had aided the optimates. Therefore, he prepared to celebrate triumphs over Gaul, Egypt, Asia and Africa.

Antony had no formal part to play in the triumphs beyond his positions as a senator and an augur, despite his key role in two of the campaigns. Still out of power and out of favour, he had spent the last few months morosely considering how to revive his fortunes, with Fulvia alternating skilfully between sympathy and gentle chiding to keep him out of the worst depths of depression and prevent him returning to his old ways. Her announcement that she was pregnant earlier in the year had temporarily buoyed him, and he had celebrated with a now rare bout of drinking and parties, but with the hangover had returned the despondency that accompanied his reduced position and influence. Nevertheless, his priesthood and rank allowed him a prime view of the proceedings, and he watched, awed despite his simmering resentment at being left out, at the staggering display that Caesar had arranged.

The first triumph – over Gaul – set the tone for the rest. The Senate had allowed Caesar an extraordinary number of lictors: seventy-two preceded his chariot, which was drawn by a team of white horses. The procession of legionaries, prisoners in chains, Vercingetorix – who by then had been imprisoned for five years – most prominent among them, all the spoils of war that could be displayed, and soldiers carrying banners and posters illustrating famous quotes and battle scenes, assembled in the Campus Martius and entered Rome through the Triumphal gate. The streets were tightly packed with revellers; all of the city was in attendance to enjoy the spectacle and to benefit from the traditional largesse, be it cash gifts or lavish banquets. They were not disappointed when Caesar announced that each one of them would receive one hundred denarii, donations of oil and corn, and a fine open-air banquet serving the best quality food and Falernian wine. It was baking hot, but Caesar had arranged for silk awnings to shade the crowds from the sun.

Everything seemed perfect until shortly after the start of the procession, when the axle of Caesar's chariot broke just as he passed the Temple of Fortuna – a terrible sign of ill omen. A replacement was quickly found, and Caesar propitiated the bad luck by, at the end of the route, climbing the steps to the Temple of Jupiter Optimus Maximus on his knees, where he set his laurel wreath on the altar.

Vercingetorix was then strangled, the executioner garrotting him from behind. Antony watched the death of the proud Gallic chieftain, as he kicked his legs, grasping the cord around his neck, with awe and some pity. It was a sad end, but an emphatic statement of Caesar's complete domination of the land of Gaul.

The other three triumphs followed a similar pattern. They took place with a gap of a couple of days between each, to allow the streets to be swept and preparations begun anew, so the full set of parades were strung out over ten days. Fulvia became restless during the second triumph, and since she was heavily pregnant by then, she could plausibly excuse herself from the last two on grounds of her health, though Antony suspected it was mainly boredom, since her expectant state did not seem to have slowed her in the slightest. Antony himself had to concede that the whole thing was becoming a bit repetitive, but he was duty-bound to attend every moment, and Caesar had done a good job of keeping as much variety as possible in the entertainment to stop boredom setting in.

Generally the crowds adored almost every moment, and they adored Caesar for his generosity and god-like power. But certain aspects were not so well received, and Antony wondered at Caesar's judgement for including them. They loved the paintings of the Pontic king Pharnaces fleeing from battle, and roared with laughter at the placard reading simply, 'Veni, Vidi, Vici', but showed their disapproval at gory depictions of the suicides of the Romans, Cato and Scipio, by falling completely silent. They were unhappy, too, at the pitiful sights of Cleopatra's fifteen-year-old younger sister Arsinoë and Juba's four-year-old son in chains. Mindful of what had happened to Vercingetorix, the crowd booed and jeered and pleaded for clemency for the children. Caesar may have intended to pardon them all along, but when he did so, it seemed as if he was bowing to public pressure rather than exhibiting mercy of his own accord.

Another unpopular incident was when Antony's friend, the famous mime author, Decimus Laberius, was forced by Caesar to act on stage in his own play, in competition with the mime Publilius Syrus. This automatically made the sixty-year-old equestrian infamis, losing all status, so he was on a social par with the actors, prostitutes and gravediggers. He made his resentment clear by adding lines to the play, such as, 'If one is feared by many, one must fear many,' and pointedly glaring at Caesar as he delivered them. Caesar gave the victory to his opponent, but then rewarded Laberius with fifty thousand stesterces and re-instituted his equestrian status. The Dictator apparently found the whole thing a wonderful joke.

But Caesar wasn't entirely content with everything that transpired. With thousands of drunk legionaries marching through the city, many of them sung ribald marching songs, and as was tradition, their commander was mercilessly mocked for his flaws, such as his balding head, his affairs with others' wives, and his rumoured relationship with Nicomedes, the king of Bithynia, when he was a boy. It was nothing Caesar hadn't heard before, but to have it sung at his triumphs infuriated him so much that he took a public oath that he had never had a sexual relationship with Nicomedes. Further, though each soldier was generously rewarded with five thousand denarii – three times as much as Pompey had donated when he had celebrated his last triumph – the soldiers grumbled that it would have been more if he hadn't been quite so lavish with his celebrations, and began a riot. The ingratitude drove Caesar incandescent with rage, and he had one of the ringleaders summarily executed, and two others ritually beheaded by the priest of Mars, and their heads displayed in the Forum. This soon brought the soldiers to their senses, and for the rest of the celebrations they were largely well behaved.

On the last day of the triumphs, when the final banquet was declared to be at an end, Caesar walked home, escorted by twenty elephants bearing torches in their trunks to light his way.

When it was all over, Antony returned home to his palatial dwelling and sat on a marble bench in the gardens, among the statues bathed in pale moonlight, and stared absently into the distance. Fulvia came to join him, putting her arm around his waist. They sat in silence for a while. The distant sounds of revelry floated over the perimeter walls, carrying up from the Forum and all those parts of the city that had not yet slept, and maybe didn't intend to.

'I should have been part of it,' said Antony.

'I know,' said Fulvia.

'I should have been fighting with him at Thapsus.'

'I know.'

'Is it over for me? If I am forever out of his favour, will my creditors call in my loans? Will I ever have power and responsibility and the opportunity for enrichment again?'

Fulvia grabbed his chin and turned him so he was looking into her stern expression.

'Snap out of it, Antonius. Self-pity doesn't suit you. Just remember, your fate is in your own hands. With prudence, and with my help, you can regain Caesar's trust. You can be beside him again in the Senate and on the battlefield. Just trust me. Can you do that?'

Antony nodded, and she kissed him gently.

'I'm going to bed,' she said invitingly.

'I'm going to sit here a little longer,' he said.

She pouted, then left him alone. He looked up at the stars arrayed above him. There was the constellation of Hercules, ancestor of the Antonii. And right next to it, the Corona Borealis, the Northern Crown. He sat in the warm night air, contemplating the meaning of this juxtaposition.

Kalendis Novembribus DCCVIII AUC (1 November 46 BC), Rome

It had been Fulvia's suggestion that Antony call on Cleopatra. She had arrived in Rome shortly after the triumphs had finished, since she had not long given birth to a baby boy. The infant, officially Ptolemy Caesar Philopator Philometor, and nicknamed Caesarion, was widely presumed to be Caesar's, though he had not officially acknowledged him. The timings were certainly correct – the boy would have been conceived when Cleopatra was his lover in Egypt, and the only doubt about the paternity was his seeming inability to produce a male heir over his long marriage, nor any other bastards from his many, many affairs, Julia having been his only child.

Cleopatra had come to Rome in answer to a summons from Caesar, bringing with her Caesarion and her brother, husband and co-ruler Ptolemy XIV, who was also still a child, though not far from his adolescence. Caesar greeted Cleopatra and her brother enthusiastically on their arrivals, and paid them all the honour due to a visiting monarch, and more. He presented her formally to the Senate, and pushed through a treaty that would safeguard her position if Rome decided to annex Egypt. He placed a bronze statue of the queen beside the statue of Venus in his new temple. And he installed her, her brother and her son in his own estate on the far side of the river Tiber.

It was a place that Antony had visited before, when he had been in favour with Caesar, but as it had not been Caesar's main residence, it had had an air of disuse about it. Now, as he was shown into the grandiose atrium, Antony realised it had been converted – every inch – into an Eastern, Greco-Egyptian palace. Statues of various Egyptian deities that Antony recognised from his time in Egypt lined the enormous hallway, the mosaic-lined pool seethed with brightly coloured carp, and everywhere he looked, be it tapestries, paintings, couches or tables, dripped with gold.

The benches that lined the walls were full of well-wishers and supplicants, and Antony recognised many senators and equestrians among their number. He had come without an invitation or sending a warning ahead, still used to behaving like the most important man in Rome, but he realised now that he should have known that half of the city would be wishing to pay their respects and beg favours from the richest woman in the world, Caesar's favourite. A bald-headed attendant, a man with a strong Egyptian accent, asked Antony for his name, then asked him to repeat it twice before he understood. He told Antony to take a seat, and that he was welcome to wait as long as he liked, but informed him that the queen was remarkably busy, with many others in the queue before him, and there were no guarantees she would receive him that day.

Disconsolately, Antony sat on a hard marble bench beside one of Caesar's newly appointed senators, whose name he could not recall. The man – a Gallic type, looking uncomfortable in his toga and his fine jewellery, with his long, blond hair oiled and finely coiffured – nudged him in the ribs.

'She even keeps the Master of Horse waiting, huh?' he said in his strong barbarian accent.

Antony looked at him in irritation.

'I am Master of Horse no longer,' he said.

'Of course, of course. Forgive me. But I am sure that you will be in a position of great responsibility again soon. I have seen your abilities when you were in my home country. Caesar will not leave such a one as you idle for long.'

Antony smiled at him weakly, wishing he shared the Gallic senator's confidence. His pride told him that waiting in line to pay homage to a foreigner was beneath his dignity as a Roman, especially one of high rank – he was still, after all, both a senator and an augur. But it was possible that Cleopatra could be genuinely helpful towards him. Besides, Fulvia would be none too pleased if he returned to her with his mission unaccomplished. He leaned back against the wall, and realised the frescoes smelled fresh. He dabbed it with his hand and was relieved to find the paint was dry, and his toga was unsullied. He rested his chin on his hands and puffed out a sigh through pursed lips, wondering if Cleopatra remembered their brief meeting during her childhood.

'Marcus Antonius!'

The loud voice jerked him upright. He stood uncertainly, and the attendant gestured for Antony to follow him. Ignoring the resentful glares and grumbles from those who had been waiting for much longer, he followed the servant past the burly guards at the doorway, and into the interior of the palace. He was led into what could only be described as a throne room – a sizeable chamber, with two rows of statues of various animal-headed Egyptian and anthropoid Greco-Roman gods. The mosaic floors were clearly of a high standard, consisting of multiple finely detailed scenes depicting the Nile and its aquatic inhabitants, with hippopotami and crocodiles particularly prominent. Steps led up to a gilded throne, which was flanked by four more tough-looking spear-bearing bodyguards. For all Antony's strength and skill in a fight, he was unsure if he could best any one of them, let alone all four at once.

And on the throne, wearing a headdress with a moon between two cow's horns and a shimmering purple and gold silk dress, her neck layered with gold necklaces, ornate gold earrings dangling from each lobe, and gold bracelets, anklets, and rings on each wrist, ankle and finger, sat Cleopatra.

Antony nearly tripped, so surprised was he at her appearance. The last time he had seen her, around ten years earlier, she had been at the start of her adolescence. Now she must be, what... twenty-two, twenty-three years of age? Antony recalled a spotty child with bad hair and a big nose. Before him now was a radiant woman, who exuded an allure that captured the gaze and would not let it go.

And yet, when he looked hard, he could still see the features of the girl she used to be. The liberal application of white lead covered any evidence of acne scarring, and her nose was still prominent, though not as huge and pointy as the picture in his memory. The mind was prone to exaggerate over time, he knew, and he was delighted to discover she was easy to look at. If he was being really picky, she was still no beauty – not in the same league as Cytheris, not even as handsome as Fulvia. Was it just because his memory of her was so negative that he was so pleasantly surprised now? But no, it must be more than that. She had entranced Caesar, after all, and he had his pick of all the noble women in the Empire, regardless of rank and marital status.

Perhaps it was the eyes. They were outlined in dark kohl that trailed off from the outside corners of each eyelid into delicate curls. The pupils were wide and dark, no doubt artificially made so by the application of belladonna. But there was something about the way her eyes danced, smouldered, shone with intelligence, that drew him in.

All these thoughts passed through his head in the merest of moments, but his reverie was broken by the attendant announcing a loud voice.

'Marcus Antonius, prostrate yourself before Cleopatra, Seventh of that name, Thea Philopator, Pharaoh of all Egypt, rightful Queen of the Ptolemaic kingdom, and her brother-husband Ptolemy XIV Philopator.'

Antony's eyes drifted to the side, and he realised that while concentrating on Cleopatra, he had completely failed to notice the presence of her little brother at a throne by her side.

He bowed deeply from the waist.

'Queen Cleopatra...' he began, but the attendant roared, 'I said, prostrate yourself. Get on your belly on the floor, face down, and grovel before the Pharaoh.'

Antony put his shoulders back and his chest forward.

'I am a senator of Rome. I do not abase myself before barbarian potentates, no matter how lofty in birth and position.'

As one, the bodyguards reached for their spears, and Antony tensed, wishing he had a weapon, wondering if flight would be prudent at this point, or more humiliating than prostration.

Cleopatra rose to her feet and gestured to her bodyguards to be calm.

'I do not require one who was, until recently, the first man in Rome to prostrate himself in our Eastern fashion,' she said, speaking Greek. 'Plain courtesy is all I require. Marcus Antonius. It has been a very long time. May I still call you Marcus?'

'You may. I recall I used to call you "princess", but that is no longer appropriate. What should I call you now?'

'My full title is rather laborious, so you may address me simply as "Goddess of the Two Lands".'

Her tone was haughty, but Antony saw her eyes crinkle in amusement, and he suppressed a smile himself.

'And you will address me as Ptolemy XIV Philopator, son of the avenging god, dispenser of justice, beloved of Ptah, son of Isis,' said the boy by Cleopatra's side in a high-pitched voice that squeaked as it neared breaking. It took an effort for Antony to tear his eyes from Cleopatra, and he simply gave the lad a nod of acknowledgement before turning his attention back to the queen.

'To what do I owe the pleasure of this visit?' asked Cleopatra.

'Merely a formality, Goddess of the Two Lands,' said Antony. 'To welcome you, as I'm sure many others have, to our fine city.'

Cleopatra let out a little giggle. 'Fine city? Oh, Marcus, you are still as funny as ever. Or have you forgotten the magnificence of Alexandria? What is this city of wood and dirt, compared to mine of marble and gold? What are your temples compared to the Serapeum, your places of learning compared to the Mouseion? What is your culture of mime and farce, to mine of poetry and plays?'

Antony bristled, but knew she was right. He had seen Rome, Athens, Antioch and Alexandria with his own eyes, and Alexandria was by far the most magnificent of them all. He tried to defend his home city, though it was an impossible task.

'We have the Temple of Jupiter Optimus Maximus.'

'A mere provincial shrine.'

'We have the poetry of Catullus.'

'A man who wrote about the most unseemly matters, in the most outrageous of language.'

'We have the wisdom of Cicero.' That last one stuck in his throat, but he was rapidly running out of culture to impress her with. But her face became solemn at the mention of the old ex-consul.

'I fear that the wise Cicero has little respect for me. I heard he considers me arrogant, and lets it be known that he believes I have bewitched Caesar with magic.'

Antony shook his head. 'I have little love for that man. Besides the personal ills he has done me, I find him vainglorious, disloyal and a coward. It saddens me that Caesar shows him so much favour.'

Cleopatra put her head on one side.

'Rome has this much in its favour. A great man of vision, intelligence and ability in Caesar, whom I love. And a man of strength and courage, who could yet be great, in the person of Marcus Antonius.'

Antony smiled at this. He was far from immune to flattery, and to hear it coming from a charming, powerful and wealthy woman was about as perfect as it got.

'Once, I showed you around Alexandria,' said Cleopatra. 'Maybe you could act as my guide and show me Rome.'

'I don't think that is wise, my Pharaoh and Queen and Goddess...' began her attendant, but she waved away her concerns with one hand.

'I am so cramped in here, and Caesar never has time for me. He need not know of this little excursion, and I'm sure Marcus and I could find suitable disguises, so we did not draw attention to ourselves. What do you say, Marcus?'

Antony grinned broadly, a surge of excitement bubbling up, both at the thought of spending time in Cleopatra's company and at doing something so transgressive – something that Caesar, towards whom Antony still felt resentment, would strongly disapprove of.

'I would be honoured.'

ante diem iv Nonas Novembres DCCVIII AUC (2 November 46 BC),
Rome

Fulvia was delighted when Antony told her the news of his reception and their plan to tour the city incognito.

'Political success is all about connections and allies, Marcus,' she said. 'Part of Caesar's genius was the alliances he made along the way to the top. Even now, he would struggle to rule without the loyalty of other important and powerful people. That's the mistake demagogues have been making from the Gracchi through to Catilina and Clodius – the support of the commoners is not enough on its own to grant power.'

Antony listened to the lecture dutifully, then set about making himself looking handsome, while at the same time dressing down so he looked like one of the lowest rank of freemen. Sadly, that meant discarding all of his jewellery except a single gold ring on his first finger, which was part of his dowry from Fulvia and had symbolic significance in their marriage. He wore a capacious cloak which made it possible for him to wear a sword discreetly beneath it – he was very conscious that he would have the safety of Caesar's lover in his care.

He set out with kisses and good wishes from Fulvia, who, despite her bulging belly looking as if it was fit to burst, seemed almost as excited as him, and waited at their pre-arranged meeting point on the Pons Aemilius. Even though it was past dark, the city was still busy with people going about the tasks that kept the city running – the farmers and merchants bringing in their goods, bands of slaves hurrying with buckets of water to put out fires, construction workers toiling around the clock to build the temples and other fine edifices that Caesar had decreed – as well as those just out for a good time. It was a sign of how much more peaceful the city had become since Caesar's return, that they weren't all hidden behind their locked doors and shutters all night long. That was a matter of some irritation for Antony, and though he knew he had been given a difficult task, he did wonder if Caesar was right, and he should have done better.

He was broken from his reverie by a tap on his shoulder that made him jump. He turned to find himself looking into Cleopatra's smiling face. She had done a good job of disguising herself, wearing simple Roman-style make-up and a cloak with a hood that covered her hair and threw her face into shadow. She was accompanied by one of her burly bodyguards, who looked distinctly uncomfortable, both in the simple tunic and cloak of a Roman slave, and with the situation. His eyes darted left to right, assessing threats, and seemed constantly on the verge of reaching for what Antony presumed was a concealed sword like his own.

'Goddess of the Two Lands,' said Antony. 'The simple attire suits you.'

'Marcus,' she said. 'Thank you for meeting me. But perhaps you should address me differently if we are attempting to conceal my identity.'

'Of course, Goddess,' said Antony, his lips twitching up at the corners. 'What do you suggest?'

'Something Greek, I think. We shall converse in Greek, yes? A much more sophisticated language than your brutish Latin.' She considered for a moment. 'I have it. You may call me Aphrodisia.'

Antony looked at her in surprise. It was a common Greek name, derived from Aphrodite, the goddess of love. Aphrodite had famously cuckolded her husband, the crippled blacksmith Hephaistus, with Ares. Was she hinting at an analogy: Caesar as Hephaistus, the man who was building Rome anew, Antony as Ares, the god of war? There was a crinkle to her eyes that hinted at mischief. If she had been anyone else's wife or lover, Antony might have devoted the evening to seducing her. But she was Caesar's, and the whole point of tonight's exercise was to start getting back into his favour. Sleeping with his lover would not be a good move. Besides, Antony was genuinely wrapped up with Fulvia, and though she wasn't as fun as Cytheris, or as unchallenging company as Fadia, she was more passionate than Antonia, and he enjoyed her conversation, her wit and her intelligence.

Antony offered Cleopatra his arm, and they promenaded into the city. Caesar had, of course, dutifully taken her on a formal tour of Rome, riding a grand carriage pulled by a team of white horses, his lictors and her bodyguards keeping the crowds at a distance. Antony commented that he doubted she had really experienced Rome in that manner.

'Then I am in your hands,' she said.

They walked through the new Forum of Julius. The recently completed and dedicated Temple of Venus Genetrix, with its marble facade and eight columns on each side, drew a comment from Cleopatra that it was 'quite a lovely little temple'. Antony thought that since it contained a gold statue of her, she might have been more fulsome in her praise, but then he recalled her country was the land of the pyramids and the Serapeum, and understood she might be underwhelmed.

He changed tack and took her to see a play by Plautus, which drew little amusement from her.

'It's hardly Aeschylus, is it?' she commented.

Finally, he decided to take her to a tavern and get her drunk. He selected a little *popina* on the edge of the Subura to which Sergius had once taken him, and he fed her *garum*-drenched sausages and kept her cup topped up with low-quality wine from Gaul. Now, for the first time, she showed her appreciation of Antony's home city, her eyes widening at the overwhelming flavour of the fish sauce, and her nose wrinkling at the strong drink. The bodyguard kept steadfastly sober and alert while Antony and Cleopatra became more inebriated together.

Just once did a rowdy drunkard approach them, throwing his arms around Cleopatra and attempting to give her a kiss. Before the bodyguard could react, Antony had dragged him off and punched the unwise man square in the face, knocking him out cold with a single blow.

Unfortunately, that was enough for Cleopatra, who, though seemingly unruffled by the incident, announced that she was weary and must return home.

As they walked back towards the river, hand in hand, she rested her head against Antony's upper arm.

'Thank you, Marcus. That was a lovely evening.'

'How long will you stay in Rome?'

She gave a little shrug. 'As long as I am wanted. I am a powerful woman, Marcus, but like everyone else in the world, even I am beholden to Caesar. I hear rumours he had a dalliance with Queen Eunoe, the wife of King Bocchus of Mauretania. It is necessary that I am near him to retain his affections. Without him, my position on the throne is threatened, and so is my son.'

'Your son? Caesar's son?' Antony would not have dared mention Caesarion's parentage unless he had consumed as much wine as he had, but Cleopatra did not take offence.

'I swear to you,' she said, 'I have given myself to no one else. I am a descendant of one of Alexander's generals, I am the successor to thousands of years of continued reign over the richest state in the world, I am a goddess. I would not consider anyone else who did not have Caesar's greatness within them.'

Was that a challenge? Antony wondered idly. Could he be as great as Caesar, and one day win Cleopatra's heart? He gave a little chuckle at the thought, and Cleopatra asked him why he was laughing.

'No reason,' he said casually. 'So your alliance with Caesar is purely political, not romantic?'

'I wouldn't say that. I love him, in my way, and admire him immensely.'

'But you can never marry him. Even if you weren't both already married, a Roman nobleman cannot officially wed a foreigner.'

'I'm aware of that,' she said. 'But to be acknowledged his consort would make my position unassailable, and ensure Caesarion's safety. Anyway, what about you, Marcus? What are your ambitions?'

'Honestly, I don't know. Fulvia thinks I am destined for greatness and is determined to thrust me there. For my part, I would be happy to be back in Caesar's confidence, and enjoying the prestige and comforts that come with that, with maybe not so much of the responsibility. It would certainly help my finances, too, which I fear are becoming precarious once more.'

'So was that what this evening was all about? A play to regain Caesar's favour by way of his mistress?'

'Perhaps at first. But I can honestly say I have very much enjoyed your company, far more than I expected.'

'You are too kind,' said Cleopatra, laughing lightly. They had reached the Pons Aemilius again, and she stopped.

'I shall take my leave of you here. Thank you, Marcus, for tonight.' She stood on tiptoes so she could kiss his cheek.

'And don't worry. I will put in a good word for you with Caesar.'

ante diem iv Idus Novembres DCCVIII AUC (10 November 46 BC), Rome

Antony had spent most of the day pacing restlessly. He was desperate for a drink – preferably several – to alleviate his anxiety, but he was trying hard not to be a disappointment to Fulvia; in particular, he didn't want to greet the birth of their first child together too drunk to appreciate it. Trebonius had come round to keep him company and distract him, and they talked politics, chariot racing and military tactics while sipping well-watered wine and nibbling dates, all the time trying to ignore the screams coming from the cubiculum where Fulvia had been confined with her midwives, physicians and maidservants for the last few hours.

'She will be fine,' said Trebonius, maybe believing repetition would turn the platitude into a prophecy. 'It isn't her first. And anyway, Fulvia is strong as an ox.'

Antony nodded and gave a thin smile. Childbirth was by far the biggest killer of young women, and he couldn't contemplate life without his clever, supportive, loving wife.

A particularly shrill scream split the air, and both men looked up, startled. Then there was a moment's silence and it felt as if Antony's heart had frozen in his chest.

Then there was the most delightful sound in the world – the cry of a newborn baby – and he let out a whoosh of breath.

One of the maidservants emerged from the cubiculum.

'The mistress says you may come through now, master.'

Trebonius grinned and slapped Antony on the back. Still hesitant, Antony entered the birthing room.

It looked like the aftermath of a violent struggle. The bed sheets were soaked in watery blood. The midwives' hands were gory and their faces spattered. Fulvia herself was pale and covered in crimson gloop. But her eyes were bright. And clutched to her breast was a tiny, hideous, gorgeous baby.

'It's a boy,' she said.

Antony approached and took the infant from her reverently. His first son.

'He shall be Marcus Antonius,' he announced, 'and he shall bear the *cognomen* Antyllus in honour of our ancestors.'

Fulvia smiled and closed her eyes. Antony leaned over and kissed her brow tenderly.

ante diem iv Kalendas Decembres DCCVIII AUC (Second intercalary month between November and December 46 BC), Rome

It had been a long, strange year. The traditional Roman year was three hundred and fifty-five days, with an extra intercalary month inserted every other year to keep the months in line with the seasons. But this practice had not been followed, and for as long as Antony had been alive, the seasons and the months had been hopelessly unsynchronised. It was not a situation Caesar was prepared to tolerate, and with Cleopatra's help, he found an Alexandrian astronomer named Sosigenes to advise him. Sosigenes informed Caesar that since a solar year was three hundred and sixty-five and a quarter days, that the year should be three hundred and sixty-five days, plus an extra day every four years. Caesar decreed it so, and also inserted an intercalary month after February and two intercalary months between November and December. Dates were already a complicated matter in Rome, involving counting forward to one of the three important days of the month – the Kalends, the Nones and the Ides – and the intercalary months made organising a meeting where everyone turned up on the right day next to impossible. Only someone with Caesar's vision and strength could have forced these measures through, undoubtedly beneficial as they were in the long run.

Despite all the triumphs, the civil war was still not over. When Caesar had beaten Pompey's armies in Spain as his first action after crossing the Rubicon, he had left Antony's fellow tribune Quintus Cassius Longinus in charge. He was the brother of Gaius Cassius Longinus, who had fought with Crassus at Carrhae and as a naval commander with Pompey, before surrendering to Caesar and being humiliatingly forgiven. It was a rare mistake on Caesar's part. Quintus Cassius had proved to be a greedy, cruel and bad-tempered governor, and he had drowned while fleeing from assassination attempts and mutiny. Pompey's sons, Gnaeus and Sextus, took advantage of the unrest to garner the support of the Spanish legions, and after Caesar's victory at Thapsus, the remnants of the Pompeian forces, including Labienus, joined them. Spain was an important province, rich in silver, and it could not be left in the hands of the rebels, lest they use it to grow their power and threaten Caesar's position.

Consequently, Caesar ordered the legions and prepared to march. Marcus Aemilius Lepidus was to be in charge as Master of Horse, the role that Antony had played during Caesar's last absence. Antony couldn't see how the ineffectual Lepidus was any better a choice than him, but Fulvia pointed out that Caesar's secretaries and confidants, Gaius Oppius and Lucius Cornelius Balbus, would be making many of the day-to-day decisions.

The day before Caesar was due to depart, Antony, at Fulvia's urging, went to see him. He had donned his full military uniform, making sure that he wore every decoration to which he was entitled, except the *corona muralis* that he had earned for being the first onto the wall at the siege of Alexandrium. He felt that wearing a gold crown before someone who was as near to a king as Rome had had for many centuries would be rather inappropriate.

There was one other in Caesar's atrium as Antony waited to be received: a young man – a boy, really, maybe seventeen years of age. Antony looked him over with mild curiosity. He stood against a wall, upright, hands clasped behind his back. He was slight of build and had smooth, closely shaven skin, wavy blond hair and grey eyes. In many ways, he seemed an idealised representation of healthy youthful male beauty, except that he breathed with an audible wheeze, and sometimes doubled up into an uncontrollable, spasmodic cough, before resuming his stance with a look of embarrassment.

Antony wondered how long it would be until Caesar deigned to admit him, suspecting that the more Caesar kept him waiting, the more unfavoured he remained. To ease his anxiety, he approached the young man and stuck out his hand.

'Marcus Antonius,' he said.

The youth looked down at the hand as if it was covered in dung, and shook it limply and reluctantly. 'Yes, I know.'

'And you are...?' prompted Antony, instantly irritated and wondering what made this boy feel so supercilious.

'Gaius Octavius.'

Antony shrugged, expecting more.

Octavius let out a sigh, which provoked another coughing fit.

'My mother is Atia, Caesar's niece.'

Ah, part of the royal family, thought Antony. He had better keep the youngster on side, then.

'Come to see old Uncle Julius, then?'

Antony was sure Octavius suppressed an eye-roll.

'Indeed.'

'Social visit?'

'A mixture.'

Antony gave up and went over to the *impluvium*, watching the fish swim in lazy circles.

'Caesar will see you now.'

The slave's loud voice startled Antony. He looked over to Octavius.

'See which of us?' he asked.

'Both of you.'

The two of them were led into Caesar's presence. The Dictator sat in a functional chair, poring over a document, flanked by his secretaries, Oppius and Balbus. When Antony and Octavius were announced, Caesar immediately rose and strode over to his great-nephew. He embraced him in a firm hug, and Antony could see Octavius' eyes water as he suppressed another coughing bout.

'It's good to see you, lad. How long have you been in Rome? Is your mother well?'

'Just a few days, uncle. And yes, she is very well, and sends her warmest wishes.'

Then Caesar turned his gaze on Antony. It had been a long time since they had talked, and Antony had hoped that their meeting would be private. Now he held his breath, waiting for Caesar's reaction.

Caesar held out his hand, and when Antony took it, Caesar shook firmly, smiling warmly.

'And you, Marcus. It's been too long.'

It certainly had, thought Antony. And whose fault was that?

'How is Fulvia?'

'She is a remarkable woman, Caesar. She challenges me every day, and I believe makes me a better person.'

Caesar nodded, apparently pleased with this reply.

'I hear you called on Cleopatra?'

'Yes, Caesar,' said Antony, hoping that he only knew of his visit to her in Caesar's residence across the Tiber, and not of their nocturnal excursion around Rome. 'It was a pleasure to see her again. I met her when she was a child, when I was helping to restore her father to his throne.'

'I know. She speaks highly of you.'

'She is too kind.'

'Perhaps.' Caesar looked thoughtful. 'I have heard of you from other mouths, too.'

Antony stiffened, wary.

'It does seem you've wiped the wax tablet clear and started again. Even Cicero concedes that your behaviour has improved.'

It felt like receiving a lukewarm report from a schoolmaster, especially with the young Octavius listening smugly, like the class swot.

'It is good to hear, Marcus. Truly. You have so much potential. Try to make sure your undoubted qualities keep your baser instincts in check.'

'Yes, Caesar,' said Antony dutifully.

'Now, you both asked for an audience, and I hope you don't mind I chose to see you simultaneously. Time is rather pressing – we march tomorrow. Octavius, why don't you start?'

'Uncle, I came to ask permission to accompany you to Spain.'

Antony glanced across at him in surprise. Octavius did not look in any way a soldier, though it was, of course, traditional for young men embarking on a political career to see some service with the army, using family connections to gain advancement where possible. It was irritating, though, because it was for precisely the same reason that Antony had wanted to see Caesar.

'And what does your mother think?'

Antony chortled, which earned a sharp look from Caesar, making him quickly cover it with a clearing of his throat.

'Excuse me,' he said. 'Swallowed a fly.'

'Mother has no objections.'

'She refused you permission to travel to Africa with me.'

'I am older now.'

'Very well. Permission granted. And you, Marcus? What can I do for you?'

'Well, I came to ask the same, Caesar. I hope I have proven to you my loyalty and my ability in battle over the years. If I let you down while ruling Rome in your absence, I can only say in my defence—'

'No excuses, Marcus,' interrupted Caesar with a wave of his hand. 'I can't deny that you disappointed me, but nor can I deny that the task I left in your hands was challenging even for the most experienced of politicians, which you certainly are not.'

Antony waited for a decision, his heart racing.

'Fine. You will certainly be invaluable. This campaign will be no mopping-up operation, no foregone conclusion. Given the number of men we have discharged since Pharsalus, I can only take eight legions with me, and only two of those are veteran. I could use your military experience and tactical wit.'

'Thank you, Caesar.' Antony's soul soared at the thought of not only being back in Caesar's favour, but back on the battlefield. 'You won't regret it.'

'Now, if you will both please excuse me, I have much planning to do.'

The meeting was over, and Antony hurried away to tell Fulvia the good news.

ante diem iv Nonas Decembres DCCVIII AUC (2 December 46 BC), Gaul

The legions made their way north out of Italy and through Gaul, taking the land route towards Spain. Caesar, never content to waste time, continued to attend to business matters from his carriage: answering letters, sending out directives, receiving reports of his building projects and law reforms in Rome. He even found the time to compose a poem which he called 'The Journey', and he read verses out to Antony, who rode beside his carriage, a sure sign of his return to favour. To Antony's somewhat guilty pleasure, Octavius had cried off at the last minute, claiming ill health was preventing him from travelling, and he couldn't help noticing an expression of disappointment and disapproval on Caesar's face at the news.

But then it was Antony's turn to disappoint Caesar. A courier came from Rome with an urgent message from Fulvia. He broke the seal and read the letter anxiously.

> Darling Marcus,
>
> It grieves me to write to you as you ride to war, but this matter cannot await your return. Your creditors have been calling. They have had a hearing in court, and it has been determined that your loans must be repaid. All of them. Your debts for your purchases of Pompeius' properties, the expenses you incurred when campaigning for political offices, the loans for games and religious festivals and disbursements to your clients. I don't know who is behind this, but I suspect one of your enemies, maybe Dolabella or Cicero, has taken advantage of your absence from the city to attempt to ruin you. You must return to deal with this situation, Marcus, or it means bankruptcy and exile.
>
> Your loving wife,
> Fulvia.

Antony read it through twice in disbelief. He was back in Caesar's favour. His loans should be secure. Fulvia was surely right that there was some mischief behind this. But he could not ignore it. Reluctantly, he took the problem to Caesar.

'You must return to Rome,' said Caesar. 'This must be dealt with.'

'But... could you not do something?' asked Antony. 'Send a message that you guarantee my loans?'

Caesar shook his head sadly.

'That would not be proper, I'm afraid. Besides, I think it would be informative for me to see how you deal with this problem on your own initiative.'

Antony stared. Was Caesar himself behind this? Was it a test? He supposed it was not something that could ever be proved, only suspected.

Antony bowed.

'I apologise that I cannot join you on your expedition, Caesar. I will depart for Rome immediately.'

Chapter XII

'I met your Cytheris at dinner recently,' said Cicero. 'It was rather embarrassing. I had no idea I would be dining around the same table as an actress.'

It was a savage opening thrust, implying that Cicero was too noble to socialise with the woman that Antony had treated as a wife.

'Not my Cytheris any more. I am happily married to a wonderful woman now. Talking of which, how did you ever let young Tullia marry that monster Dolabella?' Antony took a bite of a ripe apple.

Cicero looked pained. 'To tell you the truth, I had very little to do with it. I had actually received a petition from Tiberius Claudius Nero for Tullia's hand.'

'A most capable fellow, with impeccable ancestry,' commented Antony, spraying a little apple juice in Cicero's direction as he spoke, causing the venerable orator to wrinkle his nose in distaste.

'Indeed. But I was in my province, and by the time I returned, the deed had been done. I can't say I am sorry they are now divorced.'

'You never forgave Terentia, did you?'

Cicero looked at him from under his thick, fleshy brows. 'Terentia, was always a… challenging spouse.'

'Unlike your new ward… sorry, I mean wife.'

Cicero regarded Antony coolly. He had been forced to repay his dowry when he had divorced Terentia, but fortunately his new wife, Publilia, was from an extremely rich family, which had replenished his coffers substantially. Less fortunately, Publilia was only around fifteen years old, while Cicero had just celebrated his sixty-first birthday. Worse, he had had some role of guardianship for the child. The censure had ranged from mild mockery at Cicero's probable inability to consummate the marriage, to disgust at the age gap. Cicero had been defiant, though, and quite happy to risk the damage to his reputation for whatever he got from the connection, whether it was the money, love, or a genuine physical attraction, to the point that when someone had teased him on his wedding day by asking him why he was marrying a child, he had snapped back that she would be a woman by the next day.

Antony found the whole thing distasteful. Fifteen was, of course, a marriageable age in Roman society, but Antony's preference had always been for women older and more experienced – personally, he could not see the attraction of the fearful virgin. But he was here in Cicero's house on the Palatine for a reason – and that reason was not to antagonise the old senator. Since his emergency return to Rome, Antony had been fully occupied shoring up his finances, visiting influential senators and equestrians, promising future favours to all the rich merchants, taking on further loans at high interest rates. He had managed to prevent the dam bursting, but it still held back a dangerously large volume of debt, threatening to inundate him if any cracks appeared.

Fulvia had been a vital part of the strategy, and though much of the client base she had inherited from Clodius and Curio inhabited the poorer echelons of society, she was nevertheless highly connected with many important people who had been friends and sympathisers of her two deceased populist husbands. Between them, they had begged, threatened, cajoled and promised themselves to a position of at least temporary financial stability. It was still vital that Antony return to a position of responsibility when Caesar returned, or – still a possibility, despite Caesar's record – taking power in the event of Caesar's defeat and death.

To this end, Fulvia and Antony had agreed that he should approach Cicero, despite their personal animosity. They may never be friends, but it was politic for Antony to at least reach enough of a rapprochement to prevent Cicero actively opposing his ambitions. Despite his ill-advised marriage, Cicero remained the most respected, even revered, senator in all Rome.

Antony swallowed. 'Forgive me. I am not here to mock, but to mend bridges. How is Tullia? I always admired her.'

This made Cicero smile, as flattery of his daughter always did. Antony thought that Tullia may have been the only person in the world that Cicero had ever truly loved apart from himself.

'She is blooming, despite the size of her belly. She is due any day now, and she can't wait to be a mother, even after the previous tragedy.'

Antony shook his head. 'I have been through that pain myself, you know. It is no consolation to know that it is just the way of things, that so many children pass before seeing five winters.'

Cicero looked solemn. 'But your Antyllus is well? And the young Antonia?'

'Little Toni is happy and healthy, according to her mother. I do miss having her around. But Antyllus is putting on weight like a prize piglet. He never seems to be off the teat. Honestly, I don't know where he learned to drink like that.'

Cicero chuckled at this, despite himself.

Antony leaned forward.

'Listen, Cicero. We haven't always seen eye to eye in all matters, but that doesn't mean we cannot work to each other's advantage.'

'How so?' asked Cicero, the suspicion evident in his tone.

'Your consulship, the high point of your career, is nearly two decades behind us. But Gaius Marius held his seventh consulship when he was ten years older than you are now.'

'And he was dead two weeks later.'

'That's not the point. All I'm saying is, you still have so much to offer Rome. And Rome has so much to offer you. That triumph that Cato denied you, for example.'

'That is long past,' said Cicero, but Antony could tell he had touched a nerve. 'What do you want from me, Antonius?'

'Just a truce, for now. Then let us see what the future brings. Both of us are men of power and influence.'

'I think you overestimate your position.'

'I believe that when Caesar returns you will see the favour he still bestows on me. And if he doesn't return… Well, let's just say I am more of a soldier than any Clodius or Dolabella.'

Cicero sat back.

'Then, as you say, let's see what the future brings. Would you like your cup refilled?'

Antony forced himself to smile. When he left Cicero's house, he felt sick and it wasn't due to the wine.

News arrived in Rome in late April that two days after the Ides of March, Caesar had won a great victory at Munda in southern Spain. It was a rare mistake by Labienus that had gifted Caesar victory. His former second-in-command turned worst enemy had moved his cavalry to counter a breakthrough by Caesar's Mauretanian army, but he hadn't informed the rest of the army, who thought he was retreating and broke. Labienus was killed, and Caesar had him buried with full honours.

The war was still not over. Pompey's sons, Gnaeus and Sextus, had escaped, and the city still held out against Caesar's forces. Antony, with his finances precarious but stable, decided it was time to join Caesar, either to assist him in the last stages of the war, or to be the first to congratulate him on his ultimate victory. He bade farewell to Fulvia, who embraced him tenderly, clearly concerned for his safety, despite his reassurances of the lack of danger, especially to one as strong and capable in a fight as him. Then he set out on horseback with a small bodyguard.

He had not made his way far beyond the border of Italia with Cisalpine Gaul when he encountered a group of Gallic traders heading in the direction of Rome. He hailed them and asked them for news.

'You haven't heard? Caesar is defeated. He is dead!'

The words hit Antony like a sledgehammer to his face. It wasn't possible. The great man was indestructible. He pressed the traders for more details, but they knew little else – just that there had been a further battle outside Munda in which Caesar's forces had been beaten and Caesar had been killed.

Antony's first thoughts were for Fulvia. When news reached Rome, there would be chaos. Caesar was the glue holding the fabric of the city together, just by his mere existence. His death could cause economic instability, riots, even a new civil war. He called for his servants to fetch him writing materials, and he hastily wrote a letter, warning her of the news and declaring his undying love for her. He rolled the papyrus, sealed it and held it out for one of his servants to take. Then he paused. His servant was not as accomplished on horseback as Antony himself, and it was vital that Fulvia received his message before the rest of Rome heard about the disaster. He decided to take the message himself and, as an extra precaution, took his servant's clothes to disguise himself. If Caesar was dead, his close association with the Dictator might make him a target for malcontents with a grudge.

He rode as if a pack of wolves was at his heels, and with regular changes of horses at way stations, made his way back to Rome faster than even he thought possible. It was dark when his mount thundered across the Pons Aemilia, and he cursed the nocturnal traffic – the merchants and farmers with their wares, and the drunken partygoers and patrons of the theatres and brothels – and yelled for them to make way. There was a chill in the spring air, and Antony pulled his cloak tight around him, his face swaddled in hood and scarf.

When he reached his home, he leapt off the horse and hammered on the front door. He heard the bolts drawn, the lock turn, and the door swung open. The night porter held up a lantern and peered at Antony suspiciously.

'What do you want?'

Antony realised his servant hadn't recognised him in the dark, with his lowly costume and half-hidden face. A sudden thought crossed his mind.

'Message for the mistress,' he said, mumbling into the scarf. 'From Marcus Antonius. Urgent.'

He showed the porter the scroll with his own seal. The porter inspected it carefully, then allowed Antony into the atrium.

'Wait here,' he said, and went off to find Fulvia.

He had only been gone a few days, but he was excited to see his wife again, to hold her, to feel her close. But did she feel the same about him? She made him believe so, but she was an intelligent woman, with ambition and cunning. Was he just a useful tool for her to play out her own schemes, realise her own dreams? Maybe he would find out now.

Fulvia came hurrying into the atrium. Antony kept in the shadows between the lanterns, his head bowed.

'What news?' asked Fulvia urgently.

Antony held out the letter.

'Just tell me,' she said. 'Does Antonius live? Is he hurt?'

'It's all in the letter, mistress,' he said.

Seemingly oblivious to the unconvincing common accent her husband had adopted, she grabbed the scroll, broke the seal and unrolled it impatiently. She scanned it quickly, and when she reached the lines where he had written of his love and passion for her, she put her hand to her mouth and let out a sob. Tears welled in her eyes, overflowed, and unable to hold back any longer, Antony took two quick steps forward and grabbed her, embracing her tightly.

She stiffened, but then he said, 'My darling, it's me,' pulling down his scarf to reveal his face. A single cry was all she could manage before Antony pressed his lips to hers, kissing her long and slow, luxuriating in the feel of her body as it melted into his.

Then she took a step back and slapped him hard. He grinned and rubbed his stinging cheek.

'Marcus, you are such a fool,' she chided, then grabbed him and kissed him again.

When they broke apart, she put her hands on his shoulders and looked earnestly into his eyes.

'Is Caesar really dead?'

'That's what I was told. It's not confirmed, but I wasn't taking any chances. I needed to know you were safe.'

'Oh, Marcus.' She shook her head. 'You really are quite soft, aren't you, for all your reputation as a warrior?'

'Just don't tell anyone,' said Antony.

'We need to make plans, in case he really is gone.'

'We do. But now I know you are safe, and I am here to protect you, there is no hurry.' He took her hand and led her towards the bedroom.

'Marcus,' she protested weakly, then gave up. Antony laughed, picked her up in his arms, and took her to bed.

ante diem vii Kalendas Maias DCCIX AUC (27 April 45 BC), Rome

Gaius Trebonius called on Antony early the next morning.

Antony embraced him and invited him to walk through the extensive gardens in the villa that had once been Pompey's.

'This is really quite impressive,' said Trebonius. 'Are you intending to pay for it one day?'

'How did you know I was back in Rome?' asked Antony, avoiding the question.

'You know how the slaves gossip. I heard it from my cook, who heard it from his assistant who heard it from the vegetable seller in the Forum. Presumably one of your slaves shopped there this morning?'

'Gods, my household is leakier than the roof of a Suburan insula.'

Trebonius laughed, then turned serious.

'So, do you think it's true? About Caesar?'

Antony shrugged. 'It seems impossible. But no one is invincible. And Caesar has had many favours from Fortuna in the past. Maybe she ran out of patience with him.'

A slave brought them well-watered wine and dates as they chatted and speculated as to the direction events in Rome would take now.

'I suppose Cicero will have a role to play,' said Antony.

'I doubt it,' said Trebonius. 'He has been a wreck since Tullia died.'

Antony shook his head. 'A genuinely lovely young lady, despite her father.' Tullia had died not long after Antony's meeting with Cicero, from complications associated with giving birth to a rather sickly boy. Cicero had been inconsolable, and had left his young wife – whom he suspected had been jealous of his relationship with Tullia, and was pleased she had died. He had moved in with his friend Atticus, to spend his days reading treatise after treatise by the Greek philosophers on all subjects relating to death and grief.

Fulvia came to join them, and after greeting Trebonius courteously, she said, 'While you two have been gossiping, a messenger arrived. From Caesar.'

'He lives?' asked Antony sharply.

'Well, he was alive when he sent the message informing the Senate that he was on his way back to Rome. It seems your news was false, Marcus.'

Antony felt an immediate flood of relief. He had high hopes that he would be restored to Caesar's favour, but he had no official position yet, nor had Caesar apparently named an heir, unless there was a successor mentioned in the will he had deposited with the Vestal Virgins. Antony needed time to improve his position before Caesar departed for the underworld.

'Well,' he said. 'I suppose I should recommence my journey to meet him on his way back, and offer my congratulations. Trebonius, would you care to join me?'

Trebonius nodded. 'Thank you. Now he is truly unchallenged, I suppose we all need to grovel before the great man. Excuse me, I will prepare for the trip.'

Antony and Fulvia watched him go, and then exchanged a glance, with no need for words to express their concern.

Kalendis Maiis DCCIX AUC (1 May 45 BC), Cisapline Gaul

'It's like old times,' said Antony, lying on a hard mat under a leather tent, covered by a woollen blanket. 'We just need some terrible food and a hundred thousand enraged Gauls to complete the ambience.'

Trebonius laughed. 'I don't remember the weather ever being this good in Gaul, though. All I can recall is that if it wasn't raining, it was snowing.'

They had had a pleasant journey thus far, stopping in small towns and roadside inns for the night when possible, but not being concerned at spending the night, as on this occasion, in a tent in a field. Both were seasoned soldiers, and had no fear of the discomforts of being on the road.

'It's hard to imagine what we put ourselves through for him, looking back, isn't it?' said Antony. 'And not just us. Countless legionaries were prepared to give their lives for him.'

'And many did,' said Trebonius.

'Was it worth it, do you think?'

It was an idle question spoken to an old friend, but Trebonius propped himself up on one elbow and looked at Antony intently through the gloom.

'What do you mean?'

'Oh, nothing. I was just speculating. How would things be if Pompeius had been victorious, instead of Caesar? Better? Worse? Or just different?'

'There are many who wished we could have found out,' said Trebonius.

'That's true, but those who aren't dead are thoroughly cowed. Who would oppose Caesar now?'

'He is unassailable in battle, that is for sure. But in Rome? Maybe that is a different matter.'

'In the courts, you mean? He is untouchable legally...'

'Not the courts. I was thinking more of dark alleys.'

Now it was Antony's turn to sit up. 'You think his life is in danger?'

Trebonius was quiet for a moment, and when he next spoke, his voice was lower in pitch and volume.

'There are some who still think freedom is worth fighting for.'

'Freedom? From what?'

'From tyranny.'

'I see,' said Antony. 'And are you one of those people?'

Trebonius hesitated, then said, 'Are you?'

Antony reached out and put a hand on Trebonius' shoulder.

'Let me be very clear, Gaius. I am loyal to Caesar. He is my friend. Yes, he is a man, and men have flaws. But I believe he is what Rome needs. The Senate under Pompeius showed what can happen without a strong and insightful leader – infighting, lawlessness, anarchy. Rome faces enough threats outside its borders without continual strife within them.'

'You make your position perfectly plain,' said Trebonius, and Antony could hear the disappointment.

'I'm going to sleep now. I suggest you do the same.'

Antony rolled over and pulled the blanket close. For a while, sleep eluded him, Trebonius' words circulating inside his head. He could tell from Trebonius' breathing that he was not asleep either. Sure enough, a short while later, Trebonius spoke.

'Marcus.'

'Yes, Gaius?'

'You aren't going to mention this conversation to Caesar, are you?'

'No, Gaius. I am not going to have my old friend condemned to death for idle words that, taken out of context, could sound treasonous.'

Trebonius let out a breath. 'Thank you.'

'Just don't do anything stupid. I would not be able to protect you.'

With that, Antony closed his eyes, and slept.

Iunius DCCIX AUC (June 45 BC), Narbo

Antony and Trebonius finally intersected the path of Caesar's return at the city of Narbo in Transalpine Gaul, on the crossroads of the Via Domitia, leading to Spain, and the Via Aquitania, which led to the western coast of Gaul. A large number of other senators had had the same idea, but since Antony and Trebonius had preferred to travel fast and rough, they had their pick of the accommodation in the city, while the later arrivals who had travelled in comfort by litter and carriage found they had to take rooms they felt way below their station and dignity.

When word came that Caesar was approaching, Antony rode out to meet him. Despite his current lack of formal political position in the Senate, it was acknowledged that his augurship and his previous role as Master of the Horse made him the foremost of those gathered, and so he led the delegation. Caesar's bodyguards indicated Antony should approach, and he dismounted and walked to Caesar's carriage. Caesar pulled back the curtains and smiled broadly, greeting him warmly, to Antony's great pleasure.

Much less pleasing was the shock of realisation at who was in the carriage with him.

'Marcus, you remember my great-nephew, Octavius.'

Antony had heard that Octavius had recovered from his illness and set out for Spain after Caesar had left, but knew little else.

'Octavius showed great initiative in making his way out to join me. He gathered a small band of companions and, despite getting ship-wrecked along the way, managed to reach me, though he was sadly too late to take part in the battles themselves. Still, he has been invigorating company, and he has been challenging me with his ideas on how Rome should be run all the way back.'

Antony grunted a greeting with as much good grace as he could muster, which Octavius reciprocated in similar fashion.

'But now, we have much to talk about, Marcus. I must greet some of these senators, who – unlike Octavius – waited to see which way the campaign would turn out before they set out to pay me their respects.'

Antony presumed Caesar wasn't slighting him personally – after all, he had been quite prepared to go to battle with Caesar until circum-stances, possibly of Caesar's own devices, had forced him back to Rome.

'When we set off again, you will ride in my carriage, Marcus. Octavius, you will take the carriage behind with Decimus Brutus. He is a man with much talent, and much to teach you. Especially about boats. Off you go.'

Octavius bowed, gave Antony a look full of adolescent sulk, and got down from the carriage. Caesar rearranged his scarlet tunic and adjusted his laurel wreath.

'Am I presentable?'

'Certainly, Caesar.'

Caesar descended and approached the waiting senators, shaking hands and clapping backs, accepting congratulations and deflecting petitions with promises of audiences at a later date. Antony waited patiently, and after Caesar returned, he climbed into the carriage beside him. Caesar ordered his driver to carry on, and as the horses picked up the slack in the harnesses, he pulled the curtains closed, so that at long last, the two men were alone.

--

They rode for days, with Antony in Caesar's carriage the whole way, leaving him in no doubt that not only was he back in Caesar's good graces, but was, in fact, his favourite once more – particularly reassuring given the evident interest the Dictator had taken in Octavius' career. Caesar had several themes that he kept bringing the conversation back to, particularly the subjects of greatness, legacy and mortality. Antony listened and contributed where he felt able. He was well educated in philosophy, but he knew he was no Cicero, and it was galling that Caesar would no doubt have preferred the old orator's opinion on those subjects.

When it came to Caesar's military plans, though, it was a different matter. Caesar had never forgiven the Parthians for their treatment of Crassus, and considered them to be a serious threat to Rome's Eastern provinces.

'If they really got themselves organised, they could take Syria and Judaea and extend their empire into Asia, or even Egypt. The loss of Egyptian grain would be an existential threat. People would starve to death on the streets of Rome.'

They discussed strategy, tactics, logistics: fields in which Antony excelled, and in which it was clear Caesar genuinely valued his opinion. They dissected the battle of Carrhae and the mistakes that Crassus had made; they talked about ways of combatting skilled mounted archers, and they batted ideas back and forth for supplying a major force with food, fodder and water in the Eastern deserts for a lengthy campaign.

Then one afternoon, Caesar suddenly went still.

'Caesar, what is it?'

'Hold me down,' said the Dictator through clenched teeth. 'Say nothing. It will pass...'

And then, suddenly, his entire body went rigid. His eyes rolled up into his head, he began to judder spasmodically, as if the carriage was rolling at high speed over rocky ground, and foam appeared at the corners of his mouth. Antony stared in surprise, then, as Caesar's thrashing began to tip him out of the carriage, Antony grabbed hold of him and kept him secure.

The whole episode lasted a hundred heartbeats, if that, but it seemed like an eternity to Antony, as he held his commander, his friend, this colossus at the peak of his powers, and cradled him like a baby.

The convulsions ceased, and Caesar was still. His wandering eyes came back and fixed on Antony, and his expression took on a furious mien.

'Take your hands off your king,' he growled.

Antony made sure Caesar was secure on his seat, then sat back, equally shocked by the event, the sudden anger and the words he had uttered. King?

Caesar's face cleared, like storm clouds blown away to reveal a gentle evening sun. He blinked, then smiled uncertainly. 'It happened again, didn't it?'

'Again?'

Caesar rubbed his face. 'Fetch me some water, would you?'

Antony pulled aside the carriage curtain and called for a flask of water, which he passed over. Caesar drank thirstily, then nodded gratefully.

'This has happened a few times now, unfortunately,' he said. 'The first time was in Egypt. Cleopatra saw it. Her physician said it is the falling sickness, caused by a distemper of the head. There were other episodes in Spain and Africa, which a few witnessed. But I do not want it generally known that I have an illness. It would undermine confidence. This must remain between us, Marcus. Is that clear?'

Antony nodded emphatically. 'Of course, Caesar. You know I would do nothing to make your position difficult.'

'Not intentionally, anyway,' said Caesar, and a rueful smile took the sting out of the words. 'You know, Marcus, I believe my time is short. I am not a young man any more – I have seen fifty-five years pass by. And this sickness... Does it portend my death?'

'Would you like me to take the auspices?'

'Don't be ridiculous,' snapped Caesar. 'You believe in divination as little as I do. And even if there was truth in that superstition, you are the least qualified augur in the history of the priesthood.'

Antony had to concede this point. He had spent very little time attending to his official duties as augur, nor even bothering to find out too much about what those duties actually entailed, though he was happy to utilise his position when it was advantageous.

'I have so much to do, Marcus. I need to reorganise the government and the law. I need to develop the amenities of the city, so it can continue to function as it grows. I need to defeat Parthia for our security, and maybe even add the ancient lands of the Persian Empire to Roman territory. I pray that the gods grant me the years I need to achieve all I wish, but if they dictate otherwise, I need someone to take over from me who shares my vision.'

'Yes, Caesar,' said Antony, daring to hope that this conversation was going in the direction he deeply desired.

'You will be my colleague in the consulship for the coming year, Marcus.'

'Thank you for the honour, Caesar,' he said, keeping his face neutral, while internally his heart soared.

'I had promised the position to Dolabella – he has been of use to me recently. But I must concede your good services far outweigh his. I will have to think of some other reward for him. And when we are back in Italy, I need to update my will.'

Antony sat back, stunned by this turnaround in his fortunes, despite his usual self-belief. He was to be consul four years before the legal minimum age – the highest peacetime position it was possible to hold – with a guarantee of a governorship and a military command to follow, which would bring him untold riches. What's more, he was the man in Caesar's private carriage, while all others followed behind. He was back in Caesar's confidence, his right-hand man. He had no wish for Caesar's early demise, but he was ecstatic to be the one that Caesar was favouring to look after his legacy.

Only one thing lingered at the back of his mind, threatening to spoil his mood. That word Caesar had spoken in an unguarded moment.

King.

Chapter XIII

Antony pulled his toga tightly around him. It was the first day of the new year, and with the calendar now in line with the seasons, it was midwinter. The traditional venue for the first Senate meeting of the year was the Temple of Jupiter Capitolinus, which was on the top of the Capitoline hill, and quite draughty. Rome, of course, was never as bitterly cold as Britannia or the north of Gaul, but still, a chilly wind whipped around them, and all the assembled senators were wrapped up warm.

Antony sat before them in his curule chair, his first day in the post of consul, and reflected on some of the great names from history who had occupied this position: the first consul, Lucius Junius Brutus, who over-threw the monarchy; Scipio Africanus, who defeated Hannibal; Gaius Marius, who had reformed the army; his own grandfather, Marcus Antonius, one of the greatest orators of all time. It was hard not to be overwhelmed by the sense of history, and the sense that he didn't belong there, but he quickly quashed those feelings. He was the right-hand man of the first man in Rome, and he had been pivotal in bringing Caesar to that position, by his actions both in the Senate and on the battlefield. There was no man alive who deserved to be consul more than him.

Caesar was talking at length to the Senate about his achievements and plans, and the conscript fathers listened dutifully and attentively. The bulk of the Senate membership were firm supporters of Caesar now. His diehard opponents were in exile or dead. His less obstinate detractors were quiescent, or had overtly changed allegiance. And Caesar had also appointed many new senators to swell the ranks of the loyalists. He was therefore received with all due respect and honours, to the point of fawning sycophancy. Every announcement of a new project was greeted with rapturous applause and standing ovations, and there were so many, Antony thought their throats must be hoarse from cheering and their palms red from clapping. Caesar informed them of the awarding of new citizenships and Latin rights for whole swathes of the population, plans for settling veterans, a law forbidding wheeled traffic from the city during daylight to alleviate congestion, marshes to be drained, temples and libraries to be constructed. His reforms and projects ranged from the hugely ambitious – such as diverting the Tiber to prevent it regularly bursting its banks, and a canal to be dug through the Isthmus of Corinth – to the absurdly detailed, such as a new law that flock-masters must employ at least one free worker for every two of their slaves.

Most popular of all was the announcement of his expedition to Parthia, set for the month of Aprilis, during which he would avenge the humiliating defeat of Crassus. But not everyone applauded. Antony noted that Gaius Cassius Longinus sat in sullen silence while the rest cheered. Given that he had single-handedly rescued the remnants of Crassus' army from absolute destruction at the hands of the Parthians, he might have reasonably expected to be part of Caesar's expedition. But the Dictator had other plans, and though Cassius had been appointed as the Praetor Peregrinus for the year, and promised the governorship of Syria for the following year, he was clearly dissatisfied with the snub, which was compounded by the appointment of one of Caesar's favour-ites, Marcus Junius Brutus, who was junior in both age and previous offices to Cassius, to the superior position of Urban Praetor.

Caesar's speech drew to a close, with some words asking the house for their blessings on his past actions and future plans. It was a relief to Antony, since his bladder had been steadily filling all morning. Although he had moderated his drinking considerably, he had had a few cups of wine the previous night that were still working their way out of his system.

Caesar sat to rapturous applause, and Antony stood to give thanks. It was his maiden speech to the Senate as consul. He cleared his throat, drew himself up to his full height, puffed his chest out, and began to recite the words that Fulvia had helped him prepare.

'Conscript Fathers, neither our plain language, nor the eloquent Greek, or any barbarian tongue, could properly express the honour Caesar and your revered selves have done me by electing me as consul. I swear to carry out my duty—'

'Shame!' came a cry from the floor. Antony peered out to see who was the source of the interruption. Dolabella stood.

'Shame!' he cried again. 'Unfit. This man should never have been elected consul. It is a stain on our hallowed institution.'

'Dolabella, be seated,' said Antony, his voice low and threatening.

'I shall not.' Dolabella strode out onto the floor in front of the consul's chairs and turned to face the senators, who looked on with bemusement. His supporters cheered, Antony's supporters booed, but most felt they did not have a dog in this fight and were happy enough to watch the entertainment play out before them.

'How can a man such as this hold the highest office the Republic can bestow? In what way is he worthy of our distinguished ancestors, who sat there over the history of our Republic. This is the man who consorted with a mime actress as if she was his wife. This is the man who tried to rule Rome in Caesar's absence, but simply used his office as Master of Horse to indulge in orgies of gambling, drinking and whoring. This is the man who cannot control his own finances, much less those of the state. This is the man who commanded soldiers to massacre unarmed civilians peacefully protesting in the Forum!'

'These are lies!' roared Antony. 'That was an armed insurrection, which you incited, and this body gave me authority to use force to put it down.'

'You are a wastrel, Antonius, who debases this house by your mere presence.'

Antony took a step forward, fists clenched. To his credit, the much smaller Dolabella did not flinch, even when Antony drew his arm back to strike.

'Enough!' cried Caesar, and the tone of command made the soldier in Antony obey immediately. He let his hand drop to his side and took a deep breath. From the corner of his eye, he noticed Cicero, arms folded, chuckling quietly to himself. Had he put Dolabella up to this?

Caesar rose and walked sedately onto the floor of the chamber.

'Antonius, Dolabella, please be seated.'

Reluctantly, the two men parted and returned to their respective seats.

'It goes without saying,' said Caesar, 'that Rome will need dynamic and energetic leadership to carry through all my designs and projects. And sadly, I will be leaving Rome for the East in just a few short months.

We are fortunate that we have Marcus Antonius' capable hands as my co-consul to guide you in my absence.'

Most of the Senate applauded politely, while Dolabella's supporters glowered in silence. Antony inclined his head in acknowledgement, slowly recovering his equilibrium. It was a shame he wasn't accompanying Caesar to Parthia, but with the Dictator gone, he would once again be the foremost citizen in the city, and he could look forward to his own governorship and command the following year. He had been promised the militarily vital province of Macedonia, which was being raided by barbarians from the north and east, and Antony couldn't wait to lead his legions against them. He may even be able to conquer new territories for the glory of the Empire and himself.

'But even Antonius cannot do everything himself. Therefore, I will resign my consulship when I leave Rome in favour of Publius Cornelius Dolabella.'

What? Over my dead body, thought Antony. He looked over to where Dolabella was smugly soaking up the congratulations, and felt a renewed surge of anger. It was not unheard of for consuls to be replaced mid-office, although usually it was because of death or ill health. Caesar, however, had given up his sole consulship the previous year in favour of his generals Gaius Trebonius and Quintus Fabius Maximus, which had not been well received. He had provoked even more anger among the traditional Republicans just the day before, when Maximus had died suddenly on his last day of office. Caesar had replaced him with Gaius Caninius Rebilus – who had served him as a legate in Gaul, Africa and Spain – for just a single day, as a way of rewarding his service. The misuse of the office for the awarding of honours had not gone down well, and Cicero had joked that the new incumbent had been so vigilant that he had not closed his eyes for the entire term of his office.

So Caesar resigning his position in favour of another follower was not unheard of, nor even unexpected. But Dolabella? It was insupportable.

Antony stood, and raising his voice and using all his oratorical power to project it across the Senate floor, he called out, 'Veto!'

The hubbub immediately dissipated into confused murmurings. Caesar turned to Antony in astonishment.

'What are you doing?' he demanded.

'I will not allow this to stand.'

'You are not a tribune. You do not have the power to veto.'

'That may technically be so. Nevertheless, he is wholly unsuited to be consul. Only eighteen months ago he rebelled against the state, and the Senate decreed that his revolt be put down with force.'

'I have pardoned him since then,' said Caesar. 'Like I have pardoned many who have committed crimes against the state and me.'

There was an uncomfortable silence. There were few in the Senate who had not had cause to avail themselves of Caesar's mercy at one time or another, and Antony himself had only just been forgiven for the mistakes he made when he was Master of Horse. Then someone – Antony wasn't sure who, but the voice came from near Dolabella, so was probably one of his friends – shouted, 'You are just jealous because he screwed your wife.'

The Senate erupted in laughter, with a few making the sign of the cuckold's horns in Antony's direction. He stood, spine straight, face red, trying to let the mockery flow over him, wishing he had a sword in his hand so he could silence those who thought it prudent to make fun of him. Even Caesar had a thin smile on his face, which was unbelievably hypocritical since the Dictator had divorced his second wife on suspicion of adultery.

Enraged even further by this, Antony roared 'Silence!' His fury and the menace that radiated from him quieted the entire Senate.

Antony stalked up to Caesar, his anger overcoming his better judgement, and said, 'In this house, if nowhere else, I am your equal. I will not permit you to use your power as consul to promote this unfit man to the same rank as me.'

'You will not permit it?' gasped Caesar, stunned by this defiance.

'You heard me.'

'It is not in your power to forbid the election of a consul if this house decrees it and the people vote for it.'

'You forget, I am an augur. No election can be confirmed if I decide the omens are not propitious.'

'You wouldn't dare,' said Caesar.

'Try me.'

The two men glared at each other as the Senate watched in amazement. Surely no one had defied Caesar to his face in this way since he had departed for Gaul many years ago. Everyone waited for the explosion, almost as if the man with supreme power could summon lightning and strike Antony down where he stood.

Instead, he said, 'The elections for a *suffect* consul will take place on the Kalends of March. This meeting is now at an end.' Then Caesar turned to Antony and embraced him, and as he did so, spoke into his ear.

'Do not oppose me again, Marcus.'

'I have no wish to do so, Caesar,' replied Antony, equally softly, 'but I am not your slave, I am a consul of Rome. Do not expect me to roll over and do your bidding if it is against my interests.'

Caesar pulled back and put his hands on Antony's shoulders. They looked at each other, eye to eye. Antony did not blink, surprising even himself at his audacity. Then Caesar gave a nod, and clapped him on the back.

'Very well. You are a man with a stiff backbone. It's one of the reasons I chose you. But do not abuse my patience, Marcus.'

'I will try very hard not to, Caesar.'

As Caesar left the temple, Antony felt a cold sweat prickling his skin. He wondered if confronting Caesar in public in that way had been the bravest and most stupid thing he had ever done, especially since he had only just been restored to favour in the Dictator's eyes. But he didn't regret his actions. There was no way he could rule jointly with Dolabella. He hated the man almost as much as he hated Cicero. Still, he had some bridge-building to do, and he walked home, deep in thought about how to make it up to Caesar for his defiance.

pridie Idus Ianuarias DCCX AUC (12 January 44 BC), Rome

The consequences of Antony's confrontation with Caesar in the Senate had been minimal, at least outwardly. Fulvia reported to her husband that she had heard someone had warned Caesar of the ambition of Dolabella and Antony, and he had replied that he did not fear those long-haired, well-fed men, but the pale and hungry-looking ones. Antony had wondered if Caesar was implying that he was getting fat, and asked Fulvia if she at least liked the way he had let his hair grow out lately. She had snapped that he was missing the point, and that while it was good that he retained Caesar's confidence, he should keep an ear out for rumblings of rebellion from others. Cassius, in particular, was being mentioned as a malcontent, but others were talking about

Marcus Junius Brutus and his illustrious ancestor, who had thrown out the kings and founded the Republic.

Nevertheless, Antony would be foolish not to try to make amends. The obvious way for him to ingratiate himself with Caesar was to use his position as consul to encourage the Senate to vote Caesar new honours. This was easier said than done, since they had already rewarded him so highly. Since Pharsalus, Caesar had been granted the right to make war and peace with whoever he liked without consulting the Senate, a ten-year dictatorship, titles of Imperator, Liberator and Father of the Country – which could be handed down to his children, should he produce any – a curule chair in the Senate even if he wasn't consul, the right to speak first in debates, and innumerable awards of festivals of thanksgiving, properties and statues.

Antony convened a meeting of the Senate in Caesar's absence, with the express purpose of voting him further honours. None would dare oppose such a measure, and so, with no votes against – although a few abstentions – it was decreed that Caesar would be made Dictator in Perpetuity, awarded the consulship for ten years, tribunician sanctity, permission to wear triumphal dress whenever he performed a sacrifice, a throne of gold and ivory, more statues, temples dedicated to him as a god, recognising that he would ascend to divinity upon his death, and even the renaming of the month of Quintilis, in which he was born, to become Iulius.

The entire Senate set out in a procession to present Caesar with these awards. Crowds gathered to watch hundreds of the most important men in Rome in full formal dress, preceded by lictors to clear a path, wend their way down from the Temple of Jupiter Capitolinus to the still under construction Julian Forum. Here they found Caesar in the forecourt of the Temple of Venus Genetrix, seated on a golden throne on an elevated platform, assigning contracts for building work for his various and many construction projects. He was flanked by his secretaries, Oppius and Balbus, as well as the jurist Gaius Trebatius, and was deep in conversation with them as the senators arrived and came to a halt in the Forum before him.

In fact, he was so involved with what he was doing that, at first, he didn't notice the hundreds of senators who had just appeared before him. Trebatius leaned forward to whisper in Caesar's ear, and at last he looked up, surprise registering in his expression as he took in the huge senatorial deputation.

Antony spoke up loudly.

'Caesar, the Senate has voted you an extraordinary number of new honours, and we come to you to humbly request you accept them, for the greater good of the Republic and the people of Rome.'

A look of confusion crossed Caesar's face. There was a silence as everyone waited for his response, but nothing came.

'Caesar,' hissed Trebatius, quiet, but loud enough to be heard by the front ranks of the senators. 'Stand up. Show your respect.'

Caesar looked up at Trebatius, then to Antony, with a faraway look in his eyes. Still he did not move. The senators exchanged puzzled glances. Antony had a horrible suspicion he knew what was happening. He swiftly mounted the platform and called out, 'O Caesar, thank you for accepting our gifts and blessings.' One of his attendants passed him a laurel wreath, which had been delicately crafted in gold, and he placed it on Caesar's head, adjusting it to neatly cover his baldness. It suddenly struck him that it looked rather like a crown – something no Roman wanted to see – but Caesar's behaviour diverted the crowd's attention.

Antony looked into Caesar's eyes and saw no recognition there. He was not jerking or drooling, as in the previous episode Antony had witnessed, but there was no doubt in his mind that Caesar was undergoing some sort of seizure. He turned to the senators and the people and cried out, 'Let us repair to the Temple of Jupiter Capitolinus to give thanks for the gift of this great man whom the gods have chosen to bestow upon our nation.'

Some made to go, but others were clearly angry at Caesar's apparent disrespect. Cicero was whispering to Marcus Junius Brutus. Cassius was exchanging angry words with Decimus Brutus. Gaius Trebonius, Antony's friend, who had talked so treacherously to him a few months before, was apoplectic. He strode up the steps to the platform and looked down at the seated Caesar, jabbing a finger at his face.

'Remember, Caesar, you are just a man,' he spat. 'You sit on your throne by dint of your victories in battle – victories earned as much by your generals and your soldiers as by your own efforts. You are not a king. You are not a god. How dare you ignore your peers in such a way?'

Caesar actually seemed to shrink back from Trebonius, and Antony put an arm around his friend's shoulders.

'Come. Caesar is not himself, I think. He works too hard.'

Trebonius allowed Antony to usher him down the steps, though he grumbled and cursed the whole way.

'Caesar has accepted our gifts. Let us return to the temple and offer sacrifices of praise and thanksgiving.'

The senators reluctantly turned away and began to depart, the crowd being dispersed at Antony's instruction by the numerous lictors. As the Forum slowly cleared, Caesar suddenly came to his senses. He reached up and touched the golden wreath on his head tentatively, then looked up at Antony.

'What happened?'

'The Senate presented you with awards, Caesar,' said Trebatius, 'but you were unable to receive them appropriately. Antonius did an admirable job of protecting your dignity, but I'm afraid they were dissatisfied.'

'Dissatisfied, were they? Dissatisfied? Maybe they wish to replace me. To strike me down and put another in my stead?'

Caesar's emotions were clearly disturbed after his episode, and Antony reached out to put a gentle hand on his shoulder, but Caesar batted it away and leapt to his feet. Dramatically, he pulled his toga down, exposing his neck.

'If anyone wants to cut my throat, I am ready,' he cried out.

Those still remaining in the Forum looked on in incredulity as Caesar raved at them about traitors and assassins. Fortunately, most had already departed, and Trebatius and Antony managed to calm him down and get him into a carriage to convey him home. Oppius and Balbus accompanied him, leaving Trebatius and Antony alone. They looked at each other, but said nothing. What was there to be said?

ante diem xix Kalendas Februarias DCCX AUC (14 January 44 BC),
Rome

Fulvia had laid on a sumptuous feast for Antony's thirty-eighth birthday. She had spared no expense, to the extent that she had bought a new chef, whose previous owner had only reluctantly parted with him on payment of an eye-wateringly vast sum. He had been worth every copper coin, though, and each mouthful was an ecstasy, whether it was swan breast, trout pie or pomegranate sorbet. Unfortunately, the guest of honour was Caesar, who ate parsimoniously, preferring bread and water to the delicacies before him.

Antony refused to copy the Dictator – it was his celebration, after all – and his other guests followed his lead, enjoying all that was on offer. Antony's two brothers, Lucius and Gaius, as well as Fulvia, his mother, Julia, and Fulvia's eldest son with Clodius, Publius Claudius Pulcher, were also reclining on the dining couches. Notably absent was Antonius Hybrida, Antony's uncle – Caesar had recalled him from exile and he was back living in Rome. It would have been rather embarrassing to have invited him, since Hybrida was, of course, also his former father-in-law.

Hybrida had just failed in his attempt to be made censor, but the rest of Antony's family was thriving with the support of both Antony and Caesar. Gaius had been rewarded for his service as a legate in the civil war, despite his lack of success, with the position of praetor, and Lucius had become Tribune of the Plebs, the role that Antony had occupied at the start of the war. With Fulvia's loyal client base that she had inherited from Clodius and Curio, the Antonii were now a clan to be reckoned with, and in normal times, a family boasting a consul, a praetor and a tribune would be the most powerful in Rome. These were, of course, not normal times. Caesar had broken the model of power, and Antony wondered if it could ever be restored. Did he even want it to be? The old system had not served him particularly well – he could not deny that everything he had now, he owed to Caesar, even if he felt he had earned those rewards.

While they ate, they talked of simple matters such as the welfare of elderly family members, possible future matches for Fulvia's daughter Claudia, who was now twelve years old, and – more distantly – Antony's daughter, Toni, who was now six. Antony enquired after Octavius, and Caesar informed him that he had recently received a letter from the young man, who was studying and training in Illyricum, and was pleased to report he was in good health.

After dinner was finished, Caesar brought the topic round to his unfortunate episode two days before.

'Trebatius tells me you handled the situation well, Marcus. I'm sorry I put you in that position.'

'It could not be helped, Caesar. Even you cannot control when the gods will send that affliction upon you.'

'True. Hippocrates called it "the Sacred Disease", but we Romans sometimes refer to it as the *morbus commitialis* because of the way it can break up a meeting. I do sometimes wonder if our country's rigidly practical approach to matters is a blessing or a curse.'

They all laughed dutifully.

'Nevertheless,' said Caesar, 'once again I owe you my gratitude. It is much appreciated, coming so soon after our little disagreement.'

They had not talked about Caesar's proposal to make Dolabella consul since that Senate meeting, and the situation remained unresolved. As far as Antony knew, the elections were going ahead, but he had not changed his position. But this was not the time to reopen that debate.

'I have been considering this proposal of the Senate to vote me divine honours,' Caesar continued. 'If I am to become a god when I die, then I will need a priesthood, and a high priest. As Pontifex Maximus, I wish to propose that you, Marcus, become my first *flamen Divi Julii.*'

Antony smiled and inclined his head in thanks. It was a genuine honour, to be the high chief priest in a new cult. There were only three other major priesthoods: those of Jupiter, the *flamen Dialis*; Mars, the *flamen Martialis*; and Quirinus, the *flamen Quirinalis*. A flamen had some important powers, such as the ability to pardon criminals, the right to sit on a curule chair in the Senate, and to be awarded a lictor. But two problems immediately occurred to Antony.

'Without wishing to seem ungrateful, Caesar, doesn't the role of flamen come with some rather severe restrictions? If I recall rightly, the flamines are unable to touch metal or ride a horse. That might rather hinder my use in war.' Antony was aware of a story, possibly apocryphal – Caesar neither confirming nor denying – that Sulla had tried to make Caesar flamen dialis when he was a young man, to prevent Caesar being a future threat to him or the Republic.

Caesar laughed. 'I would like to see the man who thinks he could take your horse or your sword from you, Marcus. I don't think anyone would expect you to obey those archaic traditions.'

'That's good to know. But there is also the matter that a flamen must be a patrician. Despite my family's descent from Hercules and noble ancestors such as my grandfather, we are a plebeian family.'

'That is true, and I have also considered this matter. I will therefore make the entire Antonius family patrician.'

Antony's mother gasped and put her hand to her mouth, and Lucius and Gaius looked at each other, grinning broadly. Although once the patricians had been the ruling class and the plebeians the masses, by Antony's time, there were few practical differences between the two groups in society. They certainly could not be told apart by wealth or rank – there were as many impoverished patricians as there were rich plebeians, and the consulship was supposed to be held by one patrician and one plebeian. But there was still a certain something – an indefinable superiority – that came with being of a patrician family, which was why it was so shocking that first Clodius, and later Dolabella, had given that status up.

'That is an honour, Caesar.' Antony meant it. It was even more gratifying to know that his infant son Antyllus automatically inherited the honour.

'From a bankrupt in a dishonoured family, to a consul and a patrician, Stepfather,' said young Claudius in a sarcastic tone. 'Where will it end? Will you be king?'

'Claudius, do not take that tone,' snapped Fulvia, but Antony held up a hand.

'Don't worry,' said Antony. 'He is just of that age. I didn't always see eye to eye with my stepfather, bless his departed shade.'

'What does it mean to be a king anyway?' asked Caesar, musing. 'Marcus, you have seen at first hand, as have I, what power a king holds in the East. Is it a power worth holding, do you think?'

Antony hesitated, pondering whether there was a correct answer.

'I have seen the difference between the paralysis in our Senate as small men argue,' he said cautiously, 'and I have seen the decisiveness with which an absolute monarch can wield authority. Perhaps as our borders expand, our system of government, devised to run a single city, is no longer fit for purpose. Yet it seems to me that Rome would tolerate almost anything except a king.'

Caesar stroked his chin and looked pensive. He was already a king in all but name, Antony reflected, with his unlimited power for an unlimited term, and the hereditary nature of at least some of his titles. So why would he want the title?

'It has been said that the Sibylline books predict that only a king of Rome may conquer Parthia,' said Caesar.

Was that where this was coming from? It was true that the *quinde-cimviri sacris faciundis*, the priests who guarded the Sibylline books, had recently declared they had discovered these words in the text. Antony thought it highly coincidental that they had only just found this out, and suspected some mischief, a way of pushing Caesar to take a step too far. That the discontented Cassius was one of those priests added weight to his suspicions. But Caesar seemed to be taking it seriously.

'I would not pay too much attention to those prophecies, Caesar. My stepfather did, and look where it got him.'

'Of course, it's nonsense,' said Caesar. 'But if the people believe it to be so...' He contemplated the liquid in his cup of water. Then he looked up, and said brightly, 'I will give it some thought. Let's discuss other matters. Fulvia, your chef has excelled himself. Congratulations on your purchase.'

The evening returned to small talk, but Antony could not help dwelling on Caesar's musings. Surely this path could only lead to trouble?

ante diem xv Kalendas Martias DCCX AUC (15 February 44 BC), Rome

The Lupercalia was one of Rome's oldest religious festivals. Also known as the Februa, since it was celebrated two days after the Ides of that month, its ancient name was associated with purging and its newer name with the wolves. The religious rites and sacrifices centred around the statue of a lupine Pan, naked except for a loincloth, situated in a cave at the foot of the Palatine hill, which was purported to be the site where the she-wolf had suckled the infant twins Romulus and Remus.

There were two ancient schools of the Lupercal priesthood, the *Quinctilliani* and the *Fabiani*, associated with Romulus and Remus respectively, but this year a new one had been instituted in honour of Julius Caesar, the *Juliani*, with Antony as its first chief priest or *Magister*. It was thus his role, that late winter morning, to begin the ceremony by conducting the sacrifices at the altar in the Lupercal cave. He was completely naked, as the ritual demanded, and he tried to suppress a shiver as the wind whipped around his genitals.

Two Luperci priests led out a male dog and a male goat on leads. Antony picked up the sacrificial knife from the altar and slit the throats of the victims with grim efficiency, the blood spurting over his torso and face. He held them firmly until their death throes had ceased, while a priest collected the lifeblood in a bowl. The youngest initiates, all adolescent boys, then hesitantly stepped forward, and Antony smeared blood over their foreheads, after which they gave a ritually proscribed forced laugh. Antony passed the corpses of the victims over to the priests, who efficiently flayed them and cut the skin into thin strips, which were passed out among the celebrants.

Then there was the feasting: liberal amounts of wine and roasted flesh passed around and enjoyed by all. Antony was no stranger to ritual and ceremony – religious observance was a part of everyday life, whether it was a casual daily offering to the household gods, the religious rites that accompanied every gladiatorial contest or chariot race, or the formal observances at the frequent religious festivals. Antony had presided over many observances in his various roles as Master of Horse, consul, or simply paterfamilias. But though he had taken part in the Lupercalia in his adolescence, this was his first time in charge of the ancient ritual, and he felt unsettled by the whole odd experience. Even worse was the thought of the ridiculous role that Caesar had designated for him at the end of the ceremony. Almost without realising what he was doing, he finished several cups of wine in quick succession and soon felt more at ease.

The second part of the ceremony involved the Luperci, as the young men taking part were known, running through the city. They were given skimpy goatskin loincloths to provide a semblance of modesty, and Antony thought it was strange how even that tiny piece of material made one feel so much less exposed and vulnerable. Not that he felt he had anything to be ashamed of between his legs – quite the contrary.

He led the Luperci out of the cave at a loping run past the cheering crowds. Young women of marriageable age stepped out into their path and extended their hands, and the Luperci whipped their palms with the strips of skin they all carried. The ladies giggled, gasped; some even wept. Being struck with the skin was supposed to bring fertility, and clearly many of the recipients of the blessing sincerely believed this. Antony suspected that in times past, the young men would take the young women aside to ensure they became pregnant in more practical ways, but these days the ceremony was more civilised.

They ran up the Via Sacra and back down into the Forum, and Antony had worked up a decent sweat despite the cold. He led them to the Rostra, where he called a halt. Looking down on them, Gaius Julius Caesar, Dictator in Perpetuity, sat on his golden throne. He wore a golden wreath, the purple cloak of a general celebrating a triumph, and the high red boots traditionally worn by the kings of Alba.

Antony swallowed. Now came the moment he was dreading.

Caesar had become obsessed with the concept of monarchy, but his position seemed to vacillate between a rejection of its necessity – stating that if he had the power of a monarch, what need had he of the title – and the notion that as the supreme power in Rome, why should he not be granted the title "king"?

Recently, a crown had appeared on a statue of Caesar, and two tribunes had ordered it removed. Then a couple of days later, while Caesar was celebrating the Latin festival in the Alban hills, a man from the crowd had hailed Caesar as Rex. Caesar calmly replied that his name was Caesar, not Rex. But the same two tribunes who had had the crown removed ordered the arrest and flogging of the man who had dared to address Caesar as a king. Caesar was furious, and in a specially convened Senate meeting, had the two tribunes stripped of their posts and sent into exile, once again showing that his outrage at the abuse of Antony's tribune sacrosanctity at the start of the civil war was a mere casus belli and not a belief he actually held.

So now, at Caesar's insistence, Antony had to play his role in a farce, the purpose of which he wasn't even sure. One of the Luperci priests produced a laurel wreath, within which a crown was clear to see. Lifted up by others, he placed it at Caesar's feet. Caesar commanded Lepidus, who as Master of Horse was standing beside him, to usher the priest away, but as had been pre-arranged, Lepidus didn't move. Then Cassius Longinus, another of the Luperci, was lifted up and placed the crown on Caesar's lap.

Now the crowd became aware of what was happening, and shouts broke out. Although some urged Caesar to accept the crown, most of the voices were calling for him to toss it aside.

Then it was Antony's turn. Boosted by his colleagues, he leapt nimbly up onto the Rostra, snatched the crown from Caesar's lap, and placed it on his head.

There was a moment of stunned silence, then the crowd erupted into uproar. Some cheered and called out, 'Caesar Rex, Caesar Rex!' but the dominant sound that echoed around the Forum was a deep groan. Caesar gestured for Antony to remove the crown, and the crowd cheered enthusiastically. As Caesar had pre-arranged, Antony waited and once more crowned him. The crowd reacted similarly, but the disapproval was louder, and those hailing him as king were more subdued. Once more, Caesar commanded Antony to remove the crown, to ecstatic cheers; once more, Antony replaced it, to boos and jeers. He took it off one last time, and amid the tumult, Caesar stood and raised his arms for quiet so he could be heard. The crowd slowly calmed.

'Take this crown to the Temple of Jupiter Capitolinus. Rome has only one king, and he is the King of the Gods, not I, Caesar.'

Antony passed the crown to Lepidus and dismounted from the Rostra. Caesar got into his litter and was carried away, and the crowd followed him, cheering him and singing, 'Not Rex but Caesar.'

Antony felt someone at his shoulder, and he turned to find Cassius and Brutus regarding him with expressions of wry amusement.

'Did that go as planned, do you suppose?' asked Cassius.

'Perfectly,' said Antony, with more confidence than he felt. In truth, he had no idea what Caesar had had in mind when he proposed this odd spectacle. Caesar had explained it as an opportunity to publicly refute the rumour that he wanted to be king. But Antony had his doubts. Caesar had already privately expressed the possibility of being Dictator and consul in Rome, but king in the East, which didn't help quash the rumours that he was planning on moving the capital of the Empire to Alexandria, or even Ilium.

What if the crowd had cheered their approval of his coronation? Would he have rebuked them and rejected the crown just the same? Or would he have claimed it was the will of the people, and allowed himself to assume the title of king – maybe something he had secretly desired all along?

What Antony did know was that Caesar had changed over the last year. Whether it was the effects of his illness, his impatience with anything that impeded his plans, or an increasingly grandiose view of himself, now that he had no opponent worth the name, it was clear that he was behaving more and more like an autocrat – a Greek-style tyrant or an Eastern potentate. The question for Antony was whether this was a situation he should support. Being right-hand man and heir apparent to an absolute ruler was not a bad position to be in, but were there risks? Moreover, did he care enough about the Republic to be concerned if Caesar chose to destroy it?

Clearly Brutus and Cassius had their own opinions.

'Well, it was good to see Caesar and the unwashed masses in agreement that kingship is not to be tolerated,' said Brutus haughtily.

'Indeed.' Antony waited to see if they had anything else to say to him. The two praetors looked at each other, then bade Antony farewell and walked off together, deep in discussion.

That night, someone daubed graffiti on the statue of Lucius Junius Brutus, the ancestor of Decimus and Marcus Brutus, who had overthrown the last Roman kings: 'If only you were alive now.' Soon similar graffiti was widespread and anonymous pamphlets were circulating, reminding Marcus Brutus who his ancestor was, telling him he was no true Brutus or asking if he had taken a bribe.

Antony felt Rome was becoming less and less secure for Caesar, and he looked forward to the moment when the Dictator would depart for Parthia and leave behind the vipers in the city who might do him harm.

Chapter XIV

Caesar continued to press ahead with all his ambitions with a speed and energy that completely belied his age. Among his plans was the desire to pass his consulship on to Dolabella. Antony wondered now if that was more about a stubborn refusal to be thwarted rather than any clear desire for Dolabella to be consul. He was not aware of any service that Dolabella had done for Caesar that would make the Dictator go to these lengths and expend so much of his precious time on the matter.

So the Tribal Assembly and a large crowd of onlookers dutifully gathered on the Campus Martius to vote for the single candidate whom Caesar, as Dictator, had nominated to take over his role of consul. Antony watched impassively as the first and second classes filed through the voting pens. Dolabella stood beside Caesar, a smugly satisfied look on his face as the votes mounted, though his election was unopposed. A few lictors guarded Caesar, but he had recently dismissed his sizeable Spanish bodyguard, against the advice of Antony and others, declaring that as the Senate had sworn to protect him, he need have no fear.

Once the second class had finished voting, there was no need to continue; though the lower classes were more numerous, their voting power was so much lower that they rarely played a role in elections, even when there was more than one candidate. Caesar stood preparing to announce the outcome, but Antony got in first.

'Wait,' he called out. A crow flew overhead, turned in a circle, cawed and then flew west. 'Look!' He pointed at the crow, flapping lazily away towards the river. 'A portent.'

Caesar frowned, but the crowd had all turned.

'What does it mean?' someone shouted.

Antony held both hands aloft, tilted his head back to the sky and closed his eyes. He remained like this for a dozen heartbeats, judging the moment to perfection. His head snapped back down, he surveyed the crowd, then stabbed a finger dramatically towards Dolabella.

'I have taken the auspices,' Antony said in his best priestly, mystical voice. 'They are unfavourable. Caesar must not surrender his consulship to this man, or the gods will show their displeasure.'

The crowd groaned their dismay. Caesar's brow furrowed in anger, but the gathered masses were beginning to chant, 'No Dolabella, no Dolabella!'

Dolabella leapt up to remonstrate with Caesar.

'This is ridiculous,' he said. 'He just made that up. He has no skill as an augur. He is a fraud.'

Antony crossed his arms and regarded Dolabella with satisfaction.

'I have observed the birds. The signs are clear. Another day.' These last words were the official sanction of the augur, stating that the business could not be concluded on that day, and, of course, Antony had shown that he would not allow it be concluded on any other day either.

'Cicero,' said Dolabella, gesturing to his former father-in-law, who had been observing the proceedings with a body of other senators. 'You are an augur. Don't allow him to do this.'

Antony tensed. This was the weak part of his plan. He was not the only augur. What would happen if another priest contradicted him?

But Cicero spread his hands helplessly.

'The augury may be false. The augur himself may be a fraud. Nevertheless, I respect the sanctity of the office, and I will not gainsay the decision of Marcus Antonius.'

Dolabella balled his fists, and Antony willed his wife's ex-lover to strike him. He was a small man, and Antony could knock him down with a single blow, maybe even kill him, with a thousand witnesses to testify it was self-defence. Dolabella clearly realised this, too, and after a moment's indecision, he turned and stalked away.

Caesar held up his hands and the crowd hushed to listen.

'The augur has spoken. There will be no election this day. This now becomes a matter for the Senate to discuss. I hereby call a meeting of the Senate for the Ides of March, for the purpose of discussing the suffect consulship of Publius Cornelius Dolabella.'

Antony cursed. Caesar was being as stubborn as him in this matter. Well, the game was not yet over. Caesar could ask the Senate to back him in promoting Dolabella, but Antony had a not-so-secret weapon.

His youngest brother Lucius was Tribune of the Plebs, and could veto any senatorial decision. He almost relished the prospect – the thought of the coming battle on the Senate floor.

He had a feeling that the Senate meeting of the Ides of March would be one that went down in history.

pridie Idus Martias DCCX AUC (14 March 44 BC), Rome

There was an odd mood in Lepidus' triclinium, Antony thought, as he chewed on some dates after the main meal was finished. Decimus Brutus seemed on edge, though he was acting as if nothing concerned him, making idle jokes at the expense of the likes of Cicero and Cato. Caesar, the other guest of honour, paid little attention to the conversation as he continued his unceasing business of government, dictating letters to his private secretary and signing contracts and deeds. The mention of Cato caused him to purse his lips, however, and make a tutting sound. Both Cicero and, less skilfully but more passionately, Marcus Brutus had written pamphlets praising Cato posthumously as a model Roman citizen. It was perhaps understandable that Brutus wished to pay respect to his deceased uncle, but not particularly diplomatic given Cato's and Caesar's implacable hatred of each other, and the strongly implied criticism of Caesar's role in his death. Caesar had been restrained in his response, however, partly because of his traditional clemency, and partly because he was a great admirer of Cicero and loved Brutus like a son. He had satisfied himself with writing his own pamphlet, the *Anticato*, a polemic against his stubborn, self-righteous enemy.

Lepidus seemed put out that Caesar was not joining in the general conversation, and was all but ignoring them, though he should have been used to it by now. Caesar was rarely at rest, and was entirely capable of doing several things at once, such as that moment, when he was monitoring the topic of discussion, replying to a letter from the governor of Macedonia, and arranging for a gift of flowers and perfume to be sent to Cleopatra, whom he had been neglecting.

Perhaps to get a reaction from Caesar, Lepidus turned the conversation to some of the odd omens that had been recently reported across the Empire.

'Did you hear what Cornelius Balbus said the veterans found in Capua?' he asked.

'Do tell,' said Decimus, and Antony was sure he detected a hefty dollop of sarcasm. Lepidus was generally considered a man promoted above his ability, and Decimus and others often found it hard to disguise their contempt.

'They were breaking up some ancient tombs for building material, and they found one belonging to Capys, the founder of Capua. In it was a bronze tablet with an inscription saying that disturbing these bones would cause a man of Trojan descent to be murdered by his kin, and then avenged at great cost to the country.'

Decimus rolled his eyes, but Caesar did not react. Antony thought the story implausible, but Balbus was a generally reliable source, so it could not be completely dismissed.

'What else, Lepidus?' asked Decimus with mock eagerness.

'Well, the horses that Caesar dedicated to the river Rubicon and allowed to roam free in the Rubicon valley are apparently refusing to go near the river, and are openly weeping.'

That seemed just silly, but Antony listened politely.

'And then there is that soothsayer, Spurina.'

Spurina was a *haruspex*, a priest of minor importance, whose role was to make prognostications by examining the entrails of animals. The method of Antony's own priesthood, the augurs, of making predictions by observing the flight patterns of birds, was much less messy, he reflected. But this haruspex had accosted Caesar at a ceremony just after the Lupercalia, and warned him that a terrible fate would befall him by the Ides of March. Caesar had laughed this off, and had seemed genuinely unaffected by it. Antony's attitude to gods and superstitions was to be sceptical, but respectful, just in case. Caesar seemed to think that belief in the magical and the supernatural was just a tool for him to garner power and control the masses.

'Seriously, Lepidus,' said Decimus. 'If you paid attention to every prophecy that spewed out of the lips of every priest and holy man in Rome, you would never leave your house for fear of disaster. It is not a way to live one's life, don't you agree, Caesar?'

Caesar looked up, grunted, took a sip of water, then bent his head back down to peer at the scroll in his hands.

'Well, I agree with you, Decimus,' said Antony. 'Death lurks around every corner. You can die of illness, you can die in battle. You can be mugged and murdered as you walk home at night. A roof tile might fall on your head and strike you dead. Very rarely can you take any precautions against your fate, so why waste your days in terror, heeding every terrible portent? Who would want to know the hour of one's death, in any case?'

'I would,' said Lepidus. 'So I could make preparations.'

'Not me,' said Decimus.

'Nor I,' said Antony. 'But if you had to choose, which manner of death would you pick?'

'A sudden one.'

The words came from Caesar – unexpected, since he had said so little that evening.

The other three nodded agreement. There was not much else to say to that.

The conversation drifted aimlessly for a little longer, but the morbid discussion seemed to have subdued everyone, and soon Caesar rose, claiming to have a headache.

'Thank you for hosting me this evening, Lepidus. I apologise that I have not been better company.'

'You honour me with your mere presence, Caesar.'

He shook Lepidus' hand, embraced Decimus, then turned to Antony.

'Are you prepared for the Senate tomorrow? You know the reason for the meeting.'

'I know the reason, and yes, I am prepared. My position has not changed, Caesar. Clodius was my friend, but can you imagine what chaos he would have wrought as consul? Dolabella would be worse. And he has a cruel streak about him that is distasteful.'

'Well, let us hear what the conscript fathers have to say on the matter. Perhaps they will change your mind. Or mine. Either way, we must not fall out over it. You are my co-consul, my friend, and throughout my struggles and tribulations you have stuck by me, served me loyally and with distinction, despite our occasional disagreements. I owe you much.'

'And I you, Caesar,' said Antony, feeling a little lump in his throat.

Caesar opened his arms and they hugged, rough and firm, holding for a heartbeat longer than was customary, before separating. Caesar looked a little embarrassed at his uncharacteristic display of emotion, but he held Antony's gaze for a moment.

'Call on me tomorrow at dawn, Marcus. You, too, Decimus. I have a ceremony to perform with Calvinus on the Capitoline first – he lives not far from my house, so we will collect him on the way. Then we will go together to the Senate. And with that formality out of the way, I march against Parthia. I bid you all goodnight.'

'Goodnight, Caesar,' they all replied.

-

Antony couldn't sleep. He sat on an upholstered wooden bench in a garden room, looking out at the statues and shaped bushes that cast sinister shadows in the flickering light of the torches and lamps. The orange glow of a brazier kept the night chill at bay, aided by the body of Fulvia, who sat beside him, cuddled close, her head on his shoulder.

'How will it be when he is gone?' asked Antony.

'Very much as before,' said Fulvia. 'While Caesar is in Parthia, you will once again be the first man in Rome. Only this time, you will have me, and together we will do great things. We will rule wisely and fairly, and make ourselves rich and powerful at the same time.'

'No,' said Antony. 'I don't mean when he has gone to Parthia. I mean when he has departed this earth – gone to the underworld, or up into the stars, or wherever it is great men go when they become gods.'

Fulvia sat up and looked at him sharply. 'Have you heard something?'

'No.' Then a sudden suspicion occurred to him. 'Have you?'

'Not exactly,' said Fulvia cautiously. 'But there are murmurings. Nothing I can pin down, but some of my clients have heard rumours. Secret meetings of high-ranking officials. Whispers of conspiracies. Part of me dismisses them as the usual paranoia of the city, but some of the same names keep coming up.'

'Who?'

'I have no evidence against these people, Marcus.'

'Tell me, Fulvia. Who is plotting against Caesar?'

Fulvia sighed. 'Pontinus Aquila is angry because Caesar confiscated some of his land to give to Servilia. Then there is Tillius Cimber, who unsuccessfully petitioned Caesar to have his brother recalled from exile. Lucius Municius Basilus is said to be frustrated by his lack of promotion, and Gaius Cassius Longinus feels snubbed because Marcus Junius Brutus was promoted above him to Urban Praetor, and is not being taken to Parthia despite his experience and expertise.'

'Are these people conspirators, or just malcontents? Talk is common, and Caesar's clemency does not exactly discourage it.'

'I don't know, Marcus, I really don't.'

She looked at him, hesitated, then said, 'If you were asked to join a conspiracy against Caesar's life, would you?'

Antony's instinct was to act shocked. But this was Fulvia, and they were alone, so why pretend he hadn't thought about it?

'I can't see it happening. If there is a plot, they couldn't trust me not to betray them. I am too closely associated with Caesar.'

'But it's common knowledge that you don't always see eye to eye.'

'Neither do we,' said Antony. 'But you are stuck with me.'

'And you are stuck with me. As long as you behave yourself and do as you are told.'

Antony laughed, though he wondered if her words weren't a little too close to the truth for comfort.

'But hypothetically, would I support a conspiracy to murder Caesar?' he mused, stroking his beard. 'I suppose there are two aspects to that. Would Caesar's death benefit the state, and would it benefit me? As to the first, I can't see it. Most of the opposition to Caesar seems to come either from people with personal grudges, or those with unrealistic concepts of freedom and an idealised version of the Republic which has never really existed. Caesar brings a stability and a unity to our government that we haven't had since Hannibal invaded. I don't believe the empire would long survive with its current political system. There is too much short-term self-interest to consider what is truly best for Rome. Caesar has unique vision and ability, and can deal with our problems, big and small, whether they concern the threat of invasion from Parthia or the state of our roads and drains.'

'And for the second? Would Caesar's death benefit you?'

This was the more difficult question. Antony took his time before replying.

'We cannot divine the future...'

'Not even you, augur?' Fulvia's tone was gently mocking. She had even less belief in magic and superstition than he did.

'Not even I. Where would I be if I helped kill Caesar? Maybe Dictator in his stead. Maybe tossed off the Tarpeian rock by a furious mob.'

'You don't think it's worth the risk, for the possibility of ultimate power?'

'I am a Roman. A consul. Even a patrician now. Of course I would love to rank beside Marius and Sulla and Caesar in history. But is that potential within me?'

'Yes, Marcus, it is. I see it. You are by far the best of my husbands. The best man I know.'

Antony patted her arm. 'Thank you, my dear, but I think you are biased. Maybe I can be great, but I would prefer power to pass to me peacefully, in due course, with the support of all, and when I have had more time to learn from Caesar how to rule.'

Fulvia smiled indulgently, but he could tell she wasn't convinced. He wondered what sort of a ruler she would make, if she had not been born into the feeble body of a woman. Perhaps greater than all of them.

Antony sighed. 'It's all mere conjecture anyway. Nothing will happen to Caesar. He leaves in three days. He has asked me to call on him in the morning. I will escort him to the Senate meeting. It would be a brave and foolish person to make an attempt on Caesar's life with me by his side.

Fulvia smiled and squeezed a firm bicep.

'My brave, strong husband.'

He put an arm around her shoulders and pulled her close.

'My beautiful, clever wife.'

They held each other in companionable silence until finally Antony felt tired enough to suggest they try to get some sleep.

Idibus Martiis DCCX AUC (15 March 44 BC), Rome

Dawn found Antony waiting in Caesar's atrium, feeling blurry – not from the relatively modest amount of wine he had drunk the night before, but from lack of sleep. He tried to stifle a yawn, realised he was unable to, and gave in to it.

'Bad night?' asked Decimus Brutus, who was waiting with him.

'Just one of those things,' said Antony. 'I've had worse.'

He had expected Caesar to appear promptly once their arrival had been announced. He was usually up before the sun and raring to go. But time passed, and Antony settled himself on a bench, legs stretched out before him, back against the wall, and closed his eyes.

He wasn't sure if he was dozing, but Calpurnia's voice brought him back to alertness.

'Marcus Antonius, Decimus Junius Brutus, Caesar apologises for keeping you waiting,' said Caesar's wife.

Antony leapt to his feet, bowed, and kissed her hand.

'It is no matter,' he said. 'We are at Caesar's disposal, aren't we, Decimus?'

'Of course,' said Decimus. 'But there is an important meeting of the Senate today. When can we expect him?'

'Soon, soon. He is not fully well this morning, and I fear that is partly my fault.'

'How so?' asked Antony.

'I kept him awake with my nightmares.'

'Anything portentous?' Many people believed in the prophetic power of dreams, and even if Antony had his doubts, others would not.

Calpurnia hesitated. 'I dreamed I held Caesar's pierced body in my arms, while he bled out over my breast. Oh, you must think me a foolish woman.'

'Not at all,' said Antony. 'It sounds distressing.'

'Indeed,' said Decimus. 'Dreams can seem very real, even when we know they are pure fantasy.'

Now Caesar did finally enter the atrium, and Antony and Decimus bowed deeply.

'Apologies,' said Caesar. He was not yet dressed in his formal robes, but wore a simple tunic. His thinning hair was dishevelled and he had dark bags under his eyes. 'I am really not myself today.'

'You have nothing to apologise for,' said Antony. 'We are at your service.'

'Nevertheless, the Senate will soon assemble,' said Decimus.

'Gaius,' said Calpurnia, 'if you aren't well, perhaps you should not attend today.'

'Perhaps you are right,' said Caesar, his voice hoarse. 'I have three days before I leave for Parthia. We could reconvene another day before I go.'

'You look strong to me,' said Decimus. 'I have no doubt a man of your constitution is capable of sitting through a tedious meeting while old men pontificate.'

'Gaius, remember my dream,' said Calpurnia. 'I don't think you should go to the Senate today. You know I am not a superstitious woman, but this has troubled me.'

'It's true,' said Caesar to Antony and Decimus. 'Calpurnia is not prone to dreams or flights of fancy.' He seemed undecided. It was a measure of how much his health had declined, Antony thought. The man who fought off Vercingetorix at Alesia and Pompey at Pharsalus would never have let a bad night's sleep and a woman's nightmare stop him from doing what he wanted.

'Caesar,' said Decimus. 'Some of the senators are beginning the day by attending the ceremony in which Cassius' son dons the *toga virilis*. They will convene at Pompeius' theatre after that. And you have some sacrifices at the Temple of Jupiter Capitolinus to attend, do you not? You could be carried there first in a litter and then see if you feel up to the Senate meeting afterwards.'

Antony looked at Decimus curiously. He seemed very keen to get Caesar to the Senate. Had he done some sort of deal with Dolabella to help him get the consulship he craved? If so, he would find Antony would put up a good fight.

'Yes,' said Caesar. 'I could do that. Marcus, could you ask one of my lictors to organise me a litter?'

Antony went out into the street to do as he was instructed, leaving a pale-faced Calpurnia wringing her hands.

–

The Ides of every month were a public holiday dedicated to Jupiter, and the Ides of March were also sacred to Anna Perenna, the goddess of the year, an archaic ritual dating back to when March was the first month of the year. The rites of Anna Perenna were held at her sacred grove at the first milestone on the Via Flaminia, and this year Caesar declined to make that journey. However, he was content to supervise the sacrifice on the Capitoline hill.

First, they called upon Gnaeus Domitius Calvinus, whose house was on the way. Calvinus was being rewarded for his loyalty and his important role in the battle of Pharsalus by being nominated as co-successor to the position of Master of Horse after Lepidus' term expired, his colleague to be young Octavius. Caesar was keen that Calvinus show himself to be publicly involved in the affairs of state, to show he was worthy of the title. From there, they processed formally up the Via Sacra to the top of the Capitoline hill, the white lamb to be sacrificed led before them by some priests of Jupiter.

At the top of the Capitoline hill, on its northernmost spur, was a citadel called the Arx Capitolina, which was where the ceremony was to be carried out. A large number of priests were present, of various ranks and positions – Vestal Virgins, flamines of Jupiter, augurs to read the portents in nature, and *haruspices* to determine the signs within the entrails of the sacrifices.

The ceremony did not start well. The white lamb kicked out just as the priest's knife was descending, and the cut was not true. The lamb bleated pitifully, a non-fatal gash displaying the muscles of its neck, and it struggled, almost breaking free of the priest's grip. Another priest helped secure it, and the second strike bit deep, arterial blood spurting out, the poor young beast's cries and convulsions quickly subsiding. One of the haruspices then stepped forward, cut open the lamb's belly and plunged his hands inside, pulling out a large, floppy brown liver dripping in gore. He turned it this way and that, then pronounced, 'It is rough and the head is missing. The omens are bad.'

Caesar looked at Decimus and Antony doubtfully, but Decimus called out, 'Fetch another. Repeat the sacrifice.'

Another lamb was brought forth, and this time the killing went more smoothly. But the haruspex once again declared the entrails were not auspicious. Caesar began to look impatient, but Decimus insisted a third sacrifice take place. When this, too, was declared to contain no positive signs, Caesar had had enough.

'Antonius, go to the Senate. Convey my apologies, but inform them that the omens are not favourable, and our meeting must be postponed.'

Antony hesitated. He had not intended to leave Caesar's side. The Dictator had a couple of dozen lictors as bodyguards, but though they were useful in keeping overenthusiastic petitioners at bay, Antony had no confidence in their fighting ability, and indeed wondered how easily they could be bribed to stand by, or even to take part in any assassination attempt. But Decimus spoke up again before Antony could react.

'Caesar, are you really asking Antonius to tell the Senate that you are cancelling a meeting that you yourself convened because of some bad omens? Do you wish him to tell them to come back when your wife has had some better dreams? They will ridicule you.'

Caesar looked as indecisive as Antony had ever seen him. He waited for Caesar's response, but Decimus spoke up again.

'I should not tell you this, Caesar, since it was supposed to be a surprise, but I know that the Senate this day are prepared to declare you king of any province outside Italy, and allow you to wear a crown whenever you go abroad.'

Caesar's eyes opened wider.

'Is that so?' asked Antony. 'It is news to me.'

'Of course, Antonius,' said Decimus smoothly. 'You are Caesar's closest confidant. It must be a surprise to you, too.'

The offer of a crown seemed to sway Caesar. Decimus took him gently by the hand and led him back towards his litter. 'Come, Caesar. And if you get before the Senate and still feel the day is inauspicious, at least you can dismiss the meeting in person, which will offend no one.'

Caesar allowed himself to be led back to his litter, and Antony could not help thinking about the white lamb on its lead being led to its doom. He pressed himself close to Caesar's side, and got into the litter with him. Four burly slaves picked up the poles, and they began to make their way back down the Capitoline hill towards the Theatre of Pompey on the Campus Martius.

One of the haruspices standing by the roadside caught Caesar's eye.

'Spurina,' called out Caesar, with something of his old confidence. 'The Ides of March have come.'

'They have, Caesar,' replied the priest. 'But they have not yet gone.'

It was not a cold day, but Antony felt a chill run down his spine.

–

Multitudes cheered Caesar rapturously on his way to the Senate meeting. The incident with the crown at the Lupercalia had, if anything, increased his popularity with the masses, who appreciated his public show of rejection of the ultimate symbol of the monarchy. The masses were easily swayed, though, as Antony had seen at first hand in observing Clodius and Curio, and by his own efforts as tribune and when he was in charge while Caesar was absent from Rome. It seemed equally likely that they would have been content with Caesar as their Rex. After all, if anyone deserved the honour, it was him, and the lower classes had always appreciated his generosity and the easy manner that this most noble of all Romans could mix with them. It was different from Antony's rapport with the common man. When he went dancing with actors and drinking in rough pubs, they treated him as one of them. When Caesar interacted with them, it was as a clear superior, delighting his subjects by deigning to gift them some of his precious time and attention.

They wended around the base of the Capitoline hill and east to the Campus Martius, to Pompey's theatre, situated at the southernmost part of the estate that Antony had taken over from Caesar's murdered enemy. Permanent stone theatres were technically forbidden in Rome, so Pompey had got around this by locating the structure just outside the pomerium, and by building a temple to Venus Victrix within the complex to turn it into a sacred space, as well as incorporating four pre-existing temples. A colonnaded quadrangle behind the stage sported statues, fountains and arcades where sculptures and paintings were exhibited, and also enclosed a spacious public garden in which theatregoers could wander before and after the productions or between acts.

For the purpose of the Senate, however, the most important part of the complex was the Curia, the meeting hall situated at the opposite end from the theatre itself. It had been a useful and common place for the Senate to meet in the years since the Curia Hostilia was burnt down during the riots around Clodius' funeral, especially since its replacement, the Curia Cornelia, had been closed by Caesar to be turned into a temple, and the new Senate house, the Curia Julia, was still under construction. It was also a sign of respect from Caesar to Pompey Magnus, that he had chosen that location in which to convene the Senate, not least because the entire proceedings would be overlooked by an enormous statue of Caesar's old friend and enemy.

When they reached the complex, Caesar alighted from the litter and drew himself up straight, clearly determined to show no sign of fatigue or infirmity. Antony leapt down beside him, making a conscious effort not to offer a supporting arm that would have humiliated his friend. The sound of trident clashing against shield made Antony turn sharply, but it was only a group of gladiators practising in the grounds for the later show. Still, Antony felt his heart speed up, and felt a sudden itch to be holding his sword. Previously he had gone about the city armed and armoured, but Caesar had made it clear he regarded that not in keeping with the office of consul, and so Antony wore just his formal toga, a comfortable tunic beneath, and leather sandals.

A man pushed through the lictors and lunged for Caesar, and Antony tensed, ready to spring. But he was just passing a note to Caesar – likely one of the many petitioners who accosted the Dictator everywhere he went. Caesar pushed the note into the large collection of similar papers he carried under one arm, to be attended to later.

'Caesar, I implore you, read my note with utmost urgency,' said the man. 'It is a matter of great importance to you.'

Caesar nodded benignly, and gestured to the lictors to drag him back into the crowd.

'He looked familiar,' said Antony. 'Wasn't he one of Brutus' Greek tutors?'

Caesar shrugged. His lictors lined up to make a corridor through which they could enter the Curia. The lictors would remain outside – though, technically, since they had all taken an oath to protect Caesar's person, the entire Senate was his bodyguard. Still, Antony was glad he would be close at hand.

They mounted the first step together, when he felt a touch on his arm. He turned to see his old friend and comrade-in-arms, Gaius Trebonius, looking at him anxiously.

'Forgive me, Caesar, for disturbing the consul, but there is a matter of great urgency about which I must speak to him.'

Antony looked uncertainly at Caesar, who had hesitated and was looking back at them both. Then Decimus Brutus, who had been walking behind Caesar's litter, came up and said, 'It's true, Caesar. This matter cannot wait. But it is personal to Antonius, you need not bother yourself with it. Please, continue on, and we will join you shortly.'

Caesar nodded, and walked up the steps alone. Antony watched him disappear inside the Curia, feeling an increasing sense of unease.

'What is it, Trebonius?' asked Antony.

'It's about your debt, Consul.'

Antony was immediately concerned. If there was one thing that made him feel vulnerable, and always had since his childhood, it was money. Since the death of his father, he did not think there had been a single moment when his tangible assets had outweighed his liabilities. Even now, when he had so much spending power at his fingertips, he still relied on the good will of his creditors, and on their belief that he remained creditworthy.

'Go on,' he said.

'Maybe you should be the one to tell him,' said Trebonius to Decimus Brutus.

'I would gladly take on that burden,' said Decimus. 'But I think it would come better from you.'

'Stop beating about the bush,' snapped Antony. 'Out with it.'

'Well, Antonius, it is like this,' said Trebonius. 'We fear that Dolabella has been spreading false rumours among your creditors.'

'Like what?'

'That Caesar is about to sack you from the consulship in favour of Dolabella.'

'Sack me? Even he does not have the power to sack a consul.'

'Of course he doesn't,' said Decimus. 'As Trebonius said, we know the rumour is false. But creditors are easily spooked. If they think you are out of favour with Caesar yet again, they may start to agitate for a repayment of your debts. If they take you to court and you default, it means exile.'

'I know that. Curse Dolabella. He is likely in there now, agitating to be consul. I need to get in there.'

He made to mount the steps, but Trebonius put a hand against Antony's chest, restraining him.

'No, Antonius. That is playing into his hands. If you show violence – or even just anger – towards him, it will add credence to the lie. Moreover, it might actually turn Caesar against you, and so become a self-fulfilling prophecy.'

Antony took a deep breath, walked away a few paces, then back again. He heard some shouts coming from within the Curia. The arguments had obviously already begun. He needed to get in there, to defend himself. Concerns about conspiracies against Caesar had vanished from his thoughts.

'So what am I to do?' he asked, almost begging his two friends and brothers in arms for their counsel. 'Advise me.'

Trebonius and Decimus looked at each other, then up the steps towards the entrance to the Curia. The shouts and cries were becoming louder, more outraged. Antony thought he heard a cry for help, a roar of outrage, or even pain. Then a senator – one of the new Gauls, Antony thought – came running headlong through the doorway, clutching his toga to lift it clear of his flapping sandals. Another followed, then another, until the trickle turned into a flood, and a deluge of balding and grey-haired men rushed out and down the steps.

'Treachery!' one cried.

'Murder!' yelled another.

Trebonius put his hand on Antony's shoulder and said earnestly, 'If you want my advice, old friend, you will run.'

Antony stared at them, a horrible certainty flooding over them.

'What have you done?'

Trebonius gave him a half-smile and a shrug, and then the two of them melted away among the fleeing senators.

Anxiety elevating towards panic, Antony forced his way against the current, thrusting the terrified conscript fathers aside, until he had made his way into the Curia.

Marcus Junius Brutus was the last senator standing on the chamber floor. He was holding a knife that was coated in blood. Antony tensed, ready to fight, confident he could best Brutus if necessary, even if he was unarmed. But Brutus looked at Antony with a sad expression.

'I tried to explain to them,' he said, gesturing at the backs of the slowest senators to flee. 'They wouldn't listen. You understand it is for the best, though, don't you, Antonius? The others wanted to kill you, too, you know, but I forbade it.'

'Brutus, what did you do?' growled Antony. 'Where is Caesar?'

Brutus shook his head, and stepped aside. Behind him, at the foot of the statue of Pompey, was a pile of torn, bloody rags. Antony approached tentatively, willing what he knew to be untrue, refusing to believe until he had confirmed it with his own eyes.

He knelt down. The rags were a toga, pierced over and over, pulled up to hide the body beneath. He tentatively pulled away the wool that covered the head.

Caesar's sightless eyes stared up out of a chalk-white face. Antony realised his knees were wet, and when he looked down, he saw that there was a large pool of blood spreading around him.

Still, he found it hard to accept. This man – such a dominant and influential force for all Romans, but for Antony especially; this great man, who had raised Antony up from nothing, who had conquered every foe, surmounted every challenge – was no more, struck dead by jealous cowards who had sworn to protect him. He grasped Caesar's body, pulled it to him, and wept, sobs erupting from his very core.

After some moments, he realised he had left his back exposed to the armed Brutus, and he looked around, but Brutus had gone. He was alone in this cold, empty chamber, with the murdered body of the greatest Roman who had ever lived.

Contradictory thoughts swirled through his head. Caesar's voice chided him to get a grip of himself. Fulvia's voice told him to be a man. Cicero's mocking laughter echoed around him. He gently re-covered Caesar's face with the bloody toga. Then he slowly stood. There would be time to grieve, time to honour the man whom the Senate had both murdered and decreed that on his death would become a god. For now, he must look to himself.

But what did this mean for him? He was now sole consul, and so technically in sole charge of Rome, since Lepidus' title of Master of the Horse would lapse with the death of the Dictator. He was also a target on the list of the conspirators, who had considered themselves powerful enough, untouchable enough, to murder the Dictator in the Senate itself.

Antony had a sudden vision of a path – a broad cobbled road – forking: to the left, ascending to the heights of Olympus, to the right, a sheer drop into Hades.

It was not yet noon, but by the end of the day, Antony knew he would be the true master of the Roman Empire.

Or he would be dead.

Author notes

A note on women's names

Roman naming conventions are confusing at the best of times, but no more so than when it came to women, who were only given a single name, usually taken from the name of the broad family group or *gens*, from which the *nomen* was derived. Marcus Antonius came from the gens Antonia, and his nomen was Antonius. All the women in this gens were named Antonia. Thus his wife, who was also his cousin, was called Antonia, as was his daughter. To distinguish between these two, I have invented the nickname of Toni for Antony's daughter from Antonia. He will go on to have three more daughters, two of whom will also be called Antonia. Furthermore, he had a sister called Antonia, who does not appear in these books. I feel a little bad about leaving her out, but she seemed to play no major role in Antony's life or in the events of these books, and I felt there were already enough Antonias kicking around. For completeness, Antonia, Antony's sister, married Publius Vatinius, who was a supporter of Caesar and consul in 47 BC.

Chapter notes

As in the previous book, I have organised my historical notes by chapters, to help the reader look up specific queries without using footnotes that would interfere with the reading experience. These notes are intended to provide sources, or just to expand on aspects of ancient Roman history and culture that I think are interesting. I hope you find them useful.

Prologue

There were a large number of tribes in northern Gaul at the time of Caesar's conquest. In this chapter, the Atrebates, the Bellovaci, the Carduci and Senones are mentioned. The Atrebates held territory in modern-day Artois, as well as some land in England. The Bellovaci were located in the Picardy region. The Carduci held lands along the river Dordogne and the Senones dwelt in the Seine basin.

The defeat of the Gallic chieftain Vercingetorix at Alesia is described in detail at the end of *Caesar's Soldier*.

Hercules (Greek Heracles), the mythical son of Zeus, was renowned for his strength, courage, ingenuity and sexual prowess. He was supposed to have fathered a large number of children, known collectively as the Heracleidae. Mark Antony claimed his family was descended from one of these children, Anton. Whether Antony made this story up, or it was an older family tradition, is uncertain, but given Antony's character and physical build, a descent from Hercules would have been plausible to the common Roman.

Liber Pater – the free father, the god of viticulture and wine. In modern times, the Liber Pater is considered the most expensive wine in the world, with a 2015 bottle selling for £36,000 see worldoffinewine.com/homepage-featured-articles/liber-pater-most-expensive-wine-world).

In Caesar's commentary on the Gallic Wars, *De Bello Gallico*, Volusenus' skirmish with Commius and Antony's action in accepting Commius' terms is the last action of the war, underlining its importance, and the responsibility Caesar had already entrusted in Antony.

The 'prosecution theory' is generally accepted as one of the reasons Caesar was wary about returning to Rome as a private citizen, but Morstein-Marx argues against this theory in *Julius Caesar and the Roman People*.

Chapter I

There were three successive consuls called Claudius Marcellus: Marcus in 51 BC, his cousin Gaius in 50 BC, and another Gaius Claudius Marcellus, Marcus' brother, in 49 BC. All three were vehemently opposed to Caesar.

I couldn't find out where the meeting of 1 March took place, but it had to be outside the pomerium, within a mile of Rome, in a temple or other religious place, so I have placed the meeting in a fictional generic Roman temple.

Cytheris is an important figure in the life of Mark Antony. Cytheris was her stage name, her freedwoman name of Volumnia being derived from her former master, Publius Volumnius Eutrapelus. Much of what we know about her comes from Cicero's invective, aimed at discrediting Antony. Nevertheless, she seems to have been a talented actress and highly desired by Rome's elites. She was also a lover of Marcus Brutus. The poet Gallus was another lover of Cytheris, and he named her Lycoris in his poetry of the 40s BC. In 1978, nine lines of poetry written by Gallus were discovered, and are thought to be the oldest Roman manuscript of poetry in existence. The first line of this says that he is sad because of Lycoris' wanton behaviour. Cytheris was likely to have had some influence in political circles, despite her *infamis*. Even Cicero wrote to his wife about a failed attempt to curry favour with her, although on another occasion he describes his horror at finding himself attending a dinner party where she was also a guest.

I should take this opportunity to correct an error from *Caesar's Soldier* in which I refer to pantomime. Pantomime was probably not being performed in Rome at this time, but mime was common. Pantomime involved a solo dancer portraying mythological themes without speaking, supported by musicians and a chorus. Mime was similar, but the actors in pantomimes wore masks, unlike those in mimes, and pantomime – in contrast to modern shows – tended to have higher themes and less farce and vulgarity than mime.

The augurs were originally self-selected, but by the time of the late Republic were elected by seventeen of the thirty-five tribes which were selected by ballot.

According to Cicero, in 249 BC Publius Claudius Pulcher, the consul and admiral, sought an omen before a battle. He consulted the sacred chickens which were carried on the ships for this purpose. However, they refused to eat, which was considered a bad omen. Claudius threw the chickens overboard, declaring that if they would not eat, they could drink. He went on to suffer a catastrophic defeat.

Chapter II

I couldn't find the date of the election of the tribune of the plebs. It seems to have varied each year, but was probably after the election for the consuls.

Mutina becomes important later in Mark Antony's story, but had already been the scene of a siege by Pompey, and of one of Spartacus' battles.

The scene with the false rumour of Caesar's advance is described in Appian's *Civil Wars*.

The wearing of mourning clothes by senators, *mutationes vestis*, heightened tensions just prior to the start of the civil war.

Chapter III

A cultivated cherry was first brought to Rome in 72 BC by the great general and horticulturist, Lucullus.

Cicero's defended Gnaeus Plancio in 54 BC on charges of illegal electioneering. The prosecution demonstrated his character by accusing him of raping a mime actress. Cicero commented that this was a custom that was allowed at the games, especially in country towns, and was a sign of an honourably conducted adolescence. He chided the prosecution for accusing Plancio of something he was permitted to do. This commentary highlights both the horrific abuse that even free actresses could be subjected to with impunity, and also Cicero's own attitudes to women, or at least those of lower rank, which contrast markedly with Antony's.

Cicero quotes Pompey as calling Antony a worthless quaestor in his letter to Atticus, vii.8, dated 25 or 26 Dec 50 BC.

The Vicus Tuscum, the street of the Etruscans, was an ancient street in Rome that led south-west out of the Roman Forum towards the *forum boarium*.

Chapter IV

Some authorities state that after fleeing Rome, Mark Antony reached Caesar after he had already crossed the Rubicon, but others say he met Caesar north of the river. Antony left Rome on 7 January, and using fast horses in a relay, he could have arrived in Ravenna by 9 January, according to the Stanford Geospatial Network Model of the Roman world at orbis.stanford.edu, and so could have witnessed the crossing. As a fiction writer I have the luxury of choosing which to use in the story, so have chosen this latter interpretation, so that the reader can witness this momentous event through Antony's eyes. Note that Ravenna would for a while be the capital of the late Roman Empire.

Mare Adriaticum – the Adriatic Sea

Rubicon – the location of this small river is lost to history. The crossing is often imagined in popular culture as a grand fording of a deep river, with Caesar on horseback. In fact he crossed the small waterway in a carriage via a bridge.

Alea jacta est has been variously translated as 'The die is cast', 'Let the dice fly high', 'Let the game be ventured', or 'Let the die be cast'. *Alea* can also refer to the game of dice as well as the die itself. It has been pointed out that as the Greek for dice is *kubos*, Caesar's quote refers to the first Rubic Cube.

Ariminum – modern-day Rimini.

Arretium – modern-day Arezzo.

Iguvium – modern-day Gubbio.

Pisaurum – modern-day Pesaro.

Fanum Fortunate – modern-day Fano.

Cingulum – modern-day Cingoli.

Corfinium – modern-day Corfinio.

Sulmo – modern day-Sulmona. Caesar says Lucretius and Attius threw themselves from the walls, but Attius must have survived since he was brought to Antony.

Labienus' desertion of Caesar has surprised historians ancient and modern. Two main reasons are proposed for his betrayal – his resentment of being overlooked for glory given his achievements in Gaul, especially when Antony was promoted so rapidly for doing much less on the battlefield, and enticement from agents of Pompey. See Syme, 1938 and Tyrell, 1972.

Chapter V

Antony's chariot was supposedly pulled by lions, but this seems unlikely and may just have been exaggeration.

Antony's letters are at least partially preserved in Cicero's correspondence.

According to legend, the Roman statesman Cincinnatus was summoned to the assistance of the city to protect it against invasion, although he was a farmer. He laid down his plough, took the title of Dictator, and fifteen days later laid down his command, victorious, and returned to his plough.

Quintus Fabius Maximus Verrucosus was given the name Cunctator for his delaying tactics which kept Hannibal at bay after the disastrous defeat at Lake Trasimene.

Decimation was an ancient and brutal punishment where groups of ten soldiers were forced to draw lots, with the unlucky fellow beaten to death by his nine comrades.

Chapter VI

Brundisium – modern-day Brindisi. The island in the harbour of Brundisium is now called Sant Andrea, but I could not find a record of its name in Roman times.

Epirus – north-western region of Ancient Greece.

Aetolia – a region of Ancient Greece on the north coast of the Gulf of Corinth.

Dyrrhachium – modern-day Durrës, Albania.

Lissus – modern-day Lezhë, Albania.

Chapter VII

It has been suggested that chara is a wild tuber known as *kelkasa* in Albanian, similar to potato (see Galassi and Ashrafian).

Fornax – the divine personification of the oven and the goddess of baking.

Fans of Roman fiction dramatised on the screen will be interested to know that Titus Pullo – along with Marcus Antonius and Atia, my favourite character in the HBO/BBC series *Rome*, portrayed so brilliantly by the late Ray Stevenson – was based on a real centurion. Caesar's own commentary *De Bello Gallico* mentions Pullo and his comrade Vorenus fighting together with Caesar in Gaul. But in Caesar's *De Bello Civili*, he mentions that Pullo joined Pompey, and was responsible for many soldiers switching sides, causing the capture of Antony's brother Gaius. At Dyrrhachium, it was Pullo who led the ferocious defence of the 'hedgehog' that delayed Caesar long enough for Pompey to bring up his main forces.

Apollonia – there were a number of cities called Apollonia in the Greek world. The one referred to here is probably situated in modern-day Albania.

Aous – the modern-day river Vjosa in Albania.

Drino – a river in Albania, still bearing the same name.

Aeginium – a town in Thessaly.

Gomphi – this ancient town was situated near modern-day Mouzaki in Greece.

The Second Macedonian War was fought between Philip V of Macedon and Rome and its allies Rhodes and Pergamo from 200 to 197 BC. It ended with Philip's defeat and expulsion from Greece, and with Rome becoming more involved in the affairs of the Greeks.

Chapter VIII

Two towns, Pharsalus and Palaeopharsalus (old Pharsalus), existed in ancient times. The so-called Battle of Pharsalus may have actually taken place nearer Palaeopharsalus. Either way, the site was near modern Farsala.

Although Newton's laws of motions were not yet described, Antony would have known from practical experience what happened when opposing masses crashed into each other.

As a young man, Caesar was sent to the court of King Nicomedes in Bithynia to raise a fleet. Rumours persisted throughout his life that the two of them had a sexual relationship, and Caesar was sometimes called the Queen of Bithynia.

Lucius Domitius Ahenobarbus was the Emperor Nero's great-great-grandfather.

Corcyra – modern-day Corfu.

Chapter IX

It's uncertain why the augurs opposed Antony's extension of his term as Master of Horse, when they had already agreed to twelve months for Caesar. They might have just been making a point that Antony was not exceptional in the way that Caesar was.

The October Horse was a ritual animal sacrifice carried out on the Ides of October. It is also the title of Colleen McCullough's novel dealing with Caesar's assassination, comparing Caesar's murder to the death of the noble horse.

The Plebeian Games were a religious festival taking place in November, with theatrical performances and contests to entertain the masses.

Caesar's stay in Alexandria contributed greatly to the fascination with both him and Cleopatra throughout history, with his involvement in the civil war between Cleopatra and her brother (which included the accidental burning down of the Library of Alexandria), the way she was smuggled into the city to come into his presence, their romance, the birth of their child Caesarion, and their holiday cruising down the Nile.

The Marcus Octavius who fought Gabinius does not seem to have been a close relative of Gaius Octavius/Octavian.

The vomiting incident is described in Plutarch.

Antony did not recall his uncle Antonius Hybrida from exile. Maybe he preferred his uncle to remain outside the city with Antony's ex-wife.

Chapter X

Lictors were bodyguards of Roman magistrates holding *Imperium*. Different ranks of magistrates were allowed different numbers of lictors, from two for a *curule aedile* to twelve for a consul. They carried bundles of sticks called fasces (origin of the word fascist), sometimes containing axes.

The Tarpeian rock is a steep cliff on the south side of the Capitoline hill, still clearly visible today, from which traitors were thrown as a form of execution. The street of the yoke-makers was an ancient street leading into the Forum.

Veni vidi vici. Literally 'I came, I saw, I conquered', a neat Caesarian aphorism that encapsulates the speed of his victory over King Pharnaces of Pontus.

It has been argued (Ramsay, 2004) that Antony did not really fall out with Caesar, but that he was tasked with remaining in Rome without an official position to act as a property speculator on Caesar's behalf, in order to raise funds, service for which he was handsomely rewarded when he returned to Caesar's side in 44 BC.

Chapter XI

Roman weddings were full of violent symbolism, such as the simulated abduction, the spear in her hair and the ritual and vocal lament of the bride. Much of the ceremony seems to have been a re-enactment of the mass abduction of the Sabine women at the time of the founding of Rome.

Cleopatra's title, Goddess of the two Lands, refers to Upper and Lower Egypt.

The emperor we call Augustus was known by a number of names throughout his life, and historians often use these different names to indicate which stage of his career he was at. He was born Gaius Octavius, which is how he is referred to in this book. To avoid spoilers for those who haven't studied this period of history, I'll discuss his other names in the next book, *Caesar's Avenger*.

The date of Marcus Antonius Antyllus' birth is uncertain. Some contemporary sources state that he was born in 47 BC, while Tatum says he was probably born in 45 BC. The 47 BC date may derive from the fact that Antony gave Antyllus the *toga virilis* of manhood, normally worn at sixteen years of age, after the Battle of Actium in 31 BC. However, after Actium, Antony may have suspected he would not survive to see Antyllus' sixteenth birthday, and so, wishing to see his eldest son become a man, brought this ceremony forward. It seems unlikely that Fulvia had a sexual relationship with Antony before their marriage – there was never any hint of impropriety about her – and since I have placed their marriage (date also unknown) at the beginning of 46 BC, I have given Antyllus a birthday of November 46.

Cicero's Phillipics state that Antony did set out for Spain with Caesar, showing his continued loyalty at this point in time, but that he failed to complete the journey. See Ramsey, 2004.

Since the Roman calendar had only 355 days, it was the job of the Pontifex Maximus to insert an extra month, known as an intercalary month, every two to three years to keep the calendar aligned with the seasons. However, this wasn't always done, for political reasons or inertia, and so by the time of the late Republic, there was a large disparity between the season and the calendar, which is a headache for historians and writers. (Many historians seem not to take this into account when saying what the season was when describing events of the late Republic.) Fortunately for me, Julius Caesar fixed this, and so from *Caesar's Avenger* onwards, the calendar months will correspond to the seasons in the way we know it today.

Chapter XII

Antony's practical joke on Fulvia is mentioned in Plutarch.

Narbo – modern-day Narbonne.

Much ink has been spilled on the subject of Caesar's illness, often called the 'Falling Sickness' from the term used in an early translation of Plutarch. There are, in fact, a number of publications speculating on the nature of the disease, with most agreeing that it was a form of epilepsy, but with many possible causes suggested. Since there appeared to be a large amount of mental illness in the Julio-Claudian dynasty, a genetic aetiology is certainly quite possible, but given the late onset, it has been variously suggested that the underlying reason for the seizures could be head injury, brain tumour, syphilis, an arteriovenous malformation, vascular disease, coeliac disease, or even a tapeworm in the brain acquired during his travels in Egypt. If this was an epileptiform illness, it's unclear what form the seizures took, whether they were generalised ('grand mal') or complex partial, which can involve absences and hallucinations. Interestingly, both seizures themselves and their underlying causes can lead to behavioural changes, which some think might explain Caesar's increasingly autocratic and megalomaniac behaviour, although, of course, that could also be a result of his victories going to his head. On the other hand, Caesar may have known or suspected that he was dying, and if not, he was no longer young and he didn't have many years left to him. He might therefore have been simply in a hurry to get all the things done that he desired, for the Republic and for his legacy, before he popped his *caligae*.

Chapter XIII

Horns are common symbols associated with cuckoldry. Graber, 1987 notes that the first mention in history of this association is by Artemidorus in the third century AD. It therefore seems plausible that the symbol was in use and understood in Antony's time.

The date of Caesar's rudeness is uncertain; some place it on 31 December 45 BC. Further, some authorities suggest it was due to his epilepsy, which he himself seems to blame, while others think it was a sign of his arrogance at this stage (which might in itself have been a consequence of his epilepsy – see notes on chapter XIII).

In the time of the kings and the early Republic, patricians were the noble class and plebeians were the common man, mostly farmers working for patricians. Your status as patrician or plebeian was determined by birth, or occasionally adoption. Originally, patricians had many more rights than plebeians, but this was eroded over time, so by the late Republic there was little difference between the two classes in wealth or privileges. However, being of patrician stock was still highly valued.

The *quindecimviri sacris faciundis* was a college of fifteen priests that guarded the Sibylline books, ancient prophecies, and consulted them at the behest of the Senate. Their findings were taken seriously, although they often seemed to be suspiciously partisan in favour of one cause or another, even when the source material was ambiguous.

Chapter XIV

The festival of Anna Parenna, the goddess of the circle of the year (the name is related to 'per annum' and 'perennial') took place on the Ides of March, usually at the first milestone on the Via Flaminia. The celebrations are described by Ovid. In addition, the Ides sheep, the *Ovis Idulis*, was sacrificed to Jupiter on each Ides.

The Romans took dreams very seriously, and in the second century AD, Artemidorus of Ephesus, a professional dream interpreter, wrote a five-volume treatise on the interpretation of dreams.

It is unclear whether it was Decimus Brutus, Trebonius, or both, who intercepted Antony outside the Senate house on the Ides of March. I suspect it was both, not least because it would have taken two men to subdue Antony if things had turned violent. What they talked about is also unknown, but if there was one thing that would have distracted Antony enough to leave Caesar's side, it would have been his debts.

Glossary

Aedile

An elected official responsible for maintaining public buildings, ensuring the accuracy of weights and measures, and organising public games.

Agora

The main central open area in a Greek city, serving political and economic functions. The origin of the word agoraphobia.

Agnomen

A fourth name given to a Roman, often for some exploit. The Scipio who defeated Hannibal was called Publius (praenomen) Cornelius (nomen) Scipio (cognomen) Africanus (agnomen).

Atrium

The first room in a Roman house after the entrance, and one of the most important, a place for meeting guests and conducting ceremonies.

Auctoritas

A Roman virtue. Prestige, necessary to be respected in command and to be able to exert influence in society.

Ballista	An artillery weapon that could launch large stones or bolts over great distances.
Buccinator	The man who blew the *buccina*, a curved brass instrument.
Bulla	Charms worn around the neck, usually worn by boys until they reached manhood.
Capsarius	A trained combat medic who could provide first aid and basic care, often under the direction of a *medicus*.
Cella	The inner chamber of a Roman temple.
Centurion	Commander of a century of men, originally numbering a hundred men, but in late Republican times numbering eighty.
Circumvallation	Field works around an enemy fortification to help maintain a siege.
Colonia	A settlement of Roman citizens.
Consul	One of two annually elected leaders of the Roman Republic.
Contio	A public meeting in which the magistrates could inform the people of important news and events. It often took place after a Senate meeting.

Contravallation	Field works outside a circumvallation to protect the besiegers from attack from without.
Contubernium	A unit of eight soldiers who shared a tent. Not to be confused with the quasi-marital relationship between a freeman and slave, which has the same name.
Corona muralis	The mural crown awarded to the soldier who first climbed the wall of a besieged fortification.
Cubiculum	A small room in a private house that acted as a bedroom, as well as a place for private meetings.
Cursus honorum	The course of honours, the ladder of offices that Senators in the Republic had to ascend to reach the ultimate prize of being elected consul.
Decurion	A Roman cavalry officer in charge of a *turma*. Also an official in provincial towns.
Dignitas	A Roman virtue, incorporating dignity, charisma and respect.
Equestrian	The second highest rank of nobility among Romans, behind the senatorial rank (Latin, *equites*, sometimes called knights in English). Originally the cavalry was drawn from the equestrians, but by the time of the late Republic, it was a purely honorary

title. Equestrians were wealthy and provided many of the senior officers of the legions.

Fasces	Bundles of wooden rods carried by lictors as a sign of their authority. They could be used to administer corporal punishment, although when more severe danger threatened, the lictors could carry axes within the *fasces*, which symbolised the consuls' power to administer capital punishment.
Forum boarium	The original cattle market in Ancient Rome, and the site of the first gladiatorial contest in the city.
Garum	A highly popular sauce made of fermented fish guts. May have tasted like soy sauce, and provided a large dose of umami flavour to whatever it was poured over.
Hasta caelibaris	A bent iron spear decorated with flowers and placed in a bride's hair during the wedding ceremony, possibly as a reminder of the violent origins of marriage, or to drive out evil spirits from the bride's hair.
Imperium	Generally, the scope of a man's power. More specifically, the legal right to absolute authority within the scope of one's magistracy or promagistracy (eg consul or proconsul).

Impluvium	A pool that captures rainwater from the roof, often found in the centre of the atrium.
Infamis/Infamia	Infamia was a loss of social standing, and one subject to infamia was known as infamis. Certain professions were automatically infamis, such as prostitutes, actors, dancers, gravediggers and gladiators. Certain criminals and people caught in certain sexual situations may also be considered infamis. The status of infamia meant the loss of many legal protections that were owed to the other Roman citizens.
Interrex	Literally between kings. In archaic Rome, he acted as a regent. In the time of the Republic, he was appointed to hold the election of the new consuls when the previous consuls had been unable to do so during their time in office.
Lararium	A small shrine to the household gods, the Lares.
Legate	Senior Roman military officer, often in charge of a legion, usually of high political rank.
Lictor	The attendants and bodyguards of a consul or other magistrate.

Lora	A cheap, bitter wine made from the leftovers of the grape pressing process such as the skin husks and seeds.
Mare Nostrum	The Mediterranean Sea, literally, 'our sea'.
Medicus	A physician.
Mos maiorum	The customs of the ancestors. It was important to Romans to follow the traditions of their fore-bears.
Murus gallicus	The Gallic wall, a form of defence constructed of earth, stone and wood.
Nomenclator	A slave whose job was to remind their master of the names of people they met.
Nundinum	A Roman week, consisting of eight days (or nine in the inclusive Roman way of counting). Markets were generally held once every nundinum, and a market day was called a nundinae.
Optimates	The 'best people', the conservative faction in Roman politics.
Optio	Second-in-command of a century.
Palla	A headcloth or shawl worn by women.

Patera	A bowl, part of the legionary's marching pack.
Paterfamilias	The head of a family, with absolute power within the household.
Peristylium	The garden of a Roman private house, enclosed, often with ornate gardens, often colonnaded with various small rooms leading off.
Pilus prior	The senior centurion in a cohort.
Pilus posterior	Deputy to the pilus prior.
Pomerium	The sacred boundary of Rome, originally and traditionally the area within the line ploughed by Romulus on the founding of the city. It had religious and legal significance. For example, holders of proconsular power could not cross the pomerium into Rome, the dead could not be buried within its boundaries, and there were restrictions on the carrying of weapons.
Populares	The liberal popular faction in Roman politics.
Praefectus equitum	an officer in charge of a cavalry unit.
Primus pilus	Commander of the first cohort and most senior centurion in a legion.

Principium	The headquarters in the centre of a Roman legionary camp.
Pronaos	The inner area of a temple that leads to the *cella*.
Quadrireme	A large warship.
Quindecimviri sacris faciundis	The fifteen members of the college who guarded the Sybilline books.
Regifugium	An annual religious festival held in February to mark the flight of the last king from Rome.
Rostra	A platform for speeches in the Forum, built from ship's rams captured at the Battle of Antium.
Scutum	A large, curved, rectangular shield, made of sheets of wood glued together, covered with canvas and leather, around a metre tall and weighing 10 kg.
Senatus consultum ultimum	Extreme and final decree of the Senate. The Latin term is a modern derivation from Caesar's description of the decree in his *Civil War Commentaries*.
Sestertius	A coin worth a quarter of a denarius.
Signifer	Standard-bearer.

Spatha	A long sword, probably used by cavalry in the Republican period, coming to replace the *gladius* in the late Empire.
Stola	A traditional female item of clothing, a long sleeveless robe.
Strophium	A breast band, serving as a type of bra.
Terminalia	A religious festival celebrating Terminus, the god of boundaries, held in February the day before the *Regifugium*.
Toga Praetexta	A white toga with broad purple stripe worn by free Roman boys and some magistrates.
Toga Virilis	A plain white toga worn by free adult males.
Tribunus angusticlavii	A junior military tribune, usually of Equestrian rank, wearing a narrow stripe on their tunic or toga.
Tribunus laticlavius	A senior military tribune, usually of Senatorial rank, wearing a broad stripe on their tunic or toga.
Triclinium	Dining room, taking its name from the three couches surrounding a central table on which diners reclined.

Trireme	A warship.
Turma	A cavalry unit, thirty strong, commanded by decurions.
Vestibule	The entrance hall to a private house.
Veterinarius	A Roman soldier who performed the functions of a veterinary surgeon, working mainly with the horses.
Via Lactea	The Milky Way.

Bibliography and references

Appian (2020) *Civil Wars* Books 1–2. Translated by McGing, B. Cambridge, Mass: Harvard University Press.

Baca, A. B. (1966) 'The Identity of Gallus' Lycoris', *The Classical World*, 60, pp. 49–51

Ball, W. (2016) *Rome in the East*, 2nd edn. Abingdon: Routledge.

Beard, M., Crawford, C. (1999) *Rome in the Late Republic*, 2nd edn. London: Duckworth.

Betts, E. (2017) *Senses of the Empire: Multisensory approaches to Roman culture*. Abingdon: Routledge.

Bevan, E. R. (1927) *The House of Ptolemy*. London: Methuen. (available at https://penelope.uchicago.edu/Thayer/E/Gazetteer /Places/Africa/Egypt/_Texts/BEVHOP/home.html)

Broughton, S. (1951 & 1952) *The Magistrates of the Roman Republic*, Vols I and II. New York: American Philological Association.

Bruschi F. (2011) 'Was Julius Caesar's epilepsy due to neurocysticercosis?' *Trends Parasitol.* 27, pp. 373–4.

Bumpus, K. (2004) 'Early Life of Mark Antony.' Honors Thesis. Paper 264. Southern Illinois University.

Caesar, G. J. (1951) *The Conquest of Gaul*. Translated by Handford, S. A. Harmondsworth: Penguin.

Caesar, G. J. (1967) *The Civil War*. Translated by J. F. Mitchell. 1967, Penguin Books, Middlesex.

Carandini, A. (ed.) (2017) *The Atlas of Ancient Rome*. Translated by Halavais, A. C. Princeton, NJ: Princeton University Press.

Cary, M., Scullard, H. H. (1975) A History of Rome. Macmillan Press, London.

Cicero, M. T. (1969) 'Against Sergius Catilina' and 'The first Phillipic Against Marcus Antonius.' In Cicero, *Selected Political Speeches*, translated by Grant, M. London: Penguin.

Cicero, M. T. (1969) 'The Second Phillipic Against Marcus Antonius.' In Cicero, *Selected Works*, translated by Grant, M.. London: Penguin.

Collins, J. H. (1952) 'Tullia's Engagement and Marriage to Dolabella.' *The Classical Journal*, 47, pp. 146–168.

Cook, S. A., Adcock, F. E., Charlesworth, M. P. (1932) *The Cambridge Ancient History: Volume IX*. Cambridge: Cambridge University Press.

Cowell, F. R. (1948) *Cicero and the Roman Republic*. Harmondsworth: Penguin.

D'Amato, R., Gilbert, F. (2021) *Armies of Julius Caesar 58–44 BC*. Oxford: Osprey.

De Ruggiero, P. (2013) *Mark Antony: A plain blunt man*. Barnsley: Pen & Sword.

Dighton. A. (2017) 'Mutatio Vestis: Clothing and political protest in the late Roman republic. *Phoenix*, 71(3/4), pp. 345–369.

Dixon, K. R., Southern, P. (1997) *The Roman Cavalry*. London: Routledge.

Dunn, D. (2016) *Catullus' Bedspread*. London: William Collins.

Edwards, I. E. S., Gadd, C. J., Hammond, N. G. L. (1970) *The Cambridge Ancient History*, 3rd edn. Cambridge: Cambridge University Press.

Everitt, A. (2001) Cicero: A turbulent life. London: John Murray.

Everitt, A. (2006) *The First Emperor*. London: John Murray.

Feufere, M. (2010) *Weapons of the Romans*. Stroud: History Press.

Fields, N. (2008) *The Roman Army: Civil Wars 88–31 BC*. Oxford: Osprey.

Galassi, F. M., Ashrafian, H. (2017) *Julius Caesar's Disease: A new diagnosis*. Barnsley: Pen & Sword History.

Goldsworthy, A. (1996) *The Roman Army at War, 100 BC–200 AD*. Oxford: Oxford University Press.

Goldsworthy, A. (2002) *Caesar's Civil War*. Oxford: Osprey.

Goldsworthy, A. (2003) *In the Name of Rome*. London: Weidenfeld & Nicholson.

Goldsworthy, A. (2003) *The Complete Roman Army*. London: Thames & Hudson.

Goldsworthy, A. (2006) *Caesar*. London: Weidenfeld & Nicholson.

Goldsworthy, A. (2010) *Antony and Cleopatra*. London: Weidenfeld & Nicholson.

Goodman, M. (2007) *Rome & Jerusalem*. London: Penguin.

Goodman, R., Soni, J. (2012) *Rome's Last Citizen: The life & legacy of Cato, mortal enemy of Caesar.* New York: Thomas Dunne.

Graber, R. B., Richter, G. C. (1987) 'The Capon theory of the cuckold's horns: confirmation or conjecture?' *The Journal of American Folklore*, 100, pp. 58–63.

Grant, M. (1972) *Cleopatra*. London: Phoenix Press.

Grant, M. (1974) *Caesar*. London: Weidenfeld & Nicholson.

Grant, M. (2008) *Roman Cookery*. London: Serif.

Frederiksen, M. (1966) 'Caesar, Cicero and the problem of debt', *The Journal of Roman Studies*, 56(1–2), pp. 128–141.

Hersch, K. K. (2020) 'Violence in the Roman Wedding', in Beneker, J., Tsouvala, G (eds.) *The Discourse of Marriage in the Greco-Roman World*. Madison, Wis: University of Wisconsin Press.

Holland, R. (2004) *Augustus, Godfather of Europe*. Stroud: Sutton.

Holland, T. (2003) *Rubicon*. London: Abacus.

Holmes, T. (1923) *The Roman Republic and the Founder of the Empire*. Oxford: Clarendon Press.

Hughes, J. R. (2004) 'Dictator Perpetuus: Julius Caesar – did he have seizures? If so, what was the etiology?' *Epilepsy Behav*. 5E: pp. 756–64.

Hughes-Hallet, L. (2006) *Cleopatra: Queen, lover, legend*. London: Pimlico.

Huzar, E. G. (1978) Mark Antony. Beckenham, Minn: University of Minnesota Press.

Huzar, E. G. (1985) 'Mark Antony: Marriages versus careers', *The Classical Journal*, December 1985/January 1986, 81, 2 pp. 97–111.

Jeppesen-Wigelsworth, A. (2013) 'Political Bedfellows: Tullia, Dolabella and Caelius', *Arethusa*, 46, pp. 65–85.

Keith, A. (2011) 'Lycoris Galli/Volumnia Cytheris: a Greek courtesan in Rome', *Eugesta*, 1.

Kelly, R. (2012) *Wine, despair and women's clothing: gender anxieties in screen representations of Marcus Antonius*. PhD thesis, University of Ulster.

Madsen, D. W. (1981) *The Life and Political Career of Marcus Caelius Rufus*. University of Washington ProQuest Dissertations Publishing.

Matyszak, P. (2009) *Legionary: The Roman Soldier's Manual*. London: Thames & Hudson.

Morstein-Marx, R. (2021) *Julius Caesar and the Roman People*. Cambridge: Cambridge University Press.

Nicolaus of Damascus 'Life of Augustus', in *Fragmente der Griechischen Historiker*, translated by Hall, C. M.

North, J. (2008) 'Caesar at the Lupercalia', *The Journal of Roman Studies*, 98, pp. 144–160.

Patterson, J. R. (2000) *Political Life in the City of Rome*. Bristol: Bristol Classical Press.

Pollard, J. & Reid, H. (2007) *The Rise and Fall of Alexandria*. London: Penguin.

Plutarch (1959) *Lives of the Noble Romans*. Fuller, E. (ed.) New York: Dell.

Ramsey, J. T. (2004) 'Did Julius Caesar temporarily banish Mark Antony from his inner circle?' *Classical Quarterly*, 54.1, pp. 161–173.

Ramsey, J. (2008) 'At what hour did the murderers of Julius Caesar gather on the Ides of March 44 BC?', in Heilen, S., Calder, W. M. (eds.) *In Pursuit of Wissenschaft: Festschrift für William M. Calder* III zum, 75, pp. 351–363.

Rawson, E. (1985) *Intellectual Life in the Late Roman Republic*. London: Duckworth.

Roberts, A. (1988) *Mark Antony: His life and times*. Upton-upon-Severn: Malvern Publishing.

Roller, D. W. (2010) *Cleopatra: A biography*. Oxford: Oxford University Press.

Rosenstein, N., Morstein-Marx, R. (2007) *A Companion to the Roman Republic*. Chichester: Wiley-Blackwell.

Sampson, G. C. (2023) *The Battle of Pharsalus*. Barnsley: Pen & Sword.

Schultz, C. E. (2021) *Fulvia: Playing for power at the end of the Roman republic*. Oxford: Oxford University Press.

Seagar, R. (2002) *Pompey the Great*, 2nd edn. Oxford: Blackwell.

Sewell, J., Smout, C. (eds.) (2020) *The Palgrave Handbook of the History of Women on Stage*. Oxford: Palgrave.

Sheppard, S. (2006) *Pharsalus 48 BC*. Oxford: Osprey.

Southern, P. (1998) *Augustus*. London: Routledge.

Southern, P. (2012) *Mark Antony: A life*. Stroud: Amberley.

Stockton, D. (1971) *Cicero: A political biography*. Oxford: Oxford University Press.

Stothard, P. (2020) *The Last Assassin*. London: Weidenfeld & Nicolson.

Strauss, B. (2015) *The Death of Caesar*. New York: Simon & Schuster.

Suetonius, G. S. (1957) *The Twelve Caesars*. Translated by Graves, R. London: Penguin.

Summer, G. *Roman Military Clothing (1) 100 BC–AD 200*. Oxford: Osprey.

Syme, R. (1938) 'The Allegiance of Labienus', *The Journal of Roman Studies*, 28, pp. 113–125.

Syme, R. (1939) *The Roman Revolution*. Oxford: Oxford University Press.

Tatum, W. J. (2024) *A Noble Ruin: Mark Antony, civil war, and the collapse of the Roman republic*. Oxford: Oxford University Press.

Tempest, K. (2017) *Brutus, the Noble Conspirator*. London: Yale University Press.

Treggiaria, S. (2007) *Terentia, Tullia and Publilia: The women of Cicero's family*. Abingdon: Routledge.

Trow, M. J. (2013) *A Brief History of Cleopatra, Last Pharaoh of Egypt*. London: Robinson.

Tyrrell. W. B. (1972)'Labienus' Departure from Caesar in January 49 BC', *Historia: Zeitschrift Für Alte Geschichte*, 21(3), pp. 424–440.

Van der Blom, H. (2016) *Oratory and Political Career in the Late Roman Republic*. Cambridge: Cambridge University Press.

Watterson, B. (2017) *Cleopatra: Fact and Fiction*. Stroud: Amberley.

Welch, K. (1995) 'Antony, Fulvia, and the ghost of Clodius in 47 BC', *Greece and Rome*, 42(2), pp. 182–201.

Yaple, L. E. (2022) *The Impact of Women on the Life and Legacy of Mark Antony*. Honors Thesis, University of Nebraska-Lincoln.

Acknowledgements

Thanks as always to everyone at Canelo, especially my new editor Craig Lye, who has ably taken over from my long-serving former editor Michael Bhaskar, who has moved on to explore his own creative pathways. Thank you to Steve O'Gorman for an incredibly thorough copyedit. Thanks to my agent Ed Wilson at Johnson & Alcock for advice and support. Thanks as always to family (Nome and Abbie) and friends (particularly my fellow Roman fiction authors). Thanks also to everyone at the Soap Bar Café, where most of this book was written, especially Sakina and Zantore for running such a lovely establishment, and most of all Tash, Bryony and Liece, for keeping Ivy and me supplied with coffee and dog biscuits! And thank you to my readers, who I hope are enjoying learning more about the fascinating Marcus Antonius.